Denise Robertson is Britain's favourite TV agony aunt. She has worked extensively on television and radio and as a national newspaper journalist. She has also been a prolific short story writer and her first television play won the BBC's review play competition. Starting with *The land of Lost Content* in 1985, which won the Constable Trophy for Fiction, she has published eleven previous novels. Denise lives near Sunderland with her husband, one of her five sons, and an assortment of dogs.

A RELATIVE FREEDOM

DENISE ROBERTSON

POCKET
B O O K S

New York   London   Toronto   Sydney   Tokyo   Singapore

First published in Great Britain by Simon & Schuster Ltd, 1994
First published in Pocket Books, 1995
An imprint of Simon & Schuster Ltd
A Paramount Communications Company

Simon & Schuster Ltd
West Garden Place
Kendal Street
London W2 2AQ

Simon & Schuster of Australia Pty Ltd
Sydney

A CIP catalogue record for this book is available
from the British Library.

ISBN 0-671-85261-2

Printed and bound in Great Britain by
HarperCollins, Manufacturing.

To Jack
whom I love

PROLOGUE ·
OCTOBER, 1993

Kate could smell autumn when she opened the garden door. The robin was waiting on his perch in the apple tree, head cocked, as she spread nuts and crumbs on the bird-table. She moved back to the door and watched as first blue-tits and then the robin came down for their breakfast. She had been awake since dawn, contemplating what she had done, wondering where it would all end. Now, she shivered, feeling not the touch of autumn but the chill of winter so that she clutched her dressing-gown to her neck and turned towards the house.

As she waited for the kettle to boil in the primrose and white kitchen, she listened to the radio: genocide in the former Yugoslavia, a further bomb outrage in Northern Ireland. The same mixture as always.

The first time she had heard of a killing in Belfast she had been peeling potatoes at the sink; it was 1972 or 1973, and she had been so shocked that she had clutched the sink for support. Today a death in Northern Ireland was simply another statistic. That was what time did to everything: robbed it of meaning. Except that last night had meant something.

Kate realised that she was smiling foolishly, alone in her kitchen, and busied herself with scalding the tea, noticing, as she raised the kettle, the ridged veins on her hands, the prominent knuckles, the faint patches of pigment that came with age. And yet, last night, she had felt no different to the girl she once had been. The smile threatened to recur and she raised the cup to her lips to quell it. On the wall, today's date was ringed in red: October the twenty-fifth. She had marked it as being important to Sophie without realising how momentous it was going to be for all of them.

Geoffrey was gone from the bed when Elizabeth woke up but he had replaced the duvet carefully to keep her snug. She turned on to her side, eyes tight shut, as though, by ignoring daylight, she could hold back the day itself. October the twenty-fifth: she had been dreading this day for weeks but now she was glad it had come. She reached for the radio and listened to the jumble of sport, weather and dire warnings about the economy. Nine deaths in Northern Ireland were listed as casually as the price of bananas.

Around her the bedroom sparkled in the autumn sunshine. Usually the patina of wood, the gleam of glass, gave her pleasure; but not now. October the twenty-fifth: a time for endings and beginnings for Sophie, and for herself. Elizabeth pushed aside the duvet and prepared to face the day.

Sophie was silent as the taxi sped through the London streets. Once Chloe reached out and squeezed her hand but she didn't speak, just turned away and stared out of the window, occupied with her own thoughts.

Familiar buildings loomed up and then receded, glistening in the sunshine, not nearly as huge and imposing as they had been when first she had come to London. That had been eight years ago. Everything diminished with time, and that was sad. She turned to look at Chloe, wanting her friend to say something flippant, something that would make her laugh and ease the tension, but Chloe remained silent.

Instead, Sophie closed her eyes, trying to remember the moment it had all begun, the day she had walked into her office and seen a stranger there, behind her desk. It had been summer . . . August . . . and she had woken that day to the sight of her lover, asleep on the pillow beside her.

BOOK 1

———————•———————

SOPHIE'S STORY

London
August 1993

1

SOPHIE LAY WITH HER EYES shut, ears alert for the early morning sounds from the mews. Beside her Paul was still asleep, and she resisted the impulse to slide her hand under his arm and over the smooth skin of his chest. If he awoke he might be over-amorous and this morning there was no time. This morning she might find out that she no longer had a job. It was not the day to be late.

Below the window a chain rattled. Mr Plumley was lowering his hanging basket, that noon haunt of bees and butterflies. She strained her ears for the sound of water swishing from the long spout of the green watering can, but there was nothing until the rattle of the returning chain.

Paul moaned slightly and turned over. Sophie raised herself on her pillow and regarded his sleeping face. He looked like a young version of Peter Hall . . . or else a Rubens cherub. She gave up being sensible and put out a tentative finger to trace his jaw, the lobe of his ear, and then the crisp, dark hair that always curled, however hard he tried to stop it.

As usual, when she thought of how much she loved him, her eyes pricked. That was the worst thing about love: it rendered you vulnerable. Her fingertip returned to his ear, touching the gold stud he wore there. A man with an earring – and in her bed! She smiled, thinking of her mother's face the first time she had seen it: not shock, not horror – just absolute disbelief. Most men had abandoned earrings nowadays, but Paul was not most men.

I am lucky, Sophie thought, subsiding on to her pillow. Once I know that my job's safe, I'll have everything. She raised her hands above her head and chuckled aloud at the thought.

Suddenly a door banged down below. Someone, presumably the new lover-boy, was leaving Chloe's flat.

'What are you laughing at?' Paul was awake now, raising himself on the pillow, reaching out to pull her into the circle of his arm.

'You,' she said. 'You look like an angel when you're asleep. Shows you how deceptive appearances can be.' He smelled of sleep and sweat and faintly of garlic from last night's lamb. 'Pooh,' she said, and buried her face in the sweetness of his flesh.

They kissed for a while but when she felt an urgency enter his kisses she pulled away. 'Not now,' she said. 'This could be a difficult day for me. Remember?'

In the street below someone was whistling – the postman, probably. The rap of a returning letter-box confirmed her guess. Sophie pictured the mews: *Le Grand Plaisir* on the opposite corner, shuttered now in the early morning; number eleven with its yellow shutters and green door; the salon, with its photographs of beautifully coiffured gods and goddesses; the wine shop; numbers thirteen and fourteen, each with its neat row of bells and nameplates; the pub, its window-boxes a riot of geraniums and lobelia in the third week of August; and on this side doors in every colour; tubs of petunias; and the antique shop, a feast for peering eyes.

'We ought to get up.' Paul had propped himself up on his elbow and was looking down at her. 'You look fourteen,' he said.

Sophie shook her head. 'I always feel old on Mondays. And *this* Monday . . . '

'It'll be all right.' He meant to be reassuring but his nonchalance irritated her.

'Oh yes,' she said. 'My firm has been taken over by the Yanks, redundancy looms, but it'll be *all right*.'

Somewhere in the mews a radio started up, too far away to hear the words but the measured tones probably meant it was something like a weather forecast. 'What time is it?'

Paul rolled away from her and checked the clock on the bedside table. 'Ten past seven.' Sophie groaned and closed her eyes again until she felt him leaving the bed.

'I'll make the tea,' he said. 'It's the least I can do, considering your ordeal. Plush office, secretary, coffee in bone china, bloody sugar lumps, for God's sake. We have a machine that spews out gunge in plastic cups, and the studio used to be God knows what . . . an abattoir, for all I know. It certainly smells like one. You don't know what hardship means.'

The pillow caught him squarely on the chin and he tottered backwards. It was a mistake and Sophie knew it even as the missile left her hand. 'Right,' Paul said, diving down on her. She protested for a second, just to keep up appearances, and then he was over her and around her, and all thoughts of her job and the day ahead had fled.

It was seven forty-five when Sophie reached the shower, turning her face to the flow, blessing the shortness of her brown hair that would permit fingertip drying. She soaped and lathered, her mind racing ahead: the tube at Notting Hill, people swaying and shuffling in the crammed aisle; the city street crowded with workers and early shoppers; and then the store. The House of Ascher had survived as an exclusive family business for one hundred and fifty years, only to be bought out by the Americans. Her boss, David Lister, had been in New York for the last week. Today she would hear from him what was to happen to the store and everyone who worked in it.

As Sophie stepped from the shower and began to towel dry herself she thought ruefully of the inevitable changes. Even if she kept her job, it wouldn't be the same. They were bound to send over new management, someone called Hiram P. Hirsch the Third or some such name, with a crew-cut and rimless specs and a steely determination to demolish tradition.

'Calm down,' Paul said, as she hurled herself into the kitchen. 'Coffee's made. Muesli or yoghurt? It's still only five past eight.' He looked slightly shame-faced at making her late, today of all days, and Sophie sat down at the pine table to please him, although every fibre of her body was longing to be under way.

'Yoghurt, please. Banana. And the coffee is gorgeous. I must be out of here in five minutes, though.'

'Sod the Yanks,' Paul said amicably, spooning marmalade on to toast with one hand and tightening the belt of his towelling robe with the other. 'If this was a decent government, there'd be a law to keep out foreign money.'

'Don't start,' Sophie said. 'I'm too weak for politics at the moment.'

Paul smiled seraphically. 'Yes,' he said. 'I was at my best just now.'

'Conceited twit.' Sophie was gulping coffee between mouthfuls of yoghurt. 'My knees are shaking in anticipation, my darling. Not in retrospect.' She started to laugh suddenly, knowing she had played into his hands once more.

'I'll be here waiting,' he said, with an attempt at a lascivious leer.

'Idiot!' Around her the kitchen glowed orange and cream in the morning sun and she felt a return of the sensation of well-being. As long as she had Paul, what did anything else matter? The radio was murmuring about conflict in Azerbaijan, death in Bosnia, anger in Northern Ireland, but here – in the home she shared with Paul – all was harmony.

She drank the last of her coffee, rose to her feet and reached for her briefcase. 'How do I look?' She had put on her new grey suit with the longer jacket and mid-calf skirt, moved by some strange impulse to power-dress while Ascher's was under threat.

Paul was looking her up and down. 'I prefer more leg. On the other hand, do I want my woman on display for all the world to see?'

'Hah! That's enough to make me hitch up the skirt.' She reached across to kiss his cheek. 'I'll be home when I get here. Let's eat out. Book a table as you pass *Le Plaisir*.'

'When for? Eight?' Paul came with her to the top of the stairs and stood watching as she clattered down to Chloe's landing and turned for the second flight.

Outside, the street basked in the morning sun. Blue lobelia trailed from window sills, and tubs overflowed with August plenty. We're so lucky to have the flat, Sophie thought, turning to look back. She and Paul had the top floor of number five, above the bow-windowed flower shop on the ground floor and Chloe on the first. The cost of the top floor in a neighbourhood that was only a stone's throw from Holland Park might have been beyond them, but the flat belonged to a friend of Paul's boss, and they had it on a peppercorn rent until the real tenant returned from the Far East.

Notting Hill tube station came into view. With luck she'd be in her office on time, Sophie thought, glancing at her watch, ready for the good or bad news, whichever it might be. If she had to change jobs she would survive, but leaving Ascher's would be a wrench.

Sophie had worked for Ascher's during her university vacations for three years, coming to London to find a job for adventure the first time, and discovering that she liked it. At first she had been a packer in Goods Delivery, then briefly a sales assistant, and finally she went to Personnel. Daisy Ascher had still been with the firm then, a frail, eighty-three-year-old who could spot an undusted counter or a sloppy display at a hundred paces. Sophie had been bag-carrier and general factotum to the old lady – who was the last surviving Ascher – until it was time to return to Leeds for her final year.

'Come back to us when you've done your finals,' Daisy had said, and Sophie had accepted, sure that she would fail and be jobless and glad of a refuge.

11

In the end she'd obtained a First, and had come back to Ascher's merely to regain her breath and to honour, at least in part, her obligation to an old lady who had been kind to her. That was 1988, the year that Eddie the Eagle found fame by losing in the Olympics, three IRA members were shot dead in Gibraltar and George Bush became President of the United States.

It had been wonderful to be in London then, with her own money in her pocket, which meant being really independent for the first time. Her mother had been shocked that her only daughter did not come home and job-hunt in the town where she had grown up, but her father had understood Sophie's need to spread her wings.

As she boarded the tube she thought of her father. He would be getting out of the car now, kissing her mother on the cheek, and patting Pepsi's head before he drove to his office in Dereham's civic centre. He had been deputy town clerk when first they came to Dereham. Now he was chief executive, and there were lines of fatigue on his face to prove it.

He had taken leave and come down to London when Daisy Ascher had offered Sophie a permanent post. 'Perhaps you should shop around a little?' he'd suggested, but Sophie had been excited by the prospect of power in the store where she had held such lowly posts, and once her father realised the depth of her resolve there'd been no further argument. She had gone home every second weekend and whenever else she had a day or two's leave, and gradually her mother had accepted that her links with Dereham were merely familiar.

Eighteen months later Sophie accepted an invitation to dinner at the home of a colleague and fell into a furious argument over, of all things, the film *Fatal Attraction*. Her opponent was a good-looking guy in a denim shirt and Levis, with an earring in one ear and a soft Liverpool accent, and he'd countered her every criticism of the film's production with what she'd thought was arrogance but which turned out to be a professional interest.

'He fancies you,' her friend said as she left, and Sophie pulled a face.

'That's why he chewed my head off, I suppose.'

'He'll ring you. I've never seen him so keen,' said her host.

'He can ring. I can't bear men who sport earrings.'

The next day a florist delivered a splendid specimen of cactus, done up in Cellophane and tied with red ribbon. On the card was written, 'Enjoyed last night. When can we have round two?' She had looked at the cactus, bristling proudly in its earthen pot, and then she had thrown back her head and laughed aloud.

Three years on, she and Paul were installed in a Notting Hill flat, Daisy Ascher was dead and she, Sophie, was assistant deputy manager at Ascher's of Bond Street, which now belonged to Littlecamp Inc of New York, Boston and LA.

Outside the store now, Sophie paused to inspect the windows. There were suits and jackets displayed on elegant models, striding amid heather and pine logs and piles of autumn leaves. Tweeds were certainly in this year. She gazed longingly at a Givenchy checked tweed jacket with a velvet collar, until a plain taupe flannel jacket, worn over a box-pleated skirt and a polo-necked cashmere sweater caught her eye. The display was enticing, setting unstructured jackets in birdseye and Donegal tweeds against more formal tailoring, and everywhere to be seen was the season's 'must': the waistcoat. It came in every length and texture, in pattern or plain, worn over shirts or frilled blouses, with ski-pants or the fashionable longer-length skirts. Sophie resolved to do some serious clothes-shopping as soon as she knew she was still employed and went in by the centre door, past a magnificent display of Waterford glass on one side and fine bone china on another. It was a tempting lay-out and Sophie made a mental note to praise Display in a memo as soon as she hit her office.

Then the escalator was carrying her up, above the scents of St Laurent and Givenchy and the ubiquitous Estée Lauder, the falls of silk in Fabrics, the gleam of jewellery, hosiery and leather goods of the ground floor, on to the towers of porcelain in China and the silver and gifts and clocks on the second floor, the two storeys of fashion, men's, women's and children's, and finally the rich carpets and gleaming mahogany of the fifth.

I am lucky, Sophie thought, not for the first time. I'm in love, with my man, with my job, with London . . . with life.

She walked through her secretary's office, noticing too late that Sheila's eyes were rolling a warning. A tall lean man in a red-striped shirt and grey silk tie rose from behind the desk in her inner office, holding out one hand in greeting and removing gold-rimmed spectacles from cool grey eyes with the other. 'Gordon Sumner, from Littlecamp in New York,' he said. 'Call me Gordon. You must be Miss Baxter. Sophie . . . if I may?'

His accent was unmistakably American and Sophie felt a sudden irrational burst of anger. He was behind her desk. Her desk! How dare he walk in here and sit down as though he owned the bloody place? So this was what it was going to be like – an arrogant takeover! He had moved her African violet to a shelf and spread out his own papers. Damn cheek!

The American must have seen her eyes flickering across the desk, for he began to shuffle his papers together; but he did it calmly, not like someone conscience-stricken at squatting in someone else's place.

'I'm sorry I wasn't here when you arrived,' Sophie said lamely. It was only eight thirty-seven, so she wasn't late, but she still felt at a disadvantage.

Gordon Sumner looked up and smiled, as though he sensed her unease and was amused by it. 'You didn't know I was coming,' he said, 'so how could you have been here? I came over with David, a last-minute decision. Let's have some breakfast. I want to sample the cafeteria and I could use some coffee. I had tea at my hotel; very nice, but not what I'm used to.'

He was lifting his jacket from the chair and slipping into it with swift, economical movements.

14

He's attractive and he knows it, Sophie thought, and felt her pique grow. However she was careful not to show it. Instead, she smiled warmly. 'Shall I have coffee sent in?'

Gordon Sumner turned down her offer, saying he preferred to sample the coffee served to all personnel, and they walked down the service stairs to the space behind Luggage which housed the staff canteen. Sophie would have gone to the counter but Gordon Sumner motioned her to a red plastic bench and took his place in the queue, returning with two brimming cups and doughnuts on a plate. 'Good,' he said, biting into one and wiping jam from his chin with a tanned third finger. 'Now . . . ' He stirred milk into his coffee before completing the sentence. 'I'm here for five days – a flying visit. Here's what I need . . . '

There followed a list of demands delivered in an unemotional tone and accompanied by a hand-written list extracted from his inside jacket pocket.

Sophie glanced at it. There was nothing she couldn't cope with, but all the same, she thought, she'd better talk to David first.

She raised her eyes from the list to see that Gordon Sumner was smiling. 'I've cleared it with David,' he said. 'We talked on the plane. It's fairly ordinary stuff. I want to know about Ascher's strong points. We believe in specialties; that's how Littlecamp grew and I thought I'd like to check them at first hand.' He grinned. 'Besides, New York in August is a killer, as you probably know.'

When they'd finished their coffee, Sophie returned Gordon Sumner to the fifth floor and surrendered her office to him. 'Feel free,' she said, picking up her African violet and her pending file. 'I'll move in with Sheila while you're here. That'll give you more space.'

She arranged a place for herself in her secretary's office and then went in search of the head of display to deliver her praise for the windows in person. Besides, it was time to plan the Christmas displays. Well, almost time. She could easily leave it for a week or two, but right at this moment she felt the need to talk about something unthreatening. Pine swags and red velvet would fit the bill.

Sophie had finished with the display manager and was on her way back to her office when she saw her call sign flashing: blue and green for David, blue and yellow for her. She had time to reach her own office and take the call there, but it would still be under US occupation. She turned in to Lingerie and sought their phone.

'Sophie? It's me, darling.' As she heard Paul's voice, Sophie breathed thanks to the instinct that had kept her away from Gordon Sumner. He seemed like someone who would take a dim view of private phone calls during business hours.

'Paul?' He was usually too busy to ring her during the day.

'Yes, it's me. I won't be home on time, darling. We've lost a guest on the prison reform gig. The linch-pin, actually. Bernard's tearing his hair – well, he would be if he had some. He wants me to try and get Lord Spence but we can't find out where he is, so I'll be back when I can, but don't hold your breath.'

'Can't one of the researchers do it?' A customer had selected two or three laced-trimmed half-slips and was looking around for a fitting room. Sophie caught an assistant's eye and flashed signals until the woman understood. 'Sorry, Paul – what did you say?'

'I said it would be quicker if I did it – we've got to have someone *pronto*. We're in studio tomorrow, remember. I'm sorry, Soph, I was looking forward to tonight. I've cancelled the table. Still, when we get the last of the *Heart and Souls* in the can, I'll take a few days and we can go off somewhere. I need to go home anyway, it's ages since I saw Gary. We'll combine the two.'

They said goodbye with exhortations on her part and promises on his, and Sophie made her way towards the escalator. Damn Bernard and his unreasonable demands; any one of his researchers could track down a peer of the realm, especially one as prominent as Oscar Spence, who was famous for his prison-visiting and his odd appearance. But even as she cursed Paul's boss, she admitted that it was probably Paul himself who was obsessed with finding a replacement guest. He was totally committed to his job. We're both like that, Sophie thought.

All the same, Paul's crazy working hours were a drag and another uneasy thought was niggling at the back of her mind. Paul had said they'd soon need to visit Liverpool. Sophie's heart always sank at the mention of his home city, not because she disliked Paul's almost boundless family, his parents and siblings and aunts and uncles and cousins, once twice and three times removed. She could never remember their names but she liked them well enough. No, it was Julie she feared, Paul's girlfriend throughout adolescence, who had borne him a child when he was eighteen.

Gary was ten years old now, gap-toothed and streetwise and charming enough to wind his father round his little finger. It would be different when they had their own children, but now the sight of Paul paying rapt attention to his son made her feel vulnerable. She was always intending to quiz Paul about Julie but when first she had tried, he had shied away from the subject and gradually she had given up. They would have to talk about it one day, though. It was an important part of Paul's past and his present too.

Sophie went to the loo, repaired her make-up, fixed a confident smile on her face and made for her office, where she spent the afternoon talking easily enough about customer demand, space values and market trends. At the end of the day, she saw Gordon Sumner to his waiting cab and accepted his invitation to lunch the following week. 'I'll book somewhere nice,' he said. 'We'll relax and talk, and I'll fill you in on what you'll find when you come over.'

The cab was moving out into the traffic before his words struck home. *When you come over.* He had said it casually, but what exactly did it mean? Still, a trip to the States would be brilliant, especially if she could learn about other companies' trading methods. She went back upstairs and cleared her desk before leaving.

On her way home, Sophie decided to stop at the local Italian delicatessen and buy some of its excellent home-made pasta. Ambling back through the mews, she paused to peer in at the windows of the antique shop. One day, when they were very old, she and Paul might retire to a country town and run a shop crammed with *objets d'art* and graceful Edwardian furniture. She smiled at her reflection, thinking of Paul's response when she had first mentioned it: 'Count me out, Soph. I'm a member of the throw-away generation.'

Still, it was a nice day-dream. A papier-mâché box caught her eye; it was meant for snuff, probably, and looked as though it could be French, the lid painted with lovers embracing while cherubs gazed fondly down on them. There was a ticket attached and she craned her neck to see the price, but all she could make out was a stock number. She looked towards the back of the window, admiring a rosewood card table with sycamore bandings, its baize-lined, semi-circular top inlaid with swags of flowers.

It was Kate, her grandmother, who had taught her to appreciate antiques. Her mother was into strictly unblemished top-quality reproduction, but Kate loved and valued old wood and fragile, hand-painted china. A twinge of conscience overtook Sophie as she continued walking down the mews, remembering her mother always polishing and cleaning, keeping everything immaculate, unable to live with a spot or a stain or tolerate a cushion out of place. She must ring her tonight. After all, it wasn't a sin to want things nice. She would ring Kate too and find out what the family's *enfant terrible* was up to.

Sophie was half-way up the second flight when Chloe's voice echoed up the stairwell. 'Is that you, Sophie? You must come in and see this. And don't tell me you've got something horribly domestic to do. There's more to life than being a slave to the oven.'

'I was coming in, anyway,' Sophie protested, turning to descend again. 'And I hardly ever cook. God, you exaggerate.'

'Shut up,' Chloe said, as she ushered Sophie into her flat.

She wore a giant white T-shirt emblazoned with *Je t'aime*, and her feet were bare. Her glossy, dark hair fell free almost to her waist, hooked back behind her ear on either side of her face. She held two glasses by the base between her fingers and a half-full bottle of Chablis in her other hand. 'Drink this and look at that,' she ordered.

'That' was a dusty, rather grim-looking bottle, presumably containing wine although its uninspired label gave little indication of the contents. A space had been cleared for it among the perfume, chocolates, opened letters and discarded jewellery that littered the sideboard.

Chloe poured wine from the opened bottle into the glasses. She handed one to Sophie and then threw herself into a chair, lifting her long bare legs over the arm and raising her glass in a silent toast.

'Cheers,' Sophie said, sipping from her own glass and looking around the room. Normally it was a mass of clutter. Today it was a little neater. 'You've tidied up. What was it, a religious conversion?'

'Don't be sarky, darling. It doesn't become you. Guess.'

'You've landed a job?' Sophie suggested, leaning closer to examine the bottle.

Chloe was a freelance journalist living in hope of one of the broadsheets offering her a column.

'No, although I'm lunching with someone from the *Telegraph* on Monday. It might lead to something. If it does, we'll open that bottle.'

'What is it?' Sophie said. 'It looks like iron tonic.'

'Looks deceive,' Chloe said portentously. 'Anyway, sod the way it looks. It cost four hundred pounds.'

'You're joking.' Sophie leaned even closer. The bottle looked somehow more distinguished since Chloe's announcement, but surely no bottle could cost four hundred pounds, not even vintage champagne.

Chloe sat up, crossed her legs and held her foot with one hand, her glass aloft in the other. 'God's honour. It's incredibly old and rare, and six bottles came up for auction yesterday. They went for two thousand, four hundred pounds. Desmond, my new man, bought them and gave me one as a prezzy.'

Sophie had seen the new man on the stairs, and there had been an aura of affluence about him. 'What'll you do with it?' she asked weakly.

'Well, I shan't drink it,' Chloe said. 'It'll probably be vile, but it's not that. It's the waste. I live on a shoestring, you know that. The wolf isn't at the door, he's up my bloody backside half the time.'

'You can't sell it,' Sophie said, scandalised.

'I don't want one of your lectures on etiquette, darling. We were all well brought up but some of us have to live. I shan't sell it *now* – not while Desmond's still around. I shall put it in the cupboard. It'll probably appreciate in value with time. Maybe I'll get a grand for it and buy some decent champagne.

Sophie sat back in the comfortable chair, suddenly feeling mellow as the plonk began to do its work. 'It'll need time to appreciate. Do you anticipate Desmond being around for long?'

'Who knows, darling? He's in touch with everyone and he's thick as thieves with Andrew Neil. Besides, he's very dishy.'

'He's very married,' Sophie offered, reaching for the Chablis to refill her glass. 'Or he sounds it. Want some?'

'Ta,' Chloe said. 'Of course he's married; important men always are. He and his wife don't sleep together. They were in the same legal chambers, and it just kind of happened. She's in the spotlight at the moment . . . ' The long legs flailed as Chloe crossed the room to rummage in the paper rack. 'There she is . . . she's defending that guy who ripped off his investors.'

Sophie studied the picture of the attractive blonde with upswept hair and cool eyes under dark brows, wondering if she should point out that philanderers always claimed not to sleep with their wives. But Chloe wouldn't listen; the affair would have to run its course. Chloe would have a good time, and then there would be twenty-four hours of tantrums and weeping, from which she would emerge bright-eyed and ready for more. 'She looks a bit like Hillary Clinton,' she said instead, and handed back the paper.

'This is nice,' Chloe said, lifting her legs again and settling back. 'You're usually itching to get upstairs to Paul. God, he must be good in bed, the way you drool over him.'

'I don't! That's outrageous, even for you. I wouldn't live with him if I didn't like him, but I wouldn't even know how to drool.'

'Sorry,' Chloe said contritely. 'You *never* want to get back to him, and all those sounds of passion I hear from upstairs are really just you hoovering.'

'You don't?' Sophie said, suddenly horrified.

'No, of course I don't, you nerd. These walls are Bastille-like. So are the ceilings. Now, drink up and then tell me what you're going to cook for my supper. There's only half a bouillon cube in the cupboard – ' her voice took on a quaver – 'and I can't remember when I ate my last meal. Was it Monday . . . or a week gone Friday?'

'I've got some pasta and yes, you can have some. Now I know why I was invited in – to be your meal ticket.'

'Wash your mouth out, Baxter. My motives in asking you in were above reproach. I didn't want to drink alone and I wanted to show off my Beaujolais-not-very-*Nouveau*.'

They went upstairs together, carrying the remains of the wine and chattering about little or nothing, but as Sophie unpacked the food she kept thinking of Chloe's remark. Did she drool? Were her feelings for Paul so obvious? Chloe had been joking – she never said anything serious – but that didn't mean she might not stumble upon the truth – occasionally. Would it matter if the world did see how much she loved Paul? It's not the way I was brought up, she thought, I wasn't encouraged to show emotion.

She was manoeuvring dishes on the cooker when the phone rang in the living-room. 'It's your mum,' Chloe said from the doorway. 'I told her you were in bed with a Rastafarian, but she didn't believe me.'

'Watch the pasta,' Sophie said. 'And don't add any

spices to the sauce. I haven't forgotten the last time you "helped". We were drinking iced water for a week.'

Her mother's greeting had a faint edge of hurt feelings.

'Sorry, Mum. I was going to ring tonight, honestly! Is Daddy okay?'

In the kitchen Chloe was running through the score of *Les Miserables* and clashing pan lids for accompaniment, so that Sophie had to strain to hear.

'Who's had her baby? Oh, Sue. A boy, that's nice. I'll send a card.'

Sophie had known Susan Denham since infants' school, had sat next to her through O and A levels and bidden her a tearful farewell when Susan went into a bank and she went off to university. And now Susan was a mother!

'Is she still in Midholme Close? Yes, I've got it in my book. Of course we're coming up soon. You know we are. I can see the baby then. Give Sue my love. What shall I buy him? I'm no good with sizes for babies.'

She wrote 'baby' on the memo board when she went back to the kitchen and then, as Chloe raised her eyebrows, 'My schoolfriend's had a little boy. I'm not pregnant, and if I were I wouldn't need a reminder.'

'I hope you're on the pill,' Chloe said. 'Personally I use garlic and a crucifix above the bed. Oh, and a silver bullet for the little bastard if it ever makes it.'

'You are coarse, Chloe,' Sophie said, but she was glad of a chance to laugh. It had been a wearing day, one way and another, and it was good to unwind.

2

TODAY, SOPHIE WAS LUNCHING WITH Gordon Sumner. She decided to wear her new navy and cream linen suit, its skirt long and flared and slit to the thigh. The jacket was cream with navy binding on the revers and cuffs and the camisole she wore beneath it was striped cream and navy with a red motif on the left breast.

'You look like a French matelot,' Paul said approvingly when she was ready to leave, and kissed her warmly. She was clattering down the stairs to run for the tube when she remembered she had forgotten to tell him about the US prospect. She would tell him tonight, over dinner, and they could discuss it and make plans. Perhaps he could take a week's leave and come over with her; that would be heaven, she thought, as she hurled herself into the crowded train which reminded her that her working day began.

Gordon Sumner had booked a table at the Ritz, and although Sophie had been taken there several times before with foreign buyers she still gazed in wonder at the ornate ceiling of the restaurant and the glitter of crystal and silver below.

He ordered kir royales, and Sophie settled back to study the large, embossed menu. The restaurant had been half empty when they had arrived, but gradually the tables were filling and waiters were gliding smoothly backwards and forwards, taking orders, pouring wine, or making solicitous enquiries as to their customers' comfort. Left to herself, Sophie would have picked somewhere less grand, if only because she'd never have dared submit a Ritz bill on expenses. However David had declared that hospitality for US colleagues was to be unstinted, so she fully intended to pay the bill when lunch was over.

'I don't want anything to start,' the American said, looking at her over the top of the embossed menu, 'but I'll gladly chatter away while you have something.'

Sophie shook her head. 'No, I'll settle for one course.' They both chose steak au poivre with a green salad on the side, and a bottle of mineral water.

'With ice,' Sumner said as he handed back the menu. 'Now,' he turned his gaze to Sophie, 'before we get down to details, let me thank you for all your help over the last few days.' He glanced around. 'This is an amazing place. Do you entertain here a lot?'

Sophie had to laugh at the idea of dining regularly at the Ritz. 'Not on my salary,' she said.

It was just a throw-away remark, but he took it seriously. 'We're going to look at pay-levels,' he said. 'At first glance they're low – very low by US standards – but we don't want to start tweaking the system, a little here and a little there. I'm over here for a preliminary look-see. There'll be others following me. When things settle down, we'll adjust salaries.'

'When things settle down,' Sophie said. 'That sounds ominous. Does it mean you're going to make changes?'

His answer was direct and she liked him for it. 'Inevitably. We bought Ascher's because we liked the product. It stands for all that's upper crust in retailing. But, and probably because it's such a long-established company, some of its practices are archaic. We wouldn't have entered the bidding if we hadn't thought we could up the profit margin appreciably. Thirty per cent, probably. That will mean streamlining, job-shedding, a much faster turn around of stock – and, yes, there are some people who won't fit in to a slimmed-down company – but you needn't worry.'

Sophie was glad that the waiter arrived at that moment, saving her from a reply. She wasn't afraid of redundancy, though she wouldn't welcome it, but she didn't like the thought of Ascher's being 'streamlined'. 'Will you be glad to go home?' she asked as Gordon Sumner picked up his knife and fork and stirred the garnish around his steak.

'This looks wonderful,' he said, 'quite wonderful . . . yes, it will be good to get back to my wife, and her fried chicken! We have two boys, and I miss them. They're in Vermont at the moment, with my wife's parents. Jessica goes there as often as she can. As I told you, being in New York in August is not to be endured. The heat is almost tangible.'

Sophie nodded. 'I've never been there in August, but I can imagine. I was there briefly last September and that was bad enough.'

'But you liked it?'

'Oh yes. Brief as it was, I enjoyed it. We went on Friday at lunchtime, and had tea in Manhattan, thanks to the time difference.'

'What impressed you most?' His eyes were keen behind the rimless specs, and she took time to consider her answer.

'The Trump Tower . . . all that black glass. Very impressive. And the Helmsley building and the World Trade Center. We went up in a helicopter. Sixty-nine dollars, it cost, but we had a wonderful view of the Hudson river and the Statue of Liberty.' She grinned. 'The single most impressive sight was the stretch limos. They went on for ever.'

'What did you think of the stores?' This was business talk now.

'Good. Well laid out, with classy merchandise – I'm referring to Saks and Bloomingdales, of course – but the tops was the gift shop at the Metropolitan Museum of Art; that was something. The trip was over too soon, though. There were so many more things I wanted to do and see.'

'There'll be plenty of time when you come over.' Sumner

aligned his knife and fork and sat back. 'Tell me about your home-life. You're not married. Does that mean you live alone?'

'No, I share a flat with my partner, Paul.'

'He's not in retailing?'

'No. He works in television, as a producer for an independent company called Condor. They make quite a number of programmes for ITV and one or two for the BBC.'

'I'm impressed. British television is superb. I love the programmes we get back home. It's always easy to pick out a British product.' A waiter was hovering but Sumner waved him away.

'Paul will love that when I tell him. Does your wife work?'

'She's a baby-doctor, a paediatrician. And our two run rings round her.' He shook his head and laughed. 'I tell her, you're the expert, handle them, but she just gives in. Mother-love, I suppose.' Suddenly he was serious again. 'This Paul of yours, he'll understand when you need to move?'

'What exactly does "move" mean?' Sophie asked carefully. She felt a sudden lump in her throat and reached for her glass.

Gordon Sumner took a sip of mineral water and smiled. 'One of the reasons we wanted the House of Ascher, as I said, was because it has class, and apparently you are strong in that department. "Impeccable taste with an eye to trends", that's what David said.'

Sophie felt at once annoyed and flattered. So she had been an Ascher asset, something to trade.

'We don't intend to tamper with your management structure,' Sumner continued, 'not at first. If it ain't broke, et cetera. But we do envisage rationalisation, and the first thing is to acquaint London with our way of doing things. So you'll be coming over to work with us later this year and we'll send one of our people to replace you: we call it cross-fertilisation. You'll love New York.'

'I'm sure I will,' Sophie said carefully. Wild excitement

was gripping her but there was fear too. 'How long would this placement last?' she asked him, hating the primness of her tone but unable to help it.

Gordon Sumner shrugged. 'Who knows? CJ – that's CJ Littlecamp Junior – may want you to stay for a while. There wouldn't be a problem with Paul, would there?'

'Of course not,' Sophie said defensively. 'As I said, he'll understand. His own work takes him all over – he's recently come back from Zaire. Besides, it's understood nowadays, isn't it? That you each do your own thing, I mean.'

Gordon seemed to accept what she said and they talked shop for a while before the conversation turned to films, as she told him how much she had enjoyed the John Grisham novel, *The Firm*.

'I've seen the film,' he said, 'at a preview. It's brilliant, but I preferred the book. I can take Tom Cruise or leave him alone. I'd rather have seen Kevin Costner in the role.'

Sophie confessed to a weakness for Tom Berenger and the rest of the meal was spent discussing whether or not Madonna had painted herself into a corner. But as they talked Sophie's mind was racing furiously. New York, Boston or LA – or wherever they sent her would be fantastic. What would it do to Paul? Her mother? Her whole damn lifestyle?

'I enjoyed that,' Gordon Sumner said, as they came out into Piccadilly. He had firmly stemmed Sophie's attempt to settle the bill. 'Shall we walk back?' They began to thread their way through the early afternoon crowds, trying to keep up a conversation until they lapsed into silence and simply enjoyed the sun. But as Sophie walked towards Bond Street, the slit in her long skirt allowing her to stride freely, she felt a sense of unease. *Would* Paul mind if she had to work away? She had given Gordon Sumner the answer she'd thought he would expect, but she and Paul were more inclined to philosophise about life than actually plan its details.

She was glad when they got back to her office and Gordon was whisked away to confer with David, leaving her free to get out her file on the luxury knitwear Ascher's imported from Italy, soon to be the subject of re-negotiation. Getting down to facts and figures would calm her thoughts.

Today, though, the samples of mohair, angora, cashmere and pure merino in the season's shades failed to attract. She fingered them dutifully and listened attentively as the knit-wear buyer enthused and outlined her sales campaign, but the buzz she usually felt was missing. New York! Working in New York! Inside her, excitement still fizzed. She looked at the clock frequently, sometimes unable to believe the hands had moved so little since last she checked.

When at last she was free to sink back into her leather chair and enjoy a cup of tea she tried to analyse her feelings. In an effort to shake off her mood she went through the worst-scene scenario. If a prolonged stay in America was compulsory, she could say no. That would probably mean the end of her career with Ascher's but, in addition to her degree, she now had that precious commodity: experience. There were other stores; other careers, come to that, and if she was out of work for a while, they could cope. As she returned her cup to its saucer it occurred to her that Paul might even welcome the opportunity to be sole bread-winner for a while. There was still a streak of Liverpool patriarch under the New Man.

She worked steadily on after that, until Gordon Sumner looked in to say goodnight. Once she was sure he was clear of the building, she sought out her boss and confronted him with all that Gordon Sumner had mentioned about the trip to the States.

'Blame me,' David Lister said, throwing up his hands in contrition. 'I told them that you were the key to the operation here and – predictably, I suppose – they decided you'd be useful over there, too. I don't suppose it'll be forever. It won't be if I have any say in it. You're needed here. But you must admit it makes sense to have key personnel *au fait* with operations on both sides of the Atlantic.'

Sophie nodded. 'Yes, and I do see that it's a huge oppor-tunity. It's just the thought of upping sticks, I suppose.'

'What will Paul say?'

'I don't know. I'm sure he'll understand. That was one of the things we settled from the beginning: professional freedom for both sides. I didn't mention it when it was first suggested because it was so vague. It all depends on how long I'll be there, I suppose. He's often said he'd like to work in New York TV for a while. This might be the chance.'

David was shuffling together the papers they'd been working on. 'Try not to worry. I'll get some dates for you as soon as I can. In the meantime, keep Sumner dazzled. You have to live up to that reputation I built for you.'

It was six thirty when she got home, praying Paul would already be there, but the flat was empty, and there was no sign of life from Chloe's flat either, which was just as well. She wasn't in the mood for conversation tonight and, much as she loved her neighbour, Chloe was hard to resist when she wanted company.

As Sophie rinsed Chinese leaves and chopped fennel for salad she thought about Chloe. As yet she had no permanent job but she seemed oblivious to her state of insecurity. She was always pressing onward, following up contacts, making plans. Each freelance cheque was a cause for celebration and somehow she survived the lean weeks in between. I envy her, Sophie thought, her hands still on the chopping board, her eyes fixed on the window without seeing the rooftops beyond. Not her life – I wouldn't swop – but her *joie de vivre.*'

She returned to the salad, wondering why she took things so seriously. Her upbringing had been totally secure. The words meticulously planned rose up in her mind, but she suppressed them. It wasn't fair to think of her mother like that. She was methodical, but since when was that a crime? She heard steps on the stairs and her mood lightened.

'Soph?' Paul looked tired as he came through the kitchen door but his face brightened at the sight of the food. He reached for a knife and cut himself a chunk of cheese. 'God, I'm famished. Today has been a shit.'

They carried the food through to the living-room and

settled at the table. 'Open some wine and tell me all about it,' she said soothingly.

'Well . . . ' He heaved on the cork and it gave with a satisfying plop. 'Bernard is going to Channel Four: commissioning editor, factual programmes.'

'After all he's said about Michael Grade?' Sophie countered, forking up salad and heaping it on to his plate.

'That's the game, my love. Slag off the opposition until you get a chance to leap aboard. Anyway he's off. Which means Carl moves up and his job goes to me or Liz. You could cut the atmosphere with a knife.'

Sophie whistled. 'Nice. I mean, nice even to be in the running.' Privately she was already working out how to console him when the inevitable disappointment came. Why do I doubt his ability to land the job? she thought later, when they had fallen into a contented food-laden silence on the sofa and a documentary on Bosnia was occupying the TV screen. Paul was good at his job. He had flair and a respect for the audience which she thought lacking in some of his colleagues. So why did she take failure in her men for granted?

'Comfy?' Paul had slipped a protective arm around her and was rubbing the nape of her neck. 'You've got your knots, again.' Sophie tried to relax her shoulders, to let the tension go, but his gently probing fingers were eliciting pain deep in her muscles. 'Nice?' he asked, and she murmured her appreciation.

But even as the massage penetrated and began to work, her mind clung tenaciously to its uneasy thoughts. It wasn't that she doubted Paul, it was more a desire to protect him, to shield him from every harm. She felt like that about her father, too; had hated it when her mother had disparaged his efforts or ignored his attempts to please her. She had even felt sorry for Gordon Sumner, miles from home and family. It was silly, really. Her father was a happily married, successful man and Paul was brilliant at his job. As for Sumner, he had the power to fire everyone on the Ascher payroll, and had no need of her protection or sympathy. It's the female dilemma, she thought as she reached for the wine bottle. We're conditioned to care for the male. As she filled her glass she remembered Chloe's remark about drooling. Well, sod that, she thought, and turned her attention to the television set.

She was lying in the bath when Paul came in to rummage in the cabinet. 'I've been thinking,' he said as he found what he was looking for, 'if I get Carl's job – *if*, I say – we should look around for a place to buy. Nothing ambitious, but this is a good time with the market depressed and the sooner we get a foot on the property ladder, the better.'

Sophie pulled a face and then lifted the brimming sponge to hide her mouth while she tried to figure out her reaction to what Paul had just said. A part of her was pleased that he wanted to put their relationship on to a more solid footing. If he wanted them to buy a property it meant he was happy in their relationship; but it would be a millstone, too. Did she want a doll-sized semi in Acton? The drips from the sponge felt suddenly chill and she sat up abruptly so that the water slapped against the sides of the bath.

'We'll see,' she said. 'Now, let me get out before this water cools.' The feeling that she had fobbed him off and missed an opportunity to discuss the future filled her with guilt. 'Fancy a pint?' she said as she reached for a towel.

Paul froze and turned huge, soulful eyes on her. 'Why honey . . . ' he said, in a Southern drawl. 'I *was* hoping for an early night.'

Sophie flicked him with the towel. 'Later,' she said. 'Everything comes to he who waits.'

It took her two minutes to pull on jeans and a T-shirt and then they were out in the warm dusk, arms linked for the walk to the pub they preferred, The Star and Garter. They turned the corner and suddenly the air was heavy with the scent of honeysuckle. It was twined in and out of the railings of the second house and by unspoken consent they stood still to breathe in the aroma. 'Honeysuckle . . . it always reminds me of home.' Sophie breathed in again as she finished speaking.

'Let's have honeysuckle on our railings when we move,' Paul said. 'And a gnome with a fishing rod. I've always wanted a gnome with a fishing rod and a red hat, sitting on a little bridge.'

'How incredibly naff,' Sophie said. 'He should have a green hat and be cobbling shoes.'

'We'll have both,' Paul said grandly. 'And a rose-covered trellis . . . '

' . . . and a herb garden,' Sophie said. 'Laid out Elizabethan fashion, all squares and semi-circles.'

They walked along the scented street, trying to outdo one another, adding a ha-ha and a pergola and a pony in a paddock, and then they were blinking their way into the smoky, well-lit pub and hitching themselves on to stools at the bar.

Paul drank lager and Sophie white wine, a companionable silence between them. 'No sign of Chloe tonight,' Paul said at last.

'She's probably out with Desmond.'

Paul grinned. 'Do I detect a note of disapproval?'

'Yes,' Sophie said. 'Oh, I'm not making moral judgements. He's married, but that's not my problem. It's just that sooner or later she'll be hurt. She almost invites it.'

'She'll settle down one of these days,' Paul said indulgently. 'When she meets the right guy. There's no harm in Chloe.' There was an amused note in his voice and Sophie felt an irrational irritation. She was fond of Chloe, but all the same, she did get away with murder.

'Who is this Desmond?' she asked. 'Chloe talks as though I ought to know him, and I gather his wife's quite well known . . . '

'He acted in that libel case a while ago. Where the *Daily Globe* accused a doctor of shady practices. He specialises in that sort of thing. But it's his wife who's really high profile. She's the daughter of a former chancellor who's in the Lords now. You'd know his face. He was in one of Wilson's governments. She's a bit of a champagne socialist. They're very "in" at the moment. A "glittering" couple.'

'One of whom is playing away,' Sophie said drily. It suddenly seemed tacky.

They slid down from their stools at last and went out into the darkness. Stars had appeared above them and there was a faint chill in the air. 'Come here,' Paul said, and pulled her close. 'When we're married I will never play away. As for you, I shall only buy you the finest of chastity belts . . . '

'Ooh, ta,' Sophie said. 'Anyway, by the time I'm married sex, marital or extra-marital, will be a thing of the past. We'll all be into virtual reality.'

'Never,' Paul said. They were passing the doorway of a shop and he pulled her into its depth. 'It's years since I necked in a shop doorway. That's what we did for amusement in Liverpool.'

'Not your deprived childhood again,' Sophie began, but his lips were cutting off her words and she gave herself up to his kiss until he let her go.

'Let's go home,' he said. 'Who wants a shop doorway when they have a bed of their own?'

She smiled foolishly in the darkness, wanting him as much as he wanted her, enjoying the thought of what lay ahead but still half-wishing he'd drop the idea of house-hunting. They would do it eventually. She certainly couldn't imagine life without him, so it would all have to happen eventually. But not yet. Not for ages yet.

As they strolled towards home she tried to analyse her feelin. s. She was not the product of a broken home. Almost the reverse. Her father and mother lived for one another. She felt the faint unease she always felt when she thought about her parents. They loved one another. Neither of them could be unfaithful; they hadn't the capacity. Her father adored her mother and she was the perfect wife. Her life revolved around husband and home. It does! Sophie heard herself allowing it in her head. Mum's life does revolve around being Dad's wife. It does. There was a second voice, insidious and mean, saying, but you don't want that, do you? Sophie heard it and quelled it in the same instant. It didn't do to analyse things too much. She squeezed Paul's arm against her side and grinned up at him to show that all was well.

They were almost home how and she glanced into the basement areas of the houses they were passing. Some were dark, even shuttered, but others were lit, the life within them exposed as though on a cinema screen. In the first room a man was bent over a drawing board, a pencil poised in one hand, his head propped on the other. Next door a young girl was blow-drying her hair. After that, two houses were dark and then, shockingly, Sophie found herself looking at a man and woman, each half-naked, clasped in one another's arms. As if he sensed prying eyes, the man detached himself and crossed to the window to twitch the curtains together.

Sophie walked on but the sight had disturbed her. Would the couple make love, safe now in the curtained room, perhaps even make a baby together and thereby irrevocably change the course of their lives? It was always there, the remorseless process of reproduction, in every street in every town in every country in the world. It was inescapable as air itself: grow, love, reproduce, die. She shivered and Paul put his arm around her and drew her closer. 'Nearly home,' he said.

As Sophie pulled off her clothes and prepared for bed she again thought of her mother. She had meant to ring her tonight and once more she'd left it undone.

'You're frowning,' Paul said, coming up behind her.

'I'm not.'

'You were, I saw you in the mirror. Bringing your brows down in that executive brook-no-nonsense style of yours.'

'I was just thinking of home, that's all.'

'Ah.' Paul was distancing himself, looking around the bedroom with a theatrical stare. 'I might have guessed it. You're comparing this squalor with the Laura Ashley commemoration centre. I'm sorry this is all I can afford . . . '

'Shut up, beast. I designed this room – well, re-arranged it. And you know I loathe flowers and polka dots. I was thinking I ought to have rung Mum this evening, that's all.'

'Ring her tomorrow.' He was reaching for her, tugging

on her shoulders until she came to him, until they were subsiding on to the bed and she was trying to dispel the images of home and couples clinging in lighted rooms and semi-detacheds hung with honeysuckle that twined suspiciously like a chain.

It was afterwards, when she was drifting into sleep, that she pondered how little she and Paul fitted the perceptions of the experts. She ought to be the one who wanted domesticity, a home, a wedding ring. Paul should be the one who wanted his freedom. I do love him, she thought. Whatever else is in doubt, that at least is true.

She smiled in the darkness, remembering how it had been when she went off to university: home-baked cookies in a tin for comfort, her mother's strictures on losing men's respect ringing in her ears. She had had two serious relationships, one in her first year which had cost her her virginity and most of her illusions, and another in her final year which had been for mutual comfort while they struggled through their finals. Neither of them meant much, she thought, marvelling at the memory of the tears, the angst, the constant anxieties of partnership. What she had with Paul was so much more rounded. She turned on to her side, tucking herself against him, and gave herself up to sleep.

3

THROUGH THE GLASS PARTITION SOPHIE could see two of the canteen staff setting out glasses and trays of canapés. She tried to look covertly at her watch. Twelve fifteen. In a quarter of an hour they were to say an official farewell to Gordon Sumner. She shifted slightly in her chair and tried to look intensely interested in what the teenager on the other side of the desk was saying.

'It's not that I don't like it in Packing, exactly.' He had freckles on his nose and stubby ginger lashes which made her think of Mickey Rooney. 'It's just, well . . . ' He shrugged. 'You know . . . '

'One day's much like another?' Sophie suggested. He nodded, relieved that apparently she understood. 'I used to work in Packing.'

His eyes widened at the very idea and Sophie smiled. 'It was one of my first jobs at Ascher's and I thought it was boring – until I started taking an interest in who was buying what.' She reached for the gold-edged, mail-order catalogue. 'A third of our trade comes through this brochure, Michael. Customers as far away as Dublin or Brussels or Land's End or Inverness, all wanting Ascher merchandise.

We pride ourselves on that – that we're not just exclusive to Londoners or rich tourists.'

She saw he was dying to speak and waited until the hesitant words came.

'You've got to be well off, though.'

'True. This is an exclusive shop, and pricey. I don't deny that. But not all our customers are fabulously wealthy. Some of them save for Ascher goods because they know they'll last.'

She would have to get a move on. It was twelve twenty and she needed to go to the loo. 'You have some thinking to do, Michael. We took you on because your parents both work here and they're splendid employees. We want you to be happy here, but if you're not, you're no use to us. We're pretty benevolent employers, I think you'd agree on that, but we want one hundred per cent effort and lately you've been giving . . . ' She put her head on one side and raised her brows until he was forced to grin.

'Ninety per cent?' he said ruefully.

'That's the charitable estimate,' she said. She reached for another slim volume. 'Now, I want you to take this. It's the story of how Ascher's was established and grew. Read it, and think over whether or not you want to be part of it. If you do, I promise to move you when I can. If not, come and see me again and tell me honestly. We'll do all we can to help you change your plans. You can stay on here until you find another job, providing you give us your best in the meantime.'

Sophie rose to her feet to indicate that the interview was over and smiled as he made for the door, the Ascher story clutched in his hand. Five minutes later she was powdering her nose and touching up her lipstick, ready to face the assembled Ascher hierarchy in the boardroom which led off the outer office.

The staff stood around in groups of three or four, sipping a good quality Chablis and making conversation, trying desperately to think of what to say when Gordon Sumner joined their group. At last David was moving to the head

of the room and clearing his throat: 'Ladies and gentlemen
. . . ' He paid tribute to their American visitor, who had
been a model of tact and diplomacy, and then handed over
to Gordon Sumner himself.

The American made the usual joke about feeling like a
brash intruder in the hallowed halls of such an ancient empo-
rium, and then thanked everyone for their co-operation. He
named key individuals, Sophie amongst them, and then,
warming to his theme, threw open his arms in a gesture
of welcome. 'We are delighted that Ascher's is now part of
Littlecamp. We look forward to a trans-Atlantic fertilisation
that will benefit both companies. The first wave of that
cross-fertilisation will begin quite soon when my assistant,
Susan Goss, comes here and Sophie Baxter goes to New
York. She'll be followed by . . . ' He was moving on to other
names, but Sophie wasn't listening. Up to this point, it had
all seemed a bit vague. Now, unless she registered a protest
she was going to New York. She would have to talk to Paul
tonight and see what he could arrange.

She waited until the crowd began to disperse before
she approached Gordon Sumner. 'This exchange . . . ' she
began, but already his hand was on her arm in reassurance.

'Don't worry. You'll have an apartment and someone to
ease you into both the store routine and life in New York.
I hope you'll fix up for Susie to have the same courtesy
when she comes over. She plans to be here mid-November
so there'll be time. You'll like her. She's a great girl and she
can't wait to devour London.'

Now was the time to say, 'I'm not sure I can go.'
Instead Sophie heard herself saying, 'How long will the
exchange last?'

He threw up his arms. 'Well, it depends. You may get to
like it and stay. That was Susie's first thought. Her mother
was a GI bride, so she has connections here. But we'll see.
London and New York are both fascinating cities. You can't
take them in in a week. You're not going to back out,
are you?'

Here it was, the loophole, the escape, the opportunity

to extricate herself and keep the status quo. 'No,' she said carefully, 'I just need to know, that's all.'

He left at four thirty, in a taxi which would take him to Heathrow. 'See you in the fall,' he said. Twenty minutes later, when she was still arranging her desk, Paul rang.

'Can you come over here?' he asked. 'We're having a party for Bernard. He goes tomorrow. And . . . ' There was a long silence.

'Well?' she said at last.

'Can't you guess?'

'If I could guess, I wouldn't ask?'

'Moderate your fire, lady. You are speaking to the new executive producer of Condor Films. Watch your lip.'

'Oh, Paul! Oh, darling.' Sophie felt a sweep of emotion, joy for him, fear for herself; the exhilaration that went hand in hand with, 'Careful.' Mustn't build up hopes, mustn't be too euphoric. Lady Luck would get you if you did, turning gold to dross, joy to ashes, even as you watched. 'Wait and see.' That had been her mother's mantra all through her growing up.

'I'm *so* glad, darling. You deserve it.'

She couldn't tell him about America now; couldn't ask him to uproot himself and follow her. She ran the scenario over in her mind – telling David that she couldn't go, writing to Gordon Sumner, collecting her P45, signing on. Where was the Jobcentre? She had never been out of work in London. Or anywhere else, for that matter.

'It'll be a bit of a knees-up, so come straight here. I'm not going to get pissed, so don't worry, but I'll have to put on a show. Bernard will expect it.'

'What about Liz? How's she taking it?'

'Oh, you know – she never expected to get the job, didn't want it, wouldn't have it if it was gift-wrapped – the usual drill.'

'But she's choked?'

'Oh yes, she's choked all right. I'll give her two weeks and she'll be gone. Channel Four, probably. She's well in with Bernard. He'll see her right.'

Sophie promised to be prompt at the party and put down the phone. She'd been looking forward to doing nothing tonight. Just lazing around, nibbling leftovers, letting telly wash over her. Telling Paul about America and suggesting he take a sabbatical and come with her; better still, arrange an attachment with CBS or one of the other stations.

That would be impossible once he took up his new job, Sophie thought. He'd be like a child with a new toy now that he was an exec: doing treatments for all his pet projects, re-organising, shuffling budgets. She'd met him just after he got his first producer's job and knew the form. He'd been a runner for a Wardour Street company for a year and then gone to LWT as a researcher. Three years of doing the donkey work on *Surprise, Surprise* and *Aspel*, and then a place at Condor as a producer. And now he was executive producer with a clutch of programmes and the chance to put all his pet projects on the MD's desk.

When she had cleared her desk, she locked herself in the executive loo and tried to make herself look festive, taking off her white shirt and buttoning up the jacket of her black suit so that just a hint of cleavage showed above the single rope of pearls, each as big as a pullet's egg. When she looked in the mirror to apply eyeliner and blusher, her face looked defiantly back at her. She wanted to go to the States, wanted to see, to learn, to achieve power. If that was a sin, she was guilty.

They were sheeting the counters as she moved through the store. Soon it would be deserted, except for the cleaners moving between glass counters, flicking a duster here, polishing off a fingermark there. As she hailed a cab she tried to imagine life without Ascher's, but it wasn't easy. It isn't fair, she thought fiercely as they entered Wardour Street and she began to fumble in her purse for change. Why should I have to choose? Men could up sticks and go wherever their career took them and no one expected anything different.

Two young men were lounging in the Condor doorway, both with the unnatural tans and bulging biceps of male models. She smiled briefly and hurried through to the main office, drawn by the thud of music and the excited chatter of a workforce with something to celebrate.

Paul was on the dance floor, a Gauloise between his fingers, his eyes half closed as he gave himself up to the beat. In front of him Rosie, one of the researchers, was gyrating in time to the music, her body lithe and pliable inside the leopard-skin tunic dress, slit at the back to reveal thin bare legs ending in black, clumpy shoes. They look like surgical boots, Sophie thought sourly, half envious of the younger girl's confidence as she twisted her slim body this way and that, arms outstretched, eyes wide with booze and the pleasure of the dance. Sophie helped herself to a drink from a laden table and then leaned against a wall, unwilling to attract attention to herself. She never felt quite at home with the TV crowd, with their cries of 'Brilliant' and 'Mega' and all their meaningless insider chatter.

'Everything all right?' Paul was whispering in her ear, and when she turned to look into his face Sophie saw that his eyes were anxious. She nodded.

'Sure? You look a bit pensive.'

Sophie summoned up a smile. Now was not the time for a heart-to-heart. 'It's all your media friends. They scare me. Wait till my third drink, I'll be fine then.' He smiled his relief and hugged her. 'And I'm proud of you,' she whispered.

But as he grinned and then turned his gaze back to the throng, Sophie wondered once more how she was going to broach the subject of her going to New York.

'Come on, you two. Get on the floor.' The speaker was a laughing girl with short fair hair and ethnic earrings that almost touched her shoulders. She was reed thin, like most of the other women in the room, but she had a wedding ring and was slightly older than the rest.

'Hi, Jude.' Paul was reaching out and pulling the woman towards them. 'You've met Sophie, haven't you? No? Well, Sophie Baxter meet Judy Simpson. Judy's our celebrity booker.'

Sophie wondered if she should extend her hand but Judy was already bobbing away, smiling as she went.

'Want to dance?' Sophie nodded and they moved on to the crowded floor, where no one seemed to be partnered or to be following any specific pattern of movement. 'I've been thinking,' Paul said as they moved closer. 'Can you get some time off when I go to Paris on the fashion shoot?'

'When is it?' Sophie mouthed, as a gyrating body came between them, forcing them apart.

'The twenty-ninth. We'll be there for three days and I could probably swing a fourth. Could be nice?'

Sophie waited until they were close once more. 'You'll be working.' She could have added, 'And I might be packing for the States,' but she held back.

'I won't be working all the time, and we deserve a break. We've got to go to your folks or mine this weekend, and to whichever one we don't visit the following week. It'd be nice to have some time to ourselves, especially on expenses.'

'Let's wait and see.' She tried not to feel too dejected at the thought of a weekend in Liverpool. A knees-up with Paul's relentlessly joyful family and an uneasy outing with Gary, the small boy with a face the miniature of Paul's own. She'd been many times and she knew the form. It would only last thirty-six hours but the anticipation would feel like a lifetime.

The party wore on in a haze of disco music, in-jokes and increasingly raucous exhortations to non-dancers to join the mêlée on the floor. Sophie tried to look cheerful and succeeded best when she narrowed her eyes and saw the cavorting figures in front of her as Zulus engaged in a tribal dance. For they were a tribe, bound together by a common language and an undying fund of media stories.

At last, in a final welter of back-slapping and cries of, 'See you in the morning,' the crowd began to thin and then to dwindle and at last Sophie was out in the evening darkness with Paul, hunched in his black jacket, beside her.

There had been snacks at the studio party, nuts and crisps and dry little salty biscuits but Paul was hungry now. 'Shall we go for a meal?' he said. It was eleven o'clock and Sophie longed for home. If they ate out it would be well after midnight before they got to bed.

'Let's get a Chinese,' she said as he held up a hand for a cab. They bought crispy noodles and special fried rice, prawn and almond balls and a huge bag of prawn crackers, and carried them into the dark hall. 'Sh,' Sophie said, clutching his arm. 'Chloe'll hear, if you're not careful.' They were both a little giggly now, full of wine and post-party euphoria.

'She's not getting my prawn and almond balls,' Paul said, clutching the paper bag to his chest.

'I should hope not,' Sophie whispered, trying to remember which stair it was that creaked like a gun-shot. It was all in vain. As they reached the landing, light streamed out suddenly from the door to Chloe's flat.

'Darlings, we've been waiting for ages. Where've you *been*?' She made their late arrival sound like a major crime as she half tugged, half beckoned them through the door.

'Well, actually . . . ' Sophie began, but the words died on her lips as she saw Desmond sprawled on the sofa, the sleeves of his red-striped cuffs turned back on his forearms, his tie loosened at the open neck of his shirt.

'This is Desmond,' Chloe said, waving a hand at the sofa. 'He's been dying to meet you, haven't you, darling? Do pour some drinks. We're having . . . ' She paused for effect. 'We're drinking a Puligny-Montrachet 1987. It tastes quite nice . . . very nice . . . and Desmond says it's a state-of-the-art burgundy. Here . . . ' She took the glasses Desmond had filled and pressed them into Sophie and Paul's reluctant hands. As she did so, her eyes fell on the cartons of food. 'Is that Chinese? How heavenly. You decant it, I'll get the plates.'

'Hold on, Chloe.' Desmond had dropped his laid-back pose. 'You can't just commandeer these people's supper.'

Chloe's eyes grew round. 'There's heaps there, and we always share. Your wine, their Chinese, and I've got some grapes and a gorgeous piece of Port Salut. We'll have a feast.'

'What can you do?' Desmond said, as Sophie unwrapped the food. His mouth was soft and gentle like a woman's, Sophie thought, but his eyes were too pale a blue for comfort.

They sat around the table, eating with various degrees of enthusiasm, Chloe's being the greatest. 'Scrumptious,' she said when the last carton was empty and finger-licking could begin. Sophie took a surreptitious glance at the wall-clock. Ten to twelve. She wanted to go home, and when her eyes met Paul's across the coffee table she saw that he did too. Desmond showed no sign of leaving. Where did his brilliant and beautiful wife believe him to be? On night shift at the Old Bailey, presumably. He had opened another bottle of wine and now he made to refill all their glasses.

'Not for me, thank you,' Sophie said, and when he would've poured anyway she put her hand over the glass.

'We've got to be going,' Paul affirmed, making as though to stand up.

'Don't go yet. It isn't even midnight.' Chloe's eyes were round with disbelief that anyone might want to go home before the witching hour.

'It's all very well for you,' Sophie said. 'Some of us have to go to work tomorrow.' She looked rather desperately at Paul, hoping for back-up. 'Paul's just had a promotion. Extra responsibility. He needs his sleep now that he's a tycoon.' The moment she had spoken she realised her mistake.

'A promotion!' Chloe's voice was a shriek of glee. 'You mean he's actually been made a director or a – well, whatever – an executive producer?' she finished triumphantly. 'Darling!' This to the barrister on the sofa. 'Do go and get some champagne from the car . . . ' She turned to Sophie and Paul. 'He carries it in the boot. Isn't that sweet?'

'We *have* to go . . . ' Paul said desperately, but Chloe had gripped them both firmly by the arms.

'One drink,' she said. 'One lovely little celebratory drink, and then we can all go to bed.' She put out a hand to her lover and hauled him to his feet. 'Hurry up, darling. These good people have to get to bed . . . but we can't not drink to

44

a new job. I only wish it was mine.' As she drew them down on to the sofa, Sophie and Paul exchanged rueful glances.

'Just one,' Sophie said. 'Promise, Chloe. One drink and we go.' But as she settled back into the arm of the sofa she suddenly realised that it might be no bad thing to hang on here until there was no time to do anything except brush her teeth and roll into bed. That way there would be no chance of Paul asking her about Gordon Sumner's leaving, no necessity to mention the idea of her going to America. Tonight was a night to concentrate on Paul's career and keep her own in the background.

The next moment Desmond came back into the room, a foil-topped bottle in one hand, a slim overnight case in the other. He put the case on the chair near the door without comment but Sophie saw Chloe's eyes flick to it and then away. So he was going to stay the night. Curiouser and curiouser. Again the little irritation surfaced: in a while Chloe was going to bed with someone else's husband. Somewhere his wife would be sleeping alone, and yet here Chloe was, carefree, throwing back her head to laugh, raising her glass to Paul in tribute. She gets away with murder, Sophie thought ruefully, but I still like her.

'To Paul,' Chloe said, raising her glass. 'And to the gorgeous advance I'll get when he's running LWT or Carlton and I write him up for the Indy. I do like knowing important people!'

4

SOPHIE TOOK A LAST LOOK around the room before gathering up her jacket and bag and closing the door. In the corridor the office cleaner was assembling her tools. Sophie smiled at her as she passed and called goodnight. The woman was elderly, stooped but still lively, and had been with Ascher's for years. 'Getting off early?' she said. 'That's nice.'

Sophie smiled. 'It's been a long day. I'm going home to put my feet up.'

She hesitated at the lift and then made for the stairs that led to the floor below. She liked to take the escalator there and glide down the five floors to ground, seeing each glittering tier swim towards her and pass, to reveal another more splendid.

I love this place, Sophie thought, with a sudden feeling of exaltation. She had power here already, the power to change and influence policy. One day . . . the ground floor loomed up suddenly and she stepped on to the grey carpet. She had chosen to leave early tonight because she wanted to unwind, to cook a proper meal and laze around, listening to music or Paul's gossip before she broached the subject of New York. Two days had gone by and she still hadn't talked to Paul about the fact of her going. Stop being a wimp, Baxter, she told herself sternly, and stepped out into Bond Street.

She took the tube to Notting Hill Gate and walked up Campden Hill Road, pausing to buy a melon and a bottle of white burgundy. She was going to make Russian fish pie, a recipe of her grandmother's and a favourite of Paul's. They'd have melon to start and finish with a lemon sorbet.

She was flaking the smoked fish which she had poached in milk when Chloe arrived. 'What's that?' she asked in horror, grimacing at the milk turned bright yellow by the fish.

'It's smoked cod,' Sophie answered, turning to rinse her fingers under the tap.

'God, it looks awful. What are you going to do with it?'

'Make fish pie.'

'I never cook,' Chloe said, lifting one flake of fish from the pie dish and nibbling it. 'It puts people out of work at Marks and Sparks, and that's immoral. What happens next?'

'I cover the fish with hard-boiled egg, make a sauce with the milk and pour it over, then top the lot with puff pastry. Anything else?'

'I hate it when you're spiky,' Chloe said. 'Got any plonk?'

'I'm not opening that,' Sophie said, retrieving the burgundy from the table. 'Anyway, it's too early to drink.'

'It's never too early,' Chloe replied firmly. 'You can clean your teeth in gin, if you have to. It's lovely! Anyway, don't preach. I'm going to give debauchery up when I'm twenty-one.'

'You're twenty-four now,' Sophie said drily, but Chloe only widened her eyes.

'Am I really? God, where does time go?' There was silence for a moment until the pie was capped, the pastry brushed with egg and milk and put into the oven. 'Now,' Chloe said, 'tell me what's up.'

'What do you mean?' Sophie felt a little trickle of unease course its way between her shoulder-blades.

'Exactly what I say. You're nursing a secret. I've known it ever since the other night. Mark my words, I told Desmond, she's got something on her mind.'

Sophie sighed. 'All I had on my mind, Chloe, was extricating myself from the middle of your liaison and getting to bed.'

Chloe merely smiled knowingly. 'Come on, I know there's something. Is it Paul?'

'No, it's not Paul. And you're not going to wear me down, Chloe, because there's nothing to tell.' But she could feel the blush beginning at her neck, mantling her cheeks, making it impossible to meet her friend's eyes.

'See,' Chloe said, 'I always get at the truth. I'm going to nip downstairs for a bottle and then I'll have it all.' She turned, suddenly aghast. 'You're not pregnant, are you?'

'You asked me that the other day,' Sophie replied. 'I'm definitely not pregnant. And don't go downstairs. We'll drink this now and Paul can go to the wine shop later on.'

Chloe curled up on the settee, her thin ankles crossed above her fashionably clumpy shoes. 'Ta,' she said, when Sophie had filled her glass. 'Come on, then, I'm thirsting to hear.'

'It's nothing earth-shattering,' Sophie said uncomfortably. 'Only you mustn't say anything yet. I'm getting round to telling Paul, but I don't want you pre-empting me.'

'Would I?' Chloe was outraged. 'Discretion is my middle name. If I were to tell some of the things I know . . . actually, I've thought of doing an exposé for one of the Sundays. I'll leave you out of it if I do, though. So tell!'

'The firm wants me to go to America for a while. You know we're American-owned now? They want to exchange key members of staff, so I'm to go to New York, and someone from there comes over here.'

'New York!' Chloe's eyes had closed in anguish. 'What I'd give to be in your shoes. You can make it overnight there with one good piece. Over here, you have to slog for years before they even notice you.'

'I wonder if American women say that?' Sophie countered. 'Anyway, what's so special about New York?'

'It's travel, idiot. It's adventure. It's lying back on an aircraft with Tom Cruise across the aisle and dinky little

48

food parcels arriving every hour on the hour. It's duty free and Central Park and brownstones and the land of opportunity . . . '

Down below a door closed. 'That's Paul,' Sophie said. 'Not a word.'

She caught him on the stairs and asked him to go out again for more wine. He sniffed the air.

'Fish pie? God, I love your grandmother. Back in a tick.'

She managed to get rid of Chloe before Paul returned, exhorting her to keep her mouth shut if she met him on the stairs. 'I want to tell him myself, Chloe, so watch it!'

When Chloe was gone she finished her wine, her resolve high. She would tell Paul and he would understand and they would work it out somehow. Today she had asked David how long he thought the secondment would last. 'Make a guess,' she'd urged.

'It'd be three months at least,' he'd said. 'Probably six, maybe twelve. It wouldn't be worth it for less.'

The fish pie turned out well, the crust crisp and golden, the filling creamy and delicious. They ate it with new potatoes and broad beans and quaffs of wine, and Sophie watched Paul's tired face relax and soften. Perhaps this was how it ought to be, a man coming home from the hurly-burly of work to the smell of cooking and a welcome from a woman. Her mother had not worked since her marriage; had never appeared to miss it. But even as Sophie thought about it, she remembered the excitement she had felt a few hours ago as the escalator carried her down through her domain. She couldn't give up her job. Not now, anyway. She had worked hard to get where she was and she was glad. 'I like responsibility, she thought. I like making decisions. And she didn't want to be 'tied to a stove', as Chloe called it. I'd do it because it's expected of me, she thought. Because I'm a woman. Because it's the way Mum brought me up. But I'm not sure I like it. Not for the rest of my life.

She took a gulp of wine and licked her lips, but before she could start her confession Paul had launched into a tale.

'Anyway, they bring in this funny little American woman

– seventy if she was a day – and sit her opposite Celestine Soames, that seven-foot agony aunt from *Essential Woman*. Esme was trying to keep it civilised, but they let fly at one another. Godzilla versus the Poison Dwarf wasn't in it.'

'What was the subject?' Sophie asked, pushing forward her glass for a refill.

'Ostensibly it was where does responsibility for contraception lie, but really it was the man versus woman thing. Celestine is very much for traditional values and all that, and the other one sees every man as a marauding penis.'

'So who won?'

'Esme. Liz was telling her to bring it to a dignified end, and she tried to get a word in once or twice, but they just ignored her. In the end she looked straight at camera and said, "Well, there we must leave it for the moment. I'd like to thank my . . ." There were about thirty seconds before she said "guests", and everyone knew she meant "shits". While the credits were rolling she just kept looking straight ahead, none of the noddys right and left to say, "Well done".'

'So they won't be asked back again?'

'They will if I'm still exec,' Paul said gleefully. 'It was bloody marvellous telly. Celestine has a bosom like a pouter pigeon. The face is all right – a bit like Antonia Fraser, actually – but the tits are a shelf, I kid you not. And when she draws herself up, it's *formidable*.' He uttered the last word in a French accent and rolled his eyes. 'And then there's this gibbering little granny spitting pure Brooklynese, and Esme sitting in between trying to maintain a semblance of order. God, it was marvellous.'

'Speaking of Brooklyn,' Sophie said, suddenly liberated, 'David says I might have to go to New York for a while. A kind of familiarisation session, get to know Littlecamp's methods and that sort of thing.'

'Nice,' Paul said. 'You deserve a trip. I could probably get a few days off myself, if it's after I've settled in.'

'It might be more than a few days,' Sophie said carefully. 'I mean, it wouldn't be worth re-locating – '

Paul was frowning. 'Re-locating? You mean it'd be more than just a look-see – what Sumner did, only in reverse?'

'No, well, I mean yes – it would be more. He was only having a preliminary look from a great height. I'd be there to learn their buying techniques, work out what would succeed over here and what wouldn't. And there'd be someone from over there doing my job here. David's already looking at flats for her.'

'Why you?'

Sophie was saved from having to reply by the ringing of the telephone. 'Kate! It's lovely to hear from you.'

At the other end of the line her grandmother was asking after everyone's health. 'We're fine. How are you?' Her grandmother, or Kate, as she preferred to be called, was sixty-six going on fourteen, as unlike her daughter, Sophie's mother, as it was possible to be.

'Bearing up,' Kate said at the other end of the line. 'How's your mother? Still up to her neck in committees? I've rung her twice and got your father. It seems she's never in.'

'She's okay. What about you? Made any good deals lately?' Her question launched Kate on to her favourite subject, antique china. The line throbbed to Copeland and Garrett, Coalport, Minton and signed Moorcroft.

'I can't part with the Moorcroft. Oliver is adamant, but I won't budge. It's so beautiful, Sophie . . . all those deep blues and maroons and olive green. Wonderful!'

'How is Oliver?' Sophie liked the quiet, greying giant who was her grandmother's partner. As a child she had hoped that they would marry and she could be bridesmaid. 'He's much younger than Gran!' her mother had said in horrified tones when she suggested it but to Sophie, at thirteen, they had seemed of an age, the ten years between them unimportant because they were both old. She still cherished the idea of their getting together but it had been pooh-poohed so many times by both mother and grandmother that she was resigned to the non-fulfilment of her wish.

'Oliver's fine. I forgot to tell you, I got a set of six – six, mark you – wheelback dining chairs in red mahogany.

Original seats, not a mark on them. America will love them.'

There it was again. America. Did everything have to go there, drawn like a magnet?

'That sounds quite a find. When are you coming down? I miss you.'

'Why don't you come here, you and Paul? We could show him around, and I could get to know him better. Is he still sporting the earring?'

'It's still in place,' Sophie said carefully, aware that Paul was half listening to the conversation. 'We're going up to Liverpool next weekend, I think, but after that . . . '

They chattered on for a while, making more promises to meet, and then Paul took over the phone for a final goodbye. He was laughing when he put down the receiver.

'She's wicked, your grandmother,' he said. 'She asked after Chloe, and I said she was behaving herself – well, it doesn't do to be too truthful – and Kate said, "Behaving is she? It won't last. That one's had so many conversions her road to Damascus is a five-lane motorway." They both laughed and relaxed a little, thinking of Kate.

'Want the last of the vino?' Paul asked, suspending the bottle over Sophie's glass. 'Tell me something . . . ' He was going to ask about New York and she was too tired for discussion. 'Tell me why your mother and Kate are like chalk and cheese. I mean, there's not even a point of reference, let alone a familial resemblance.'

'They do look alike,' Sophie protested.

'They do, but that's not what I mean. You all resemble one another a bit, and you've all got terrific legs. But Kate's a free spirit and your mother has more hang-ups than the Sock Shop.'

'What about me?' Sophie had hoped for a swift reassurance that she too was a free spirit, but instead Paul put his head on one side and considered. 'Come on,' Sophie urged.

'Well,' he was teasing her now, his eyes twinkling, 'you're so multi-faceted, it's difficult to tell.'

They passed it off as a joke, but as she got ready for

bed Sophie pondered. Was she like her mother? She liked
a tidy home, that was true. She didn't disapprove of much of
which her mother disapproved, but there were times when
she caught herself being . . . well, a little narrow-minded.
Take her view of Chloe, for instance.

'About this American thing . . . ' Paul had come up behind
her as she brushed her hair. He was damp from the shower
and the dark curls surmounted his head like a coronet.
She turned in his arms and pressed her lips to his moist
shoulder.

'I won't be away for long,' she said. He hugged her.

'We'll work something out if we have to. I'll commute –
Concorde every second day. Or I'll get a secondment of my
own. They're hungry for talent out there.'

'You couldn't leave Condor now,' Sophie protested, but
even as she spoke she knew that it hadn't been a serious
suggestion on Paul's part. He was lapping up his new job,
loving every minute of it, just as she had when she made
manager.

'Let's not talk about it,' Paul said. 'We're going to Liverpool
this weekend. God knows, that's enough to cope with. When
we get back, we'll talk. Anyway, it might have fizzled out by
then. You know what Americans are like – they talk big.'

Sophie wanted to protest. Gordon Sumner didn't talk big.
He was enthusiastic, expansive, he *thought* big, but he meant
what he said. The way Paul was dismissing what was a career
move for her as little more than a myth was irritating.

'Anyway,' Paul was moving away now, 'it's too late to
think about it tonight. I'm bushed, I don't know about you.'
Down below there was a sudden thrum of music. 'Oh God,
she's not going to serve up heavy metal tonight, is she?'

'We won't hear it in the bedroom,' Sophie said soothingly.
But when the lights were out and they were safe beneath
the sheets the music could still be heard, more melodious
now but penetrative just the same. It was Sting, breathing
menace: *'Every step you take, every move you make, I'll be
watching you.'*

Paul turned in the bed and slipped his arm around her,

nudging her round as he moved so that they were lying together like spoons.

'Know something?' he said drowsily. 'You'd never survive without me. You couldn't manage it in Newcastle, never mind New York. True?'

He's wrong, Sophie thought, watching the shapes of furniture loom up as her pupils grew accustomed to darkness. I love him, but I could survive without him – without anyone – if I had to.

'Know what?' Paul's voice was drowsy, so that she had to strain to hear.

'What?'

'I'd like to ravish you if I had the strength.'

'Go to sleep,' she said, patting his arm where it curled round her belly, glad that he was as tired out by his day as she was by hers, saving her the need to respond.

5

B Y EIGHT THIRTY THE OUTSKIRTS of London were petering out and the M1 lay before them.

'What time will we get there?' Sophie asked. She felt tired still and her eyes were itchy with lack of sleep.

They had intended to have an early night, but in fact it had been one o'clock by the time they had got to bed and the alarm was set for six thirty. When it had pinged Paul had groaned in disgust and it was left to Sophie to draw back the curtains and make him get up.

The fear Sophie always felt about facing up to Paul's home-ground had transmuted itself into anger. Why should she have to take responsibility for getting them under way, when it was his child, his background, that necessitated the journey? But even as she fumed she acknowledged the fact that a part of her liked to organise. It was the same with shopping. Each week Paul offered to do the supermarket trip for her. Each week she made an excuse, feeling it was her job to keep a well-stocked cupboard, unwilling to risk his coming home without one or other important staple. The fact was that she would feel less of a woman if she surrendered all the reins of running the house. But did acting as a human alarm clock fall into that category?

For a moment she had contemplated snuggling down, but if they didn't go today he would be consumed with guilt for a week and then they'd have to go next week. Seven more days of miserable anticipation; it wasn't worth it. She had contented herself with counting the hours until they would be on their way home and set about making breakfast, hearing Paul singing in the bathroom as she broke eggs into a pan to scramble. He had been full of good humour when he had emerged, and his face now, eyes fixed on the road, was bright with anticipation.

'What time will we get there?' she asked again.

Paul glanced sideways, pursing his lips. 'Half-eleven, thereabouts.'

'Where'll we go first?' Sophie hoped he would say his sister Maria's. She liked Maria and her husband, and anything else that would put off the moment when Paul crouched down and held out his arms for his son to leap into.

'Probably dump the bags at home and then go straight round to Julie's. She says Gary plays her up when he knows I'm coming, so the sooner we get there the better.'

It was the only time Sophie ever felt broody: the moment when she saw Paul's face soften as he spoke of his child. Outside the car were fields raped of their crops, looking pathetic and useless with their patterns of stubble. Everything was meant to bring forth. If she didn't go to America, she and Paul could have a child. Paul would be scared at first, but then he'd be pleased, especially with the new job and its extra income. But a baby would be a side-road for her, a cul-de-sac from which she might never escape. She shivered and then shifted in her seat so that Paul looked at her.

'Okay?' he asked, and she nodded.

'Just cramp in my leg. Where are we going to take Gary?'

They had been to the Beatles museum and crossed the Mersey on the ferry twice. What was left?

'I thought we might try the Maritime museum. I don't expect Julie's taken him there. McDonald's or the swingy park, that's about the limit of his perambulations with her.'

56

There was a degree of contempt in Paul's tone and for the basest of reasons it cheered up Sophie.

'How did . . . how was it . . . ' She wanted to say, 'Why Julie?' but it was hard to find the words. 'You've told me how it happened, but never why.'

'Julie and me?' He pursed his lips. 'I don't know, really. I mean, looking at it now I can't understand it myself. It was peer pressure, I suppose. I was labelled "bright", and when that happens the other lads move off you a bit. Well, they do in comprehensives.' This was a dig at her own private school background, but Sophie let it go. 'Anyway, Julie was the girl everyone lusted after. I'd never've tried anything . . . I wouldn't've dared. You wouldn't have recognised me then, I was totally self-effacing. But she made it obvious she liked me, and that was it. We went about together for a year before anything happened. The lads were all saying lucky sod, and that sort of thing, but there wasn't anything to it. And then one night there was. After that, there was no going back. Oh, I was tempted, all right, but I couldn't've stopped. And I felt very protective of her. Tender. Grateful, I suppose. I bought condoms, and what a pantomime that was.'

They slowed down because of a patch of roadworks and Paul was silent for a while, concentrating on the car and changing lanes. Sophie wanted to hear more but was afraid of appearing nosy, so she stayed silent.

'Anyway,' he said at last when they were past the cones and out on the open road again. 'I can't remember when it began to go stale. Five or six months later, I suppose. Julie got possessive and I got restive, and in the end I had to psyche myself up to the sex. I couldn't walk away, because it would've looked as though I'd got what I wanted and that was that. I had this desire to be grown up and responsible, or that's how I saw it. So it went on. I was starting A levels and I wanted out. I'd almost reached a point where I could say it, and then . . . '

' . . . and then she told you she was pregnant?'

'That's right!'

'Do you think she did it deliberately?'

'To keep me? I doubt it. She was probably as sick of me as I was of her. Anyway, from the moment it was out we hated the sight of one another. She felt I was getting away scot-free. I felt she'd shackled me.'

'What happened then?' Sophie probed.

'There was a meeting of the two families. She was only fifteen, remember, so marriage was out of the question. So was abortion, as far as the parents were concerned. They were Catholic, too. So my dad forked out with expenses, and when I got my grant I chipped in a few bob. By that time she was on social security, so she managed.'

'It must've been hard for you. A grant's not lavish.'

'I worked in a bar at weekends . . . and the family were good. Maria used to knit me lovely pullies, and I got Gerard's cast-offs. That's why I buy so many clothes now.' He turned to grin, and then put a quaver in his voice. 'I was deprived, your honour, that's what it was.'

Sophie sat back, reflecting on what he'd told her, thinking how different her adolescence had been from his. She had gone to the church high school in a blue blazer with a gold crest on the pocket and a grey felt hat with a blue-and-gold band. There had been ballet lessons and riding at weekends, and she had never had to wonder where the next outfit would come from. Her father was town clerk of a prosperous market town, and her mother kept the home immaculate, helping out on a voluntary basis in an Oxfam shop on Tuesdays and Thursdays.

She put out a hand and rested it on Paul's jean-clad thigh. 'I love you,' she said, and felt her eyes prick with emotion. How could she even think of leaving him, even for a week, let alone six months. She closed her eyes and tried to think of the weekend ahead and what she could do to make it successful.

It was twelve o'clock when they drew up outside his parents' terraced house. In the distance the tops of the Anglican and Catholic cathedrals could be seen, one ancient and four-square, the other spiked and futuristic. If they got married, where would it be? The Register Office probably, which would mean they both compromised.

Paul's mother kissed Sophie's cheek and put a cup of tea in front of her almost as she entered the room. It was small and cluttered, with Catholic emblems on the walls and mantelpiece, and an ornamental mouse cowering in a glass bowl on the sideboard, a Siamese cat ready to pounce from the rim.

'Good journey?' Paul's father was a retired docker, with a paunch of Henry VIII proportions beneath his striped sweatshirt. He was obviously determined to make conversation, and Sophie racked her brains for a suitable subject.

'It wasn't too bad,' she said. 'How's Liverpool doing at the moment?' They both knew she meant Liverpool FC, his passion. His face lit up with relief and gratitude that his son's posh girlfriend wasn't going to lead him into unknown territory. As he chattered about goals and friendlies and Graeme Souness, Sophie thought of how the two families would get on when eventually they met. Kate would make an effort, and Dad was too nice to upset anyone, but her mother would be restrained. Not rude, not icy; just withdrawn.

'We've got to dash,' Paul said, when the tea was drunk.

'Gary's had a bit of a cold.' His mother's face showed concern. 'I met him with Julie in the market. His eyes were streaming, poor little soul. But he was looking forward to you coming.'

The boy was at the window when the car rounded the corner. Sophie saw him turn into the room to tell someone behind him, and then he was erupting from the front door, only stopping when he was almost upon them, suddenly looking abashed at his own haste. He's growing up, Sophie thought, marvelling at the change in his demeanour since the last time she had seen him. He looked at her and grinned, a little uncertainly. 'Hi,' she said. 'Good to see you.' Gary was small for his age, or so it seemed to Sophie, but the small body was muscular, the face round and glowing with health beneath the dark thatch. He was becoming more and more like Paul, and she had to resist an impulse to reach out and hug the child to her.

Paul was looking towards the house but there was no sign of Julie or her boyfriend, who rejoiced in the nickname of Mojo.

'Where do you want to go?' Paul asked when Gary was safe in the front seat which Sophie had vacated for him. 'I thought we might take in the Maritime museum?'

'Mam said you'd take me to see *Jurassic Park*,' the boy said, his face alight with enthusiasm.

'*Jurassic Park*?' Paul's eyes met Sophie's in the rear-view mirror. He pulled a quizzical face but she stared blandly back. If Paul was expecting her to tell Gary it wasn't a good idea, he was wasting his time. 'I thought we might go off for a run somewhere after the museum? Seeing as it's such a nice day.'

'I want to see *Jurassic Park*.' Gary's tone brooked no refusal. 'Everyone at school's seen it. They say its wicked.'

'I could leave the money for your mother to take you next week,' Paul said desperately.

'I want to see it today.'

They sat through Spielberg's spectacle, watching Gary devour a giant carton of popcorn and two ice-creams.

'It wasn't bad, was it?' Paul said, as they made for the exit.

'It was wicked,' Sophie said. 'And I use that word advisedly.'

Outside the sun was still shining and Liverpool city centre was emptying of Saturday shoppers. 'What now?' Paul said and then, before Gary could reply, 'I know, McDonald's!'

They sat in a tiny booth, Paul and Sophie eating fries and the gherkins from Gary's cheeseburger. 'I don't like pickle,' he said, blowing down the straw until his Coke frothed and bubbled. When the food had been consumed, Gary indulged in an orgy of tidying up, carrying their litter to a swing-bin.

'I'm glad you're here,' Paul told Sophie gratefully. 'It was awful when I had to do this on my own.'

Sophie squeezed his arm and smiled, genuinely pleased that her presence made a difference.

Gary came back and slid on to his seat. On an impulse, Sophie put out a hand to ruffle his hair. I like him, she thought. I feel as though he's a foreigner . . . almost from another planet . . . but I like him. I could even love him, given time. The fear was ebbing with familiarity, the terrible fear that had gripped her on that first visit; a fear born out of the belief that Paul was bound to be drawn to his child more than to her and that, if it came to conflict, he would inexorably take his son's side. But there had been no conflict, only a wary truce that was turning, gradually, to friendship.

They walked in the park after the meal, Paul asking the occasional question, Gary chattering away about school and home and the antics of his friends. 'I saw me Nana in the market the other day,' he said. 'She bought me a wicked T-shirt with dinosaurs.'

Sophie was content to watch them, noticing the points of similarity between father and son. The boy was bright, but his conversation was limited to his own world, and it was obvious that his television viewing was strictly game shows and soaps. If things continued like this, he would never achieve his potential. For a crazy moment she wondered if they could accommodate Gary in the flat; broaden his horizons; send him to a good, demanding school. But even if such a thing were possible, Julie would never let him go and Sophie was ashamed of how relieved that made her feel.

As the time for returning Gary to his mother drew near, Sophie felt the usual unease. If she accompanied him to his door she would look bold, even threatening, as though she were taking his mother's place. If she stayed in the car she looked unfriendly or disapproving. And exactly how should she bid Gary farewell? He was too old for a goodbye kiss, and too young for a formal handshake. Each time she dithered and chose a different path. Today she got out of the car, put her arm round Gary's shoulder and hugged him. She got a fleeting grin for her pains and a nod when she said, 'See you soon.'

Paul went into the house and she knew he would hand

over money. Maintenance for the child was paid by direct debit but after a visit to Liverpool Paul was always hard-up, or 'skint', as he called it. Sophie didn't begrudge anything he gave his son but sometimes there was a stirring of resentment, a wish that his life, like her own, was a nice, clean copy book waiting to be written on. I'm getting more like Mum, she thought, and grinned to herself as she turned away.

Back in the car, she fiddled with the cassette player and tried not to look too obviously at the house. She mustn't seem impatient or nosy. Nevertheless, she was curious about the house where the mother of Paul's son lived. It had net curtains at all the windows, elaborate nets with embroidered hems which were looped up in the centre with a frou-frou of pink and green. Her mother would have condemned them instantly as common, but at least they were eye-achingly white and matched those of almost every other house in the street.

There was a satellite dish on the wall and a rambling rose between the door and window, past its best now but still sporting the odd yellow blossom. Sophie tried to think of the girl Julie must have been, but however hard she tried she couldn't banish the picture of the reed-thin, sharp-faced, twenty-five-year-old whom she had glimpsed from time to time, endless legs in pipe-cleaner jeans, hair held back in a ruffled tie, eyebrows raised in a permanent, supercilious stare.

It was a relief when Paul emerged from the house, turning to wave to Gary in the doorway, going back once to ruffle the boy's hair and bend to whisper something. I want his child, Sophie thought, feeling a sudden longing deep within her. But it was just a reaction; she knew it wouldn't last. One day there would be children for them but not yet.

A huge high tea was laid out at Paul's parents' home when they got back. Ham and pease-pudding, salad and coleslaw, a dish of beetroot and another of huge pickled onions, cheese in a cheese dish, and great wedges of white bread with butter spread thick upon them. Do what you can,

Paul's eyes beseeched her, and Sophie tried to eat with gusto, but it was too soon after the McDonald's fries. When the meal was over they all slumped about the room in various stages of torpor. Sophie, as an honoured guest, had one easy chair. Paul's father had the other, and no sooner occupied it than he was fast asleep, his lips reverberating gently, his false teeth slipping down to give him a horsey appearance.

Paul's mother got out her photo albums then. There were photographs of various family weddings to see, and nephews and nieces looking angelic at their first communions. The TV blared in a corner, and a dog and cat wound in and out of knees and arms and looked longingly at the food-laden table.

'It must be hard for you, all this,' Paul's mother said sympathetically to Sophie. 'You being from a small family.'

'There aren't many of us,' Sophie agreed. 'Just Mam and Dad,' – she had bitten back 'Mummy and Daddy' just in time – 'and my grandmother, of course. You'd like her. She's a good sport.' She tried to imagine her grandmother in this gathering and found she could do it easily. Kate could be grand, grander even than her mother at times, but she had a much greater appreciation of other people.

Just thinking like this made Sophie feel guilty. Why couldn't she feel closer to a mother who had always striven to give her every possible opportunity in life, who had understood her needs and anticipated many of them? Guiltily, Sophie acknowledged that her own attitudes left room for improvement. She didn't look down on Paul's family but she did see them rather as alien beings. There were so many of them: Maria, Antony, her husband, and their two children; Gerard and his wife, Angela. Claire and Patrick and Paul; all, with the exception of Paul, Liverpudlians to their fingertips, laughing and joking and almost overwhelmingly friendly.

It was a relief when eight o'clock struck and Mr Malone awoke and gave a gentle belch. He looked at the clock. 'Is that eight o'clock?' he said. 'We're wasting good drinking time.'

They walked to the pub, arms linked, in twos and threes: two parents, five siblings, three partners. 'We're a bit of a clan, aren't we?' Paul whispered in Sophie's ear. 'Don't let it put you off.'

And then the warm fug of the pub enfolded them, where she could cuddle close to Paul, sip her lager and think of tomorrow, when they could both go home.

'I've got a bit of news,' Paul said when everyone had a glass in their hand. 'You're looking at an executive producer!' There were oohs and aahs of delight. 'And,' Paul said portentously, 'this one is going to America to show them how to run a proper store.'

Sophie smiled self-consciously until her eyes met the eyes of Mrs Malone and she saw doubt.

'That's nice,' the older woman said. 'As long as you're not away for long.'

6

I T WAS TRADITIONAL FOR THE Malone women to cook the
massive Sunday lunch, called dinner in their household, while the men went off to the local and washed down
their hearty breakfast with ale. Paul made a half-hearted
attempt to persuade Sophie to accompany them, but it was
easy to resist. She was stiff from a night spent clinging to
the single bed she shared with Paul in a bedroom belonging
to his youngest sister, which was decorated with posters
of Take That and Madonna clad in a metal corset with her
basilisk stare.

Th, first time they had come to Liverpool, Sophie had
half ex₁ected to be put in a separate bedroom. Paul had told
her of his family's deeply held Catholic beliefs, so it was a
surprise when no one mentioned where she would sleep
and at bedtime Paul simply took her hand and drew her
up to the bedroom Claire had obligingly vacated. She had
thought of the guest-room at home as they climbed into the
slightly rumpled bed, obviously unchanged since the night
before. Her mother had special guest linen and towels, laid
neatly at the foot of the bed and changed daily during the
guest's stay. There was a selection of books at the bedside
and cotton wool balls in a jar. Here there was a Mickey

Mouse alarm clock and a pile of *True Romance* magazines on a chair.

'I'm going to help your mum,' she said when she declined the trip to the pub. 'Don't drink too much . . . remember the drive home.' She would never have ventured such advice in London but here, among the cheerful chiding and forthright exhortation of the Malones, it seemed quite natural.

In the tiny kitchen, the windows were steamed with heat from the oven and the huge aluminium pans that hissed and bubbled on the burners. There was much talk of 'the Yorkshires', and ceremonial beating of the batter. Sophie watched almost aghast as two pints of milk and one of water were put into a huge earthenware bowl, along with a dessert-spoon of salt and then a pinch more, six eggs, and finally twenty-four spoonfuls of plain flour, measured with a generous hand. 'It looks a lot,' she said weakly as the whisking began.

When Mrs Malone's wrist tired, her eldest daughter took over. 'Beating in the air,' she said economically, and Sophie nodded, ashamed to mention the occasional and meagre Yorkshire puddings of her own upbringing: five fluid ounces of milk and five of water, one egg, a pinch of salt, the flour carefully weighed, and all blended in the food processor.

At last the joint was removed from the oven – a huge piece of beef, spitting in the meat tin – and it was time for the batter to be poured into tins which had been preheated in the oven and then made almost glowing on the rings.

'Set the table,' Mrs Malone said with a glance at the clock. 'The men'll be in directly.'

When the last fork was set in place they trooped through the door, father and sons and sons-in-law, gravitating to their seats while the women hovered like maid-servants. Not for the first time, Sophie marvelled that Paul had come from such a background, loving though it might be. He shared the chores with her; he was careful of her feelings; he supported her in her career. At least she had thought he did. Deep down was he still primitive man, seeing his woman as wife and mother, loving her, but only as an adjunct of himself? One way or another she would soon know.

When the men were seated the women took their places, slipping in next to their men, helping them pile their plates with mountains of food. The mammoth pile of individual Yorkshire puddings disappeared like snow on a griddle, along with huge wedges of the big puddings, crisp and rounded at the edge, soggy and pale yellow in the middle until they were drowned in thick, glistening gravy and buried under piles of mash and greens.

'I don't want to eat again, ever,' Paul said when they had bid their goodbyes and were safe in the car, speeding south. He burped with gusto. 'All the same, I miss those dinners.' He put out a conciliatory hand. 'Not that I'm not mad about your cooking.'

Sophie did not have the energy to take offence. She settled her head against the rest at the top of the passenger seat and closed her eyes. In retrospect she had enjoyed the weekend, in spite of the hurly-burly of the home and family. For a while she had suspended anxiety, forgotten about authority and decision and the hectic pace of life in London.

'Happy?'

She opened her eyes to find Paul looking at her. 'Yes,' she said, slipping her hand on to his thigh and squeezing gently. 'Very happy.'

She closed her eyes again and calculated their time of arrival. They'd be on the outskirts of London by six thirty if they met no unexpected obstacles. Another half-hour to get home . . . seven. Plenty of time to ring her mother, have a bath, catch up on chores and get ready for tomorrow. Perhaps she should tell her mother about the suggested trip to the States? She opened her eyes and looked at the landscape flashing past. That was the worst of motorways; you never had time to appreciate the view.

She closed her eyes again and imagined what her mother would be doing now. If her father had brought in flowers from the garden she would be sitting at the kitchen table, wearing household gloves, cutting the stems of small flowers and crushing the stems of others. Sunday afternoons at home had always been peaceful: picking over fruit gathered by her father in the morning and arranging the flowers in summer; writing cards in November; wrapping gifts in December or pouring brandy into the cakes and puddings, safe in their foil-lined tins. It was so different from what they had left behind in Liverpool! And yet that was a warm and loving home.

'Just tell me if you want me to drive for a while,' she said aloud. It was the only thing she could think of immediately to assuage her feelings of guilt at making comparisons.

'Do you want to stop somewhere?' Paul asked. 'We could have an early drink on the way or press on home and go down the Garter later on?'

'Let's get home,' Sophie answered. She wanted to ring her mother, and to talk to her father, too. He would understand about America, help her to weigh the pros and cons. Her mother would be sure to advise caution. She never really wants anything to change, Sophie thought. It's almost as though she's afraid of it. And yet Kate was restless, just the opposite of her daughter. I love them, but I don't understand them really at all, she reflected.

Her reverie was interrupted by the sound of Paul's voice. 'Are you awake?'

She sat up in her seat and turned to him. 'Yes. I can't doze off in the car like you. Wish I could, but the fact that I'm driving probably calms you.'

'*Au contraire*, my pet. I go to sleep when you're driving because I daren't stay awake. Anyway, I've been thinking some more about looking for a place of our own.'

'To buy?' He had her full attention now.

'Yes. It couldn't be much of a place to begin with, but the sooner we get into the property market the better.'

Sophie was trying to think of a decent excuse. She didn't want a mortgage at this juncture. Her mother would wail about entanglements without a marriage certificate, and there would have to be an orgy of nest-building shopping. She'd seen it happen to others, their desks buried under swatches of material and colour cards and carpet and wallpaper samples. The furniture and decor of the flat was elegant enough, and it wasn't even theirs. The most onerous lifestyle decision she had to make at the moment was where to site a pot-plant. 'There's no harm in looking,' she said aloud. 'I expect it'd be quite a while before we found the right place.'

Paul was smiling to himself now, putting his foot down so that the speedometer climbed. 'Steady on,' Sophie said mildly. 'I'd like to live to see this rose-covered cottage you're thinking of buying.'

London was slow and sleepy when they reached it, as befitted a late Sunday afternoon. 'It's a glorious city, isn't it, when it isn't choked with traffic,' Paul said.

'Yes,' Sophie said absently. 'What shall we eat? And don't say "anything", because that puts all the responsibility on to me.'

'I'm still digesting that dinner,' Paul said.

'Lunch!' She was teasing.

'Not in Liverpool.' He lapsed into broad Liverpudlian. 'What's lunch, whack? And where's me dinner? Anyway, I bet our neighbour is waiting with a delicious repast all prepared. If she's not, I'll knock up an omelette.' They were in Baker Street now, ready to turn into Marylebone Road, and suddenly Paul's voice was serious. 'What did you think of Chloe's bloke? Desmond?'

'I didn't like him. Oh, not just the fact that he's selling his wife short. Who doesn't, nowadays? He's just . . . well, oily. Too smooth, too pleasant, you know what I mean. Why do you ask?'

'We're thinking of using him in *Speaking Out*. He's got the gift of the gab. What do you reckon?'

'He'd be all right, I suppose,' Sophie said.

'He's too bloody arrogant for me. Knows everything, speaks in that silky voice and never raises it because he's so convinced of his own superiority. What do you mean about everyone selling people short nowadays? I don't.'

'Sure?' Sophie met his gaze and saw that his eyes, unlike her own, were not twinkling.

'Very sure, Sophie. Nor will I when we're married. I hope you know that, and I hope you feel the same.'

'Don't be silly.' She moved closer to him. 'Anyway, what brought this on?' She felt uncomfortable, wanting the conversation to cease, but at the same time there was a certain satisfaction in knowing she held him so securely.

In the evening sunshine the mews looked idyllic. Moths had ventured out and hovered above the flowering tubs, there was a smell of good food in the air and a lazy calm overall. I like this place, Sophie thought. I want to stay here. The question of just why she wanted to stay was put off as Chloe emerged in a cream chiffon trouser suit, the scent of Givenchy's Ysatis preceding her, gilt clips in her ears matching the gilt strap of a bag that looked suspiciously as though it was from Chanel.

'Darlings! I'm glad I caught you. I got you a pint of skimmed and a granary loaf, and I watered the plants both days. My God, the feeling of virtue . . . I'm off to a do at some film producer's house . . . he was at Winchester with Desmond so he won't tell the lady-wife. Not that she cares, Sophie, so don't be so po-faced. How do I look?' She did a twirl. 'You never know who you might meet. I could come back with my own column. Remember Jilly Cooper? One drink with Beaverbrook or someone and she was a household name.'

'You look gorgeous,' Paul said, lifting the cases from the boot. 'You'll probably come back half-cut, as usual.'

'Pig!' Chloe said. 'Must rush.' There was a honk from the end of the mews and a sleek grey car appeared.

'I might've known he'd have a Mercedes,' Paul said bitterly. 'And all off the backs of the criminal classes.'

Chloe's slingbacks were clicking on the pavement as she hurried to the car, folding into it as easily as a clasp-knife.

'She is stunning,' Sophie said. 'You can't deny that.'

'Lovely to look at but not to touch,' Paul said firmly. 'Now, get these cases upstairs, woman, and let me get at the eggs. Omelettes, my God, what a come-down after beef and three veg.'

When supper was over and Sophie had bathed and washed her hair, she dialled her mother's number. 'Mummy?' At the other end of the line her mother sounded a little abstracted and the TV was burbling in the background. 'Are you watching something good? Oh, well, I'll keep it brief.' There was demurring at the other end but it lacked conviction; no chance to mention America tonight. 'I just wanted to say that we're safely back and we'll be coming home soon.'

When did you stop saying 'home' when you spoke of your parents' house? You weren't really grown up until 'home' meant where you lived, but when did you make the transition? She could hear Paul clattering dishes in the kitchen as he washed up and she tried to concentrate on what her mother was saying. 'Yes. Yes, it was good news. Not a surprise, because he's terribly good at what he does. But it means extra money and a company car. Oh, I don't know. What they give him, I expect. But it'll be nice. We'll keep the Renault so it'll mean more freedom for me. Yes, of course I want to talk to Daddy.'

As her father came to the phone Sophie felt the familiar welling-up of love. 'Daddy? Yes, lovely to hear you too. How's Pepsi?' Her face drooped as she listened to details of the dog's failing health. She had been fourteen when they got her the poodle puppy, so the dog was twelve or thirteen now. She made a firm promise to come home as soon as possible to see Pepsi, and blew a kiss down the phone before replacing the receiver.

'Sloppy,' Paul said, coming up behind her and twining his arms around her neck. His forearms were strong and muscular, with a faint patina of dark hairs, and he smelled of lemon washing-up liquid. She leaned her cheek against the moist flesh and closed her eyes.

'You can talk. I thought your lot were going to hug you to death when we left.'

'That's family solidarity, whack.' His Liverpudlian act again.

'What's mine, then?' He was slipping over the arm of

the settee, shifting to make room, folding her into his body.

'Yours is slop.' He put on a genteel accent. 'Goodnight, Daddy darling.' There followed smacking noises with his lips. 'Yum, yum, yum!'

'Shut up,' she said lazily. 'Let's get to bed. I'm bushed.'

In the glow from the streetlights in the bedroom they shed their wraps, without putting on the lamp, and moved to the bed.

'You're beautiful,' Paul said, looking at her across the expanse of duvet.

'I'm getting fat,' she replied, looking down at the length of her body, knowing it was not getting fatter, simply riper.

'No you're not,' he said, kneeling on the bed and reaching for her. There was a sudden chuckle. 'Of course, you are twenty-six,' he said, 'and they do say that after twenty-five gravity comes into play. It's not fat, my darling, it's droop.'

She cut his words off with a kiss and began to push the duvet off the end of the bed with her feet. No need of a cover on such a night as this.

7

SOPHIE LAID ASIDE THE MAGAZINE the hairdresser had provided and looked around the salon. It was one of the most profitable Ascher departments, but that was not the most important reason for its existence, which was to bring women – women with money and leisure in which to spend it – into the store. The salon was set back on the third floor. To reach it you had to wend your way past perfume and jewellery to the escalator or lift, and when you reached the third floor you passed the separates department and a handful of fashion boutiques before entering the pink and grey portals of Hair and Beauty.

Sophie's gaze ranged around. Everything seemed in order. The assistants were trim in their grey dresses or trouser suits, with pink edging at cuffs and collar, and a pink A embroidered on the left breast. They wore regulation grey kid pumps with the trouser suits, or low-heeled grey kid court shoes and toning tights if they chose dresses, except for one junior assistant who wore black clumpy boots. They were the height of fashion but they struck a wrong note, and Sophie resolved to mention it to the salon manageress.

The plastic cap was tight around her temples and she put up a finger to ease it. She had reverted to the old method for highlights because the foil strips didn't reach the roots quite so well. She had it done at regular intervals, her staff discount making it more affordable, and, like many women, she enjoyed the time spent like this. Whatever problems you brought into a hairdressing or beauty salon, you had to abandon them once you surrendered to the assistant's capable hands. Phones might ring, businesses crumble, dynasties fall – but while you were under the spray or trapped in the dryer, there was damn all you could do about it. Sophie closed her eyes and snuggled down for a precious moment of doing precisely nothing.

Her worries returned as she signed the bill and added her staff number. Tonight she and Paul were going to view a flat in Finsbury Park. Three rooms, kitchen and bathroom, and at an almost affordable price. Already Paul was pausing at style pages in the supplements. What's the matter with me, Sophie wondered, as she was borne upwards on the escalator to the office floor. She ought to care about home-making, but she didn't. Perhaps she had overdosed on it in childhood. There had always been one room in a state of flux, awaiting a new carpet or coving or shelves in an alcove. Her mother was a harmony junkie; everything must tone. If a treasured old possession did not fit the new decor, it was doomed.

As a result, Sophie had grown up in a succession of perfect shop-window sets with nothing shabby or very familiar or distressed by time and loving usage. Only in Kate's home had she felt a sense of permanence, and that was strange, because Kate traded in antiques and items often came and went. But there was a sense of security there, of a home lovingly created over time. I must ring Kate tonight, Sophie thought as she settled behind her desk and began the business of the day.

It was almost midday when Chloe telephoned. 'Darling? It's me! Are you booked for lunch? Good. Can I take you somewhere wonderful with my new card? It really is a flexible friend, with a huge limit and bare as a badger's bum at the moment. I want you to help me launch it. And there's something else I need to discuss.'

Sophie winced at the thought of another flexible friend. Chloe already had a fistful. 'Yes, but I won't be able to take more than an hour,' she said.

They met in Alfredo's, where you had to duck to avoid the greenery that hung from the ceiling, and the air was redolent of olives and garlic and the rich, spicy home-made sausages that were an Alfredo special.

'This place is horrifically over-expensive,' Sophie said, looking down the menu.

'It's outrageous,' Chloe agreed. 'That's why I adore it. Now, don't look at the prices; choose anything. I'm having prawns in garlic for starters, and then the osso bucco. And we'll have oodles of wine, and then armagnac. It's heaven with those little almondy macaroon things.'

Sophie chose antipasto and penne, and asked for a bottle of water. 'One of us has to keep her head,' she said.

Chloe leaned closer and peered into Sophie's face. 'What are you looking at?' asked Sophie.

Chloe straightened. 'Signs of the stigmata. I know they're supposed to show on the hands, but it does no harm to check elsewhere. Well, I am not a saint, I am a human being verging on amoral, and, as I've said before, I'll give it up when I'm twenty-one. Now, will you listen? Desmond is off to San Francisco next week – some lawyers' convention or other – and he wants me to go with him.'

'Is that wise?'

'It's perfectly safe. They're all supposed to take their spouses, so for ten days I'll be Mrs Desmond Bowker.'

'You're mad,' Sophie said as the antipasto was placed in front of her. She moved a whole small fish to the side of the plate, unable to meet its reproachful eye. 'You'll never get away with it.'

'Of course we will.' Chloe was twirling prawns around in the garlic butter and lifting them, dripping, to her mouth. 'The people attending the convention will be mostly Americans; he's checked. And in the unlikely event that one of the foreigners turns up over here and meets Hilary, they'll just think he's changed wives. They do it all the time over there. More importantly, darling, if I'm to play the doting wife I have to look the part. I've got a two-grand limit on this card. I don't intend to spend a penny more than five hundred. So you see why I need you. What can Ascher's come up with, and is there any chance of your staff discount?'

Sophie had to grin, in spite of herself. She disapproved entirely of what Chloe was about to do – getting into debt on account of an affair – and she couldn't rid herself of the feeling that she was confronted by a naughty child with its hand in the cookie jar. But this was a very elegant, red-tipped hand, raised now to the up-swept hair, as if to tuck in an imaginary strand.

They went straight to the French salon when they got back to Ascher's. 'You can't have my staff discount,' Sophie said. 'That's strictly forbidden, and you should know that. However, if you smile very nicely at Harriet she can, if she chooses, give you a good deal. Don't go mad.'

'*Moi*? Do have a word with Shoes and Handbags as you go, darling. I don't want to spoil things for want of the right et ceteras.'

At four forty-five Chloe appeared in the doorway of Sophie's office. 'It was wonderful, darling. As usual, Ascher's came up trumps.' There was a slightly disturbed air about her and at some stage she had unknotted her upswept hair so that it tumbled down about her flushed cheeks.

'How much?' Sophie asked.

'Oh, about what I said.' Chloe was definitely distracted now.

'How much?'

'My God, you can be relentless. I *have* spent a little more but . . . I'll work harder to pay it off. You have a beady eye and a caustic tongue, Sophie. You're like that ghastly columnist, Cindy-Lou Pitter, or whatever her name is, always thinking the worst of people. If I had her page I'd grip people, but not by the jugular.'

'Get out,' Sophie said, struggling not to laugh because, as

she reasoned when she sat down, the whole thing was far from funny.

Paul was waiting for her at the staff entrance when she left on time. 'Good,' he said. 'I said we'd be there by half-six and it's going to be a near thing in this traffic.'

As the car wove in and out of the rush-hour chaos, Sophie glanced through the estate agent's literature and tried to sound enthusiastic. 'I'm glad it's three rooms. They're small, of course, but at least you can . . . ' She paused, trying to rephrase what she had intended to say.

'Get away from one another?' Paul said cheerfully.

'I didn't mean that, *dumkopf*. The truth is that at home we always had a room that was tidy, ready for visitors, and I liked that. It meant you could really relax.' It hadn't meant that, at all, but this was not the time to go into the inner workings of her childhood home.

'Well, there *are* three. And an airing cupboard, and a fitted kitchen. In other words, this is what we're looking for. *And* we can afford it. The only thing we have to worry about is whether, at that price, it's situated next to a kebab house or a brothel.'

The flat was at the bottom of a cul-de-sac of small Victorian terraced houses, each three storeys high with a tiny front garden. The stairs were narrow and the rooms identical in their waxed pine floors and stark, white walls.

'It still needs a lot of work,' the owner said, deprecatingly, 'but there's huge potential.'

Sophie smiled and nodded and tried not to look as claustrophobic as she felt, but it was a relief when they were out in the street, a street that seemed to be full of jeans-clad children on expensive bicycles.

'What d'you think?' Paul asked when they were in the car and driving back into town. The enthusiasm had left his voice, and Sophie tried to be gentle.

'It would do . . . but perhaps we should keep on look-ing?'

'It's out in the sticks, anyway,' Paul agreed gloomily. 'Imagine making this trip morning and night. And the old flat's spoiled us; it's too bloody spacious by far, that's the trouble. That kitchen was like an aircraft galley.'

'How did today go?' Sophie asked, to divert him.

'So-so. Bloody awful, actually. We had that terrible Shu Harmon woman in, the one who says all males are child-molesters. We're signing her up for the next series of *Hearts and Souls*, although whether she has either is debatable after that last documentary she made for Four. And we got two episodes of *Have We Got Words For You* in the can.'

'Who was on the panel?'

'The same old smirkers. Greasy Leighton in the chair and Digga and Forbes as team captains. They chewed up almost everyone, as usual.'

'There's a whole industry of spite in this country now,' Sophie said. 'As long as you can be vicious enough, you're a star.'

'It's not a modern phenomenon, Soph. Remember the old pamphleteers? They could be scathing.'

'Scathing in a cause, darling. Nowadays the only cause is self-advancement, the furtherance of their own careers. That's the difference.'

They were on the Bayswater Road and Sophie sighed, thinking how nice it would be to get home. 'I must ring Kate tonight. Remind me.'

'I'll tell the agent we're not interested in that flat tomorrow,' Paul said, as he put his key in the front door. 'And I'll pick up details of anything else he's got.'

So he wasn't going to let the idea go. Sophie followed him up the stairs, trying to think of the meal ahead, reminding herself of the call to her grandmother, wondering if Chloe was out or in the flat below exulting over the afternoon's haul.

'Did you hear what I said, Sophie?' Paul had stopped ascending and was looking down at her.

'Yes,' she said. 'You're going to get some more bumf from the estate agent. Hurry up and get the door open.'

He was fumbling with the key but she could see that his mouth, usually so pleasant, was firmly set.

'What's the matter?' she asked, when they were inside the flat.

'Nothing.' The way he said it meant, 'Everything.'

'Come on, I know something's up. I said we'd look at other places.'

'With as much enthusiasm as you might look at abbatoirs! This is our future, Sophie. You ought to be keen.'

He flung himself on to the sofa but his eyes were fixed on her face, awaiting a reply. She didn't want a confrontation now so she sank to the floor beside him and looped her arm over his knee.

'It's not that I'm not keen, darling. It's just that now, when you've taken on more responsibility and I'm going away, I wonder if it's the time to take on a property.'

'You don't have to go away.' So it was out at last, the suggestion she'd always sensed was lurking beneath the surface.

'I do,' she said quietly. 'It's important for my career.'

Paul threw his head back and stared at the ceiling for a moment, and then he leaned forward and put his arms around her.

'I understand that, darling. You know I do. I've always accepted your right to be as ambitious, as keen to get on as me. But think. If you go to the States, what then? You come back better equipped . . . for what . . . further promotion? But is that what we want? You know I'll move eventually, probably to America – its logical – but if we're committed to one another – to us – we'll want a base. Permanence. Children. I thought we were both committed, Sophie. I am. So if you're committed too is there any point in gadding about?'

'Gadding about'. It was too much. She could go to the States eventually, but on her man's arm, not in her own right.

'Why do I have to be the one who forgoes a career, Paul? Why not you?' He sat back, detaching himself from her.

'For the simple reason that I don't have childbearing hips, Sophie. Don't be bloody silly. If we want a family, you

79

have to be the one. All the feminists in the world can't change that.'

'I can still work.'

'And turn my kids over to a nanny? No thanks.' He paused, struggling to be reasonable. 'Let's have a drink and talk this through. We both want the same thing in the end, don't we?'

'Apparently not.' She had scrambled to her feet so that she could glower down at him. 'I just want to get on with my life and take advantage of a golden opportunity. You're the one who's obsessed with settling down. What's wrong with this flat? I love it.'

'Hah!' He stood up now, gripping her arms. 'Now we have it. You don't want to move; you're perfectly happy to camp out in someone else's place. And why? Because you don't really want a relationship. Not with me, anyway. You don't want *us*.'

'You're being ridiculous.' Sophie was angry now, spitting her words at Paul because he was being so unfair. 'I'm tired and I don't want to argue. If you want to think all sorts of things into that, you can. Now, if you'll leave go of my arms, I want to ring my grandmother.'

He let go of her instantly, and for a moment she saw indecision in his eyes, as though he regretted a row that had blown up out of nothing. But the moment passed. He turned away and she knew she had hurt him.

'Look,' she said, reaching for his arm.

He shrugged off her hand. 'I'm going out for a beer,' he said. 'Don't cater for me. I'll fend for myself.'

'You're so childish,' Sophie said bitterly. 'Yes, go and sulk in the pub. Better still, ring up some of your colleagues and have a good old moan about how hard done by you are. I'm sure there'll be no shortage of willing listeners. You might even get some real consolation, if you put your mind to it. Media people are generous with their . . . sympathies. You never know your luck.'

'You are a bitch sometimes, Sophie,' he said, and this time his voice was quiet. She stood still as he clattered down the stairs, then she walked to the phone. It would blow over. He would settle down in his new job and forget the delusions of ownership it had aroused, the US trip would turn out to be a damp squib, over in weeks, and they could both go back to being happy.

She dialled 091 and then her grandmother's number. 'Kate? Yes, too long. How are you? Good. Paul's fine. He's just been promoted to executive producer. Yes, awfully grand. And he's off to Paris soon, to film. I might go with him. Things are a bit tricky at work at the moment. Yes, the takeover. There's talk of me going over to the States for a while.' It was a relief to tell someone who could take in the idea in their stride. 'No, not particularly. Well, not for too long. Still, it may not come off. What are you up to?'

Kate was off to Nice in a couple of weeks' time, to stay in a hotel by the sea. 'I envy you,' Sophie said. 'I've never been to the South of France.'

Her grandmother's response was swift and Sophie smiled. 'I'd like nothing better than to come with you, darling. Sun and nice food . . . do they have cicadas there? If I get an unexpected week off, I might join you. If not, I'll come up to Durham for the weekend as soon as I can. How's Oliver? Has he proposed yet? Don't say he's young enough to be your son. Biologically, almost, but socially no. And you don't look your age, or act it, you reprobate.'

Sophie was smiling when she put down the receiver, as she usually did after talking to Kate. It would be nice if her grandmother got together with Oliver one day. I could go up and play Cupid, Sophie thought. Although if she was as successful with Kate's affairs as she had been with her own, tonight, she'd better leave well alone.

She was in bed, tense at the extreme edge, with the room in darkness, when Paul returned. She heard him enter the flat and make himself a coffee. There was the low sound of the television for a while, and then noises from the bathroom that meant he was coming to bed. Half of her wanted to make up, the other half was still furious with him. He had taken it out on her because the damned flat hadn't come up to his expectations. As if you get the house of your dreams at the first throw. He was childish. All men were childish.

When at last Paul slipped into the bed, Sophie held her breath, half hopeful, half apprehensive. At last his hand came out, touching first her arm and then slipping between arm and side, towards her breast. For a moment she hesitated, and then she remembered his angry face only hours before and tensed herself so that his hand could move no further. After a few seconds it was withdrawn. He turned away from her and punched his pillow for sleep. Sophie was left, wide-eyed in the darkness, wondering how things could have gone so wrong when neither of them had wanted it to be that way.

What I want is reasonable, she told herself. I want to go as far as I can. I want what he wants, that's all. There was an ocean of time for children. Twenty more fertile years. Other women ran career and family in tandem, women she knew. When she saw Paul with Gary she felt strange. Not broody, exactly, nor jealous. Just strange. Do I want his children? she asked herself, feeling suddenly as though the man lying beside her was a stranger. Could you know someone for years, live with them, and still not know them? She was almost ready to turn to him and take up the conversation when she heard a gentle expiration and realised that he had fallen asleep.

8

PAUL LEFT FOR HEATHROW AT six thirty a.m. 'Sorry about the last few days,' he said, as Sophie stood in her dressing-gown to wave goodbye.

'It was my fault.' Sophie thought of the armed neutrality of the previous week and grimaced.

'No, it was me,' Paul insisted. 'I just got daft . . . blame it on promotion. It went to my head. Let's talk when I get back.'

'Yes, let's talk.' She kissed him and stood on the landing until he disappeared from sight. She was leaving herself for the north in a couple of hours, and there was a lot to be done. The antagonism between them had been resolved too late to think of her accompanying him to Paris, so she was going home for the weekend alone.

As the car ate up the miles on the A1, she worked out how to tell her parents about America, and indeed the whole direction of her life. If only she could have a real talk with her mother, but at the first hint of anything in the least flaky her mother's eyes would flicker with alarm and there would be a swift change of subject. It was always the same.

As an adolescent, Sophie had resented it. I need you, Mum, had been her unspoken plea. Now she accepted it, along with her mother's polite but relentless urging to conform, not to rock the boat. As a teenager, Sophie had sometimes been tempted to adopt a Mohican haircut or get tattooed, or flagpole-sit; anything to disturb the ocean calm that her mother was so determined to maintain. And yet her mother had been a child of the Swinging Sixties. It didn't add up.

Her harsh thoughts on the way home made her feel guilty when she saw her mother in the doorway, obviously delighted to see her. She allowed herself to be clutched, and hugged back in turn. After that she was enfolded in her father's arms. 'It's good to see you, Sophie,' he said lovingly.

She walked past him into the hall, looking for the big white dog with the ridiculous pom-pom tail.

'Where's Pepsi?'

The hush told her the worst.

'What happened?' she asked.

'It was for the best.' Her mother's face was set. 'It's heartbreaking. We both cried, but it wouldn't've been fair, darling. To keep her alive, I mean. She could hardly raise her head at the last.'

Sophie looked at her father and saw that his eyes were bright with tears. 'Surely there was something you could've done?' she said, but he only shook his head. She moved to him and squeezed his arm. 'I'm so sorry, Daddy. You'll be lost without Pepsi.' She wanted to cry for the loss of her beloved pet, but some instinct made her want to console the man. She would not have been insensitive enough to suggest one dog to replace another, but in any event her mother forestalled her.

'We're not having any more dogs,' she said firmly. 'They cause altogether too much heartache.'

Sophie carried her case up to her old room, fingers crossed that it had been left untouched. It was still intact, the paper with its delicate shell pattern, the magnolia paintwork, the matching curtains and duvet cover printed with swags of flowers. She moved to the window and looked down on the garden. Was it really eight years since she had sat in this window, alternately revising and breaking off to daydream? Eight years full of events: university, Ascher's, Paul . . . almost all the major events of her life had been crammed into a relatively short period. What would happen in the years ahead?

She shivered slightly and opened her wardrobe to find a cardigan. Was it just her imagination or was it colder in the north? She slipped into the comfortable old garment and went downstairs in search of tea.

As usual her mother had prepared a feast fit for a brigade of guards. Cheese straws, melting moments, crumpets with apple jam; all Sophie's old favourites. She tried to sample everything and murmur appreciation while catching up on her mother's news.

'Sue's baby is lovely, apparently. I haven't seen it yet, but everyone says it's her image. She's expecting you round, so don't forget. I expect she wants to show off her house as well. They've got one of those Dutch bungalows in Midholme Close.' She looked directly at her daughter, as though deciding whether or not to speak out. 'I do long for you to get married, Sophie. I know all the stuff about it being just a bit of paper, but a mother can't feel really settled till she sees it all tied up. It's not a moral thing – well, it is in a way – but, really, it's security. I mean, what kind of commitment have you and Paul made?'

'Not again, Mum.' Sophie tried to keep the irritation out of her voice. 'We are committed. We were flat-hunting last week.'

A look of bliss flitted across her mother's face. 'Were you? Well, this is news. You never tell me anything on the phone.'

Should she say she had hated the flat, didn't want to move, would like to live like a snail with her house on her back? Should she say that she would soon be crossing the Atlantic? Sophie looked around at the velvet three-piece suite with its fringed hem, the matching china on every surface, the dried flower arrangements on the wine-table, the Chinese rug at the hearth . . . and surrendered.

'We looked at a flat in Finsbury Park: quite small by northern standards, but big for London. The trouble is, the rooms were tiny. So we're still looking.'

'Well, I must say I'm pleased. Will you have a flapjack? Don't eat too much, I've planned a lovely meal later. Can we expect a wedding when you get settled, then?'

The impulse to be craven for a second time came and went. 'I don't know, Mummy. Perhaps, but one way and another we've got our hands full at the moment, you've got to understand that.'

'I do. We're so pleased about Paul's promotion. Daddy says he must be doing well. It cheered him up. He's been lost without Pepsi to make a fuss over.'

'You must get another dog for him. Not straightaway, I know, but eventually.'

'No.' Her mother's voice was sharp. 'I'm too old to cope with a puppy now, and you never get loyalty from a grown dog. Besides, we've just got the house right, and Daddy has such a lot on with Rotary and his voluntary work.'

'Too old? You're forty-five!'

'I'm forty-six.' Her mother had the grace to look discomfited. 'I know it's not old, but it's not an easy time of life. You'll know when it happens to you.' As if a warning light had suddenly flashed she changed her tone. 'We must try and get into Lewis's while you're here. They have the most heavenly hats in that shop, and hats are back with a vengeance.'

When tea was over Sophie looked at the clock. Usually, when she came home, Pepsi leaped and whimpered until she gave way and took him for a walk. But there was no Pepsi now. 'I might just pop out and see Susan, if you think there's time?'

Her mother was only too keen for her to visit her friend, in the hope that sight of a Dutch bungalow *and* a baby might bring her to her senses. Sophie had to conceal a wry smile. It would take more than a glimpse of someone else's domestic bliss to change her, she thought smugly, as she walked the half-mile to Susan's house.

But she was unprepared for the sensation that swept over her as the minute, warm bundle of Susan's son was placed in her arms. 'He's lovely,' she said, but in fact the baby was so much more. Mysterious, complicated, perfect in detail, suddenly opening his blue eyes to stare fixedly at a point beyond Sophie's face.

'He lost six ounces,' Susan said, 'but he's put it all back since. I'm feeding him myself, which makes life easier in one way, 'cos it's all on tap. On the other hand, I never know how much he's had, which is a bit worrying.'

Sophie looked at her friend. Susan's face was pale, her hair stringy, her hands unnaturally white and wrinkled slightly at the fingertips, as though they'd been in water too much. She wore a cotton sweater over breasts that bulged and leaked, in spite of the clear outlines of a brassiere that looked as though it were made from whalebone and sailcloth. Sophie found herself fascinated by the spectacle of these huge globes which had replaced her friend's modest 34B breasts. She's been taken over, Sophie thought, and was at once both horrified and awestruck.

'What about you?' Susan said, when the baby had been put back in its blue-and-white Moses basket and they were settled on the beige Dralon sofa with coffee in yellow china cups set out on the teak coffee-table in front of them.

Looking around, Sophie noticed how everything matched here, too. Aloud, she said, 'Well, I'm still with Paul, and we've got a flat in Notting Hill Gate. That's sort of off the Bayswater Road. Quite central.'

'A flat,' Susan said brightly. 'That's nice. Is it self-contained?'

They talked about houses for a while and then Susan suggested a conducted tour of her house. Sophie had never been particularly interested in other people's homes, but there was no escape.

They moved from lounge to dining annexe, to kitchen, to utility room, to patio and tiny immaculate garden. After that it was upstairs to master-bedroom, guest-room complete with paperbacks on the bedside table, loo and bathroom combined, with colour-co-ordinated towels, and finally the nursery, a mass of ruffles and fluffy toys and dangling mobiles. 'Michael did most of it,' Susan said modestly. 'He's wonderful with his hands.'

'You're lucky,' Sophie said, managing to inject a note of envy into her voice.

When she was out in the street, Susan's kiss still warm on her cheek, she tried to examine her own feelings. Prior to the visit she had, if she was honest, felt superior to Susan. She, Sophie, had escaped; Susan had been left behind, trapped. But Susan was obviously happy; blissfully happy. And the baby was . . . Sophie sought for the right word . . . the baby was wonderful. It had gripped her finger at one stage, with fingers tinier than a doll's and looked up at her with the face of a wise old monkey.

'Well?' her mother said when she came in at the kitchen door.

'Well what?' Sophie said, smiling. 'The house is lovely and the baby is scrumptious. Will that do? Sue looks a bit washed-out, but I suppose that's only to be expected.'

'I'd never had a tooth filled till you were born.' Her mother was piping duchesse potatoes on to a blue willow-pattern dish. 'Then I had seven fillings within a year. It's all the calcium you give the baby, or so they say. You do feel washed-out . . . and a bit low, sometimes.'

The last thing Sophie wanted was a discussion on post-natal depression. She went up to her room on the pretence of freshening up before dinner, but instead leaned out of the window to look at the garden and smell the honeysuckle that trailed the wall. She had dreamed her girlhood dreams in this window-seat but now they were strangely hard to remember. Had babies figured in them? If so, it had been in a very chocolate box way, herself in a Janet Reger bedjacket holding a tiny bundle in her arms while a Robert Redford figure stood at the side of the bed, eaten up with admiration. What tripe adolescent dreams were! She leaned her forehead against the glass and looked down on a lawn striped by mowing, surrounded by hydrangeas and buddleias, marguerites and hybrid tea roses. An English garden, straight from a seed catalogue.

In ten years' time Susan would have a detached house and garden like this one. There would be one point four more babies, Michael would be grey at the temples and Susan would be chairwoman of the Ladies Circle and watching out for crowsfeet. And where would she, Sophie, be? Her life was not laid out; at least she could choose that it wasn't. She could be a world away if she so desired. She heard her mother's voice below, calling her to table, and abandoned her uncomfortable thoughts.

9

I T WAS STRANGE TO WAKE up in the single bed and hear
familiar sounds of Sunday: lawn-mowers and children
and somewhere hymns from a church service on the radio.
The smell of bacon drifted up from below and Sophie thought
of Paul, drooling over bacon butties. He would be waking up
in Paris now, drinking rich, dark coffee from a white jug, and
lifting croissants laden with apricot preserve to his mouth.

Once – the first time they had gone to Paris – they had
stayed in bed for two days, reading, laughing, making love
and eating from trays, until an irate manager with a Hercule
Poirot moustache had rapped on the door to demand entry
for the maid.

I should have gone with him, Sophie thought, regretting
the bad feeling of the past week. They should have been
able to sort it out. They were both adult, intelligent human
beings. Why had they resorted to abuse when honest
discourse would have served them better?

She snuggled down and imagined Paul's homecoming.
She would be welcoming, he would be randy. They would
both be forgiving. He might even phone her tonight, when
she got back to the flat. She had hoped for a call last night, but
she knew the kind of hours he worked on a shoot; perhaps

he had finished too late to disturb her parents' household. Tonight would be different. She would be in her own place and he could ring her at any hour.

Sophie was suddenly filled with an impulse to create. It came over her sometimes, and it was a good feeling. Perhaps if she made the flat more theirs – hers and Paul's – he would settle for a while. She could stock the freezer before she went away, as evidence that his comfort mattered, that she was his woman no matter where she might be. She had intended to stock the freezer when they moved in – casseroles and soups and pasta dishes – so they could enjoy home-cooked food at the touch of the defrost button on the microwave. She had just never got around to it and it had remained a fantasy of domesticity. She had a few days' leave coming up soon. She could indulge in an orgy of baking then, using all the glossy coffee-table cook-books she had bought and never opened since.

She was still on the same high when she came downstairs and decided to go for a walk. If only Pepsi had still been there, but her father was eager enough to accompany her. They strolled down the garden and out of the gate at the bottom, which gave on to woodland and then an expanse of fields. Most of them had been raped of their crops now, but there had not been time for them to blacken and the stubble still glowed golden. Sophie loved the landscape of North Yorkshire, even without the white dog trotting ahead; she loved each hedge, each sloping field, each patch of trees against the skyline.

'I wish Pepsi was here,' she said, without thinking.

Her father nodded, swiping a patch of nettles with the stick he carried. 'Yes. You can't have a beast that length of time and not feel the loss. I feel it at nights, too. That last-minute walk round the block . . . it helped me to sleep.'

'You'll get another dog eventually,' Sophie said encouragingly. 'Mum'll come round.'

Her father shook his head. 'She won't. She's quite adamant, and I can see her point. I'm not far off retirement –

I can go at fifty-four or fifty-five – and she thinks a dog'll be a tie if we want to see a bit of the world.'

'Mum hates foreign travel,' Sophie said, filled with a sense of injustice. If that was the best excuse her mother could come up with, it wouldn't wash. 'I could get you a puppy for Christmas. She'd have to accept it then.'

'No.' There was a touch of authority in his voice, 'No, Sophie. It's kind of you, but it wouldn't do. I wouldn't want a dog to be resented and . . . well, I'll adjust. Pepsi was your dog after all, not mine.'

It was there again, the feeling of compassion for this man – for all men – the feeling that rendered her vulnerable. If she went to America, Paul would be wounded by her choice. I'm tied, she thought. It isn't fair.

As if he'd read her thoughts her father spoke. 'How's work going, then? You've been bought out, apparently.'

'Yes. We belong to Littlecamp Inc of New York, Boston and LA. So far they've been okay – quite nice, really – but there'll be changes.' She hesitated. Was this the moment to mention going overseas? 'Actually, I might be sent over to the States. Just temporarily. It's all a bit up in the air at the moment. If I do go, you and Mum must come and visit.'

'I'd like to see Vermont.' Her father laughed. 'Blame Cadbury's. Someone once gave my mother a box of chocolates – Cadbury's, or it might've been Rowntrees – anyway, it had this fabulous picture of Vermont in the fall; utterly beautiful. I've longed to see it ever since. One or two trips have come up – conventions or Rotary exchange visits – but you know your mother. She likes her own home. Unlike *her* mother, who can't sit still. Have you seen Kate lately?'

'I spoke to her last week. She's fine. Off to the South of France soon.'

'Yes. Lucky Kate. Perhaps your mother'll change when I retire. Not that she welcomes it, I fear.' There was real anguish in his tone and Sophie looked at him sharply.

'You're not serious, are you, Daddy? She loves you being at home at weekends.'

'Yes. I'm making too much of it.' He stopped suddenly

and gestured. 'Look, there's a baby rabbit over there.' The rabbit was small and pale brown, staring at them from the field edge. 'It's had a scare,' her father said. 'See how fixed its expression is? I could probably walk right up to it and pick it up.'

'It looks mesmerised,' Sophie said. 'Has it seen a stoat?'

'It'd be dead now if it had encountered one of those evil little beasts. I think it's just bewildered by the field, dazzled by space. It wants a nice narrow path between greenery, something to scuttle down, out of sight.'

I know how it feels, Sophie thought. It has too many choices, too many ways to run. Aloud, she said, 'Can we do anything for it?'

'Only frighten it further, darling. Best to leave well alone.' Her father spoke with conviction and Sophie walked on, but not without a backward glance. Let the rabbit be all right! Let everyone bemused by choices be all right.

In the kitchen, as she helped to dish up lunch, she spoke to her mother. 'Dad says he might retire before too long.'

'Oh, he's always talking about it. He'll never do it.'

'He'll have to do it one day, Mum!' Sophie was shocked at such an airy dismissal of the inevitable. She was ready to paint a glowing picture of what early retirement could mean to them both, but she had reckoned without her mother's capacity to terminate a tricky conversation.

'Really, darling, as if we didn't have enough problems without dwelling on something ages away. I'm forty-six, remember. That's a bad enough time for a woman without being told she's ready for the scrap-heap.'

'No one's saying that. Anyway, you're not menopausal, are you?' It was amazing, but her mother's neck was flushing red.

'If you mean have I stopped menstruating, the answer's no. But . . . well, as I said, it's not the easiest time. Now do pass that colander, darling, and don't harp on. I don't know what your father's thinking of, talking of such things on your weekend home.' She made it sound as though Sophie had not visited for a decade and was unlikely to visit again, but Sophie let it go. There were more important issues to pursue.

'I wish we could talk sometimes. Not just about you and Dad, but about me . . . and Paul . . . and life.'

'We do talk!' Her mother was shocked. 'I've gone on about you and Paul and the future till you must be tired of listening.'

'But we don't discuss. You don't listen.'

'I do. I don't always agree with you, but I always listen.' Her mother looked up from the gravy she was stirring to thickness. 'Why? Is something wrong?'

'No, not really. Not specifically. I just feel there are so many decisions to make. A woman nowadays has so many choices. I looked at Sue yesterday and . . . yes, I can see why you go on about marriage and children. I felt quite broody actually, but only for a minute. I just wondered what you felt when you were my age. How did you feel about Dad, and your job and . . . well, everything?' She wanted to confess about America but couldn't find the words.

'Pass the plates. Thank you.' Her mother had recovered her composure now. 'I was settled down by the time I was your age. Long settled. You were . . . you must've been five or six, and Daddy was moving from Gloucester. And then we moved again to this place. It wasn't a case of choices; I had to get on with it. It was all terribly tame.'

'But when you were single? Before you settled down?'

'It was still tame, darling. I was only nineteen, remember, and I doubt I'd ever have made a good nurse. I didn't have the dedication. I met your father at a rugger club dance. We fell in love and there I was, a married woman with a tiny little house to keep and a baby on the way. It wasn't a shotgun wedding, if that's going to be your next question. You were born two days before our first wedding anniversary. Now call your father and let's eat this meal.'

But as Sophie left the kitchen, Elizabeth remembered. 1966: the soundtrack of *Dr Zhivago*, 'Lara's Theme', sounding from every radio and TV set; Britain in the grip of World Cup fever; and then the horror of Aberfan, the black tide of the slagheap engulfing a school and its children, providing a grim backdrop to her own misery.

She looked down at the diamond solitaire on her finger and remembered.

BOOK 2

———————•———————

ELIZABETH'S STORY

Sunderland
1966

10

THE FRACTURE CLINIC HAD GONE on for two hours and left a trail of chaos for Liz to clear up. She looked at her watch. There ought to be some X-rays coming through soon. If not, she would go in search of them. She sat down on one of the couches and wiggled her toes inside her regulation black lace-up shoes. When she got home she would take them off and simply let her feet breathe for hours and hours and hours.

The footsteps on the marble corridor outside were too brisk for Sister's stately tread and it was red-haired Staff Nurse Harker who appeared and looked around the clinic. 'Nice,' she said, 'everything ship-shape,' at the same time hitching up her apron and scrabbling in her pocket. 'Want some gum?'

Liz accepted a piece of chewing gum and popped it into her mouth. 'Ta,' she said.

Harker scowled as she unwrapped the gum. 'Heard about Sinatra? He's married that Mia Farrow. It'll never last.'

Liz was sure the remote and dreamy Mia would reform Frank, the hell-raiser, and it would end, like all good fairy tales, with the lovers living happily ever after, but it didn't do to argue with staff nurses so she nodded agreement.

'Right,' Harker said, replacing her apron and settling her cap. Her jaws moved as her eyes ranged round the clinic for a final check. 'I'm going to Break now. Keep out of Sister's way and take care of the waiting-room. I'll swing for that houseman if he doesn't turn up soon. I won't be long.' She was gone in a whirl of pink uniform dress and black stocking-clad legs, and Elizabeth got rid of her gum and went about her duties.

Down the ramp, in the waiting-room, there were three patients awaiting their X-rays, one of them a toddler cuddled into his mother's side. Elizabeth was about to reassure them that they wouldn't have to wait much longer when Harker reappeared on the ramp. 'I've seen Dr Quezi and threatened him with Sister if he doesn't get a move on. He's only talking to the porters about the flaming World Cup. It'll probably be a forearm plaster for the kid so just shunt him along to Mr Greenfield. I'll be back to check it. Sister's on the phone to her mother so that'll keep her busy for the next hour . . . ' Her voice trailed away as she hurried up the ramp.

A moment later the X-ray technician appeared, holding some dripping wet-plates well clear of her white coat. 'It's a greenstick radius,' she said. 'Don't forget to return them for fixing.'

Liz carried the X-rays up to the clinic, hung them on the viewer and switched it on. In her second year of training now, she could distinguish the two bones of the forearm and see that the larger of the two, the radius, was slightly curved, still pliable enough in a three-year-old to bend, not break. She switched off the viewer and made her way back to the waiting-room.

The child with his arm in a makeshift sling saw her coming. His eyes widened in fear and his lip began to tremble. He turned an imploring face towards his mother. 'I want to go home, Mammy.'

Liz was careful not to touch him. That would only make matters worse. Instead she crouched down an inch or two away from him, lifting the hem of her pinafore to keep it clear of the floor. 'I've got the pictures of your arm now, Martin. I'll let you have a look at them later on. There's nothing broken. One of your bones is a bit bent but it'll be all right.' There was a pause and then he turned to look suspiciously into her face. So far, so good. 'The doctor will be here in a moment. He'll have a little look at your arm and then a look at the X-rays and after that he'll tell me what to do.'

'What do you mean?' More progress.

'Well,' Liz said, 'he might say, put a nice, soft dry bandage all the way around your poorly arm, or he might say use a wet one. The wet one is a bit cold but that's all, and when it dries, it's hard and it stops anything from hurting your arm till it's better. And,' she paused for effect, 'we can write your name on it – in red pen.'

She was never to learn which treatment Martin would prefer. At that moment the door of the waiting-room was thrown back and two figures appeared in the entrance. One of them looked anxious and the face of the man he was holding up was contorted in pain. Instinctively Liz moved to the wheelchairs parked at the side of the room.

'Get him into this,' she said, propelling a chair towards them and holding it steady while the injured man was manoeuvred into it. 'Thanks,' they said in unison, and the patient managed a grin through stretched lips.

'Have you got an admission chit?' Liz asked.

The man grasping the handles of the chair shook his head. 'No, I'm just a cabbie. I brought him in, that's all.' He was already backing towards the door and the patient was pressing what looked suspiciously like a fiver into his outstretched hand.

'You should have gone through Admissions at the lodge,' Liz said, 'but it doesn't matter. I'll take your details here and we can get you a number later on.'

The man in the chair was smiling at her, putting up a tanned hand to smooth his fair hair. Now that his face had relaxed there was a confident, almost teasing quality in the way he looked at her. 'Well,' he said, 'I can see I'm in good hands.'

Liz felt her cheeks flush. She was used to patients who

made passes but there was something different about this one. He was the patient, she was in charge . . . but it didn't feel like that. It didn't feel like that at all.

She took refuge in flight, moving back to the greenstick patient and bending close to him. 'Not much longer now, and then you'll be able to go home.' His mother flashed her a look of gratitude and one of the other patients, a man in his sixties, cleared his throat.

'What about me, nurse? Any signs of the doctor yet?' It was useless to explain that junior housemen came and went as they pleased unless there were consultants about, at which time they hovered like bluebottles around fresh meat. She murmured a soothing platitude and took a blank admission sheet from a drawer in the desk.

'Can I have your name?' she asked, sitting down next to the wheelchair.

'Hartley-Davis,' the man said. 'Bruce Hartley-Davis.' He threw back his head and looked at the ceiling. 'Date of birth October the twenty-eighth, 1937. Do you want my address? It's the Palatine Hotel – I'm staying there at the moment.'

Liz wrote steadily, glad that her bowed head concealed her mounting excitement. There was something about this patient, something different . . . and he liked her. She could tell, even without looking into his face. She tried to think about Geoffrey and the fact that they were nearly engaged, but it didn't help.

'Occupation?' she said.

'Business . . . ' She looked up, confused, but before she could speak he smiled. 'Wheeling and dealing, actually, but just put Chartered Accountant.'

'Thank you,' Elizabeth said. 'Nearly finished. I need your religion and your doctor's name.'

'Religion . . . God, the family is C of E. As for my doctor, he's in London, but his name is Christopher Proud. I'd like you to hold my hand, nurse, while they amputate, and then let me take you out to dinner to say thank you.'

'There's not much risk of amputation if you could hop up the corridor,' Liz said briskly, but her heart was racing uncomfortably. It was a relief when the tall figure of Dr Quezi half ran down the ramp, his white coat flying behind him.

'Where's this greenstick, nurse? Hurry up, I'm wanted in theatre!' He saw the wheelchair and halted. 'What's this?'

'Nothing for you, doctor.' Sister had appeared from nowhere, the bow of her white cap quivering beneath her chin as she took command. 'Mr Hartley-Davis?' She smiled benignly at the man in the wheelchair. 'Your hotel rang through and Mr Hinckley is on his way.'

So he's a private patient, Liz thought. Nothing else would bring Mr Hinckley back once the clinic was over. She snapped to attention as Sister spoke.

'Take Mr Hartley-Davis into the clinic, nurse. Put him in a cubicle.' She turned to the rest of the waiting-room, taking in the picture in a second and turning to Liz for information, which she demanded with the lift of an eyebrow.

'The little boy's wet plates are in the clinic, Sister. The others shouldn't be long.'

Sister's white cap bobbed graciously above her navy-blue shoulders. 'Right. Dr Quezi, take your patient with you. Off you go with doctor, mother, you'll soon be on your way home. Nurse, the wheelchair! Where's Staff Nurse Harker?'

'Here, Sister.' Harker had returned in the nick of time. Elizabeth manoeuvred the chair towards the ramp and was grateful for Dr Quezi's help in pushing it up towards the curtained cubicle, which, out of clinic hours, was allocated only to the very injured or the very important.

She helped the patient on to the examination couch, self-consciously because he was deliberately staring at her now, trying to force her to meet his eyes as she busied herself with placing a pillow for his head and folding a blanket across his legs.

'You'll know me next time,' she said, regretting the banal expression the minute it left her lips.

'I'd like to know you.'

'Well,' she said briskly, to cover her discomfort. 'You'll just have to wait for Mr Hinckley now. I don't expect he'll be long.' She knew from experience that paying patients usually brought forth the senior consultant with the speed of light, but she forbore to say so.

She was leaving the cubicle, twitching the curtain into place behind her, when Mr Hinckley appeared at the clinic door, unusually dressed in an open-necked shirt and slacks.

'Sister.' He bowed his head to the casualty sister and ignored Liz, as consultants always ignored junior staff. At the other end of the clinic the greenstick fracture began to cry as the house surgeon's fingers probed his arm. Sister smiled grimly and leaned towards Liz. 'Tell the doctor to take his patient to the dressing-room, nurse. Mr Hinckley doesn't need interruption at the moment. When you've done that, chase up those other X-rays and tell the staff nurse to see to things. I'll be busy here for the moment.'

When Liz returned from X-ray the three-year-old had gone off to Mr Greenfield, the plaster technician, and the cubicle that had held Hartley-Davis was empty, its curtains drawn back to reveal a vacant couch.

'The PP's gone up to PP1,' Staff Nurse Harker told her. 'It's only torn ligaments but you'd think he was a compound the way they're all going on.'

'Who is he?' Liz's eyes were round.

'Some kind of businessman, up here on a big scheme, apparently. Something to do with the river, or so he was telling Hinckley.'

'I thought he must be a nob of some sort, the way Sister was going on. Red carpet wasn't in it,' Liz said.

'He was good-looking.' Harker's eyes rolled. 'I wouldn't mind a night out with him. That shirt he had on was silk – very sexy. And don't purse your lips, nurse. We're not all nuns like you.'

Liz would have protested but she knew the folly of bandying words with senior staff, Harker in particular. She kept out of harm's way as much as she could until her shift was over and she could hang up her apron and cap and slip into her navy gaberdine coat for the journey home.

A bus-ride later, she let herself into her mother's hair-dressing shop, her nose wrinkling at the mingled smells of ammonia, peroxide and perm solution. She could hear her mother in the flat above, singing 'Alfie', the Cilla Black song that seemed to be on the radio non-stop nowadays.

'It's only me,' she called as she neared the top of the stairs. The singing stopped and her mother appeared in the doorway of the kitchen, still in her pink overall, her face damp with heat and exertion, her hair curling around it like a halo.

'It's toad-in-the-hole for tea, pet. I had a perm in till quarter to six but it's nearly ready. Have you heard what Wilson's done?'

Privately Liz couldn't have cared less what the Prime Minister got up to, but her mother's face demanded some response. 'What?'

'A six-month standstill on wages and dividends and probably another six months after that. Still, he's frozen prices; that's something. The paper says George Brown'll probably resign over pay restraint. Not that he'll be missed. He's never sober, or so they say.'

'That's just talk. You want to buy a better paper,' Liz said. 'You only get rubbish in that one. Can we eat now? I'm starving.'

'All right, if you want it half cooked,' Kate said. 'You'll have to use a spoon to the batter, though. It won't be set.'

'Sorry.' Liz pulled a contrite face. 'It just seems a year since lunchtime. I'll go and get changed.'

'Everything all right at work?' her mother asked later, as she lifted wedges of sausages in batter pudding on to their plates.

'Yeah, fine. We had a severed radial artery this morning. Blood everywhere. And a lovely little boy with a greenstick radius.'

Her mother looked up from shaking the tomato ketchup bottle. 'A what?'

'A greenstick radius . . . it's this bone here, in the forearm, only in kids it bends rather than breaks. He was lovely.

Somebody called Hartley-Davis was brought in this afternoon. Everyone was making a fuss. You'd've thought he was Antony Armstrong-Jones.'

'What was the matter with him?' Kate Lucas was toying with her food and Liz could see that her mother was too tired to eat.

'You can put your feet up after tea. I'll do the dishes. He had torn ligaments. Worse than a fracture, they can be.'

Her mother's face brightened. 'You are clever. It beats me how you take it all in.' She began to eat again and Liz kept the conversation going, seeing that it was an aid to appetite.

'He's staying at the Palatine Hotel. That must cost something. He's in Sunderland to do with the river Wear . . . some business scheme, they say.'

'One of the shipyards, probably,' Kate said. She put down her fork and knife and rested her chin on her hands. 'I wish you'd seen the Wear in its heyday, Elizabeth. Sunderland was the biggest shipbuilding town in the world. Everybody worked for the Thompsons or the Doxfords or the North Eastern Marine. They had great big houses, and their workers lived in little terraces, just like miners. Still, they gave employment, you have to give them that. Your grandad was apprenticed to Player's but he went to Greenwell's in the war as a riveter. I think it was Greenwell's – anyway, he wound up at Austin and Pickersgill's.' She clicked her tongue against her teeth in disgust. 'You could stand on the bridge once and hear the river lifting. Riveters, platelayers, caulkers . . . they produced a million and a half tons during the war. The King and Queen came twice to say thank you, and she launched a ship in '46.' Kate lapsed into silence and Liz knew she was remembering. Her father had come home in 1946, or about then.

'Come on, Mam,' she said after a while. 'You're letting your food get cold.'

They had tinned fruit salad for afters with Carnation milk poured from the tin.

'Seeing Geoff tonight?' her mother asked as Liz stood up to make a pot of tea.

'Not tonight. He's gone for that interview, remember? Weights and Measures in Gloucester. It'll be a big promotion if he gets it. He went this afternoon so he could get a good night's sleep in a hotel before tomorrow.'

'He's a sensible lad,' her mother said approvingly 'He'll make a good husband for someone.' Liz smiled at the veiled hint in her mother's words.

'I dare say he will,' she said. 'Now get this tea down you so I can get washed up. I've got to think through my essay for Sister Tutor.' But it was not the facts of haematology which ran through her mind as she rinsed the dishes. She'd been going out with Geoffrey ever since school and they'd probably get married at some point. As she scrubbed the remnants of batter from the oven-tin she thought about engagement rings. If they did get engaged she'd have to wear her ring on a chain for work. Matron was mustard about jewellery. If you got your ears pierced she wouldn't even permit sleepers while your holes healed.

An emerald would be nice, Liz thought as she dried the dishes. An emerald flanked with diamonds. Or a diamond cluster. As the suds ran away down the plug-hole she grinned. Diamond clusters? How daft could you get. Geoff was in local government, not the oil business. Still, he was good with money so she might get a nice little solitaire with an illusion setting. That was what most girls got . . . or opals, but opals meant tears . . . or was that pearls?

If Bruce Hartley-Davis had a fiancée she'd probably have a ring like a football. Private patients always had lovely jewellery; tiny little watches and thin platinum wedding rings, and the men had gold signet rings on their little finger. They never wore too much, though. That was the main thing.

'Have you finished?' Kate had taken off her overall and tidied her hair. 'I've got something nice to show you. Come into the living-room.'

The 'something nice' was a large and shiny jug in a strange shade of pink.

'It's lustre,' Kate said in tones of awe. 'It might be

Sunderland – the pottery did a lot of lustre before it closed. I'm going down to the library tomorrow to see if they've got a book on it.'

'It's chipped,' Liz said dubiously.

'Only the bottom rim.' Kate picked up the jug and held it to her breast. 'Anyway, I love it.' She put the jug to her lips and kissed it. 'I really love it.'

'Where did you get it?'

'Jacky White's market. A woman brought it in to sell but they didn't want it so I gave her five bob for it.'

'Five bob?' Liz was scandalised.

'I know.' Kate put up a guilty hand and shook her head. 'We can't afford it and I should be shot. But if it *is* Sunderland, Elizabeth, my pet, it's probably worth ten bob or more, so I'll make a profit.'

'If you sell it!' Liz's tone was scathing. 'This flat's filling up with junk and we both know you'll never part with it.' Her face softened as she looked at her mother. 'Still, if it keep you happy . . . '

'One day I'll sell the salon and go into antiques,' Kate said, setting the jug back in place. 'Nothing pricey, just bric-a-brac. And when I'm rich, we'll both have a musquash coat.'

'You could probably get a night class,' Liz said, rolling down her sleeves as she spoke. 'Furniture restoration or ceramics or something like that. It'd do you good to get out.'

'We'll see.' Kate winced and lifted one foot from her shoe, rubbing it against her other calf for relief. 'After nine hours on my feet each day, my pet, all I want to do is flop. You get your homework done and then we'll have some cocoa. Right now, I'm going to soak my feet in Epsom salts.'

11

L IZ GATHERED UP THE CASE notes and carried them
down the ramp to the receptionist's desk. Behind her
the clinic was winding down. The last new patient was
behind screens with Mr Hinckley and the registrar was
working his way through the other patients. When she
reached the waiting-room it was almost empty.

'There's a PP coming in any minute,' Staff Nurse Harker
told her when she returned to the clinic. 'Get a cubicle ready,
and I mean ready, Lucas. You know what Sister's like about
her precious private patients.'

'Who is it?' Liz asked, as casually as she could.

'It's that Hartley-Davis,' Harker said. 'What a right charmer
he is.'

Liz was tempted to mention the half joking offer of dinner
made to her, but she refrained. Harker could be spiteful if
she turned awkward. Instead, she said, 'He was all right, I
suppose.'

'I wonder who he is exactly?' Harker mused as they
began to tidy the instruments trolleys. 'He's bound to be
well-heeled.' There was a sudden sharp intake of breath.
'Watch out, here's Sister.' When Harker spoke again it
was in her cut-glass professional accent. 'Nearly finished,

Sister. Two to come back from X-ray and one in the plaster-room.'

Sister's head inclined but her eyes continued to rake the entire clinic. 'I've Mr Hinckley's private patient in my office, Staff Nurse. Clear a cubicle as soon as you can.' She turned to Liz. 'Tea, nurse. For three. Use the china cups. Get milk from X-ray if you have to, but hurry.' She moved towards the consultant, who had emerged from the cubicle, and stood, hands folded in front of her, until he deigned to notice her presence.

'Sister?'

'Your patient, Mr Hartley-Davis, is in my office, Mr Hinckley. I've sent for tea and told him you'll be coming directly.'

'Thank you, Sister.' The consultant returned to interrogating his patient and Sister spun round on her cuban heels, pausing only to glower at Liz, who was finishing what she'd been doing to the trolley.

'I want that tea today, nurse, *if* you don't mind.'

'And we know where we'd like to put it,' Harker said, *sotto voce*.

Liz went off to the kitchen to plug in the kettle and set about assembling a tray fit for visiting royalty, which was what PPs were, if the truth was told.

When she carried in the tea, Mr Hinckley was already there. 'Thank you, nurse,' Sister said, in a tone of dismissal. Liz put down the tray and turned, but the patient's leg, encased in plaster, was sticking out now, preventing her from getting through the door.

'Sorry,' he said, trying to hitch it out of her way. Mr Hinckley was holding forth about somewhere called Antibes, and Hartley-Davis was nodding slowly, as though he agreed with every word, while Liz eased round the plastered leg and out of the door.

'How long are they going to be?' Harker asked when Liz got back to the clinic.

'Ages, I should think.'

The staff nurse consulted the watch pinned to the top of

her apron. 'It's half past twelve. They can't be ages, he's got theatre at two and you know he likes his lunch.'

'You go off if you want to,' Liz said, suddenly anxious to be the one who assisted when Hartley-Davis came to be examined. As if she read her junior's mind, Harker grinned.

'Want rid of me? I'll stay, if you don't mind. If he needs his hand held, I'm the one to do it.' But when they were finished in the clinic it was not Harker who pushed the patient to the plaster-room to have his cast trimmed to the ankle. It was Liz who was summoned by Sister and Liz who brought the wheelchair alongside the patient so that he could ease himself off the couch and on to it. He was heavy. Six foot, Liz guessed, and muscular, and the wheelchair rocked until Liz braced her foot against it.

'Thanks, Nurse Lucas,' he said, when he was safely seated. She was startled at his use of her name and he smiled. 'I asked. Now . . . ' He was taking a slim gold pen from an inside pocket. 'Write your telephone number on my cast. You have got a telephone?'

'Yes,' she said, giving silent thanks for the salon and the black telephone on its counter. She felt sick suddenly and scared, and tried to think of a put-down. 'I've already got a boyfriend,' she could say – or, 'Sorry, but I'm busy tonight,' – but before she could speak he intervened.

'Come on, do it before the dragon comes back.' There was an imperious tone in his voice and Liz found herself uncapping the pen and inscribing the salon number on to the chalky surface of the plaster. Thank heaven no one would recognise it as hers or it would be all round the hospital that she was fast.

As if he had read her thoughts, Hartley-Davis chuckled. 'Good girl. Now, not a word to anyone. I'll be in touch. Wheel me away!'

As she pushed him along the corridor, Liz reflected that what was happening must be because of fate. In the ordinary course of events she'd never have met someone like Hartley-Davis. But he had come to Sunderland and played squash and injured his leg, and all the cogs of fate had clicked into place.

In the plaster-room she steadied the wheelchair again as he hoisted himself on to the couch, the muscles hardening in his brown forearms as well as the inch or two of thigh between plaster and groin.

Hartley-Davis grinned at her. 'You look much too fragile for this job, nurse.' There was a teasing quality to his voice as he continued and Liz felt herself blush. 'I can't keep saying "nurse". It makes me sound infantile. What's your name?'

Liz was saved from having to answer by the advent of the plaster technician, but before she could melt away she felt the patient's cool fingers brush her arm in what might have been accidental contact but felt more like a caress.

The rest of her shift passed in a blur of tidying and sluicing and casting anxious eyes along the corridor for fear of seeing Sister in pursuit. It was a relief when the end of her shift came and she could shrug into her outdoor clothes and head for home. As she walked she tried to work out what made Bruce Hartley-Davis so attractive. He wore marvellous clothes, quite conservative but beautifully cut and finished, and the thin gold watch on his left wrist must have cost a fortune. Yet it wasn't the outward trappings or even the sleek fair hair that impressed; it was his supreme confidence that came across most of all. Like President Kennedy, she thought, as though he was born to it.

She was almost at her own bus-stop when a figure fell into step beside her. It was Geoffrey, his face bright and earnest above a neat collar and tie, leather patches on the elbows of his tweed jacket.

'I was hoping I'd catch you. If not, I was going to ring.' There was an air of suppressed excitement about him and Liz guessed the job interview had gone well.

'How did yesterday go?' she said, but she could see the answer in his face.

'I got it!' His cheeks, which were normally rosy, were glowing. She thought how handsome he was, but today he looked boyish. Even the way he stood was gangling, his dark hair somehow spiky and falling across his brow.

'Oh Geoff, I'm so pleased for you. You deserve it. When do you start?'

He had fallen into step beside her and they walked on, moving apart to miss oncomers, forming up together again when they passed. She might have held out her hand and let it slip into his but somehow, it didn't happen.

'I go in November, Liz. It seems a long way off but the time will fly, I expect.' He was smiling at her, shyly, as though he was hugging a secret to himself, and suddenly she wished she was safely on the bus without the need to make conversation.

'Well, it's wonderful,' she said lamely. 'You'll be a town clerk before you've finished.'

'That's why I'm moving. You've got to move if you want to get on.' He reached for her hand now, and she let him take it. 'I thought we might do something special tonight . . . to celebrate.'

'That would be nice,' Liz said, but the thought of Hartley-Davis robbed her voice of enthusiasm. What if he chose to ring tonight and she was out? 'Come round ours,' she said timidly. 'Mam'll want to congratulate you anyway. We can decide what we're going to do then.' If Geoffrey was there and the phone rang down in the salon, she would make an excuse to answer it and no one would hear what she said from upstairs.

'I was thinking we might go out early and have a meal?'

'No,' she said firmly. 'Call for me about eight o'clock and we'll see.'

Long after her bus had pulled out of the bus-stop she could see his crestfallen face mirrored inside her guilty eyelids. Then she remembered Hartley-Davis and excitement began to consume her, so that she had to press her knees together and grind her nails into her palms to stop herself from smiling like an idiot.

She felt strange as she let herself into the shop and hurried up the stairs. Her mother met her on the landing, eyes dark in a stark white face. 'I haven't joined the black-and-white minstrels, I'm having a Yeast-pac. My face feels filthy.'

'You don't want a bath, do you?' Liz asked anxiously. There would barely be enough hot water for one and she must have a bath tonight, in case Hartley-Davis wanted to see her tomorrow, straight after work.

'No,' her mother said. 'I suppose you're meeting Geoffrey. Did he get the job?'

'Yes . . . I've just seen him on my way home. He's coming round later.'

'Well, I'm really pleased.' Her mother's eyes shone in the dead-white face. 'When does he go?'

'November. It seems a long way off.'

'Six or seven weeks. You want to make the most of them.' Kate reached out and patted her daughter's arm. 'I know you'll miss him . . . but you can write and there's the telephone.'

'Yes,' Liz said, trying not to meet her mother's eye. She usually confided in Kate but some instinct told her to keep quiet about Hartley-Davis and the fact that she had given him their phone number.

In the bath she thought about a date with a stranger. She had only ever been out with boys she knew from school or her neighbourhood. This would be different. If he was a Londoner he would be sure to be fast. Everyone knew what London was like: drugs, all-night parties and sleeping around. Especially now. It was in the papers every day. She sank lower in the water, wondering if she would be out of her depth with him. Quite apart from being a southerner, he was posh. He had a double-barrelled name, and that wasn't the only thing. Everything about him was classy.

Her eye was caught by the patch of damp in the corner by the window. The distempered wall was bubbling and flaking, the colour falling away to show the white plaster underneath. The rest of the flat wasn't much better, try as they might to cover things up.

Liz felt herself go hot at the idea of being shown up. If

Bruce asked her about her mother, she would be straightforward about the salon and she would tell him about her father, who had died when she was five as a result of three years in a Japanese prisoner of war camp. She would say her mother was a trained beautician, rather than a hairdresser, who occasionally did eyebrow shaping and blackheads. Later on, when he came and saw things for himself . . . By then it wouldn't matter, because if she lasted that long with him it would mean that he loved her, and nothing else would count.

On an impulse, she tipped the rest of her Boots bath crystals into the water and stirred until it was a deep pink. Even before her father died – they had been hard up: always the unpaid bills behind the clock, the struggle to keep a fire going in the grate, to pay the rent for the council house they had lived in then. She had dreaded being asked to take anything into school: cotton wool for Easter-bunny making, crêpe paper at Christmas, extra textbooks so she would do well in the eleven-plus. In the end she had preferred to take punishments at school for forgetting to bring them rather than ask her hard-pressed mother to provide them.

They had moved into the rented salon seven years ago, and things had looked up since she started work, but it was still hard. When – if – this was going to be a real romance she would have to get clothes from somewhere. Bruce had only ever seen her in uniform. Everything else she possessed was either cheap or shabby. She thought longingly of the wonderful fashion shots in magazines; clothes by Mary Quant and Biba, hair by Vidal Sassoon. Her mum could do her hair but her clothes were from C & A or catalogues. Her thoughts ran round and round her head like rats in a cage, until she snuggled down in the water, remembering how Scarlett O'Hara had made a magnificent outfit from old curtains in *Gone with the Wind*. But all their curtains were threadbare and flower-patterned, and Liz laughed aloud at the thought of what a fool she'd look in them. Perhaps she might open an account at Dunn's and get a new wardrobe on the never-never? In the end she daydreamed to such an extent that there was barely time to get dressed before Geoffrey was due.

Mick Jagger was singing of his 'Nineteenth Nervous Breakdown' on her mother's transistor when Liz emerged from her room. Kate's face was restored to its normal hue and she was curled up in a fireside chair, a book open in her lap. She looked up as her daughter entered. 'You look nice. I've always liked that dress.'

Liz was about to moan that the dress was old when the phone rang in the shop below. 'It'll be for me,' she said, already half-way to the door. 'Sheila Harker said she'd ring.'

It was dark in the salon, the air still redolent with the acid smell of perm solution. 'Hello,' she said into the receiver, and then, collecting herself, 'Five four nine two.'

'Elizabeth?' So he knew her first name too.

'Yes.' It was almost as though he was laughing at her, there at the other end of the line.

'It's your favourite patient here, and I'm sadly in need of your nursing skills.' As his teasing voice talked on, Liz found herself promising to be at his hotel the next night. 'I can't really do much else at the moment, you see, with this blessed plaster, but we can have a meal and I can get to know you.' Bruce made the simple words seem full of import, and when Liz put down the phone the palms of her hands were moist, so that she had to rub them down the sides of her dress to dry them.

She mounted the stairs, trying to compose her face, wondering why she didn't just tell her mother about Bruce Hartley-Davis. She might even be pleased about it; understand and help. I'll tell her tomorrow, she decided. If it really happens – if he doesn't call it off – I'll tell her as soon as I get home.

And then Geoffrey was bounding up the stairs, his face still glowing, a bottle of sweet sherry in his hand so they could drink to his new job.

'To Geoffrey,' her mother said when they each had a glass. 'And a glittering future.'

They drank, and then Kate was withdrawing, pleading that she had things to do in the kitchen.

'What are we going to do then?' Liz said brightly, willing to go anywhere now that she'd had the all-important phone call.

'Anything you like.' Geoffrey put down the glass, taking time to position it carefully before he stood up and moved to face her. 'Actually, before we decide . . . ' He reached out and held her elbows in his cupped hands. 'I've been thinking, Liz. We could get engaged before I go. I'd like that, and I think my parents would too. And your mother. So that only leaves you.'

Liz had often thought of this moment, had imagined a dozen versions of her own joyful acceptance. Now, she was simply embarrassed. She moved nearer to him, thinking to hide her face against his shoulder, feeling his arms come round her while she sought desperately for the right thing to say. 'We'll see,' she said at last. 'Let's not rush things.' She raised her face. 'I want to go out now – somewhere nice like the Victoria Hall. I feel like dancing.'

She saw that he felt let down by her lack of response and she gave him a quick peck on the cheek. 'Come on, silly. Let's get out of here and then we can talk.'

It would all be all right in the end, she thought, as they called out their goodbyes to Kate and hurried down the stairs. Geoffrey had a new job and would undoubtedly do well. He'd meet heaps of girls in Gloucester and make a happy marriage and they'd both live happily ever after, like everyone should.

They sat upstairs on the bus, looking out on the lit-up windows of the town shops, seeing the river Wear glinting below as the bus crossed the bridge and then turned east, towards the sea-front and the Victoria Hall.

Liz loved the dancehall with its whirling ceiling light that left the edges of the floor dark for smooching. Sometimes the bands were really good. Most of the people who came to dance used buses and a fleet of them stood in the car park, ready to transport everyone home at the end of the evening.

I wish it was hometime now, Liz thought guiltily, and smiled at Geoffrey to make up for her treachery as he shepherded her past the doorman and bought their tickets at the kiosk.

'See you in a moment,' he said, and turned towards the toilets. Liz went into the Ladies and shut herself in a cubicle. The place was a hive of primping, perspiring girls, bemoaning bra straps that would keep slipping into view or petticoats that dipped below short skirts.

Liz queued to rinse her hands and dried them on the roller towel. Then she took a sixpence from her bag and inserted it in the perfume machine with its three choices of fragrance. She bent to the nozzle marked Christian Dior and pressed the button, turning her head quickly so that the perfume landed on both temples. She held the insides of her wrists against the wet patches and wiped them on her neck so that the fragrance was transferred, then she checked her hair and make-up in the mirror and went back into the foyer.

Geoffrey was waiting under the clock, one hand in his trouser pocket, his jacket looped over it. Usually Liz would move towards him, linking her hand in the crook of his arm, smiling at him in a way that told the outside world they were a pair. The eyes of other girls would flick towards him in a way that signalled interest and Liz would tilt her chin to show pride in possession before they moved away.

Tonight was different. His jacket, with its leather elbow patches, looked wrong; his brogue shoes were clumpy and his haircut was too neat – too short, too ordinary. Around him flowed a motley collection of styles, some sticking to the old ways, others in the uniform of Carnaby Street, which was everything from pink hipster jeans to beads. She had always been glad Geoffrey scorned such things but tonight she felt a profound dissatisfaction with his appearance. He's stuck in the mud, she thought. That's what it is. She pictured Hartley-Davis, sleek and so well finished off. There was no comparison.

'All right?' he asked as she went towards him. She smiled and moved ahead of him into the semi-darkness of the dancehall.

He danced well and for a little while she gave herself up to the pleasure of movement, held on a strong arm as their feet made intricate patterns and the crooner sang of dreams and love.

Eventually the waltz gave way to a Latin-American number and they left the floor and moved to the café area. 'Coffee?' Geoff asked, and ordered two frothy cappuccinos. Usually he would chat easily, about his parents and younger sister, about work, about her work at the hospital and her life at home. Tonight he twiddled with his coffee cup, eyes downbent, and Liz did not feel able to ask him why he was silent.

At last he looked up and grinned. 'I'm a bit lost for words,' he said.

Liz tried to summon up an interested smile. 'Oh,' she said. 'Perhaps it's yesterday catching up on you.'

Geoff shook his head. 'No, it's not that. It's just that I'm realising what a big step this move is. I'm going to miss you a lot, Liz, and it would help to know we were both committed.'

'Geoff . . . ' She felt her mouth go dry, knowing she must try not to hurt him, knowing she couldn't say yes. Not now. She was mad not to jump at the chance of a ring and a good catch like Geoffrey, but it was no good. 'It's lovely of you to ask, but there's Mam, you see, and then my SRN matron doesn't approve of it – not even courting, really – not when you're coming up to your final year. After that . . . ' She left it vague, hating herself for disappointing him. 'When you come home for Christmas, let's talk about it then.'

They danced again but there was a stiffness in their movements now, an unwillingness on both parts to touch or be touched so that it was a relief when it was time to board the homebound bus and drive along the illuminated sea-front, back towards the town centre. There was a ship leaving the river, low on the water, with a light at its masthead, and Liz felt a sudden kinship with that little vessel, moving out, like her, into uncharted waters.

12

L IZ GAVE A FINAL SQUIRT of lacquer to her bouffant
hairstyle and teased the side curls a little further on
to her cheek, unsure whether or not the style suited her.
Harker, who was good with the new hairstyles, had done it
for her in the nurses' changing-room before she came home.
It had looked all right at first, perfect to go with her mother's
black sweater and the pink gingham skirt she had made for
herself. But Bruce Hartley-Davis was classy. Would he expect
her to be more restrained? Her mother had offered to do her
hair, but Kate only had two styles and both of them were
old-fashioned.

In the end she wore her navy suit with a low-cut, white
camisole underneath instead of the usual blouse with a Peter
Pan collar.

'How do I look?' she asked when she came into the
living-room, and saw alarm flare up in her mother's eyes
at the hairstyle and the extra make-up. But all Kate said
was, 'I've seen worse. Don't be late coming home. We've
both got to get up in the morning.'

Liz could see that her mother was making an effort not to
seem disapproving but that she was still shocked at the idea
of Liz going out with someone else behind Geoffrey's back.

'I hope it won't end in tears,' she'd said when Liz had told her about her date for the evening.

'It's only one night, Mam,' Liz had protested, but the hope that it would turn out to be much, much more was in her voice and she knew that Kate had detected it.

Liz was gathering up her bag and door-keys when her mother spoke again. 'I suppose you'd better bring him in one of these nights. If you see him again, that is.' It was said without a great deal of enthusiasm. Her mother had not yet come to terms with the fact that Geoffrey could be supplanted.

'He'd never get up those stairs with his plaster on.' Liz was glad of a watertight excuse. It was impossible to say that she couldn't bear the thought of Bruce Hartley-Davis seeing how they lived, in a flat that had a kitchen where the hallway should be, and leatherette chairs and odd tables her mother had picked up here and there, all of them a bit worse for wear. When I'm married, Liz thought, as she picked her way downstairs on thin stiletto heels, when I have a home of my own, everything will be brand new.

She felt sick on the bus-ride into town, burping guiltily behind the cover of her hand, her tea uneasy on her stomach. She was sure the hairstyle had been a mistake, had known it even before her mother's shocked expression. Still, it was done now. The lacquer had set in a transparent shield that wouldn't shatter if a brick were applied to it. Apart from the uncertainty about her appearance, Liz was worried at the thought of walking, unaccompanied, into the Palatine Hotel. Everyone would turn and look at a woman on her own. She'd seen it happen to other girls when she'd been out with Geoffrey, and felt a comfortable sensation of superiority at her escorted status.

In the end, it wasn't as difficult as she'd imagined. Bruce was there, just inside the door of the cocktail bar, rising awkwardly to his feet as soon as he saw her in the doorway. 'Good,' he said, not subsiding until she was seated, then raising a nonchalant hand to summon the barman.

She had intended to ask for a sweet sherry, but Bruce

persuaded her to try a Pimm's, an exotic concoction in a tall glass with a swizzle stick and a sprig of mint rising up from a dark sweet liquid with fruit in it. There was a frosted rim to the glass and the whole thing looked and tasted expensive. She wrinkled her nose when she was half-way down the drink. 'It tastes a bit like Tizer.'

'Tizer? What's that?' When he laughed his eyes narrowed and crinkled, like one of the French film stars whose name she couldn't remember. Liz felt a fool for mentioning something as common as Tizer but he continued to smile so it didn't seem to matter. She had another Pimm's, and then a third.

'They're not alcoholic, are they?'

'A bit,' he said, 'but not enough to matter.'

He was easy to talk to, questioning her first about the hospital, making her laugh when he called Sister 'the juggernaut', and asking then about home and her life with her mother. Finally he asked her about any boyfriends, and Liz shook her head, feeling a faint fullness in her ears so that her own voice sounded strange to her. She was laughing a lot but this seemed to please him, and everything seemed to be deliciously funny. At last Bruce leaned forward and pretended to tease a stray hair from her eyes. The touch of his finger on her skin made her mouth go dry, and she half pulled away. She had a sense of excitement, of release.

'What are you doing?'

Bruce didn't answer her question. Instead he asked her if she wanted another drink and when she said no he leaned towards her again. 'Let's get out of here, Liz. I'm beginning to feel submerged by the *hoi polloi*.'

She went ahead of him, trying to clear the way, but he managed to negotiate the chairs and tables, smiling charmingly as people stood aside, saying, 'I'm terribly sorry,' or 'Thanks so much.'

'You'll never win the Grand National at that rate,' a woman at one of the tables said, and he joined in the laughter.

'You never know, madam. I might surprise you yet.'

'Yes please,' the woman said, and the laughter followed them out into the foyer.

'Do you want to eat?' he asked, and Liz shook her head. The idea of sitting opposite him across an elaborately set restaurant table terrified her. 'Okay, we'll go up to my room and have a drink there.' He was holding her elbow now and she let him lead her towards the lift, hoping no one was watching because going up to a man's room was asking for trouble. And then they were safe inside a huge suite and Bruce was moving closer, fingering the nape of her neck with one hand, taking her bag from her with the other and lowering it to the floor.

'What are you doing?' Liz asked, not particularly wanting an answer, more anxious to keep a barrier of conversation between them for as long as she could.

He smiled. 'Did anyone ever tell you that you look like a worried nun? A Capucin.' He moved to accommodate his bad leg. 'Damn this plaster!' Liz felt his hand cup her breast and tried to draw away. 'It's all right, Liz. You know it's all right.' He was kissing her. 'I don't want to scare you. Anyway, I'm harmless with this stupid plaster on.'

He let her go then and moved away, and Liz felt guilt flood over her. He really cared for her, and she was behaving like a silly kid. She moved closer and put up her face to be kissed again.

'That's better,' he said. 'That's much better.' And Liz was filled with a sense of power that she could make him happy so easily.

It seemed as though they kissed for a long time. Her mouth grew wet and she longed to wipe it dry, but that would have been rude. His chin seemed to grow bristly suddenly and her face felt raw, but somehow the discomfort was thrilling, making her feel adult and in the swim of things. When his hand came again to her breast she let it stay and he murmured, 'Good girl,' against her neck.

She began to wonder where it was all leading, even toyed with the possibility of giving way there, in the quiet of this room. Other girls did, with far less reason to feel safe than she had with Bruce. Suddenly he was drawing away, looking at his watch and shaking his head. 'Time you were in bed. I'll ring for a cab and we'll have a drink while we're waiting. They'll charge the fare to my account, so don't pay the driver.'

Liz was filled with an overwhelming sense of disappointment that the evening had come to an end.

13

Liz unpinned her cap and stuck the white-tipped pins that held it in place into the folded material. Her apron was soiled and she stuffed it into the laundry bag. At the opposite locker Staff Nurse Harker was changing too, belting in her navy gaberdine, jamming her hat to the back of her head until it almost disappeared in the red hair. 'So the PP got his plaster off?' she asked.

Liz nodded. 'Yes. He's got viscopaste on, and he'll be back in a week.'

'I'll expect he'll be seen at Denton Street,' Harker said. She moved to the mirror and began to apply lipstick. 'PPs don't come back here once they don't need hospital facilities. He'll go to Denton Street unless something goes wrong.'

Denton Street was where Mr Hinckley had his private consulting rooms with a private secretary, a lady of indeterminate age whose nickname was Marblegob because of her precious enunciation.

Harker bit her lips together and rubbed her teeth clean with a forefinger. 'Don't worry,' she said. 'He won't fancy Marblegob. She looks like the north end of a southbound cow.'

Liz shut her locker door before she replied, hoping her

face was not as flushed as it felt. 'He can please himself, as far as I'm concerned,' she said.

As she said goodbye to Harker and came out into the courtyard, she wondered when she should let out the truth. She had kept it quiet in case things fizzled out, but the romance was lasting. Until now their meetings had been confined to his hotel, but she had never minded. It had been fun to play at house in his suite, eating room-service meals and watching the telly. Now that he was out of plaster they would have more freedom, but it wouldn't change things. He wouldn't have bothered with her in the first place if there hadn't been something special, not when he could have had any girl. She had seen the way women eyed him and men deferred to him.

Last night he had shown her some of the plans for the new marina. 'There's five million in this deal,' he'd said. 'And it's almost in the bag.'

Liz had looked at the blueprints, trying to make sense of them, and marvelled that anyone could think up such an ambitious scheme. She would have to tell everyone soon, because after tonight, unless she was much mistaken, their relationship would have moved on to a more serious footing.

She was almost down to the town centre, the bus-stop in sight. She glanced at her watch. Plenty of time to indulge in a little window shopping. She needed clothes desperately. It was getting harder and harder to permutate what she and her mother possessed to look new and fresh for each date.

She would have liked to patronise the trendy boutiques that had sprung up in the town centre, but all she could afford were the chainstores. Black stockings for work cost a fortune, and God help you if Matron caught you with a ladder. She gazed longingly at a window displaying hipster jeans and crocheted see-through mini-dresses. She'd never dare to wear one, but she liked them on other people. She was saving up for some wedge-toed pumps, but what she really needed was one good classic dress. She'd seen one in a boutique in a lovely butter colour, but it was seven guineas and out of the question.

It was her mother's half-day, the time when Kate was supposed to do housework and keep her books. The books were usually done in a last-minute panic when the accountant was threatening gaol, but there was always a proper meal on Wednesdays, sometimes Irish stew with shin beef or a meat and potato pie. Liz licked her lips as she opened the front door. She wanted a comforting meal, something warm and solid and safe. Food had always comforted her, as far back as when her father was dying in the front room while her grandmother fed her Turkish delight, and the times after that when her mother had lost a boyfriend and cried, or people had banged on the door for money and she and Kate had cowered in the corner, behind the window, until the onslaught ceased and the disappointed creditor could be heard to drive away.

She mounted the stairs, sniffing as she went, but it was the smell of disinfectant that assailed her nostrils, not stew. As she reached the landing she saw her mother on her knees in the kitchen doorway, scrubbing brush in hand, wiping hair from her eyes with the other hand.

'I've washed all the lino, Liz. Watch where you put your feet. Here.' She reached for a pile of newspapers and threw it at her daughter. 'Put sheets down and walk on them.' Through the kitchen door Liz could see the pages of newsprint stretching away, black-and-white stepping stones on the brown and red linoleum. 'Thank God it's done for now,' Kate said fervently.

Liz did as she was told, throwing down newspaper and stepping on it, making for the kitchen. 'Is there anything to eat?'

'Chopped pork and piccalilli and tinned rice for afters,' her mother said. And then, sitting back on her heels and smiling, 'Only kidding. There's mince and dumplings and rhubarb tart.'

'With custard?'

'With custard . . . now let me get finished.'

They ate sitting opposite one another at the kitchen table, the radio burbling away in the background.

'I had that lustre jug valued today,' Kate said, her mouth full as she talked. 'You're not going to believe it but it's worth five pounds. It'd be more if it wasn't for the chip.'

'Five pounds?' Liz's fork halted in mid-air.

'I'll go into business, one day. More dumps?' As she spooned mince and dumplings on to both their plates Kate shook her head. 'If I could make a find like that four times a week, we could manage.'

'And if you found a real gem – Ming or something – we could both retire,' Liz said sarcastically.

'All right, laugh,' Kate said cheerfully. 'I'll have the last chuckle!'

They did the washing-up between them, feeling close, both of them excited but for different reasons.

'You're serious about this lad, aren't you?' Kate said at last, draping the wrung-out dishcloth over the taps.

'He's not a lad, Mam. I keep telling you, he's a man.'

'He's not a bit flash, is he?' Kate said carefully. 'I mean, there's plenty of talk but what about his background? I don't hear much about family or friends. How old did you say he was, twenty-four? He must have someone somewhere.'

Liz had lowered Bruce's age when speaking of him to her mother and a blush threatened to develop at the thought of the lie being exposed eventually. 'He does have a family. Of course he does, I mean, everyone has a family.' Bruce had never mentioned relatives, only friends from his days at public school, but he would, eventually. 'Remember he's away from home, Mam. He's not like us. He moves around.'

'Well, that's another thing . . . all this business thing at twenty-four. Isn't that a bit young?'

Liz was regretting the lie about Bruce's age but now was not the time to confess. 'He's got contacts,' she said desperately. 'People he met at school and everything.'

'Well, you'd better invite him home soon and let me see for myself. Where are you going tonight?'

'Out somewhere, I think. He can move about a bit more now he's got the plaster off.'

Liz looked down at her hands, pretending to examine them for signs of wear and tear. He would have to come here eventually, she knew that, but not just yet. It'll be all right, she told herself, remembering the way he teased her for being too shy, too self-effacing, too modest about herself. She looked up to meet her mother's eye. 'I wish I knew what to wear.'

'You can borrow my Moygashel two-piece if you like.' But they both knew the outfit was dated and beginning to go at the cuffs.

'I saw a lovely dress in that boutique in the high street. Sort of butter yellow with cap sleeves.'

'Is it in the window?' Kate was lighting a cigarette and drawing in smoke.

'Yes, but it's seven guineas. I wish you didn't smoke, Mam. It's not healthy. You should hear Sister Tutor on about it. Every drag shortens your life.'

Her mother grinned. 'There've been times, pet, when I wouldn't've minded. Now, go and get ready and let me do the receipts before I fall asleep where I stand.'

Outside, it was getting dark and Liz crossed to the bedroom window to draw the curtains before switching on the light. She looked out on the back yard and beyond it, to the close-packed roofs of the houses that made up 'Little Egyp Cairo Street, Nile Street, Alexandria Terrace. She had grown ip in this bedroom, dreamed childhood dreams there and teenage fantasies. She leaned her head against the glass and allowed herself to contemplate the thought that she had tried to block out all day.

In half an hour she would be leaving the house. She would have to laugh and smile, and be very careful not to catch her mother's eye. It must look as though tonight was just another night, a night like any other. In fact it was very different. She twitched the curtains into place and felt her way to the bed, resisting the impulse to snuggle under the blankets and pretend she was a child again and that all was well.

But she was nineteen, and after a while she switched on the lamp, seeing her ghostly image in the wardrobe mirror, the whiteness of her underwear making the skin of her body look dark and rich in contrast. She took the pink sleeveless shift-dress from its hanger and slipped it over her head, twisting to find the zip fastener and pull it up to the nape of her neck. It was a copy of a Mary Quant design, and the nicest thing she had, although the material was thin and flashy. To complement it she would do her hair in a fringe and bring a pin curl on to each cheek, sticking them down with Sellotape until they 'took' and she could gingerly peel the tape away. Her mother's black patent stilettos would complete her outfit, even though the unaccustomed spindly heels threw her forward and crushed her toes. You had to suffer a bit for fashion.

'I'm off then,' she said, when she was ready, trying to sound casual. She moved to the octagonal mirror above the mantelpiece and pretended to check her hair and make-up. Her eyes were overbright but otherwise she looked okay. She could see her mother reflected too, plumping up cushions, flicking imaginary specks of dust from any surface within reach. She knows, Liz thought; and then, why doesn't she stop me?

'I'll see you later,' Liz said quickly. 'You don't want me to be late, remember, so we don't have a lot of time.'

'Watch what you're doing,' her mother said, but when Liz turned and looked at her Kate looked away. For one second Liz hesitated, but only for a second. Her life was moving on. Bruce would take care of her now and everything would be better. In London there was a revolution going on, a liberation. Tonight she would become part of it.

She was relying on Bruce to make sure nothing went wrong this time, but after tonight she would make an appointment at Family Planning. Tonight Bruce would have Durex – men always did – and, like every woman before her she would have to take the fateful step, almost the only thing in life from which there was no going back. Virginity. It was a funny word and she rolled it round and round in her mind as the bus made its way into town. She felt special as she stood up to alight, sure that anyone looking at her would know that tonight was different. Tonight she was going to change everything, so that nothing would ever be the same again. She felt her eyes prick and then she was out on the pavement and moving towards Bruce, who was waiting in the foyer of the hotel.

His hand was warm and reassuring on hers. 'All right?' he asked and she murmured assent. 'Where shall we go?'

'Anywhere.' She didn't want to make decisions. She wanted him to take charge, not only of tonight but also of her life.

'We'll go anywhere you like,' he said grandly. 'Come on, choose. My leg feels fine so the sky's the limit.'

'Anywhere,' she said again, leaning close to him. 'We can just stay here if you like.'

'Don't you want to eat?'

'I've had something . . . but we can eat if you want to.'

He hugged her then, tut-tutting as he did so. 'So you'd even eat twice to please me. What a little mouse you are . . . that's why I love you so much.'

It was the middle of the week and the cocktail bar was half empty. They hitched themselves on to stools at the counter and Bruce looked at her fondly. 'Have a proper drink,' he said. 'Gin and tonic?'

She was thinking of all the stories she had heard about losing your virginity. They had been many and varied, but all of them had involved pain. 'Okay,' she said. 'But can you make it a gin and orange?'

Bruce drank his beer quickly, not saying much but reaching out occasionally to touch her hand or squeeze her arm. He smiled at everything she said, whether or not it was amusing, and once he laughed softly and said, 'You are a little idiot, Liz,' in tones so loving that she felt close to tears.

At one stage he took a small gold box from his pocket and shook a small tablet from it, palming it into his mouth and washing it quickly down with a drink.

131

'What's that?' Liz asked. 'Are you okay?'

'Fine,' he said, cheerfully. 'Just a bit of a headache, that's all.'

They had another drink and then, by unspoken consent, went out to the lift, not speaking but holding hands even while he unlocked the door of his room and turned on the radio. Frank Sinatra was singing 'Strangers in the Night', and Liz's eyes filled at the appropriateness of it all.

'Put the light out,' she said, still unable to meet his eyes. He went to the bathroom and emerged holding a large, white towel which he spread on the bed. He switched out the light then and Liz felt strong suddenly, almost powerful, knowing that she was going to make him happy and it would be all right because he knew exactly what he was doing. Her head was swimming but that only added to the mystery, the sense of this being a momentous occasion.

'Will it be all right?' she asked once, when he was fumbling in the dark and she knew he was using a Durex.

'I promise you.' He kissed her, but it was a hasty kiss, and then she was crying aloud, but in the end the pain was bearable. Bruce was loving too, holding her when it was over, thanking her, telling her again and again how much she was loved. She felt a sticky wetness when they drew apart and then his lips were against her ear. 'It's true what they say,' he said. 'The first time is extra good.'

She looked at him, sensing from his profile in the darkness that he was smiling. It couldn't have been the first time for him, too? He had seemed so experienced, so sure of what he was doing. But that was London, where everybody was doing whatever they wanted. I'm part of that now, she thought, feeling her heart thump uncomfortably in her chest. I'm part of the new revolution.

As if he guessed what she was thinking, he drew her back into his arms. 'I hope you feel proud?'

'Proud?' She couldn't understand his question.

'Yes, proud, you little silly. Proud of what you've done tonight. You've proved yourself a real woman, and you've given me the very best thing you can give a man.'

'Yes,' Liz said. 'I suppose so . . . '

'No "suppose" about it!' He was brusque now. 'You've given yourself to me and I'm going to love you for ever.' His lips brushed her forehead, causing little bursts of static electricity to prickle over her skin so that she let out a small gasp.

He switched on the bedside lamp and raised himself on his elbow to look at her. 'You'll have to tidy up a bit before you go home, darling. You look like a fallen woman.'

He was smiling so indulgently that she felt no fear at the enormity of what she had done. She lay still, looking at the cream walls with their gilt panelling, the huge drape of the chintz curtains, the ornate hotel furniture, wanting to imprint it on her memory so that she would remember this night for ever.

At last, though, she got up, clutching the clothes she had discarded, and padded to the bathroom. She felt sick suddenly, so that she had to sit down on the toilet basin and rest her head on the sink. She waited for panic to come, thinking of that mythical thing she had had when she entered the hotel and had no longer. But there was no panic and in the end she got to her feet, seeing a stranger in the mirror with streaked mascara and hair awry so that the task of tidying herself up brought her to her senses.

He was waiting when she came out of the bathroom, a sly smile on his face, a small box in his hand. It contained a ring, a beautiful thing of pearls in a twisted gold setting.

'It's not an engagement ring,' he said. 'Not yet. But it's for you because you're special. It belonged to my mother. Don't flash it around, not for the moment. And now I'm going to take you home in a cab because I don't want to be separated from you until I must be.'

As they sped back through the starlit night, his hand tight on hers, Liz felt a growing contentment. She'd done it. It was over, the endless debate about whether or not you should and who with if you did. She had chosen well. There would be no disastrous pregnancy with Bruce. Eventually they would marry. He'd promised her that tonight when he had said he would love her for ever and ever. So really all she had done was anticipate things. He would be the only man in her life and they would have lovely children. She wouldn't like them to go away to school, as Bruce had done, but that could be discussed later on, when she was his wife.

She saw herself suddenly in a grey suit, very fine gaberdine, with a white lace blouse and a solitaire diamond and a tiny, tiny watch, letting her children out of her car at the school gates. In the darkness she opened her bag and felt for the ring box, solid and square and reassuring, and the dream carried her through the goodbyes and into the flat, lasting until she was locked in the bathroom and the stains on her underclothes brought her back to reality.

14

THERE WAS A WONDERFUL SMELL of frying bacon in the air when Liz woke up. It was Sunday, she had the day off, and in the living-room her mother's treasured cut-glass vase held a dozen dark red roses. Best of all, this wasn't a dream. She turned on her side and burrowed down to extract the last glorious ounce of pleasure from this fact.

She ate breakfast in her dressing-gown, feeling sloppy and lovely and full of goodwill. 'I'll go round to Grandpa's when I get ready,' she said, knowing this would please her mother. Her grandfather had lived on his own since her grandmother's death and she knew Kate worried about him.

'Tell him to come round for his dinner,' she said now.

'I'll tell him, Mam, but it won't do any good. He'll have his bit of meat in and his pudding tins ready and he won't budge!'

'Well, try.' Kate looked across at the sideboard. 'I can smell those roses over here but when I think of what they must've cost! Still, red roses . . . every woman should have red roses once in her lifetime.'

'Did you?' Liz said it light-heartedly but, to her surprise, her mother's eyes filled and she had to blink to clear them.

'Yes,' she said. 'I did once. Now, go and get cleaned up and get round to Dad's. Dinner'll be ready one o'clock sharp.' She made to start clearing the table but Liz could see that she was not far from tears. She got up from her chair, tightening the belt of her dressing-gown, and moved to hug her mother.

'We'll have a nice day today, Mam, and we'll talk about when Bruce comes to meet you. He'd've been here before if he wasn't so busy. He says the phone never stops all day long.'

As she walked the half-mile to her grandfather's home she thought about her mother. Kate had been a teenager when she married, younger than Liz was now. Then her father had been captured by the Japs and imprisoned till the end of the war. I couldn't live through that, Liz thought, being separated from the man I love. Even when her father had come home he'd been ill. 'Never the same again,' her grandmother Lucas used to say. Still, Liz thought, at least Mam has me. She was passing the allotments and on an impulse she bought a shilling's worth of marguerites for her mother from one of the gardeners.

'They're not for you, Grandad,' she said, when she let herself into her grandfather's kitchen. 'I bought them for Mam.'

'Just as well,' her grandfather said cheerfully. 'I can't be doing with flowers. Get yourself a cup. I've just mashed this tea.' He waited until she was seated opposite him, cup in hand, and then he eyed her with a twinkle. 'Talking of flowers, your mam says you've had some roses sent. Looks as though it's serious, the price roses are. Who is the lad? Do I know him?'

'He's not from round here, Grandad.' In spite of the late summer weather, her grandfather had a coal fire burning in the grate and the walls, papered with garlands of flowers on a white background, were smoke-grimed. For a fleeting second Liz wondered what Bruce would make of this room, with its chenille over-mantel and heavy furniture. Bruce could cope with anything, she was sure.

He'd be wonderful with her grandfather because he loved her.

'Up here for the college, is he?' There was a School of Pharmacy in the town that brought students from all over.

Liz shook her head. 'No, he's not a student. He's here on business. It's a project at the North Dock.' Her grandfather's eyes gleamed at mention of the dockside.

'It's not the marina, is it? The new marina . . . ' He was levering himself out of his chair and crossing to the mantelpiece to fumble behind the clock. 'I cut something out of the *Echo* just the other night.'

It was there, in black and white: pictures of the plans she had seen in Bruce's hotel room; pictures of the area where the projected marina would be; and a picture of the councillor who headed the relevant committee, talking to Bruce.

'That's him!' Liz said, suddenly embarrassed. She could hardly believe it: a man who was pictured in the *Echo*, involved in town affairs, and he was hers.

'Well, mind,' her grandfather said at last. 'It sounds grand, and he's your lad. It's nice somebody's doing something for this town.' He was launched into his favourite subject now, the mighty river Wear and its ships.

'Six hundred years of shipbuilding, that's our record. Right back before Napoleon. There was seventy-six yards in the middle of the last century, and everyone a good-un. Most of them went in one slump or another but the thirties was a killer. I was laid off then and your mam just a bairn. I was a riveter, you know.' Liz had heard this a thousand times but she managed to look absorbed. 'We earned good money on piece work. Boilermakers, riveters, caulkers, platers – the lot – but it was welders that took over in the end, especially after the war. We specialised in colliers in the early days but the Liberty ship was a Sunderland invention. They'd never've won the war without Liberty ships.'

'It must've been dangerous in wartime,' Liz said. 'They bombed the yards, didn't they?'

'They tried to,' her grandfather said scornfully. 'They couldn't hit a goal-mouth from a yard off, the Jerries. We never worried, not even the women. There was women in the yards in the war, you know. Canny workers an' all.'

He leaned back in his chair, puffing contentedly on his pipe. 'I always wanted to work in the yards, right from being a little lad, taking me dad his breakfast in a blue-and-white cloth, stotties and a can of tea. And when I was out of me time, by lad, I thought I was King Dick, thwacking them red-hot rivets in. I'd be walking to work, half past six in the morn, hearing the men's boots on the cobbles and then the buzzer, seeing the smoke belching out and then the racket starting. Mind, we couldn't work unless we got the weather. If it was raining or icy or windy, we had to pack in.'

'It must've been hard,' Liz said, knowing what was expected of her.

'Hard? It was bloody terrifying sometimes! Don't tell your mam I swore, mind. I got started as a rivet-catcher boy and I used to sit there in the dark, seeing the glare off the fire, hanging on to the tongs I had to catch the rivets with. I would put them in the hole, red hot, mind, and the riveter would hit it with a longshaft, a great big hammer. I used to go home black as the ace of spades. After that I was a rivet-beater, and then they let me serve me time. Aye, I can remember when you couldn't stir for shipyards, right up as far as Hylton. And now this lad of yours is going to build a marina. Well, good luck to him, but it'll never beat the old days. By, they were grand.'

He was still singing the praises of the Sunderland yards when she made her exit. 'I wish I was back there now, our Elizabeth. The comradeship . . . you couldn't whack it.' He came to the door to wave her off. 'Take care of your mam. She hasn't had it easy.'

Liz felt proud as she walked home. Sunderland was a good place. If Bruce's project came off, perhaps he would stay and become important, like the owners of the yards and the other big families? She turned the corner, still clutching her marguerites, anxious to get home and tell her mother about the cutting and all the other things that were crowding her mind. She was almost up to the shop door when she saw

Geoffrey, walking towards her, his face earnest above an open-necked shirt.

'Liz!' She had tried to let him down lightly, but still he persevered.

'Hello, Geoff. Nice to see you.' She kept on making for the shop door but he was barring the way.

'What about coming out tonight, Liz? We need to talk.'

It was now or never. She took a deep breath and forced herself to meet his eye. Fleetingly, she admired his steady gaze. He had kind eyes and they weren't flinching now although he must have an idea of what was coming. 'Geoff, I'm sorry, there's no point in talking. The fact is . . . ' She put up a hand to her throat, to bring out the ring from its chain around her neck, but some instinct stopped her. She mustn't be too cruel. 'I'm seeing someone else, Geoff. I'm sorry, I hope we can be friends, but that's all it can be, I'm afraid. Friendship.'

She had expected his face to crumple but instead he squared his shoulders and half smiled.

'I see. Well, I'm glad you told me. Thanks. That's it then. I thought it was worth one last effort.'

Liz felt a small pang of regret that he was taking it so well but it didn't last. If he had persisted it could have been awkward, especially if her mother had been involved.

'I hope Gloucester turns out okay.'

'Thank you. It seems a nice place. I hope everything works out for you.'

They were marking time now. One of them would have to turn away.

'I've got your Beatles album still.'

'Keep it. You're keener on it than I am.' She was shaking her head and he shrugged. 'Well, I'll get it back sometime. No hurry.'

'We'll always be friends, I hope?'

'Of course.' He was already turning away and Liz clutched the marguerites defensively, trying to think of something she could say to lessen the blow without raising his hopes.

'See you, then.'

'Yes. See you. You know where I am, Liz – if things change.' He was walking away, head up, his long legs devouring space so that soon he was turning the corner and was out of sight, and she was left feeling oddly disappointed that he hadn't turned back for one last look at her.

She dreamed the early afternoon away lying on her bed, her stomach full of food, her head full of the evening ahead. She felt good about being honest with Geoffrey and grateful that he had taken it so well. When it was time to go and turn on the immersion heater for a bath she felt almost euphoric. Life really was wonderful. She was meeting Bruce early because he had a surprise for her, something that would be revealed as soon as she reached the hotel.

The surprise was a long, sleek, open car, dark blue with leather seats and a snarling jaguar on its bonnet. 'I had it sent down from London,' Bruce explained. 'I've been without wheels too long.' They drove over the bridge and down to the coast road, attracting admiring glances as they went. Liz felt the wind ruffle her hair, blowing it sometimes across her eyes until she had to hold it in place as the car accelerated.

Since Bruce had been out of plaster they had gone everywhere by taxi-cab. She had visited her first Chinese restaurant, trying to eat the unfamiliar food with *savoir-faire* in spite of all the stories she had heard about cat food, and eaten in two other restaurants where they'd served English food. She had thought them grand enough, but drawing up outside an expensive hotel on the sea-front at Tynemouth capped all her previous adventures.

Bruce half ran round to open the door and hand her out of the car, as though she was Princess Grace. There was a commissionaire to hold open the hotel door and a waiter in evening dress to escort them to their table. He held out her chair for her and when she was seated, another waiter flipped out her linen napkin and draped it across her knee.

Liz gazed around at the mirrored walls, the subdued lighting, the banks of flowers, as Bruce held a long conversation about wines with the first waiter, who was obviously the boss. I'm doing fine, she thought in wonderment. I can manage all this. I can even enjoy it.

Bruce guided her through the menu and plied her with wine, and then they drove back through the gathering dusk and walked, hand in hand, from the car park to the hotel. 'Life will be easier now,' he said. 'I'll collect you next time and I can meet this mother of yours.'

In the lift, as they ascended, he kissed her forehead and held her close, but there was something perfunctory about his kiss and Liz could sense something different about him, a kind of tension that had not been there before. It was so apparent that he was on edge that she found courage for a question. 'Is everything all right?'

'All right?' He stood back from her, his eyes suddenly wide and half angry. 'Why do you ask that?' And then, as suddenly as the hostility had arisen, it subsided. 'Of course I'm "all right", when I'm with you. We're going to have fun tonight. You'll see!'

In the room Bruce poured two drinks and then fished in his pocket, producing the small gold box. He touched it and the lid sprang back to reveal four small yellow tablets. He handed her a glass and then shook two tablets into his palm. 'Try one of these.' Liz had been about to say she'd had enough to drink at the restaurant. The tablets were an unexpected complication.

'What are they?' They looked uncommonly like saccharin, except for the colour. 'I haven't got a headache.'

He was laughing now, throwing back his head as though at some enormous joke. Liz felt suddenly uneasy and her consternation must have shown in her face because he stopped laughing and answered her question.

'Life-enhancers, my pet. Come on, try one. It's okay, they don't bite.' He put a tablet on his tongue and flushed it down with a sip from his glass. 'See? Harmless.' He was still proffering the tablet.

'Must I?' Liz asked.

'Yes.' He was gently insistent. 'Call it part of your growing-up. You've got to get with it, Liz. It makes everything better. Much better.'

Liz had read about drugs and heard about them from other nurses, who all said they were exciting and harmless, which must be true because Bruce was standing there before her, living proof that they didn't hurt. The tablet tasted sour on her tongue until she flushed it away. Then her mouth went dry and she was licking her lips, suddenly wanting to reach out and seize him.

Bruce was laughing at her, grabbing her questing hands, saying, 'Steady on,' but entering into the spirit of it so that they landed on the bed together.

Something was growing and blossoming inside her head and there were strange sensations in her body too, a feeling of expansion and contraction, of power and weakness, a sense of whirling around in space so that objects in the room seemed at once far away and almost on top of her. And then the room seemed to revolve around her so that she clung to Bruce, tearing first at his clothes, then at her own, saying, 'More,' and, 'More,' once twisting her fingers in his hair and shaking his head on the pillow.

Afterwards she sat on the toilet, her brain whirling, her heart thundering in her body, the beat ricocheting crazily around her chest. Each time she stood up she wanted to pass water again and when she leaned on the handbasin and looked into the mirror two eyes looked back at her, the pupils dilated into huge black orbs.

It was midnight before she felt able to go home and she had serious doubts about Bruce's ability to drive her there. The matter was settled by a phone call that came through as he looked for his car-keys. He stood up to take the call at first and then, dropping his voice, he retreated to the bed, drawing up his legs, turning away from her, hunching his shoulders as though to exclude her.

Liz stood there, her mind still racing, seeing the objects in the room almost zoom into view, as though bombarding her.

Her head felt empty, a great warehouse with only her brain inside, whirling around in the space.

At last Bruce turned, tucking the receiver under his chin, the hand-set held in his other hand. He fished in his trouser pocket and produced a note. 'Can you get a cab, Liz? Good girl. This is important.'

She slipped from the room, feeling somehow dismissed, tip-toeing guiltily down the stairs, hoping to pass through the lobby unseen. But the night porter insisted on summoning a cab for her and seeing her into it, accepting the coin she thrust into his hand as she had seen Bruce do, not knowing that it was her last two-shilling piece.

On the way home she felt a feverish sense of excitement. The streetlights seemed brighter than usual, the cab so slow she wanted to urge it on. She would never be able to sleep, not tonight. The tablet speeded up everything, even the rate at which you blinked your eyes or spoke. When she let herself into the house she could smell the roses and then light was streaming across the landing. 'Is that you, Liz?' Her mother sounded worried and she hastened to reassure her.

'Yes. Sorry I'm late. Get to bed. We'll talk in the morning.' To her relief her mother called goodnight and went back into her room. Liz crept upstairs, to lie wide-eyed for most of the night, wishing she could turn back the clock and turn down the tablet, trying desperately to remember whether or not they had taken precautions tonight when they had made love.

15

THE GIRL SITTING JUST INSIDE the clinic was wearing a caftan. 'Get a look at the flower-child,' Harker hissed as she passed Liz. There were plenty of people to be seen in caftans nowadays, not to mention ethnic prints and grandad-shirts over skin-tight jeans, and beads and weird hats and any form of footwear as long as it was ugly. It was a time for being who or what you wanted, and there was no need to break the rules for the very simple reason that there were no rules.

All the same, the sight of one of these exotic creatures waiting to have a splint checked was rare. Liz studied the girl covertly as she went about her duties, wondering what Bruce would think if she dressed like that. Not that she had any intention of doing anything so silly. She had spent a sleepless night and her head thumped uncomfortably if she moved it too suddenly, but at least she had learned a lesson. If the little yellow pills were part of being with-it, she would stay without it. Her cheeks grew hot at the thought of how she had acted with abandon last night. If she hadn't been with Bruce, who understood such things, it could have been a disaster. He had been different, too; more controlled, but then he was used to the effects of the drug.

When first she had come on duty she had felt wretched. 'Wrecked,' Harker had called it, regarding her junior with a worldly eye. 'You should drink a pint of milk before you go on the batter; it puts a lining on the stomach.'

For a moment or two Liz had contemplated confiding in Harker, in the hope of her recommending a cure. She would have to come clean about Bruce soon, anyway. But some sixth sense told her to wait, and now that she felt better she was glad she'd been discreet.

She went through the rituals of the clinic, putting complicated cases behind screens, sitting uncomplicated hand and arm injuries at the desk, all the while trying to remember exactly what had happened last night. She could remember how intense everything had seemed, how every sense had been heightened, but what had gone on when they made love? Bruce had often teased her about contraception in the last few weeks. He'd pointed out how much easier life would be if she were on the pill; the magic pill that meant the end of worrying and using French letters. And it was true she worried night and day about getting pregnant. Now she regretted not taking her courage in both hands and going along to Family Planning. Even though everyone talked about those nurses who did, nine times out of ten they got given the Dutch cap instead of the pill. Tonight she would ask Bruce if he had taken care of it, and if he had she would never, ever let herself get into that state again. Some nurses took Dexedrine when they were on nights, and that was bad enough; but whatever was in the speed that Bruce had given her last night, it was an experience not to be repeated.

She felt sick on the bus on the way home and her eyelids were heavy. It was probably her imagination. She'd only had one little pill after all and, according to Bruce, they were practically harmless. She looked up to see the conductor watching her from his perch on the platform. Surely he couldn't tell? If he could he must be a user himself. No one else would know. She turned her head and stared out at the pavement until she reached her own stop and could make her escape.

Once she was home she shut herself in the bathroom and examined her face for tell-tale signs. She looked tired and a little bright-eyed, but that was all. She sluiced her face with cold water and went to greet her mother.

She tried to force down the corned-beef pie Kate had made for tea but it was an effort. She would have liked to lie down, but if she did that she might never get up again. She was cleaning her teeth in the bathroom when a tap came at the door.

'Liz, there's a phone call for you.'

She opened the door to find her mother, wide-eyed. 'It's Bruce . . . he wants to speak to you.'

'Bruce?' On the other end of the line he sounded a little breathless.

'Something's come up, Liz. Business. I'll be tied up till late – too late. I'm sorry, but it's one of those things. Let's meet tomorrow. Better still, I'll come and collect you and meet your mother – must dash – about eight, is that okay? And I'm sorry!'

He was gone and Liz put down the phone, bemused. He had been so abrupt, quite unlike his usual self.

'Something happened?' Kate asked when she got back upstairs.

'He's got a business meeting.' Liz tried to sound nonchalant. 'I'm not disappointed, so you needn't look so sorry for me, Mam. I'm glad of a night off, to be honest.'

'But you do like him? I mean, he's important?' On the sideboard the roses were beginning to bow their fragrant heads.

'Yes, he's important, Mam. I like him a lot.' For a moment Liz felt the urge to confide, to tell Kate that Bruce was the first man she had made love with; that his ring was on a chain in her dressing-gown pocket even now; that she confidently expected to spend the rest of her life with him. In the end, caution prevailed once more. Let's get tomorrow night over with, she thought. If she knows the truth now it'll put her on edge, and I want everything to be as easy as possible.

She smiled at her mother and said, 'You'll like him when

you meet him, Mam. At least, I think you will. He's coming in tomorrow, when he calls for me.'

Kate was looking anxiously round. 'We'll have to square this place up.'

'It's fine,' Liz said, hoping she sounded sincere. The room looked shabby. Nothing matched because everything had been bought piecemeal. 'Anyway, he's coming to see you, not the house.'

'Why's he coming in tomorrow, all of a sudden?' Kate had drawn her bare legs up on to the chair and was leaning forward. 'He's not going to ask for your hand, is he?' She was grinning, but Liz could sense anxiety behind the smile.

'Don't be daft. And don't you dare say anything embarrassing . . . '

'As if I would!' Kate sounded so outraged that Liz moved to her side and hugged her.

'I know you wouldn't. Now, I'm going to get into my nightie and then we'll have a nice evening in together, like we used to.' They were both silent for a moment, remembering how they had clung together in the various crises.

'I only want you to be happy,' Kate said.

'I will be!' And this time there was certainty in Liz's tone.

They had cocoa and banana sandwiches for supper, a treat from childhood, while poring over Kate's latest borrowings from the library – *Beginner's Guide to China* and *Cabinet Makers of Note*.

'I would like to have a shop one day,' Kate said, lovingly fingering the illustrated pages. 'Nothing really pricey . . . just selling china mostly, and dolls. I had one of those porcelain-headed dolls once. If only I'd kept it. It'd be worth a fortune now.'

'You've got your lustre jug,' Liz said. 'And the side table . . . and Grandma Lucas's garniture.'

They both laughed then because the garniture of vases was hideous, and hidden away in a cupboard.

'I've enjoyed tonight,' Kate said, when it was time to clear their mugs and plates and make ready for bed.

'We'll do it more often,' Liz vowed, but Kate smiled and shook her head.

'You're about ready to fly, pet, one way and another. Still, it's what every mother expects – and wants, if she has any sense.'

Long after Liz had put out her light she thought of her mother's words. She mustn't ever let her down. Last night had been silly. The thought that it had also been Bruce's fault occurred to her and was ruthlessly repressed. She was grown-up and responsible for her own actions. All the same, she would be more careful in future. Bruce is coming here tomorrow, she thought. It's all beginning to move now, faster and faster.

16

THE FLAT WAS TIDY WHEN Liz reached home. More than that, it shone. There was a bowl of fruit on the sideboard and the roses had been cut down and trimmed of dying leaves, so that they looked for all the world a fresh bouquet. A lace cloth covered the marks on the occasional table and Kate's antique books were displayed on the coffee table.

'Where am I?' Liz said, her eyes rolling in wonder. 'Because this isn't home!'

'Don't be cheeky,' Kate said. 'And tea's in the kitchen. I've had my hands full today.'

'It's lovely, Mam,' Liz said, between mouthfuls of ham and pease-pudding. 'Thanks.' She couldn't resist a little dig at her mother's passion. 'I like the books spread out there. He'll think he's in a stately home.'

Kate was leaning against the sink, her cup held in both hands. 'I wish I could get a chance to read them properly. There's so much to learn about.' She turned round to wash up her cup. 'I'll go and get ready now, then you can have the bathroom. What are you wearing tonight?'

'Is the white blouse clean?'

'My white blouse?' Kate's look was quizzical as she turned back.

'Yours – mine – is it clean?'

'I'll see,' Kate said. When she returned she wasn't carrying the white blouse. There was a dress over her arm, a yellow dress with a short skirt and cap sleeves.

'What's that?' Liz said, although she already knew it was the dress she had seen in the boutique window. Her heart had begun to pound, but something stopped her from reaching out to take it from her mother's outstretched arms.

'Well, now,' Kate said, holding the dress aloft and looking at it. 'It's a dress. A yellow dress. It's . . . '

'Oh Mam, shut up!' Liz moved forward and took the dress, holding it against her, staring down at it. 'How did you afford it, that's the point?'

'Well, I didn't pinch it,' Kate said mildly. 'I bought it.'

'What with?'

'I sold the lustre jug. The rest's the housekeeping, so it's going to be a thin week. Now, let me go and get ready.' But Liz had laid the dress reverently over the back of a chair and was hugging her mother fiercely. 'All right, all right,' Kate said, making no move to free herself. 'It's only a dress.'

'It's *the* dress,' Liz said. 'I'll pay you back, I promise.'

'I won't hold my breath,' Kate said, freeing herself and making for the bathroom, leaving Liz to scamper up to her room and slip the coveted dress over her head for a try-on.

They were both ready by seven thirty, sitting opposite one another, slightly ill at ease. Kate jumped up from time to time to straighten a vase or twitch a curtain until Liz begged her to stop. 'He's not coming to make an inspection, Mam. We'll only be here for five minutes. Besides, he's not like that.'

They sat on, trying to concentrate on a radio quiz, crossing to the window from time to time to check on cars in the street below. Eight o'clock came and went, and a growing anxiety sprang up in Liz. Bruce must be avoiding a meeting with her mother, which meant he didn't really care. On the other hand, she reasoned, lots of men worried about meeting family and getting drawn in, but they faced it in the end. On the sideboard, the roses proclaimed his interest.

Beside her, Kate made a valiant effort to take her mind off the passing time.

'Did I show you the table in here?' She riffled through one of the books. 'See this.' She was pointing to a picture of a copper kettle. 'We had one like that at home. I bet your grandad's still got it in the wash-house. It says here that it's worth thirty pounds. Thirty pounds! I'll be round there in the morning!'

They pored over the pages, admiring the table, trying not to look at the clock, both of them aware of time ticking by.

'Shall I make some coffee?' Kate said at last, an air of finality in her voice.

She thinks he's not coming, Liz thought. She looked at the clock. It was twenty minutes to nine. 'Bruce must've been held up,' she said, lifting her chin. 'He often gets people ringing up with problems.'

'Yes,' Kate said, relieved. 'I'll make us a coffee. He'll probably be here by then.'

Liz stood up when her mother quitted the room. She saw herself reflected in the mirror above the fireplace, eyes dark in a white face, the yellow dress she had wanted so much seeming to mock her now. She went quickly down the stairs to the salon and lifted the receiver. When she got through to the hotel she asked for room forty-two. There was a slight hesitation at the other end of the line. 'Whom do you wish to speak to?'

For a moment Liz was tempted to hang up, but this was too important. 'Mr Hartley-Davis, please.'

'Just a moment, madam.' In the background she could hear a whispered conversation and then another voice came on the line. 'Who is calling?'

Liz said the only thing she could think of to say, stubbornly repeating, 'Mr Hartley-Davis, please.'

'Who's calling?' The voice was more urgent now and there was more agitated whispering in the background. Liz could imagine them all laughing at her, thinking she was chasing him. She put down the phone without answering and went back upstairs.

Kate was already there, coffee in unaccustomed cups on saucers in front of her.

She's still expecting him to turn up, Liz thought, acknowledging that she herself had accepted that Bruce would not be coming. She tried to smile. 'It's like I said; something's cropped up. He'll probably come tomorrow.'

'Good,' Kate said. 'Now get that good dress off, drink this coffee, and I'll knock up a nice snack.'

But neither of them had much appetite and they were in bed by ten, to lie awake and speculate. It will be all right, Liz told herself, her arms wrapped around her pillow, her eyes screwed tight against the lamplight that came through the thin curtains. Bruce wouldn't have picked her out if there hadn't been something real between them. You read about it in books, an attraction like that. And it had lasted for weeks: from summer into autumn. He had sent her roses and spent every off-duty minute with her. Tomorrow he would ring her and explain.

On the other hand, he came from a different world. From London, where everything was happening and everyone was sure of what they were doing. And she wasn't sure of anything, not even whether or not she was pregnant. If she was pregnant . . . she thought of Kate and what it would do to her. If they could get married, quickly . . . seven-month babies could be premature. She knew of dozens of seven-month babies. People would still talk, but it would be bearable as long as she was married.

She fell into an exhausted sleep at last, waking to hear soft sounds from the kitchen that meant Kate was making tea. Turning over and seeing that it was still dark outside, she realised that it was still the middle of the night. As her eyes grew accustomed to the darkness she picked out the ghostly shape of the yellow dress, where it hung on the front of her wardrobe. I was wrong about that dress, she thought. I really don't like it at all. Remembering what her mother had surrendered to buy it for her, she found it a relief to have a good excuse to cry.

17

THERE WERE FRESH HOT SCONES on the counter and Liz took one. She felt like something warm and soggy with her coffee. She looked around for a spare canteen seat, hoping she wouldn't bump into Staff Nurse Harker. There had been plenty of questions already about the 'mystery man' who was taking up her time. Until she knew about the circumstances of last night, Liz didn't want to be cross-questioned or even teased. The pearl ring, on its chain, seemed to bulge under her uniform dress, but she hadn't dared leave it at home for fear of her mother stumbling across it.

Much to her relief, Harker was not in sight, and Liz carried her tray to a seat by the window. Outside, the hospital grounds were aswirl with leaves, brushed into piles here and there but mostly blowing freely around the lawns and flowerbeds. She liked the inner court with its arched entrances on all four sides. It was like a womb, a secret place within the mass of wards and clinics.

'Shove up, Lucas.' She turned to see a plump probationer from her own year standing there with her tray, and shuffled along the seat to make room. The girl spooned sugar into her coffee and stirred. 'There's been a disaster. It was just coming over the wireless when I left the ward. A coal tip's collapsed. They say there's hundreds dead.'

'Whereabouts?' Liz asked.

'Wales,' the girl said, her mouth full. 'I don't know where exactly, but it was definitely Wales. These scones are lovely.'

A figure had appeared in the doorway. It was Harker, searching the heads at the table. Liz turned back to the window, hoping to escape her attention, but in vain. She felt the staff nurse's presence even before she heard her voice. 'I've been looking for you, Lucas.' She was reaching inside the bib of her apron to bring out a folded sheet of newsprint. 'Remember Hartley-Davis . . . the torn ligaments?'

Liz felt blood sweeping up her neck, suffusing her face. 'What about him?'

The newspaper Harker thrust at her was folded into a square, so that one item was prominent.

A man appeared before magistrates in Sunderland today, charged with three offences of fraud and false pretences. The man, whose name was given as John Stubbs, formerly residing at the Palatine Hotel, was first charged under the name of Bruce Hartley-Davis. The magistrates adjourned the case, pending further enquiries.

The piece went on to list the prominent individuals and companies linked with the marina project. 'Large sums of money are believed to have changed hands,' the cutting concluded.

Liz went on reading for as long as she dared, seeing the names dance up at her. Bruce Hartley-Davis, John Stubbs, Bruce Hartley-Davis. 'Well,' she said at last, trying to stop her voice from trembling, 'fancy that.'

'I never liked the look of him,' Harker said. 'Too handsome for his own good.' She laughed. 'I hope Mr Hinckley got his bill in quick. He'll have kittens if he did all that bum-licking for nothing.'

Liz drained her cup and left the uneaten portion of scone. 'I've got to get back,' she said. 'Don't forget your cutting.'

As she made her way back to the clinic she felt as though she was going out of her mind. She had to clasp her hands together to stop them shaking and her legs were trembling. It couldn't be true. It was all a mistake. Except that newspapers never lied; they got things a little bit wrong sometimes, but never totally. Still, even if it was partially true . . . she heard a ringing in her ears and had to grasp the wall for support.

It was a relief when she found the clinic awash with conjecture about the Welsh disaster. There was more news available now. A giant tip had gone on the slide, crushing a school full of children in its path. An army of rescuers – many of them parents of the children – were tearing at the mud and debris in the hope of finding someone still alive. As if in sympathy the skies outside had grown leaden and a mood of misery settled on everyone, staff and patients alike.

At lunchtime Liz avoided the canteen and went out into town, moving from shop to shop, arcade to arcade, arguing with herself. At last she went into a phone box and rang the hotel once more. She wasn't sure what happened after court cases. Perhaps Bruce was out on bail. The paper hadn't said.

It was a man who answered the phone. Liz drew in her breath and then spoke quite firmly. 'Can I speak to Bruce Hartley-Davis, please?'

'Hold on.' There was a moment's hesitation and then, 'Who shall I say is calling?'

She couldn't give her real name. Not to a stranger.

'It's Liz . . . Liz Smith.'

'Please hold.' She heard the murmur of voices. 'I'm afraid he's not here. Could you give us your number?'

Liz put down the phone. She had seen the call as a solution, a means of finding out, for better or worse; but she was no further forward. Was Bruce there, or had whoever answered spoken the truth? Who had it been on the other end of the line? He couldn't have been one of the usual hotel staff, who were mostly women.

She walked blindly back through the lunchtime crowds, hearing everywhere the name 'Aberfan'. She tried to think of the tragedy, willing herself to feel pity for its victims instead of for herself, but it was useless. The enormity of what had happened in Wales meant nothing compared to the anguish she felt inside, the wretchedness of unanswered questions, the horror of what might lie ahead.

But going from daylight into the comparative darkness of the hospital entrance, and trying to work out which emotion was uppermost, she knew, without doubt, that it was fear. She thought of all the things they had done together in the last few weeks: the drinking, the outings, the expensive meals, and what it had all cost. Perhaps she would be implicated; perhaps she was guilty of something? Her name would be in the paper and everyone at work would gather in groups to laugh at her. There would be no sympathy, that was for sure. She had seen things happen to other girls, and she knew how it was. She tried to think of Bruce and what he must be going through, but all she could see was a stranger called John Stubbs, who would probably go to gaol. I ought to worry, she thought. I love him. I ought to care about what happens to him. But whichever part of her had cared yesterday had taken flight today.

Her mother was glued to the TV when she got home, a mug of tea in one hand, a hanky in the other. 'It's terrible, Liz,' she said, 'There's pannacalty in the oven. I don't feel like eating. A hundred and sixteen children missing or dead and twenty-eight adults. A whole generation wiped out. They found the deputy head with five bairns in his arms, trying to save them. And Lord Snowdon's there. He looks shell-shocked, but he's doing his best.'

The food stayed uneaten as Liz joined her mother on the settee, glad of an excuse to shed her tears.

'Going out?' her mother asked when the news bulletin ended.

Liz was about to say yes when she came to a sudden decision. 'I've got something to tell you, Mam. And it's awful.'

It came out then, the newspaper, the hotel . . . everything, except what she and Bruce had done in his room together. Finally, she took out the ring. 'He gave me this, Mam.' Her mother looked at her for a moment and Liz knew she was hurt that she had kept it secret, but it was quickly past.

'Well,' she said, putting down her mug. 'Let's turn the oven off for the meantime, and get the kettle on, and then we can sort this problem out.' She smiled. 'And cheer up, it's not the end of the world, pet. It never is.' She was trying hard to appear unconcerned but Liz could see that she was shaken.

They talked for an hour, the drooping roses seeming to mock them from the sideboard. Eventually they decided to do nothing for the moment. 'Let's wait and see what happens,' Kate said. 'You never know, it might all blow over. Now, go and bathe your eyes.'

In the end Liz put on her coat and let herself out of the flat. 'I'll only be a moment,' she called, desperate to get out into the evening air. She was grateful that it was dusk and that the streets were almost empty of homegoers. She shivered suddenly, realising that the autumn was nearly over and winter was not far away.

As she walked she counted cyclists. If she'd seen an even number it would be all right: it would be a case of mistaken identity. Bruce would turn up at her door, smiling his familiar smile, scooping her up into his arms, and life would go on as before. Eight cyclists passed but in her heart of hearts Liz knew that there would be no reprieve.

As she passed a large house the door opened and light spilled across the pavement as two girls in floating dresses flitted to a waiting car on the arms of dinner-jacketed young men. One of them was fair, like Bruce. The other man reminded her of the picture of her father that stood on the mantelpiece. She wondered if her long-dead father had ever worn a penguin suit. She could only dimly remember him. If he'd lived, wouldn't her life have been different? They wouldn't have lived above a shop, on the proceeds of perms and depilatories and face creams, made up by Kate in the kitchen from whatever came to hand mixed with a lanolin base. Even their clients were common. The better people went to the big stores with their padded chairs and uniformed assistants. I'm ashamed of what I am, Liz thought. I've always been ashamed, and now all this.

It was all so daft, really, the way you let yourself get carried away by dreams. She had seen Bruce as a prince who could rescue her from her cinders, and he had only made things worse. A phrase from Sunday school intruded: 'a mess of pottage', that was it. You traded in everything important for a mess of pottage. Any man who bothered with her now would know she was cheap. Men always recognised damaged goods. Every girl had had that drummed into her: 'No one wants damaged goods.'

It began to rain and Liz held up her face, licking the raindrops into her mouth. As she turned for home she thought of her grandfather. If Bruce went to trial and the papers were full of it, how would she face him?

She was passing a television shop with pictures of Aberfan on the lighted screens in the window; she watched as parents and police toiled in the rubble in the hope of finding someone alive. God is cruel, Liz thought. There's no mercy for anyone, not in the end.

Elizabeth looked down at her finger. The solitaire was one and a half carats. Her first ring from Geoffrey, all those years ago, had been a tiny sapphire surrounded by diamond chips. She had it in a box somewhere in a drawer. She had completely forgotten how important it had once been, a badge of safety and respectability to flourish to a hostile outside world.

BOOK 3

———————•———————

SOPHIE'S STORY

London
September 1993

18

PAUL HAD LEFT AT SIX o'clock for an early filming assign-
ment and Sophie found herself unable to go back to
sleep. She moved into the warm space he had occupied,
smelling him on the sheets and pillows, remembering last
night. If only life could be all love-making. But would that
be enough? How much identity was bound up in being an
object of desire, how much in what you made, or made to
work? And most of all, where did allegiance lie? She ground
her head into the pillow to rid it of uncomfortable thoughts,
but it was useless. There weren't enough sheep in the home
coun. s to get her back to sleep. She got out of bed and went
to swit h on the kettle.

Outside, most of the houses were still asleep, their windows curtained. She heard the rattle of a milk cart and,
far off, the screech of brakes. London was waking up.
Paul would be half-way to Kent by now, at the speed
he drove. Was he wondering about allegiance or identity?
Probably not. Men were more focused in their needs and
desires. Or were they more self-centred? Her father was an
exception, seeming to live only for herself and her mother.
How could she let weekend after weekend go by without
flying to his side? I will do better, she vowed as she scalded

her coffee and carried it back to bed to sit, arms around her knees.

The bedside radio was giving out news of the peace accord between Israel and the PLO. Who would have thought of Arafat and Rabin shaking hands? It gave Sophie a brief feeling of well-being before she returned to contemplation of the day ahead.

At eleven she was having coffee with David, and the subject of New York was bound to crop up. She was lunching with the giftware buyer and then at three she was meeting Kate, her grandmother, at King's Cross and seeing her safely to Heathrow to catch her plane to Nice. After that the day was her own. Paul had suggested eating out if he got back in time, but she felt fairly certain he would be late.

Last night she had wanted him so much she had felt savage, knowing a communion with him that was overwhelming but, in retrospect, stifling. It was frightening to think of need like that, a need that made you shed inhibitions along with clothes, desperate to be within or without another person. Now, she felt guilty, as though she had used Paul and then put him away.

Discomforted, she finished her coffee and went for a shower. There was post on the mat when she emerged; two bills and a letter with a Liverpool postmark. Surprisingly, it was addressed to her: 'Miss Sophie Baxter, c/o Paul Malone'. She took out the letter, smiling wryly at the idea that she was 'care of' her partner. A photograph was folded in the single sheet of notepaper, she and Paul in the centre of the Malone clan, taken on the Saturday of their last visit. She began to read.

Well, Sophie, I don't have much to say, you being here lately. Just that we are all well and hope you and our Paul are too. It was great to see you both and we're made up that Paul has found the right girl at last. Paul says you're making plans and this is to say that when you get married there'll be no shortage of bridesmaids, with our lot to choose from.

There were misspellings and crossings-out in the letter and Sophie winced at her own disapproval of the grammar. Why did she nit-pick sometimes? She hated it in her mother; now she was doing it herself! But the really disturbing thing about the letter was its assumption that she would soon be Paul's wife and the unreasonable irritation which that idea aroused in her.

It was natural for the Malones to think in terms of marriage and commitment; everything about their lives was traditional. The conversation of the unmarried sisters centred around the time when they would come into their own as married women and mothers. I'm different, Sophie thought. I'm capable of so much more. But the arrogance of her own assumption frightened her. Commitment kept the human race in business, so it was not to be despised.

Her remorse carried her through breakfast and out into the overcast morning. It hadn't been much of a summer, not in London anyway. It would be sunny in New York, and hot enough to walk bare-legged in the park and sleep without covers. I want it, she thought. One way or another, I have to go there.

Three hours later she was sitting opposite David and listening as he outlined plans. 'They want you in New York by the first of November. It's a Monday. You'll meet your counterpart, and she'll run you through the routine. She comes to us a week later.'

'What if I said I couldn't go, David?' Sophie asked quietly.

He looked at her for a moment before he replied. 'You can't not go, Sophie. Unless you want to ruin a very promising career.'

Elizabeth could hear the Hoover in the dining-room. Mrs Clifford always did the dining-room on Mondays. Tuesdays was bedrooms, Wednesdays the lounge, Thursdays washing and ironing and outside paintwork, and Friday the kitchen. Bathroom and toilet were done everyday, and cupboards once a month. There was order in the house. Usually this gave Elizabeth a thrill of satisfaction. Today it didn't seem important.

She walked to the window and looked out on the garden, now past its mid-summer glory but still beautiful, carefully planned to give colour all year round. Elizabeth pictured her daughter sitting at her desk, speaking on the telephone, at the very heart of a big business. She had never wanted a career herself, not after ... . she moved to the sideboard and began to straighten the artefacts on its surface. Polished wood and silver, an elegant combination. She wanted to feel her usual joy in looking at her possessions, but uncomfortable thoughts kept intruding. It had been the same ever since Sophie's visit home and the question that had stirred up so much debris.

She took a photograph album from a drawer in the sideboard and opened it. There was their first house in Gloucester, neat as a new pin and about the same size. A new beginning, that's what Gloucester had been. A chance to start again. Liz had stood at the altar and made her vows mechanically, but over and over in her head she had promised, 'I will be good to Geoffrey. I will. I will.' She had cried when he lifted the veil from her face for their first symbolic kiss as man and wife. She could see the tender expression on his face even now, the belief that she was filled with the same emotion that was suffusing him.

She carried the album to the sofa and sat down, but she didn't turn the pages that were a record of her life with Geoffrey: the move from house to house up the ladder of local government. No snapshot could compare with the vividness of the pictures inside her head. Her mother's face when she had told her that she was going to marry Geoffrey: 'Are you sure this is what you want?' And then, her eyes afraid, 'Are you pregnant?' Harker's eyes, sharp with envy, when Liz held out her hand with its tiny star of diamonds and sapphire centre, as neat as a ring from a cracker. And Geoffrey's face, when she had offered sex in an anxious attempt to contribute something to the bargain: 'I love you, Liz. I can wait,' he had responded. She had despised him for that, if she was truthful. She had been relieved, but contemptuous just the same. Elizabeth closed the album now with a snap and stood up. Damn Sophie! She had been happy until her daughter's probing.

Sophie positioned herself at the barrier with five minutes to spare. King's Cross was a great, grey hive of activity, trains disgorging one crowd of passengers, another queueing hopefully to make the journey north. There were pigeons hopping boldly between feet, fluttering up to the steel joists when something scared them, but always swooping down again. Now and again someone threw them crumbs, but the pickings were scarce and some of them had deformed or mutilated feet so that they hobbled painfully from morsel to morsel.

Sophie looked at her watch and up again, to see her grandmother's train moving majestically to a standstill, two minutes before it was due.

Kate was one of the first passengers to alight, procuring a porter as she stepped on to the platform. She's still an attractive woman, Sophie thought as she walked towards her grandmother. Kate's figure was erect, her eyes clear, her white hair cut short and curled around a face that had retained its colour in spite of ageing.

'Darling!' Kate hugged her and then stood back to gaze into Sophie's face. 'Let me look at you. A bit on the skinny side, but you'll do. Let's get out of here and then we can talk properly.'

They had an hour to spare, too short a time to stray far from a taxi-rank. They sought out a nearby hotel, seedy but clean, and ordered tea.

'Now,' Kate said. 'What's the news?'

'Paul's fine. Loving his new job.'

Kate pulled an impressed face and Sophie smiled. 'Yes, it is exciting, isn't it? And I'm fine.' She had decided not to mention America; not now, when Kate was off on holiday. Time enough to tell her when she got back. Instead she said, 'Tell me all about Nice.'

'I'm staying at the St George,' Kate said, 'on the Promenade des Anglais, which is actually the sea-front – cheek by jowl with the Négresco, which is the ritziest place apparently. You should be coming with me.'

'Ooh, yes,' Sophie said. The thought of being anywhere but home, where she had to wrestle with her problems, was more than alluring.

Kate had picked up on her mood, and now leaned closer. 'Why don't you come? Even for a day or two? I've got a double room; it could easily be arranged. I'd treat you to the air fare if that was a problem.'

'I can't get away. I'd like to – don't think I wouldn't – but at the moment things are hectic.'

'Well, the offer's there,' Kate said. 'Remember where I am: the St George, Promenade des Anglais, for the next two weeks. Sun and sea and gorgeous food and wine. It bears thinking about.'

'Why isn't Oliver going with you?' Sophie had meant to tease but she saw Kate's jaw tighten.

'Oliver is ten years my junior, Sophie. And although I have liberal ideas, they don't run to toy boys.'

'He's hardly a toy boy, Gran! What's the difference . . . only eight or nine years?'

'It's not simply a question of age, Sophie. And anyway it's *ten* years. I wouldn't dream of disrupting my life now. I don't want another commitment . . . '

There it was again, Sophie thought – that dreaded word, 'commitment'.

'I know it's no one else's business, darling,' she said aloud, 'but you get on so well together – and he's so dishy.'

'*Dishy?* What a word! He's a nice, overweight, middle-aged man who is quite content with his lot as it is. He wouldn't thank you for matchmaking, and neither do I. We're business partners, no more, no less.' There was something about the set of her grandmother's lips that said, 'Conversation closed,' so Sophie was glad that the tea arrived at that moment.

*   *   *

166

It was seven o'clock by the time Sophie got home. The flat was empty and silent. She stood in the middle of the kitchen, uncertain whether or not to start cooking. If Paul got home in the next hour or so they could still go out. She went through to the hall and pressed the button on the answering-machine. His was the fifth message: 'It's a shit, Sophi, but I've got to hang on here. I should be home, oh, eightish. See you later. Don't prepare anything. We can either go out or get a take-away. Love you. Oh, almost forgot: what did David have to say? I'll hear later. Bye.'

Sophie was on her way back to the kitchen to put on the kettle when she heard Chloe clattering up the stairs and opened the door. Her neighbour had obviously been washing her hair which hung, unrestrained, almost to her waist. 'Sophie, let me in! I'm exhausted. Is there any coffee? I haven't stopped today . . . not since dawn!'

'Doing what?' Sophie's tone was sceptical as Chloe moved gracefully to the sofa and fell theatrically along its length.

'Packing, chérie. Choosing, deciding, checking accessories, make-up, hair things . . . everything I'll need while I'm away with Desmond.'

'Oh, tough,' Sophie said, setting out mugs. 'I can see how that would be stressful. How many cabin trunks are you taking?'

'Don't be facetious, Sophie, it doesn't become you. We're flying, that's the whole problem. I'm having to pare things to the bone.'

'Drink this,' Sophie thrust a mug of coffee at her friend and sat down opposite her. 'The whole art of being well dressed is that you can do it economically. Well, not exactly economically; it costs . . . but you know what I mean.'

'What I *know* is that I have things I absolutely *need* and no room to take them. I'm distraught. Still, if I'm pushed I can buy stuff there. Everything has compensations. Besides, think of the article I could get out of this trip. More than one, probably, and definitely broadsheet.'

Outside it was growing dark but neither of them moved to switch on a lamp. 'I was offered a trip to Nice today,'

Sophie mused, her lips against the rim of her mug. Suddenly *she* wanted to be going somewhere, packing and having to decide on nothing more important than chiffon or silk.

'I hope you took it.' Chloe sat up straight. 'Don't tell me you turned it down, or I'll despair. Nice is scrumptious. All those bare brown thighs and the cicadas in the trees and wine flowing like water. Everyone's rich. You can smell affluence, you know, actually smell it.'

'Is there anywhere you haven't been?'

Chloe was spreading out her hair, lifting it on her hands to facilitate drying. 'Thousands of places, darling. Which is nice, because my life expectancy is probably eighty years. Don't want to get bored by the time I'm sixty, do I?' There was a sound of footsteps from down below. 'Here's lover-boy. Shall I tell him you're off to the Riviera for a dirty weekend?'

'Do,' Sophie said equably. 'He won't believe you. We all know you're an amoral delinquent, unable to distinguish truth from fantasy.'

Chloe got to her feet and bent down to kiss Sophie warmly on the cheek. 'That is quite the nicest description anyone's ever applied to me. It means I have the makings of the perfect journalist. I'll leave you to your lord and master. See you before I go.'

Sophie heard a moment's banter on the landing, and then Paul was coming through the door. He kissed her, shrugging off his jacket as he did so. 'What are we eating? Not that I'm hungry. I lost any appetite I might've had around six thirty.'

'Bad day?' Sophie tried to sound sympathetic but her heart was sinking. He couldn't have a crisis, not tonight. They needed to talk.

'Bad day? You might say so.' Paul was opening fridge and cupboard doors, munching whatever came to hand.

'Don't do that,' Sophie said mildly. 'Not till we've decided what we're doing. Take a piece of cheese and sit down.'

He took out a bottle of wine and poured two glasses. 'I'll skip the cheese if we're going out. Here's a glass.'

'Tell me what's been going on?'

'Well . . . shall I start with the ice-cold agony aunt? Or the mad scientist who never spoke once in an eight-minute interview except to say, "Yes," or, "Precisely"? Shall I tell you we're two cameras and one sound man down? Shall I tell you that I viewed a documentary today which bears my name on the credits and is a load of . . . bollocks?'

'Is this the Beatrice Maconochie piece?'

'You might guess. She does the usual distortion of truth. She never lies, she's too fly for that; she simply turns things inside out to fit her pet theory. No one wants truth any more, Soph. They want everything "focused". That's the buzz word. And if the focus is coming from the wrong angle, it doesn't matter a fuck as long as it's got a good soundbite you can use in the promos.'

'Drink your wine,' Sophie said. She wanted to stand in the centre of the kitchen and scream. 'What about me?' Instead she said, 'What's this about the ice-cold agony aunt?'

'Her? She comes over all warm and comforting on screen, and so anxious that you have a good sex life. Nothing's too much trouble! This morning she comes into my office with a handful of letters – fan mail – and dumps them on my desk. "Who's going to answer these?" she says. I poked at them, and then I say, "You, I suppose. That's who they're addressed to." I open one and this poor sod's asking about why he can't get it up, so I say, "And it's your subject. These people need help." And she says, "Ten pounds a letter." Just like that. Ten pounds! I nearly said, "Is that for all night?" but I restrained myself. I told her that we have no budget for answering letters, but I'll talk to Calvin – and she picked the letters up and dropped them in the waste bin. And then she walked out. Nice?'

'Charming. What did you do about the letters?'

'At the moment they're back on my desk. God knows how I'll deal with them.'

'Well, let's get out of here. We can talk while we eat. *Le Plaisir* okay?'

They ate in silence in the restaurant, until Paul's plate was clean. 'That was wonderful. More wine? I assume Kate got off all right?'

'Yes,' Sophie said. 'She looked wonderful. I hope she has a good time.'

She was hoping Paul would go on to raise the subject of her meeting with David, but instead he stared broodingly at his glass.

'Do you want a pudding?'

He shook his head. 'I'll just have coffee.'

'I talked to David today,' Sophie said when the coffee was served. 'Or rather, he talked to me. They want me to be in New York at the end of October.'

Paul grunted, without lifting his eyes from his glass. 'How long for?'

'I'm not sure.'

This time he did look up.

'You must have some idea. A week? Ten days?'

'Longer than that, I think.'

Paul leaned forward, elbows on the table. 'You mean they want you to move there?'

'Not for ever. For six months – perhaps twelve.'

'You've told them it's out of the question, I suppose?' His eyes were holding hers across the candlelit table.

'No. I've said it might be difficult . . . '

'It wouldn't be difficult, Sophie, it'd be impossible. If it was any other time, I'd say, "Do it, and I'll commute." But I can't at the moment, you know that. There's no way I could take off, even for forty-eight hours. God, I can hardly get home to kip.'

'I know.' Sophie reached out and covered his hand with her own. 'But I can't just say no, can I? Not if I want to keep my job?'

'You have to make a decision.' Paul withdrew his hand from hers and leaned back in his chair. 'We all have to make decisions sooner or later. You have to decide what matters most . . . and surely that's us? We're an item. What's the point of love at long distance? I know you find my parents a bit much, but underneath all the daftness there's something solid. They were both always there for the family, Soph. They loved one another, and when kids came along – however many – they were drawn in to that love. I haven't given Gary that, but it's what I want for our kids: a base . . . a home. Not your place, or mine, but ours. Now, let's have another drink and forget all this. Jobs can screw up your whole life if you don't watch out. It's not going to happen to us.'

Elizabeth creamed her face carefully, not forgetting the brow bone, finishing off with upward sweeping strokes to the neck and chin. Her face was thrice reflected in the triple mirror, white and shiny with cream, her eyes dark and ghostly as though in a mask. She could see Geoffrey's reflection too, as he moved about, putting shirt, pants and socks in the linen basket, emptying the contents of his pockets on to the Wellington chest, folding his trousers on to a hanger and walking through to the shower, clean pyjamas over his arm. He had carried out the same routine for twenty years – more than twenty years – wherever they were, at home or abroad on holiday. He's methodical, she thought, and tried not to feel resentful. She had wanted someone reliable, and if reliability was unexciting, that was no one's fault.

She lay down on her back and drew up the duvet. Her eyes were closed as she tried to list Geoffrey's virtues on her hand. A good provider; she had never, ever had to worry about money. It had been tight until his promotions really took off, but she had always known where she stood with him. He had been the gentlest of lovers, and he had given her Sophie. I'm lucky, she told herself, and then repeated it to reinforce the message.

'Tired?' Geoffrey was getting into bed, setting the alarm clock, putting the radio on to 'snooze', putting out his lamp; just as he always did. In a moment he would put out a hand, and she would pat it and turn away – or not, as she chose. Tonight, though, the hand didn't come. Instead he sighed. 'I still miss that dog. I used to like a walk last thing.'

If he was hoping she would weaken he was wasting his

time. Elizabeth had meant to let him make love to her tonight, but he had spoiled her mood. 'I know,' she said, 'but it would be silly to get another dog and get attached all over again.' She turned on to her side, hearing the midnight pips on the radio and the announcer reading the headlines. 'Goodnight, darling. Get a good rest.'

She kept her ears cocked to see if he replied, but there was only the gentlest of sighs, and then he too turned on to his side, leaving them back to back in the dark.

'Ready for the light?'

Sophie snuggled down and adjusted her pillows. 'Yes,' she said. Paul put out the lamp and turned over. She could feel his breath on her cheek and shoulder, and ordinarily she would have turned to him so that their breath mingled and lit the fuse. Tonight, though, she was still considering his words, spoken in the restaurant: *Jobs can screw up your life. It's not going to happen to us.* Implicit in all he had said was the fact that *his* job was sacrosanct. If their working lives affected their relationship, hers would be the one to be adjusted.

Paul slipped an arm across and drew her closer. Sophie did not co-operate, neither did she resist. 'Come here,' he said. He was kissing her neck, her ear, waiting for her mouth to turn to his. Her mind said, 'Sod him,' but her body was betraying her. When his hand moved to her breast and then down over her belly, she let her legs give way so as not to deny him entry. How could you refuse a man who loved you? It was hard enough if you didn't love him; impossible if you did.

In the end hers was the more frenzied love-making, but the image in her head when it was over was a surprise. It was Susan's baby, with its monkey face and small, wet, questing mouth.

'See,' Paul said, withdrawing and subsiding on to his back. 'You couldn't go anywhere without me. We'd both die for the want of it, if you did.'

He was only joking and Sophie knew it, but that didn't stop the resentment growing inside her.

19

SOPHIE WAS BUTTERING TOAST WHEN Paul came into the kitchen, his hair wet from the shower, curling Botticelli-like about his head. He came up behind her, nuzzling her neck, locking his arms around her waist. 'Love me?'

'I must do,' she said, waving her hand at the breakfast table.

'I'll make it up to you,' he said, sounding contrite. 'You'll see.'

Sophie was puzzled for a second, but only for a second. Paul thought he'd won the battle because she'd had sex with him last night. Typical! She hated feminists who used that word whenever men transgressed, but today it came readily to her lips.

'Make up for what?' she asked coolly. He let go of her waist and she turned to face him.

'For New York,' he said, a little lamely. 'I know it was an opportunity, but there'll be others. I'll take you there one day.' It was the wrong thing to say and she saw the realisation flash across his face even before he finished speaking.

'I haven't said I'm not going yet.' Her voice was icy and she turned away. 'Sit down and eat your breakfast. It'll be ruined if we're not careful.'

'What d'you mean, not not going?'

'Not, not going? What does that mean?' She was being petty but she couldn't help it.

Paul scowled. 'God, I hate it when you fence with words. Are you going or aren't you?'

'I'm not sure. I have to think it through. But when I do see New York, I'd like it to be on my own account, not as part of your entourage!'

She'd hurt him and she was half glad, half sorry. She tried to think of words to defuse the row, but it was too late.

'I'm sick of this, Sophie. Make up your mind. Either we have a relationship or not.' Paul was into his coat now, getting his car-keys, the breakfast table abandoned.

'And if we do, it's on your terms?'

'If you want to put it like that. Someone has to see sense.' His words were dying away down the stairs, and Sophie half ran to the landing.

'I'll go if I choose to!'

'Please yourself.' His voice was an echo now, and she beat the banister with a clenched fist, realising too late that Chloe was sitting half-way up the stairs, chin on fists, obviously enjoying the scene.

'You know,' she said, as she followed Sophie into the flat, 'you two *should* be married. You already behave as if you are.'

Sophie ignored the remark. 'There's tea, if you want it. And toast. I thought you were off at the crack of dawn?'

'We are. Eleven a.m. *is* crack of dawn, darling – at least it is to reasonable people.' Chloe switched on the TV and turned to GMTV. 'Isn't Eamonn Holmes gorgeous? He looks like a streetwise cherub.'

'Not to me he doesn't. He looks like a TV presenter.'

'Don't take your moods out on me, darling. I'm a neutral observer. I love it when you two row, though. It makes me glad I'm not into fidelity.' Behind them the TV was burbling away. Chloe spread a piece of toast with marmalade and lifted it, dripping, to her mouth. 'Ooh, lovely. I never buy proper food but when I get it here, it's scrumptious.'

Sophie didn't reply. She was suddenly fascinated by the blonde woman sitting on the GMTV sofa. 'Isn't that Hilary Purser . . . Desmond's wife?'

Chloe swung round, marmalade forgotten, eyes wide. 'My God, it is. Turn it up.'

Sophie pressed the button as the camera lingered on Hilary Purser's serene smile.

'So you see a hardening of attitudes towards women in these latest rape verdicts?' the presenter said.

Hilary Purser went on smiling, seeming in no hurry to answer. 'It's obvious that the establishment wishes to re-assert Victorian values,' she replied at last. 'Their contention is that "nice" women don't get into dangerous situations. Ergo, a woman who finds herself in danger cannot be "nice".'

'What's the solution, then?'

Again the warm, slow smile. 'The solution lies in our own hands. Women must stand by one another, demonstrate a true solidarity. We must not only be nice to one another, we must also truly like one another. Sisterhood is not a dirty word. It's a beautiful word, and better in the performance than the saying.'

Eamonn Holmes was thanking her and Hilary was smil-ing graciously. 'She looks like Angela Rippon,' Chloe said grudgingly.

'Yes.' Sophie didn't really care less about Desmond's Hilary, but you couldn't be rude. One remark, however, was irresistible. 'I wonder how sisterly she'd feel if she knew you were off to wherever it is with her husband?'

'She wouldn't care,' Chloe said. 'That's half the trouble. Desmond says she's indifferent. She even likes him to play away. It's less hassle for her.'

'If you believe that, you'll believe anything.'

'It's true.' Chloe was indignant now. 'She's so laid back, she's horizontal. Can I do these dishes for you? No? Well, it's just as well. I've heaps to do, and detergent ruins your hands.'

* * *

Elizabeth fingered the sweaters, weighing silk against cashmere, taupe against cream. She shopped frequently in this boutique and the assistants kept a respectful distance, knowing she liked to make up her own mind. In the end she bought both, paying for them with gold plastic, adding a pure silk scarf in orange and brown to her purchases before the bill was complete.

She carried the black-and-silver dress bag up to the third floor restaurant and ordered coffee. It came with a filter and a tiny biscuit wrapped in foil. She didn't feel like eating, or much like drinking the coffee either, but she sipped slowly, trying to decide what to do next. The trouble was, she wasn't in the mood to do anything. However she tried to divert herself, her mind came back to Sophie and that question: 'How was it for you?'

With that simple query, the pain and misery she had suppressed for years had come flooding back, as though a dam had burst. This morning she had cried in the bath, letting the tears flow. What she couldn't work out was why she was crying. Surely not for a humiliation almost thirty years old?

She raised the cup to her lips, gazing out above it at the busy restaurant, but the picture in her mind's eye was of roses that refused to die, a mute reminder of a lie. It had been played out in the paper over the next few days, details of the scheme which had almost netted Bruce – she still thought of him as Bruce – one hundred thousand pounds, a scheme which had been a complete figment of his imagination. He had not even had the money to pay his hotel bill. As the toll of Bruce's sins mounted, and were revealed in the newspaper, Liz had grown even more afraid of her involvement with him becoming known. He had spent money on her, other people's money, the product of criminal fraud.

Even when it had all come out and she had read about it in the papers night after night as the case proceeded, she had found it hard to believe: Bruce Hartley-Davis, the wheeler and dealer, was, in reality, John Stubbs, ex-psychiatric nurse in Slough and croupier in London. 'He fooled a lot of other people, pet,' Kate had tried to comfort her. 'Professional men . . . even they couldn't see through him.' But the words of consolation couldn't ease Liz's humiliation and fear. Her only comfort was the fact that Bruce was being safely held in gaol and could not turn up to embarrass her.

And then her mother had rung her at the hospital to tell her that the police had come to the salon in search of her. Liz had kept the receiver in her hand, not caring if Sister appeared and ticked her off for taking a private call; she hung on to it in the hope that her legs would cease trembling and she would find the strength to walk away.

Now, twenty-seven years later, she gathered up bag and parcel and made her way between the white damask-covered tables, smiling graciously when she saw a familiar face, as befitted the wife of a chief executive. She came out into the main street, intending to find another shop, another unwanted purchase. Instead she went straight to the car park, not really knowing where she was going, just impelled to get in the car and take to the road. She drove out of town and turned north on to the A1, seeing the signs flash by: Boroughbridge, Thirsk, Durham . . . and then Sunderland. She parked in a multi-storey car park and made her way down into town, to the bridge above the river.

Once you had to cover your ears to stand here, such was the clamour of the yards. Today, apart from the traffic across the bridge, the area was silent, and the river the haunt of sea-birds. She looked over to the left bank where the yards had stood, a forest of cranes and hulls and gantries. They were all gone, but something was happening: building work – a sign of regeneration. At least she hoped it was. She stood there, remembering the girl she had been once, gazing first at a sea-bird wheeling above and then down at her hands, folded now on the iron balustrade. They were the well-kept hands of a forty-six-year-old woman, pampered, the solitaire diamond dazzling in the sunshine. It had cost three thousand pounds in the year Geoffrey had moved to Westerham. She thought of the diamond and sapphire ring which had cost thirty-seven pounds and ten shillings. Above her the sea-bird swooped on huge, silent wings. She watched it soar and turn towards the river mouth until it was lost to view because tears had blurred her vision, and then, when her vision cleared, she went back to her car and drove to the Palatine Hotel. She felt a steely resolve within, a determination to probe until she touched the nerve and felt the thrill of pain. For too long she had suppressed her memories, but so much else had been suppressed along with the pain. I have never really lived, she thought, and then began to multiply and subtract. She was forty-six. If the Bible held true, she had twenty-four years left; one third of her life left, two-thirds gone. 'Wasted.' The voice in her head was a reproach: 'Wasted. Thrown away.'

Why had she done it? She parked the Volvo in a lay-by and walked the last two hundred yards to the hotel. All those years ago she had worn flimsy shoes with stiletto heels and paper soles. She had on brogued leather court shoes today. They had cost a hundred and twenty-five pounds, far more than she had earned in three months as a student nurse.

She mounted the steps and went through the swing doors. There had been a revolving door there then – or had she just imagined it? She looked for the sweeping staircase up to the cocktail bar, with the telephone box tucked beneath it, but it was all gone. The foyer had been modernised, changed out of all recognition. She found another bar at last and ordered Tio Pepe, thinking all the while of a frosted, fruit-filled glass with a swizzle stick and a sprig of mint, and a man sitting opposite her whose every word was a lie.

They had sent him to prison for six years and before his appeal was heard she was Mrs Geoffrey Baxter, whose husband was that model of respectability, a local government officer.

Elizabeth got to her feet and went in search of Little Egypt, seeing, with relief, that the houses were still cared for, the place much as she remembered it – except that her mother's salon was now a take-away kebab house with a cheery Asian proprietor.

She stood for a moment, eyes closed, remembering Geoffrey, hands in pockets, waiting in the street. He was greying at the temples now, no longer a boy. I want to go home, she thought. That's the only thing I want to do.

A case of shoplifting would normally be handled, discreetly, by security, so Sophie was surprised to receive a call from the accessories buyer, a normally calm thirty-year-old, who was clearly in a state of high agitation. 'Steady on,' Sophie urged her. 'Just tell me what's happened.'

It was a simple enough story, at first. A woman had taken a scarf, a silk scarf, and walked out with it into Bond Street. An assistant had followed her, but when accused the woman had neither denied nor admitted it. She had simply walked back into the shop, threading her way between customers on to the escalator. Neither the assistant nor the security officer, called for back-up, had been prepared for this. They had followed her at a discreet distance, and she had gone into the second-floor rest-room where she had chained herself to a water pipe.

'Chained?' Sophie asked. The woman had hooked her belt around the pipe and refastened it. Sophie sighed. 'Well, unfasten it!' But the belt had a silver clasp, and no one knew exactly how to unhook it. To fumble with it or look at it too closely might constitute assault, according to the security man. He wasn't prepared to do it; the buyer was also unwilling, and a crowd was gathering. 'I'm coming down,' Sophie said.

She sailed down on the escalator and made her way to the rest-room. Several women inside the grey-and-silver interior were ostensibly washing or drying their hands, but really gazing at the woman in the corner. Sophie made a mental note to have all the pipes boxed in, and went to the woman's side. She looked at the security man and asked softly, 'Can you empty the place? Apologise. Say it's only for a moment.'

He moved away and she turned back to the woman.

'Please, can we go to my office? I'm sure we can sort this out.'

The woman didn't answer. Sophie tried again, but still there was no response. She looked thirty, but an old thirty; the lines of her mouth turned down and her skin had a sallow tint. Her clothes were cheap; not shabby, just badly finished and skimpy.

'Why did you want the scarf?' she asked.

It was useless. Sophie could see that the woman had no intention of replying; was probably not even hearing her. She turned her attention to the buckle then, seeing that the top of one half of the clasp was clear. That meant the other side must come up to loosen it. She tried to think: was it assault? You could lay hands on someone's arm. Did a belt constitute clothing? Would undoing it equate with undressing her? A decision must be made soon, whatever the consequences.

'I'm going to unfasten you, and then we'll have a cup of tea.' She kept her voice calm as she put out a hand, praying the belt would give immediately. She felt the woman's body pulsating; trembling. The belt clicked and fell loose, and Sophie pulled it clear and held it out.

The woman took it without speaking, her eyes wide and staring. She's afraid, Sophie thought suddenly. She's out of her mind with fear. She remembered the baby rabbit, its eyes glazed with terror, its limbs unable to carry it. Motioning everyone to stand clear, she took the woman's arm, leading her gently out of the door and on to the down escalator.

'She's still got the scarf,' the buyer muttered indignantly, but Sophie shook her head.

'Never mind. Let's just get things back to normal.'

In the end, though, the woman let the scarf fall to the ground, as though she had discarded it.

'We can't do anything to her now,' the security man said gloomily, as the woman walked through the door to the street. However, Sophie felt a sudden sense of triumph; at least one petrified creature had found its freedom.

She went back to her office, desperate to tell Paul what had happened, suddenly sure of what she wanted. What did a job count for in the end? It was love that mattered; it was not waking up in the night in an otherwise empty bed.

She worked it all out on the way home, rehearsing her speech as she prepared dinner, reminding herself of all the other jobs she could get if she had to leave Ascher's. But when Paul came through the door he wasn't contrite, or loving. He looked and sounded hostile.

'I hope you're not making anything for me. I've only come home to pack a bag. I've got to go to Paris again.'

'Paul . . . must you? I do want to talk – I *need* to talk to you.'

Sophie was standing in the bedroom, almost crying with the yearning to share with him her thoughts of the afternoon.

'God!' he said, pulling open a drawer and rummaging for clean socks. 'I've got about three minutes to get ready if I want to catch that flight. I can do without you throwing a wobbly!'

His words cut Sophie like a knife. 'Sorry,' she said coolly, turning back to the hallway. 'Heaven forbid I should get in the way of *your* career.'

But the emphasis was lost on him. A few moments later he was out of the flat, tossing, 'I'll phone,' over his shoulder as he went, swinging his bag to his shoulder and patting his jacket to check that his passport was there.

20

THEY WERE ONLY A FEW miles away from Liverpool when Paul sighed and stretched away from the steering wheel.

'Tired?' Sophie asked, hoping she wouldn't have to take over now and negotiate Liverpool's traffic. There had been an unspoken truce since he had returned from Paris and she tried to keep her voice neutral.

'No, I'm fine. We're nearly there now.' Paul cleared his throat. 'By the way, Soph, I'd prefer it if you didn't mention New York to the folks.'

'Why not? They already know it's a possibility so why not mention it?'

'No reason. I just don't want a lot of hassle. We're only there for thirty-six hours.'

'Why should there be hassle?' she persisted, a sense of injustice overcoming prudence. Outside the car the city outskirts were appearing, neat houses with tended gardens and creeper-clad walls.

'They just wouldn't understand one of us going off. They'd read all sorts of things into it. You know what they're like.'

'They'll have to know when I go, Paul. Or do you intend to keep up the pretence that I'm still here? I could record some messages for the answer-phone, if that would help.'

'Don't be flippant, Sophie. That always gets me, when you make jokes about serious things.'

'All right, I'll be serious. I think it's crazy to pretend something's not happening when it is. And it's deceitful. Your mother's so honest . . . she'd be horrified to think I'd kept something like that from her.'

'There's time enough to tell her when it happens.' He swung the car on to the Toxteth Road and she stared at him.

'Don't you mean *if* it happens?'

'I didn't say that.'

'No, but you meant it. I know you, Paul. You think I won't do it, don't you?'

He didn't answer and they drove on in silence.

Elizabeth straightened up from the shrub she had been dead-heading and flexed her back. It was warm and she wiped her forehead with the back of a gloved hand. Around her the garden glowed: white Esther Reed marguerites, pink lavatera, the purples and violets of asters.

Sophie would be in Liverpool now. Elizabeth always worried about the M1, which was silly, really. It was no more dangerous than any other road. She picked up the trug of cut flowers and carried it into the kitchen, pausing on the step for one last look at the garden. She would be on her own for lunch, so a sandwich would do. She took off her gloves and put on the kettle.

Usually she drank in the charm of the kitchen, which was designed to her own specifications without an inch of wasted space. Today, though, all she could think about was Sophie. 'I'm going to New York for a while, Mum.' That had been the bald statement down the phone on Friday evening, as though New York were Brighton or Salisbury. Fear had gripped Elizabeth then, the fear that always came with anything new or strange. I want order, she thought, that's all I want, so that nothing in my world should tremble.

And suddenly it was there again in her mind's eye, the

sideboard and the wilting roses, her mother snatching them up one day and saying, 'These must go.' That was after the police had come, sitting on the edge of the settee in their highly polished shoes and belted gaberdine macs. 'Are you saying you had no inkling of what was going on, Miss Lucas?' 'Did you meet anyone else as a result of your relationship with Stubbs?'

Liz had wanted to cry out, 'Stubbs? Who is Stubbs?' But her mouth was too dry. And then it had come . . . the crunch. 'We're trying to trace the whereabouts of a quantity of jewellery belonging to Mr Stubbs's wife.' Liz had laughed, until she saw her mother's frown of alarm. A wife . . . that was the one thing she hadn't expected! He had been a free spirit, a man-about-town. How could Bruce Hartley-Davis have had a wife called Mrs Stubbs?

Liz had got to her feet and fetched the pearl ring. 'That's all he ever gave me.'

They hadn't looked as though they believed her, but there was nothing more she could do about it.

She hadn't gone out of the house for a week after that, hiding her shame in her bedroom, telling the hospital she was sick. She had emerged at last, just to go to work and hurry home again for sanctuary, painfully aware that the world was a dangerous place.

And here was her only daughter preparing to go to the other side of the world, to work and live among strangers. Elizabeth got to her feet to arrange the flowers, sick at the heart because her world was trembling once more. She reached into the trug for the first blossom and felt a thorn jab her finger. It was a rose, a white one. She never grew red roses, just as she never, ever, wore the colour yellow.

They took Gary to McDonald's when they came out of the cinema. It had seemed a waste of a late summer afternoon but he had insisted that he wanted to see an action film so they sat, munching popcorn, through a movie filled with screeching cars and grunting confrontations, and then crowded into a booth to demolish hamburgers and fries, as they had done half a dozen times before. 'That film was wicked,' Gary said, blowing down his straw so that the remains of his coke frothed and bubbled.

'Stop that,' Paul said. Gary went on blowing. 'I said, stop that.' Paul's tone was sharp but the little boy stared defiantly back. Sophie saw Paul's hand clench. In a moment there would be an explosion.

'Steady on, Doc Holliday,' she said, and saw his lips twitch. As if he sensed it was time for a mutual backing-down, Gary stopped blowing. 'Well,' Sophie continued, 'I don't know about anyone else but I want some fresh air.'

They walked, arm in arm, along the edges of the Albert Dock, Gary running ahead of them, occasionally turning to one another to smile the half-smiles of lovers, keeping up the pretence that everything was all right and their relationship not under threat.

They drove back to Gary's home, chattering about Liverpool's First team and Graeme Souness, the manager. According to Gary his days were numbered. 'Who do you want instead?' Sophie enquired.

'I want Kenny Daglish back . . . he's the business.'

'Souness is all right,' Paul countered, from the driving seat. 'The trouble with Liverpool fans is that they're never satisfied.'

Sophie got out when they reached the house and held out her hand. 'It's been good seeing you again, Gary. When are you coming to London? We could show you all the sights.' He was nodding enthusiastically when Sophie saw Paul's expression change. She turned, to see Julie coming towards them, a scarf around her fair hair, a bag of flour in her hand.

'You're here,' she said lamely. 'I just ran short of flour.'

There was a moment's silence and then Sophie held out her hand. 'I'm Sophie. I'm glad to meet you at last. You must be very proud of Gary.'

Julie transferred the flour to her other hand and took the hand Sophie proffered. 'Pleased to meet you.' Their eyes met and held for a moment, each of them searching to see just what made the other tick.

'Right,' Paul said, suddenly galvanised into action. 'I won't be a moment, Sophie. Let's get you into the house, young man.'

Sophie ruffled Gary's hair and smiled all round before stepping back into the car.

The other three walked into the house and Sophie sat waiting, Julie's face imprinted on her mind's eye. There had been strength there, but desperation too. She's pretty, Sophie thought, but she looks older than her age.

The Malones were all waiting when they got back to the house; Mr and Mrs Malone and Paul's sisters and brothers, ready for the regular family night out.

'Have you had a good meal?' Mrs Malone asked, holding up her hands in horror when they confessed to hamburgers and fries.

They sat at the table to eat spare rib chops and three vegetables, followed by apple tart and custard. If I live through this, I'll make my three score years and ten, Sophie thought, but she went on smiling until they were out in the gentle north-western darkness and making for the friendly lights of the pub.

They went up to bed at last, Elizabeth going ahead, Geoffrey pausing to put on the alarm before he mounted the stairs.

When she came out of the bathroom he was already in his pyjamas, looking out on the dark garden. 'It's chilly tonight,' he said. 'Lucky Kate to be in the South of France.'

There was a wistful quality to his words and Elizabeth felt a pang of guilt. She had always discouraged holidays abroad, choosing traditional places like Eastbourne or Southport or Bath. She wanted to make a gesture, to concede, but instead she heard herself say, 'Oh, it'll suit my mother to be somewhere lazy and extravagant.'

Geoffrey turned, frowning. 'Your mother's still working, Elizabeth, and she's old enough to retire. You can hardly accuse her of self-indulgence.'

'I know, I know.' She sounded irritable now, and she rushed to excuse herself. 'It's just that she gets me on edge, Geoff. All this business about Oliver – people will talk.'

'Who will talk, Liz?' He hardly ever used the diminutive nowadays, and it surprised her. 'You keep saying people will talk, but who? Who wouldn't be happy to see two people, who are obviously made for one another, doing something about it? Aren't you at least a little afraid that it's your carping that might be keeping them apart?'

Elizabeth was stung to answer, 'As if she'd take any notice of me!'

But after he had gone into the bathroom she stood in the centre of the room wondering if, unawares, she had become a bitter and joyless woman. Where is the girl I once was? she thought, remembering the yellow dress and her arms round her mother's neck in gratitude. Where did Liz go?

It was late when they went up to the borrowed room. 'I'm bushed,' Paul said, sitting on the side of the bed, elbows on knees.

'I'm not surprised. If you participate in a marathon drinking session what else do you expect?'

'All right. If we all stuck to Aqua Libra the world would be a better place. You made that quite plain.'

'So now I'm a killjoy, am I? Because I don't get my hand round a pint glass?'

'That isn't fair. No one mentioned pint glasses – and keep your voice down. We don't want to entertain the entire family.'

She tiptoed to the loo in the unaccustomed nightgown, wondering why they were arguing. She had quite enjoyed the evening. The Malones were uninhibited and fun to be with because they expected nothing from you, taking your participation in their enjoyment for granted. So why was she on edge? Perhaps it was that tonight she had seen what Paul had tried to explain to her, that sense of family commitment, of being part of a whole, and the spectacle had both pleased and scared her. Or was it that Paul's remarks in the car still rankled: 'I'd rather you didn't talk about New York.' In other words, she wasn't here in her own right. She was here as his appendage, the faithful girlfriend-soon-to-be-wife, and mother ten months later. They would surely allow her four weeks to conceive.

Stop it, she told her reflection in the mirror, knowing she was deliberately winding herself up because when you were angry decisions were so much easier to make. I've got to get away, she thought as she outstared herself. I need space to think.

21

S OPHIE FELT BETTER AS SOON as the plane lifted off the tarmac. She closed her eyes and let her worries drift away. The last forty-eight hours had been hectic: arranging for a long weekend off, making sure she tied up loose ends at work, packing, as well as cancelling the milk and papers because with Paul and Chloe both away there would be no one at home to take them in. And here she was at last, airborne, with nothing to do but let herself be carried towards sun and wine and laughter for three whole days.

A voice at the back of Sophie's mind reminded her that she had solved nothing, merely shelved her dilemma; but she silenced it, giving herself up to glimpses of cloud through the portholes and the ministrations of pretty air-hostesses plying her with food and drink in doll-sized portions. She had decided, lying awake after Paul's departure to Paris, that she would go to Nice. A few days with Kate had seemed the perfect answer, much better than roaming the empty flat.

She slept her way across the Alps and woke just in time to fasten her seat belt as the plane began its descent. The slow progress from plane to arrivals hall and the wait for the luggage to arrive had seemed endless, but at last she was pushing her trolley through the doors, to be hit by the solid heat of the Riviera. Kate was there, hopping up and down, looking at a distance like a teenager in her pink-and-white sleeveless shift. They hugged and allowed themselves to be bundled into a taxi, which was cool and comfortable after the heat and bustle of the airport.

Though the cab was moving along the motorway quite quickly, the driver turned in his seat to beam at them. 'Air conditioning,' he said proudly. 'Good?' They agreed it was not only good but wonderful, and he beamed again. 'Nice – *très jolie. Côte d'Azur très jolie.*' He was proud of his territory, even anxious to talk about it, which seemed amazing when he must ferry scores of people to and from the airport every day. Sophie would have liked to talk to Kate, to explain her sudden change of mind, but he continued to monopolise the conversation. When they reached the hotel, Sophie tipped him well and he beamed again before hurling the cab back into the traffic in search of more visitors to his beloved Côte d'Azur.

The hotel was old and imposing, its walls hung with huge gilt-framed mirrors and murals where nymphs flirted with shepherdesses in enchanted gardens. As Sophie registered at the reception desk, the concierge rang an imperious bell to summon the porter. No porter appeared. She rang again.

'Never mind,' Sophie said. 'I only have two bags.'

She and Kate made their way to the ornate lift, but though it was already there, when they pressed the button the doors failed to open. Sophie pressed again but to no avail. 'Could we walk up?' she said to her grandmother.

'It's on the fourth floor,' Kate answered dubiously, eyeing the bags.

A man was sitting in a gilt chair nearby, half hidden behind his newspaper. As Sophie pushed vainly at the lift button once more, he lowered his paper. 'Having trouble?' His tone was amused and Sophie felt her face stiffen.

'We can manage, thank you.'

He ignored her answer and levered himself to his feet. 'This lift is very French,' he said. 'Or very feminine. It has to be coaxed.' He put a well-groomed finger on the bell-push and wiggled it gently. There was a purr of machinery, and the doors slid open.

'Thank you so much,' Kate said. Smiling at her, and then, quizzically, at Sophie, the man returned to his chair and his paper.

'I love men when they fix things,' Kate said as they were borne upwards, but Sophie didn't rise to the bait. A moment later they were through the double doors of Kate's room and Sophie was depositing her bags on the luggage rack.

Kate closed the doors and turned. 'Now,' she said. 'Tell me, what's going on?'

'What do you mean?' Sophie was playing for time.

'I mean that a week ago you were involved in work, and in home, up to your eyeballs. Then all of a sudden, you drop everything and ring me to say you're coming. I'm glad to see you, but I still need an explanation.'

'I just felt the need to get away. I had a couple of days' leave due me, David let me tack them on to the weekend, and here I am. That's all, Gran.'

'Don't call me Gran! Well, if that's all it is, I'm glad. You're sure nothing's wrong?'

'Certain.' Sophie moved to the window. 'I noticed the palm trees as we were driving here. They're amazing!' She leaned out to look at the crowds moving beneath the window. There were neat flower beds in the middle of the road and a blue sea beyond, but what really struck the eye was the multiplicity of signs everywhere you looked: hotel this and hotel that; tourist information; Orangina; and Pepsi, Pepsi, Pepsi.

'You can't see the beach,' Kate said, from behind. 'It's only a strip of sand at the best of times, and that's hidden under umbrellas.'

A car horn blew down below, and then another, and another, till the air was alive with the cacophony. 'That goes on all day,' Kate said. 'They'd never get away with it in England.'

Beyond the blue umbrellas the sea was calm and glittering, with a single swimmer moving purposefully out to sea then turning to head for the shore. A speedboat sped from right to left, towing a paraglider on a rainbow-coloured parachute. A faint breeze was gentle on Sophie's cheeks.

'It's lovely to be here,' she said fervently, turning to her grandmother. 'Thank you for inviting me.'

Geoffrey put his briefcase by the side of the hall table and bent to kiss Elizabeth's cheek. 'All right?' She moved away from him towards the kitchen and he followed. 'Did Sophie get away?'

'I expect so. She'd've rung if anything had gone wrong.' Elizabeth donned an oven glove and opened the glass door. 'Almost ready. Shall we have an aperitif?'

Geoffrey poured Tio Pepe into two glasses and handed one to his wife. 'It was a very last-minute arrangement. Still, it'll do the child good.'

'She's not a child, Geoffrey. She's twenty-six, and I'm not sure she should be with Kate. My mother is, well . . . ' Elizabeth was suddenly defensive. 'You've got to admit she's unpredictable. I know you say I go on, but even you will admit that.'

'Because she doesn't don a shawl and support stockings and go into a home? She's still in her sixties, darling. Hopefully, we won't be moribund either when we're her age.'

'I won't be buying and selling junk,' Elizabeth said, closing the oven door and straightening up. 'I won't have a man-friend at least ten years my junior. I won't go off alone to gad about Europe. I'll have some *dignity* . . . or at least I'll try to.' Her voice had risen and her face was flushed but Geoffrey made no comment and it goaded her. 'Yes, sit there and say nothing. Let me do all the carping. I'm used to monologues.' She waited, but he didn't respond. 'Well, Geoffrey, you must have *some* views?'

'Oh, I do. I find your mother rather stimulating, if I'm truthful. And Oliver – if indeed they are involved – is hardly a boy, toy or otherwise. As for her going on holiday alone, if she'd gone with Oliver it would have upset you so what else can she do?' He spoke mildly enough, but Liz was in the mood to take offence.

'There's no point in my talking, is there? You're never sympathetic towards me.' Her voice trembled. 'I worry about Kate, just as I worry about Sophie. I wish I could be like you and switch off, but I *care* about them. About all of you.'

And I want to be sensible, she thought. Sensible was safe. Sensible was sensible . . . the only way. I was sensible, she thought. I was foolish once but then I made the right choice. Why can't they be like me, all of them, and see that there's only one way to be happy? Except that she wasn't happy, hadn't been ever since she grew up one day in a hospital canteen, looking at a piece of newspaper that turned dreams into nightmares. She must have made a sound for she felt it in her chest, but she wasn't sure that it had escaped her lips until she saw her husband's face.

Geoffrey put down his glass and moved to take her in his arms. 'Come on, this isn't like you. Why not sit down and let me dish up? If you're worried about anything – anything at all – we'll sort it out.'

Elizabeth's face was against his shoulder, and for a moment she felt like telling him about Sophie's question. But she had covered up so much over the years that now she had difficulty in distinguishing truth from fiction. Besides, how could she possibly tell him the truth about their marriage, after all this time?

She shook her head and stood upright, moving away from him. 'No, I'll sort dinner. You get changed. I'm sorry if I'm a bit overwrought. It's my age, I suppose. Men can't imagine how difficult it can be. And Kate *is* impossible, Geoffrey, whatever you may say. Has she said one word to urge Sophie to get married? You can bet she hasn't. It's all left to me.' She put up her hand and smoothed her hair. 'I'm sorry, but all this business about Oliver . . . people *will* talk, whatever you might say.'

'Who, Elizabeth? Who will talk? You keep on saying this but I wonder! Most people are taken up with just surviving. They're not waiting to cause a furore because one woman in her sixties goes to bed with a man a few years her junior. *Why* does it worry you so?'

'I wish I had your faith in human nature, Geoffrey. Still, I'm sorry, you shouldn't have to come home to this. You must be fed up with me.'

He reached out and took her arms in a firm grip, pulling her forward so he could kiss her brow. 'I'm not in the least fed up with you. I never have been, and I never will be.' He looked suddenly aghast. 'Now, why on earth does that make you cry?'

Kate and Sophie slept for an hour in the early afternoon heat, and then went out into the street in search of refreshment. Elderly couples were strolling arm in arm, accompanied always by a dog on a lead. The dogs were small and aristocratic and overfed inside their little harnesses, and the men and women had skins like hide from years of sun. 'Are they as old as I think?' Kate whispered. 'Or are they simply sun-shrivelled?'

But Sophie was looking at the linked arms, the sometimes entwined hands. The world was made for couples. A sudden panicky desire to go home came and went, and then Kate was drawing her into the cool depths of a *salon de thé*.

While Kate ordered, Sophie watched the family at the next table. A tiny little girl with gold rings in her ears and a dummy on a chain gazed solemnly back with liquid chocolate eyes. Her skin was biscuit-brown, her green dress showed matching green knickers, her dimpled wrists wore gold bracelets . . . but the set of her mouth was one of resignation as her parents argued over her head.

I'll never do that to a child, Sophie thought. The face of Susan's baby swam up in her mind, and then Gary, pugnacious in his Liverpool strip. She felt Kate's hand on her arm.

'Where are you?' Kate said gently. 'Drink your tea.'

Sophie wanted to confide in her grandmother but not here, in this crowded café. 'I'm jet-lagged,' she said. 'Well, you know what I mean. I'll pick up in a while.'

The couple at the next table were getting to their feet. The father took the child's hand but the mother yanked her free. '*Allez-vite!*' she said sharply and tugged the little girl out into the sun.

When Sophie and Kate emerged a street photographer was waiting, his camera poised. 'Submit,' Kate said. 'It's the quickest way.' A moment later they had parted with one hundred and thirty francs, and sat down on a seat facing the sea to look at the instant Polaroids. 'Not bad,' Kate said, and tucked them in her capacious handbag.

It was pleasant to sit in the sun and watch the passers-by: old women tottering on high-heeled mules, their faces, once beautiful, now caked with make-up, their hair destroyed by the sun so that pink scalp showed through the straw-like tresses. The old men looked too tired to be lecherous but the women gazed seductively up at them just the same, fluttering false eyelashes that were stuck to their crêpe-textured eyelids. 'Have you noticed,' Kate whispered, 'all the men look like Somerset Maugham?'

There were young people too, half naked, striding out on long, tanned legs. What clothes they did wear were the colours of the Mediterranean: lime and lemon and violet and turquoise.

'I won't want to go home on Monday,' Sophie said ruefully.

'You can come back, one day.' Kate patted her hand. 'You can come back with Paul.'

Sophie nodded and smiled in agreement – but would she be with Paul next summer, next year, next month? If she went to New York, would he be waiting when she got back? She had a sudden vision of herself alone. Was that a frightening thought, or an exciting one? Her mouth went dry but she couldn't make out the reason why.

She turned to look at Kate, seeing suddenly how age had touched her grandmother. Kate's bare arms were like crêpe, the flesh sagging. One day she too would be old. When that happened she didn't want to be alone. She thought of Paul in the bedroom, a short time ago, teasing her about gravity. It was true; youth did fall away. She was suddenly frightened, so that she had to look back at the bronzed beach boys and girls for reassurance.

'Come on, darling,' Kate said beside her. 'You look like a little girl who's just lost her pocket money.'

Sophie smiled apologetically. 'I'm sorry. I am mixed up, I admit. I'm going to New York – that's the trouble.'

'You've been before,' Kate said matter-of-factly. 'Where's the problem?'

'I've been there on holiday, for a flying visit, but this would mean staying for quite a while.'

'I see.' Kate pursed her lips. 'And Paul can't go with you because of the new job. How long is "quite a while"?'

'Six months, perhaps more. Paul thinks I shouldn't go. He feels the time has come for us to make a commitment to each other. Not marriage, necessarily, but all the rest of the trappings. A house, perhaps even a baby.'

'Don't you want those things?'

'Eventually.' Sophie blinked back tears and tried to keep watching the powder-puff parachutes floating across the sky. 'But I want so many other things too, Kate. I want to find out what I can do before I settle down.'

But by then Paul might not want her. That was the rub.

They watched the nine o'clock news and then a documentary.

'Night cap?' Geoffrey asked as Elizabeth changed channels in search of a little diversion.

'Nothing alcoholic. Aqua Libra, perhaps.'

He brought in a tall glass for her and a squat tumbler of whisky and water for himself, as Elizabeth switched off the TV set and put down the remote control.

'Nothing good?'

'Sport. Watch if you want to – there's golf or football. I'm going to turn in.'

'No, it's okay. I'd rather listen to some music until we go up. Anything special you'd like?'

Elizabeth shook her head, and he chose a tape at random,

a symphony orchestra playing pop tunes. She sipped the sparkling liquid in her glass and tapped her foot, thinking sometimes of her mother and her daughter together in the soft evening air of the Riviera.

She had never enjoyed holidays It was better to be at home, with your own door to shut out the world.

After the long weeks of the trial, with the *Echo*'s front page continually occupied with details of Bruce's fraud, she had wanted to escape from everyone.

It had been a struggle to keep her distress from Harker and the rest of the nurses as they pored over the details of the scandal. John Stubbs had been a former nurse among other jobs – even a disc-jockey in a fifth-rate nightclub. He'd married the daughter of wealthy parents, whose family business was yacht-building, and when her father had refused further subsidy Bruce had taken off with his wife's jewellery and what cash he could lay his hands on. The scheme for the marina had been a sham, but he had managed to persuade several reputable businesses to part with money on account of it. Even the local council had been duped.

Liz had hidden herself away, night after night, until Geoffrey had sought her out again. They had gone out twice, and then he had proposed once more and she had suddenly seen a heaven-sent escape route opening up. 'As long as we don't wait too long, Geoff. I want to go to Gloucester with you. If we're engaged, I don't want us to be apart.'

She had had a white wedding, with all the trimmings. Kate had seen to that, throwing herself enthusiastically into debt once she was sure that it was what Elizabeth wanted. Elizabeth had not restrained her, because the window-dressing was necessary. She had been the perfect bride-to-be, shy and eager by turns, reassuring Geoffrey's parents, her own mother and grandfather, kissing Geoffrey with fervour, planning their first poky flat in Gloucester, the honeymoon, her trousseau, the hymns and flowers. 'See,' she had proclaimed with every move, 'see how happy I am, how unaffected.' Had she really done all that? Were Sophie and this home and almost thirty years of marriage simply the product of one close shave?

As Elizabeth went upstairs she wondered if all this retrospection was the product of depression. It happened to women in mid-life, everyone knew that. And then, as she went into the bathroom, a melody drifted up from the stereo, a hundred strings, or so it seemed, weaving in and out of 'Eleanor Rigby', and suddenly she remembered the sixties; the smell and the feel of that decade. Eleanor Rigby – the woman who kept her face in a jar by the door.

Liz switched on the striplight above the basin and looked at her reflection in the mirror. She, too, had worn a face for twenty-seven years; a serene face, a face of middle-class respectability. In a moment she would get into bed and, unless she feigned sleep, they would probably have middle-class respectable sex. She had only fucked – the word shocked her but she made herself say it again inside her head – she had only fucked with two men. With Bruce, in constant terror of pregnancy, and with Geoffrey because she had no option. So she had never made love except in terror or indifference.

She leaned closer and stared at herself. What would it be like to love freely? With abandon? What had she been missing all these years?

She heard Geoffrey setting the burglar alarm in the hall, and then the 'pip, pip, pip' as he mounted the stairs, knowing he would reach the landing at the exact moment that the beeping stopped. We are trapped, she thought. Both of us are trapped in routine as though we were flies in amber.

Kate lifted the carafe and refilled Sophie's glass, then her own. They had dined on the terrace in front of their hotel, at tables lit by candles inside coloured glass bowls. A hundred yards away, out of sight, the sea was lapping the beach, the night sky above it banded in dark blue and violet.

'This is heaven,' Sophie said. Earlier they had walked in the park and heard cicadas in the trees and somewhere, far off, a violin playing gypsy music. They had eaten well, on coquilles St Jacques followed by cassoulet and then crème caramel.

'It is rather nice,' Kate agreed. 'Well, we're both twenty-one. Let's stay here.'

'I wish I could.' Sophie's tone was so heartfelt that Kate put down her glass.

'Your mother witters on so much I never take any notice, but this time she was sure you had problems. I should have listened to her.'

Sophie was suddenly unsure that she wanted to talk. Not again, not now. Not to spoil this magic night. 'You know Mum,' she said. 'She's got to have something to worry about. She's been imagining that I'm in peril for years.'

Kate stared out to sea. 'My daughter is married to a saint, Sophie, and that's her misfortune.'

'What do you mean?'

'I mean that any other man but your father would have cried "Enough," long ago.'

'She does go on a bit,' Sophie admitted, but Kate shook her head.

'Don't criticise your mother, Sophie. Pity her. She's like a hamster on a wheel.'

'She should come here and live like a lotus-eater,' Sophie said, uneasy suddenly, and anxious to change the conversation.

'No.' Kate's headshake was emphatic. 'The sun is fine for a while, but permanently it's only for lizards.'

Against the night sky the palm trees were exotic, the horizon tinged pink. A man was threading his way along the pavement, a basket of dried yellow-brown flowers in his hands. 'Yasmeen,' he cried and then again, 'Yasmeen.' A moment later he had disappeared in the crowd.

A monkey-faced waiter approached to hover over Kate. 'He fancies you,' Sophie teased when he was out of earshot and was amazed to see a gleam of pleasure in her grandmother's eye. Did Kate still fancy men? Surely not. 'How's Oliver?' she asked.

'I told you the other day,' Kate said tartly. 'Ask about my other friends.'

'They're not as interesting,' Sophie said. 'Well, not to Mum, anyway,' she grinned. 'She's terrified that you and Oliver are having a wild fling.'

'We're not,' Kate said, 'for reasons I've outlined before. Now, is it bedtime or shall we sally forth?'

'Let's have coffee,' Sophie said, and lifted a hand for the waiter.

The coffee came, accompanied by two small glasses containing liqueur. 'With the compliments of *monsieur*,' the waiter said, waving a hand towards a distant table. It was the man who had operated the lift for them. He raised a glass in salute and Sophie felt her cheeks flush until Kate said, 'How nice,' and bowed her head in thanks.

'Oh God,' Sophie said, dropping her head, 'he's going to come over.'

'So he is,' Kate said gleefully, enjoying Sophie's discomfiture.

A moment later the man loomed over them.

'May I introduce myself . . . Alistair Dunbar.'

'I'm Kate Lucas, and this is my granddaughter, Sophie Baxter. Do sit down for a moment.'

He eased into one of the wrought-iron chairs and elegantly disposed his long legs. 'I think we're the only British residents so I thought we should stick together.'

Around them the myriad tongues of the other guests proved his words to be true. 'I'm all for solidarity,' Kate said, leaning her elbows on the table. 'Now, tell me, how long have you been in Nice?'

Sophie relaxed now that Kate had taken up the conversation. She and Alistair Dunbar chattered on about the Riviera, where he was a representative for his law firm. Sophie tried to look interested, but his presence made her feel uneasy and she was glad when at last he got to his feet. 'I hope you have a pleasant stay,' he said.

'Thank you.' Sophie could feel his eyes on her but her lids felt heavy, too heavy to raise her own eyes to his. Why didn't

Kate step in? In the end she forced herself to look up at him. 'You're very kind,' she said lamely.

He grinned, as if he was enjoying her discomfiture. 'Well, I'm off for a stroll before bedtime.' He turned to Kate. 'I don't suppose you ladies would like to accompany me?' Sophie saw Kate's mouth opening to say yes but the pressure of her sandalled foot on her grandmother's shoe brought a swift change of mind.

'Not tonight, I'm afraid. I think we're straight for bed. Perhaps tomorrow?'

'I'll live in hope,' he said cheerfully, and moved off into the night.

'That was my bunion,' Kate said ruefully. 'He only wanted to go for a walk.'

'I'm not in the mood,' Sophie said.

But afterwards, safe in bed, Kate snoring gently a few feet away, she thought about the man. He was a few pounds below his ideal weight but there had been the suggestion of strength in the lazy way he used his body. She thought of the morning, of the beach deserted at such an early hour, of lying beside Alastair Dunbar under a blue umbrella, the skin of her bare arm touching his arm, their legs touching, entwining, the thrill of her flesh meeting unfamiliar flesh. She had been faithful to Paul for three years, and it had been no penance because the thought of anyone else had never even crossed her mind. Until now.

Outside, in the street, a girl laughed, a car door slammed, an engine revved, and then there was a squeal of tyres as the car sped away along the promenade.

Sophie turned on her side and punched the pillow into shape. Why was she thinking about another man, a stranger? As if she didn't have trouble enough already.

22

Sophie's three days in Nice passed in a delightful haze of feeling good and having enjoyable experiences. In the early mornings she sat on the balcony of their room watching water-skiers on the turquoise sea and the occasional yacht making for Monte Carlo or Cannes. They went out at ten o'clock, to shop at stores full of oriental pottery or dazzling designer clothes, and to drink tiny cups of strong coffee at kerbside tables.

Sophie hired a car and drove them up the Moyenne Corniche, the middle one of three roads that clung to the mountain. There was a Moorish influence to the pink-roofed houses dotted here and there on the mountainside, where vegetation sprang from the barren rock. And then they arrived in Eze, a town with an ancient history, its peach and apricot houses shuttered and sleeping in the midday heat.

They sought refuge in a *parfumerie*, a temple of fragrance where assistants presided over perfumes with names like *Pour Elle* and *Eve* and *Printemps Japonais*. There were soaps and scented candles, all in the colours of sugared almonds, and jars of lotions to match. A pair of blond tourists entered, looking all of sixteen, he like a peacock in pink and peach, she drab in khaki. '*She's* buying *him* scented soap,' Sophie whispered, and received a wink from Kate in reply.

The young man's gorgeous T-shirt bore the legend 'Boys of the Summer', and indeed the young giants striding about in skimpy shorts looked just that. Where did they go in the winter and what would become of them when they were old and turning to fat? Sophie thought of Chloe. If there were girls of the summer, she was surely one of them.

They scuttled from the cool of the *parfumerie* to a canopied café, where they ordered Orangina and gazed at the other customers. 'There's your true Frenchman,' Kate said, nodding towards a man hunched over a glass of *anise*. 'You can tell by the world-weary eyes.' Sophie watched him sip the milky-white liquid and then, as the noon-day gun boomed, throw some coins down and leave. He crossed the street, sauntering rather than walking, as the air took on a bloom of heat.

'I wouldn't mind coming here for a honeymoon,' Sophie said. 'Where did you go for yours?'

Kate laughed. 'Well, I went into a munitions factory, pet, and your grandpa went off to Changi for a couple of years. Not that he knew it at the time. He was a wreck when he came back.' She was thoughtful now, no longer smiling. 'Not just physically, but emotionally too. Then your mother was born, and it all came right in the end. We had a few happy years together before he died.'

'Mum was born in 1947, wasn't she?'

Kate nodded. '1947, the year of the worst-ever winter – twenty-foot high snowdrifts, no electricity, and what was the meat ration then? Tenpence per person per week, I think – and your grandfather not long home from Changi and thin as a rake. You wouldn't have liked my life.'

Sophie smiled. 'I know. But what about when you were single – before you settled down?'

'I've always been settled – at least it seems like that. I was thirteen when the war started. I married Grandpa just after my seventeenth birthday and he went overseas the next day. I didn't see him again for nearly three years.'

'Was it lonely without him? How did you bear it? I don't think I could live without Paul for three weeks.'

'We were too busy to be lonely. We all wanted the war over, especially the wives. And then it *was* over and they came back, and we had to start winning the peace.'

'I'm so muddled up, Gran.' It burst out of Sophie unheralded.

'Well, hang in there, Sophie. Everything passes, that's the one thing I do know.' Kate was waiting for her to continue, but Sophie wasn't sure she wanted to go on.

'Have you been happy?'

'Of course,' Kate said. 'I have you, and your mother, and lots of other things.'

At a nearby table a mother slapped her small son, the noise of flesh on flesh like a gunshot. No one took any notice, apart from Kate and Sophie.

Kate shrugged disapproval, but Sophie was looking at a poster pinned to the café wall. '*Grande Soirée Karaoke, venez tous chanter avec nous*.' She nudged Kate and pointed. 'Good God,' Kate said. 'Is nothing sacred?'

They drove back to Nice when the midday heat abated and parked by the sea. There was a little park alongside and they sat under the trees. The sprinklers had come into action and water was running across the mosaic path to the bases of palm trees, birds playing in and out of the spray, lifting their wings to splash. As they watched, an attendant appeared with a hosepipe to augment the flow. He was overweight and perspiring and at last he turned the hose to douse himself, letting the water run into his open mouth and over his hair and clothes.

'It must be wonderful to be like that,' Sophie said, half to herself.

'Like what?' Kate was enquiring.

'Oh, I don't know,' Sophie smiled. 'Oblivious of everyone . . . just pleasing yourself. You know what I mean.'

'Yes,' Kate said. 'You mean uninhibited. It's not always easy when there are other people to be considered, but it's what we should aim for.' She leaned forward suddenly. 'You haven't been brought up to throw off your inhibitions, Sophie, but sometimes it's the right thing to do.' She stood up. 'Now, I would like to go to the flea market.'

Sophie looked up at her. 'I love Paul, Granny.' For once Kate did not reprove her for the name. 'I love him but if I don't take this chance, I could live to regret it. What should I do?'

'I think you should make up your own mind, Sophie.' Kate's voice was gentle. 'You'll have to live with it so you must choose. I'd do anything for you – I hope you know that – but I can't make your decisions for you.'

There were dark caves of carpets and leather goods lining narrow streets that led to the Cours Saleya, a perfumed flower market for six days a week, the flea market on the seventh. The stalls of bric-a-brac stretched in every direction: jewellery, mirrors, pictures, scent bottles, bisque figurines . . .

'You're not going to go mad, I hope,' Sophie said, but Kate was already lost to the world, poking around in search of every antique dealer's dream, the unrecognised object of great value.

They came away with a bisque cherub, a silver *épèrgne* and two Imari plates, and went in search of a meal.

'I wish you weren't going,' Kate said, when they were settled at a table in sight of the sea.

Sophie nodded. 'Me too.'

Kate leaned forward and put out a hand to cover Sophie's. 'You know where I am if you need to talk – and I'll be home next week.'

Elizabeth had arranged flowers for a table centrepiece and made a special effort with the meal. As usual Geoffrey noticed the trouble she had gone to.

'This looks impressive,' he said. 'I haven't forgotten some important date, have I?' Elizabeth smiled and shook her head. 'Are we having guests?' he persisted and again she indicated, 'No.'

He smiled at her, then. 'I'm glad,' he said. 'Just the two of us. We can talk. I had some news today.'

'Good news?'

'That depends,' he said. 'I think it's good. Let me get a bottle of wine and then we'll discuss it.'

Elizabeth had cooked saddle of lamb with apricot stuffing, and broccoli and new potatoes. They talked inconsequentially until she brought in the fresh fruit salad and cream, and then Geoffrey cleared his throat. He was fidgeting with the condiments and she knew he must be nervous.

'Come on,' she said as lightly as she could. 'What's the big secret?'

'I've been offered early retirement; a very generous deal. It means I can leave in the New Year – earlier if the job goes to Alan, and I'll certainly be recommending him. How would you feel about having me at home?'

He was avoiding her eyes and Elizabeth was glad.

'It's up to you,' she said.

Geoffrey didn't look up but he persisted with his question.

'I didn't ask who it was up to, I asked how *you* felt about it.'

A week ago she would have known precisely how she felt: appalled. Now she honestly didn't know.

'I'm not sure,' she said slowly. 'I've been on my own at home for so long . . . except for holidays, of course. But we've always got on together then, and at weekends.'

'So you wouldn't mind?'

'Of course I wouldn't,' Elizabeth said, but the words sounded hollow to her and she could see, from Geoffrey's expression, that he thought so too. How would she cope with his retirement? They would be together twenty-four hours a day, seven days a week. I like him, she told herself fiercely. I like him, admire him . . . now I have the chance to make things up to him. For a second she wanted to speak out, express her gratitude, her affection even . . . but the words would not come.

It was Geoffrey who spoke, reaching for her hand as he

did so. 'You have been happy, haven't you? Have I made you happy?'

'You've been a good husband, Geoffrey. The best.' It was not a direct answer and they both knew it. I want to speak out, Elizabeth thought, but it's too late. I am walled up in silence.

'It seems a long time ago, doesn't it?' Geoffrey had released her hand and was moving the condiments again. 'The sixties, I mean.'

'The *Swinging* Sixties,' Elizabeth corrected. 'Not that I remember much swinging.'

'We were provincials.' Geoffrey was smiling. 'And the swinging was in the early sixties. We weren't old enough to swing. We belonged to the flower-power era.'

'Was it really a special decade?' Elizabeth was toying with her fruit salad, pushing aside pieces of peach and grape and apricot. 'I know fashion took off, and there was the pill . . . but I don't remember it being suffused with love and kindliness.' She shivered suddenly.

'You're not cold?' Geoffrey was concerned and she put out a hand to his.

'No. I was remembering Aberfan. That was about the time you proposed.'

'The second time I proposed, or the third. I was always proposing, I seem to remember. We talked about love a lot in those days, and there was more sex than there had been, according to the papers, although it passed me by. I'm not sure people are ever that different, not underneath. We conform to trends and we blame the politicians for making us selfish or lazy, but really we're our own men – or women. I used to kid myself I looked like John or Bobby Kennedy: the lords of Camelot!'

'And I wanted to look like Audrey Hepburn.'

'You did a bit,' he said loyally, and again Elizabeth felt a desperate urge to cry.

'You're an idiot,' she said. He had always been an idiot – a dupe, even – but what would have become of her without him?

'Let's drink a toast,' he said, raising his glass. 'Here's to retirement, if it comes off. We'll have to travel as much as we can afford. I'll never be able to fill my days unless we do.'

He fell silent then and she knew he was remembering the dog. She was remembering too . . . the vow she had made the day she married him, the pledge that if she could not give him love she would give him everything else. I will be a good wife, she had promised. Had she kept that vow?

'Coffee?' she said aloud, and made her escape to the kitchen.

It was growing dark when they returned the hire car and went back to the hotel to collect Sophie's bags. Over the sea the sky was pink around the edges and deep blue in the centre, and lights were springing up here and there on the promenade. They took a taxi to the airport and both women were silent on the way.

'What will you remember most?' Kate asked when they were seated in the restaurant-bar, sipping wine.

'The Corniche, I think. The cicadas, and the sight of Eze when I looked back, lit up like a jewel in the black sky. Oh, and the Rotonde at the Hotel Négresco; all those pink brocade chairs and life-size carousel horses. I could hardly drink my Irish coffee!'

'At fifty-six francs a cup, it's as well you did.' Kate was trying a joke to cover the parting, but neither of them laughed.

The airport was full of flowers, most of them lily-like, some strange and spiky. Soon they would announce the flight and it would be goodbye. I don't want to go, Sophie thought, and knew at once that it was not a longing for the Côte d'Azur that possessed her. It was a reluctance to go home and face up to life and decision.

'We'd better move.' Kate was gathering up her bag and sunglasses. They were walking through the restaurant doors when Sophie saw the tall man from the hotel in front of them.

'You're not leaving?' he said in mock horror. He was

carrying an Adidas bag and he saw her eyes flick to it. 'I've been to Paris on business. Where are you off to?'

'She's going home to London,' Kate said.

'Ah, I love London.' They all smiled at the old cliché and Sophie held out her hand.

'Hello and goodbye, Mr Dunbar.'

He was fumbling in a pocket. 'Take my card. When I'm in London I stay at the Marlborough, near Oxford Street. I'll be there next week if you've any free time.'

'He fancies you,' Kate said when they had taken their leave.

'Don't be silly,' Sophie replied through gritted teeth.

'You do it to me over Oliver,' Kate said. 'Still, no need to worry. You're not likely to see him again.'

Sophie's flight number was flashing its boarding gate. 'I love you, Sophie darling. Safe flight, and ring me when you get home.'

For a moment Sophie hesitated and then she was moving forward, turning again to wave, and her journey home had begun.

Kate closed her eyes as the cab sped back to the centre of Nice. She didn't open them again until they were on the Promenade des Anglais, the paragliders still in the air, like bright moths in the dusk. She thought of Sophie's face as she went into the departure lounge, clutching her duty frees and trying to wave at the same time. 'I honestly don't know what I'm going to do, Kate.' She had said that with her lips but her eyes had said, 'Help me.' Kate had wanted to say something wise and constructive, but nothing would come except, 'Don't forget how much we all love you.'

Sophie had asked about the past, about youth, and Kate had passed it off as best she could. She had said that it was grim, and that was true enough. But there had been so much more.

BOOK 4

———— • ————

KATE'S STORY

Sunderland
1945

23

Kate's ears were still thrumming to the noise of the machines when she came out of the factory gates. It was half past five and almost dark, but there was a mildness in the dusk that hinted at a spring not too far away. It was six months since 'black-out' had given way to 'dim-out' and the street lamps glowed above her as she walked to the bus-stop. There had been rejoicing when the lights came on again, even in a modified form. It was a visible sign that the end of the war was in sight, and that was something for which most people had worked and prayed for five long years.

Kate had been pleased, too, but not with an unalloyed pleasure. The war's end would mean a decision, and she was not ready to make it. Now, with Germany under attack on all sides and Japan devastated by air-raids, she was no nearer a solution. She took her place in the queue for the bus and leaned against the brewery wall. Her shoulders ached from operating a lathe all day, her fingers were calloused and sore at the tips, but it was her legs that were the worst. She smiled to herself in the darkness, remembering how she had belly-ached when she had first started hair-dressing: 'I'm on my feet all day, Mam,' she had wailed when she came home at night; but the salon had been a soft lie-down compared with a munitions factory.

'Going out tonight, Katie?' A girl with her hair bound up in a turban had joined her in an effort to dodge half the queue. There were angry mutterings from behind but the newcomer ignored them.

'I might,' Kate said. 'Depends how I feel. Are you?'

''Spect so.' The girl's name was Arlene, and since people thought she resembled Ann Sheridan, the 'oomph' girl, her face was made up like the film star. At night she wore her hair in curls on her forehead and swept up behind; by day it was skewered in metal curlers concealed in a headscarf turban. Her make-up was always immaculate. She took out a compact and checked it, putting up a forefinger to wipe the corners of her mouth and stroke an errant eyebrow into shape. 'It must be difficult for you,' she said, snapping the compact shut. 'I mean, you're only my age and you've got no social life.'

The realisation that she was spreading gloom and despondency occurred to her and she tried to redress the balance. 'Not that it won't be wonderful when your hubby comes home. And he will come home. They'll get the Japs before long, McArthur'll see to that, and then they'll all come out of the camps and fly back. There'll be some parties then, won't there?'

To Kate's relief, a bus loomed up, the tired faces of other factory hands pressed against the window. 'Room for three up top, two below,' the conductor said sternly. 'There's another bus behind.'

'Behind what?' a wag called out from the queue and Arlene shuffled on to the platform as the conductor put out a hand to bar Kate.

'That's me lot.' He pinged the bell and Arlene mouthed, 'Sorry,' as the bus pulled away. Kate slumped back against the wall, grieved to have missed the bus but relieved that there was no need to reply to her friend's question. If she had a party to mark the end of the war, would it be a fiesta or a wake?

It was twenty minutes before she got aboard a bus, and half-way through the journey before she got a seat. She slumped into it and opened her handbag. The watch Ben had given her was in there, zipped in the back compartment where no one else would see it. Ten past six. She had wanted to look special tonight, to take time over her appearance, maybe even get a bath if there was hot water, but she wouldn't manage it now.

She ran the few steps from the bus-stop to the corner house where she had been born and in which she had grown up. She had been married from it two and a half years ago, her jubilant father throwing pennies and halfpennies to the kids who had gathered round the door.

Why had she done it? As she ate the sausage and leek pudding her mother put in front of her, Kate tried to think of an answer. Because the whole country was wedding mad? That was part of it. It was patriotic to wed your lad before he went overseas, an affirmation that you expected him to survive and come home. And partly she'd done it because of the feeling it gave her of being grown-up. She had expected opposition from her parents, but their faces had simply glowed with pride when she told them, and later she had overheard her mother say, 'It's just what I'd've done in her place.'

Now, as she stood stripped to the waist, washing under-arms and breasts with a soapy facecloth, she thought of her husband. Jimmy Lucas had been the first of her classmates to get an errand boy's job at the Co-op. He had been promoted to counter-hand three months before his call-up and when he went away they had put a 'Good luck Jimmy' notice in the Co-op window. Kate had been proud to be his girl. He had taken her to the pictures, the double seats in the back row, and bought her ice-cream and held her damp hand in his wet one. He was three years older than she was and had freckles on the bridge of his nose like Van Johnson. The first time Kate had seen him in khaki she'd wanted to laugh. He didn't look like a soldier, he looked like a Co-op assistant masquerading inside a uniform two sizes too big. But once inside the uniform he had changed. He wanted more from her than holding hands.

'Let me love you, Katie. Let me do it. It'll be all right.' And then, when she resisted: 'I don't want to die without knowing what it's like.' She'd been too afraid to give way. Other girls in the street had done it, and she had seen the fruits of their sins. They went to a church home at the first showing and returned, empty-handed, seven months later, pale shadows of the girls they had been.

Jimmy had come home twice and begged for it, once almost threatening to take it by force. Then his embarkation leave had arrived and he had stood there twisting his forage cap in his freckled hands. 'I'm going overseas, Kate.' A week later they were married, she in a borrowed wedding dress and white silk shoes that kept falling off her feet. The wedding cake was a tiny square hidden inside a magnificent cardboard exterior. They had spent one night together in his sister's house, which was evacuated out of tact but still had lines of washing hanging from the pulley above their heads.

And then he was gone to war. Kate was seventeen years and two months old, and could scarcely believe she was someone's wife. She received one letter from New Delhi before he was posted to Burma, to reinforce Allied forces in the Mayu peninsula on the Bay of Bengal. In early May the fighting stopped with the monsoon, but it was too late for Pte Lucas, J. He was already a prisoner of the Japanese.

In her bedroom Kate looked at the photograph that stood on her dressing-table. There they were, looking bewildered, heads half bent to dodge confetti painstakingly cut from the coloured pages of magazines. In church she had given herself to him for better or for worse, but no one had said anything about in absence. For one night he had possessed her – taking her without preliminaries, putting a hand over her mouth when she would have cried aloud – doing it again and again, as though by sexual excess he could postpone the time when he must return to war.

He had kissed her gently enough at the station, apologetically even. 'It'll be different when I come home,' he'd said, and she'd answered, 'Of course it will,' with all the conviction she could muster. Now she stood in the bedroom, twisting the still-bright ring on her finger, trying to remember her husband's face. But all she could recall was the face of her lover, and the only touch she could remember was his touch.

Ben was waiting in the street when she got to Ranelagh Road. He had rented a room there, and she motioned to him to get inside before anyone could see him. They mounted the stairs to the first floor, giggling like the guilty children that they were, and then, as the door closed behind them, cast aside the things they were carrying to clasp one another and kiss and kiss until they were panting and laughing too much to continue.

'Put the kettle on,' he said, unfastening his greatcoat. 'I've got coffee, pineapple, sausages and muffins.'

They had met at the end of 1943, when Kate was still working in the salon, shampooing mostly for Louise, the stylist. It was Louise who had persuaded her to make up a foursome with two GIs. 'Come on, kid. You can't stay in night after night.' So she'd gone along reluctantly, to meet an equally reluctant blind date. They had danced and talked, and gradually reluctance had given way to warmth and then, a few months later, to love and sex. This time, however, she had wanted it for herself.

Now they made coffee and toasted muffins in front of the popping gas fire, feeding it with florins when the flame wavered and threatened to go out. And then, when they were talked-out and had eaten their fill, they climbed, naked, into the sagging bed, with its brass rails and faded chintzy eiderdown, and made gentle love. Afterwards, she stroked his body, feeling the faint fuzz of dark hair that covered it, the muscle and bone beneath, curving her finger into his waist and out again over his buttocks.

'You better hadn't go on,' he warned with a groan that begged her not to stop. Then they were fitting together again and he was lifting her and turning her so that she was above him and bracing herself on her arms so that he could put his mouth to her breast and complete the circle.

It was nine o'clock when they put on the kettle and tuned in to the news. Mandalay was back in British hands, taken by the Gurkhas and the Royal Berkshires. The US Pacific Fleet was continuing to bomb the Japanese mainland and Martin Bormann was exhorting the war-weary citizens of the Third Reich to rear up like werewolves and hurl back the advancing allies.

They fell silent then, Ben to thoughts of going home, Kate to thoughts of a homecoming. They drank the last of the coffee and washed up in a scarred, enamel bowl. It was a ritual, this tidying of the place they called home. The house was rented out in rooms; they could come and go without exciting too much interest, and the rent was only six and sixpence a week, which was chicken-feed to a Yank with money to burn.

Out in the dark street they checked carefully before they slipped into the back lane for one last kiss. 'We can't go on like this for ever, Katie.' Ben's lips were against her ear, his breath was warm in her hair. 'Sooner or later you've got to choose.'

'I can't,' she said. 'I can't choose, love, surely you can see that? We don't know what'll happen.'

That was when they drew away from one another, each knowing that what they were talking about was another man's survival or death.

24

THE NEWS, WHEN IT CAME on a May morning, was stark: 'The German radio has just announced that Hitler is dead. I'll repeat that.'

'That's it, then!' Kate's father said, thumping his fist on the table in triumph. 'It's as good as over.'

Within minutes, or so it seemed, people were making plans. Street parties, bonfires, American suppers where everyone would bring a plate of food; all these things were arranged as if by magic. Bunting appeared from nowhere, and where there was no bunting, people manufactured it from whatever came to hand.

The official announcement was made on the eighth of May. There was to be total German surrender. The King would speak to the nation, and so would Churchill. 'Good old Winnie's' name was on everyone's lips and everyone was laughing, even as they queued for food or buses.

Kate went into work, but no one felt like machining. They were dizzy with euphoria, awash with plans not just for a night of celebration but for the futures they could now look forward to with certainty. Only the people with either men still at the front or Japanese prisoners of war were silent. 'We don't count now,' one woman said bitterly. Her son was fighting in Burma and there had been no mention of an end to the war in the east. Kate nodded and tried to simulate a pain she could not truly feel.

Am I wicked? she thought. I don't wish Jimmy harm but I can't, in my heart of hearts, wish him home. She tried to summon up his face again, but nothing would come. There was only Ben's face. Ben, which was short for Benson: Benson H. Guyser. Ben laughing in a country lane; smiling in a dimly lit dancehall; Ben the lover, his face serious in the light of the gas fire. 'I love you, Katherine.' He was the only person who called her Katherine and he made it sound like a love song.

The woman interrupted her reverie. 'No one's thinking of you, Kath, with your man in Changi. They say it's a hell-hole. God knows what state he'll be in – if he makes it, God love him.' She had raised her voice and the group around them had fallen silent.

'Come on, Alice,' a girl said uncomfortably. 'No more air raids, no more bloody ration books . . . there'll be some nylons soon and not on the black market either. You can't blame us for being a bit pleased. Anyway,' she said, gaining confidence, 'they'll turn everything on the Japs now and blast the little buggers to hell. It won't last much longer, you'll see.'

'It won't last much longer.' They were fateful words. Kate told her mother she was going to visit her in-laws and made for Ranelagh Road as soon as she could, knowing Ben would come. He was rounding the corner as she reached the front door and he broke into a run at the sight of her. 'I knew you'd come,' she said, and he smiled to show that he thought her wise as well as beautiful. Once inside the room, he drew her down on the clippy mat that fronted the fire and took her hands in his.

'It won't last much longer,' Kate said despairingly.

'No, it won't,' Ben answered, but he spoke with conviction. 'Now that we can disengage in Europe it'll be all systems go in the Pacific, and then Jim will come home and we'll face him. We'll face him together. He'll understand. War changes things, Katherine. Everyone knows that.'

She allowed herself to be comforted and led to bed. Outside the sky was lit by victory bonfires and sounds of jubilation filled the air. Once, as his gentle fingers brought her to climax, she heard a laughing conga line pass beneath the window. Bells rang somewhere, the ringers rusty from lack of practice but doing their best.

And while they lay, contented, in one another's arms, he told her of his homeland, of the lovely old townships of New England, with their white wooden churches and houses. It was in New England, he told her, that the revolution which freed America from Britain had begun. There were families in his town descended from the pioneers, and others whose ancestors had taken part in the Civil War. 'We have our history too,' he teased her.

He promised to show her fall in Vermont; the glory of gold and crimson and brown. He told her that although the New England earth was stony, the region abounded in small waterfalls and woodland, and that until she had tasted cranberries from Cape Cod she hadn't lived. His home-state of Maine was famous for its potatoes and blueberry pie. 'You'll like America,' he said, and began to love her again.

Afterwards they went out into the street, for once unafraid of being seen together because on this night total strangers linked arms and no one cared. As they stood by the bonfire with its effigy of Hitler slowly succumbing to the flames, Kate saw a couple peel off from the crowd and make for a shop doorway. When she passed by them with Ben she heard the girl moaning in ecstasy and the boy, in khaki, grunting with effort. As she turned at the far end of the street to look back, she saw them emerge, shame-faced, and go their separate ways.

She let herself into the house and tidied her appearance in the kitchen mirror before she went through to the living-room. Her parents were seated on either side of the fire, and for once the wireless was silent. She was aware of an atmosphere as soon as she entered the room.

'How were they, then?' her mother asked, too casually.

Kate knew something was dreadfully wrong but she was in a corridor now, like the beast in the abbatoir, no other way to go but forward.

'They were fine. Pleased, you know, but wondering . . . '

'Wondering?' Her mother savoured the word, glancing at her husband to see if he too was relishing the situation. 'I bet they were wondering – wondering what you were doing sitting round there on their step while they were round here waiting for you. They've just gone.'

Kate looked down at her feet, waiting for further onslaught.

'Come on, then,' her father said. He was sitting like a judge, his feet planted in front of him and his hands curled round the ends of the arms of his chair.

'Come on what?' It was all she could think of to say but it brought her father half out of his chair, one hand raised to strike her.

'Now then, Dad,' her mother said, and stopped him in his tracks. Her hands, too, were folded in front of her in judgemental fashion. 'That won't help.' She looked at her daughter, her mouth curled in disdain. 'You might as well speak up, Katherine.' The use of her proper name struck home to Kate as nothing else would have done. Her mother never called her Katherine; always Kath or Katie.

'I went to Emma's.'

'Don't lie.' Her mother's tone was like a whip. 'If you were going round Emma's, why lie? Why say you were going to see Jim's folks if you were only popping to Emma's? Whatever you've been doing, miss, it wasn't innocent.' There was a long pause before her mother spoke again. 'You've got another man, haven't you?'

For a moment Kate contemplated lying, but it would have been useless so she said nothing.

'My God,' her father said. 'My God . . . and a decent lad penned up in a camp suffering Lord knows what. My daughter – Christ Almighty!'

At any other time her mother would have jumped down her father's throat for such blasphemy. Now she stayed silent

222

until the ticking of the clock seemed to take over the shabby kitchen, growing more deafening with each beat.

'Get out of my sight!' her father said at last. He sounded suddenly weary and he turned from her to look first at the fire and then to lean forward and riddle it vigorously with the brass poker. Kate, relieved to be released, turned away. She was almost at the door when her mother spoke.

'It's not a Yank, is it? Just tell me that. All I ask is that it's not a bloody Yank!'

Kate kept on moving, leaving her mother to construe her silence as best she might. Mounting the stairs she could hear the jollity in the street, singing and shouting and the occasional handbell, all of it in celebration of a victory. There was no victory for her; instead, all she held dear was slipping away. If she stuck by Jim, she would lose Ben. If she went with her lover, as she longed to do with every fibre of her being, no decent person, especially her parents, would ever look at her again.

25

THERE WERE ASTERS PEEPING THROUGH the churchyard railings and the August sky was cloudless. Kate's legs were bare and her feet squelched with sweat inside her canvas sandals. She stared up at the sky, wondering what a mushroom cloud would look like. That was all anyone talked about nowadays: the atom bomb and the mushroom cloud. It was a week since the first bomb had gone down on Hiroshima and four days since the second one had fallen on Nagasaki. 'They'll have to give in now,' her father had said, but the Japanese had not given in. There were tales of mass hara-kiri, of extermination in the camps; and with each tale Kate saw reproach in her parents' eyes as they remembered V.E. night and the row over Ben.

She shivered, remembering the icy, hate-filled days that had followed. Her parents could not leave it alone, picking at it like a scab whenever she came into sight. 'A Yank, a bloody Yank,' her father said each time. 'Not even proper men – they get a bleeding medal for shooting a gun. Did you know that? A fancy ribbon for their fancy uniforms. Paper soldiers!'

'Buying people!' That was her mother's contribution. 'With their cigarettes and their chocolates and their nylon stockings. It's bribery and corruption, and my daughter fell for it.'

'He's not like that,' Kate wanted to say, but words were useless in the face of such prejudice. She had her own misgivings about GIs. They were overpaid, tossing money around like water. And she didn't like their attitude to their black fellow-soldiers; Ben's arm would come protectively around her each time there was a negro soldier in sight, as though all black men were predators. But Ben was basically good and didn't deserve the abuse her parents heaped upon him. In the end she had pretended to beg their forgiveness and had promised never ever to see Ben again. 'It wasn't really anything, Mam. Just someone to go to the pictures with. He's got someone back in the States, so he doesn't want to get involved either.' They had neither of them forgiven her the disgrace of having a daughter who had betrayed her marriage when her man was suffering for King and country; but there was now an uneasy truce, as long as she kept talking of plans for her future with Jim.

'I'm going to make it all up to him, Mam. The years he's lost and everything.' How did you make up for being a faithless wife? Where could she find the answer to that? 'Anyway, when I can leave the factory I'll look for somewhere to live. If they take me back at the salon we'll be able to manage – there's our post-war credits – so one way and another we can afford to get a place. It'll be nice to make a home for him, although I expect he'll need a lot of attention at first. I know I was wrong – well, daft – but it vas the wondering all the time about Jim. It got me down.

'I know it's been hard,' her mother conceded, 'but if you do what's right, it works out in the end.'

Would it work out? Kate turned the corner and saw the salon where she had worked until she was drafted into the factory. When she had started there in 1939, it had been smart: paintwork gleaming, windows masked with blindingly white nets, portraits of ladies with their hair permed by Eugene on every wall. Now it looked like the rest of Britain; shabby, weary and down at heel. The war was almost over; six years of deprivation and danger. For most people that would mean the return of happiness. What would it mean for her?

Her father had just entered the kitchen when she arrived home and her mother was standing there, a tea-towel pressed against her lips, her eyes wide. 'The scaffolding should've been secured to the bulkhead,' her father was saying. 'There's a hole in the deck for the welders to climb through to get down into the lube-oil sump for the final welds. There's two skins to the ship – double bottoms – and the welders crawl between them, lugging their tools with them. They take an extractor pipe, an' all, to take the fumes off while they're lying there. It's only a foot and a half high, mebbe less.'

'So what happened?' her mother said. Her father shrugged. 'He took a wobbler, that's what happened. Many a one's done that in the double bottoms. It's pitch black if your light fails, and the noise is hellish . . . booming and screeching from the burners and caulkers. Reverberation, that's what does it. He blacked out, likely, and the fumes got him.'

'What's happened? Kate asked.

'Miller's lad's gone.'

'The one on the corner?'

'That's right.'

Her mother had subsided into a chair as her father shrugged himself out of his dungarees and made for the sink. He tucked in the neck of his shirt, the exposed skin white against the weatherbeaten neck, and then rolled up his flapping shirt-sleeves. His elbows were pink and crinkled above the muscular forearms as he splashed and grunted over the sink, blowing his nose between forefinger and thumb and then splashing it with water. 'Right,' he said from the folds of the striped towel, 'Where's me tea?'

There was neck-end of lamb stewed with barley – a rare treat. For a while the room was silent except for the scrape of knife and fork and the guzzling sound of Kate's father sucking the bones.

'Hoy the wireless on, lass,' he said, when the bones were picked clean. 'Let's see if the Nips've given in yet.'

There was no more up-to-date news than they had heard already, but rumours about the effects of the atom bomb were rife. People had turned to ash standing up, it was said, so that the bombed cities were a forest of upright corpses! Birds had shrivelled in the air and fallen as cinders to the ground! There was no one left alive in Japan, no one at all, but even if that were true, it seemed unreal compared to the death of the Miller boy.

'It's bound to shorten things,' her mother said.

'Bound to,' her father agreed.

Kate knew she was expected to look pleased, and she tried her best. Last night she had knelt on the cold lino and begged God to bring all prisoners home fit and healthy, and her fervour had been sincere. She wanted Jim to live, but she wanted him to have grown away from her as she had from him and be over the moon to be set free. Lots of men had come back from France completely changed. You heard stories every day.

'I'll make the tea,' she said now and pushed back her chair. She was warming the pot, turning it round and round so that the hot water reached every part, when there was a knock at the door. Her mother went to open it.

'This is nice,' she said, flashing a warning glance over her shoulder before ushering in the callers. 'Beattie! George! Come away in. We haven't seen you for a while. Our Kate's just making tea. Sit yourselves down.'

It was Jim's parents, his mother in the black coat and hat she habitually wore, a patterned scarf folded across her chest and tucked inside her collar. Mr Lucas had taken off his cap and was twisting it backwards and forwards in his hands.

'Mam. Dad.' Kate gave them their courtesy titles and reached for the best cups. You couldn't sit in-laws down to mugs. 'Nothing wrong, is there?' she asked as they slid uneasily on to upright chairs at the kitchen table.

'We wondered if you'd had any news,' Mrs Lucas said. 'It's awful this waiting; this not knowing. It'd be different if we were next of kin, but as it is we're depending on you telling us.'

'Our Kate'll come straight round as soon as she hears anything,' her father said, entering into the conversation. 'You can depend on that, George. Not that Kate wouldn't do it off her own bat, but we'd see to it, Maisie and me. We'd do it for any lad in the services, never mind family.'

'We know.' Jim's father was apologetic. 'We know you would. It's just that it gets us down, him being an only one and so forth.'

'Get your tea,' Kate said, pushing forward their cups. 'It can't be much longer now.'

'We were thinking . . . ' her mother-in-law began. 'We did wonder . . . ' Now the real reason for their visit was emerging.

'The thing is,' her husband said, 'you'll need a place. When Jim comes home, I mean. You'll get your own house eventually but in the meantime . . . '

'And he has a chance to need a lot of attention.' Mrs Lucas was picking up her cup and putting it down again, only to lift it a moment later. 'We've got the space. You could have your own room. We wouldn't interfere. We'd just like to have him back with us for a bit, while he gets built up.'

'You're sure to want him with you, it's only natural,' Kate's mother said. 'Not that he wouldn't be welcome here, but, as you say, you've got a three-bedroom house.'

'We thought we'd paper,' Mrs Lucas said. She looked towards Kate. 'You could choose it, anything you like.'

'Anything you can get your hands on, more like,' Kate's mother said matter-of-factly. 'Paper and paint's only for war damage, so they say.'

'It can be wangled,' Mrs Lucas said, 'if you've got a bob or two.'

They were all looking at Kate, all waiting.

'I wouldn't mind coming to you,' Kate said. 'For a while, anyway.'

It all seemed unreal, so it didn't matter what she said. She glanced at the clock; quarter to seven. She was meeting Ben at half past, so she would have to get them out of here. 'I'll walk round with you when you go,' she offered, and heard her father's soft intake of pleasure that he would soon have his house to himself.

They talked about decorating while walking back to Jimmy's old home, and about what would be needed to build someone up when they'd been on starvation rations for a long time.

They made an uneasy procession, Mr Lucas bringing up the rear, Kate walking alongside Jim's mother in front.

'I won't interfere, Kate. You're his wife now, but it would mean a lot to me to have Jim back in his own room for a month or two. I've already put the word about the place. It's no use looking to the council, they'll be swamped with people coming back from the front and getting wed, not to mention them as was bombed out, and evacuees. No, you'll have to go for a couple of rooms somewhere, but we won't hurry you.'

Kate felt a crazy desire to laugh aloud. All this planning, and there might not be a reunion, any nest-building, or any marriage at all to be accommodated anywhere. Instead she said, 'It'd be nice to get some wallpaper. Not that your house isn't lovely, but a fresh start would be a good thing.'

'You'll get your paper, and he'll get what he needs to build him up. I've got a cupboard full of Dorsella already, and Bert's boss can get butter and eggs from a farm Bishop Auckland way. We'll not be able to go too fast. He'll've been hungry for so long his stomach won't take it. Little and often, that'll be the ticket.'

There was silence for a while, and Kate realised the other woman was weeping silently, tears rolling down her face. 'It'll be like when he was a little babby, spooning goodness into him.' She turned suddenly and clutched Kate's arm. 'I won't interfere, but I love him. You understand, don't you?'

Before Kate could reassure her, a voice came from behind. 'Now then, mother, if you're going to take on like this you'll have Kate changing her mind.'

'No,' Kate said, 'I want you to look after him. I'm depending on you – on you helping.'

229

She tried not to sound too relieved but it wasn't easy to hide jubilation when a heaven-sent solution had fallen into your lap. Jim would come home to loving arms, and in a while he would meet another girl and be happy again.

'I won't come in, if you don't mind,' Kate said when they reached the Lucas doorstep. 'I've promised to baby-sit for a friend. Her man's home on leave, so they're having a night out.'

'It'll be your turn soon,' Mrs Lucas said, blowing her nose on a white hanky. 'Nights out – and a babby and all, in good time.'

Both of them embraced Kate before she turned away, and she smiled bravely into their faces, all the while feeling both treacherous and overjoyed.

She ran the half-mile to Ranelagh Road and fell into Ben's arms on the landing. 'I love you,' she said. 'I love you,' as if to re-affirm that this was real. This was what mattered in the end.

They shuffled rather than moved, into the bedroom, arms still entwined. 'Hey,' Ben said, smiling down at her. 'What's brought this on?' But when she looked up into his face she saw that his eyes were wary, his mouth sad.

'What's up?' she said. 'Just tell me.'

He hesitated only a moment. 'I'm being posted,' he said at last. 'They're sending me to Burtonwood.'

They went to bed, not so much out of lust as a desire to assuage their fears. They made love violently, and then a second time, more gently, glad of the noise from the wireless to drown their passion. Ben made tea afterwards and served it with sugared doughnuts from the PX. The time to go home came and went, but Kate was suddenly reckless. She was a married woman, after all, and tomorrow – when retribution would have to be faced – was a long way away.

They were lying in one another's arms, their bodies sticky with love, their mouths rimmed with sugar from the doughnuts, when the announcer introduced the Prime

Minister, the Right Honourable Clement Attlee. The mild, precise tones of the nation's leader told them that Japan had surrendered unconditionally, and the world war was at an end.

26

KATE'S MOTHER CONTEMPLATED THE TABLE, sparsely spread for Sunday dinner. 'You'd never think the war was over,' she said. 'I thought things would go back to normal. I didn't bargain for them getting worse. The Germans are getting our food now; it doesn't seem right!'

The meagre British ration had been cut to provide food for the starving people of liberated Europe, and the Germans, too, were benefiting. The situation had not been helped by America's abrupt cancelling of the Lease-Lend programme a week after the Japanese surrender. Churchill had called it 'grave and disquieting'. Kate's father's verdict was harsher: 'The Yanks don't care if we starve to death now. They don't need us any more. They'd rather suck up to the Germans.'

'We can't leave Europe hungry,' Kate said listlessly. She didn't care what happened to some far-off people, Germans or not, so acute was her own misery with Ben being far away; but you couldn't just leave people to starve. That would make you no better than the Nazis.

'That's all very well,' her mother was not about to give way, 'but sausage for a Sunday dinner. Sausage! My mam must be turning in her grave. We were supposed to be poor, but we always managed a joint on a Sunday.'

There were one and a half sausages each for the women, and two for Kate's father, with potatoes and swedes and a lump of suet pudding flavoured with leeks and covered in Oxo gravy. They were all careful not to mention the reports of the cruelty, filth and malnutrition in Japanese camps revealed in that morning's papers. Prisoners were ill or dying from having to eat rice and grass. Many of the men had dysentery as a result of the filthy conditions in which they had been housed, and there were harrowing tales of brutal Korean guards keeping the sick men working for eighteen hours a day. Instead, Kate's family talked of Rudolf Hess's forthcoming trial, of the temporary shortage of Bile Beans, and the new film at the Plaza, *Blithe Spirit*, which was apparently the funniest thing for years. Anything except the fact that thirty-six thousand Allied prisoners were awaiting liberation from Japanese camps.

'I'd better be going,' Kate said, when the dishes were dried and stacked away. 'I said I'd be round at the Lucases' about two o'clock.' Her mother was wiping down the bench, rinsing out the dish cloth and squeezing it before folding it neatly into half and draping it over the taps.

'Yes,' she said slowly. 'Yes, you'd better get off.' But something more was coming and Kate knew it. Her mother looked at her and then turned away before she spoke. 'What are you going to do about things?'

As if by mutual agreement they each pulled out a chair, the same chairs they had tucked under the table moments before. Her mother sat down heavily and put her elbows on the table. Kate insinuated herself into her seat and waited. 'How do you mean?' she asked.

'It's got to stop, our Kate.' Her mother had ignored the question, knowing her daughter knew exactly what she meant. 'I know it's still going on, whatever you may say. I've always known, if I'm honest. I suppose I thought it might stop without me interfering, but it's *got* to stop now. Your man's coming back, Kate; you'll get word any day. You'd be the talk of the place if you let him down. Any road, whether or not you care what people say, you can't turn your back on a lad that fought for his country.'

Kate put her hands to her face, her little fingers either side of her nose, her fingers and thumbs supporting her chin. She did not speak until her mother said, 'Well?' And then again, 'Well, Katie?'

Kate stood up, pushing back the chair so that the legs scraped on the flagged floor. 'It'll be all right, Mam, don't worry. It's going to be fine.' But in her heart she knew she could no more give up Ben than fly. Her conviction that she could leave Jimmy to his mother had faltered a little, but that still didn't mean she would be doing it herself.

There was an air of excitement abroad as she walked the half-mile to her mother-in-law's house. Several people were scraping off the black paint that had obscured their windows for the black-out. Others were dismantling the Anderson shelters that had taken root in their gardens six years before. Some upturned sheet of corrugated iron were already uprooted and lay scattered about, oddly puny-looking now that they were exposed and free of their covering of earth.

When she reached the Lucas house she pushed open the outer door, left ajar on a summer day, and called, 'Cooee,' to give notice of her presence. Her mother-in-law appeared in the doorway that led to the living-room, carpet slippers on her bare feet, her finger held to her lips.

'Sh,' she said. 'Dad's having a lie-down. He had a bad night, worrying over our Jimmy, so I said you'd understand. Besides, it gives us a chance to talk.' Her eyes were anxious as she looked at Kate. 'Come on in and sit yourself down. I've got the kettle on the hob.'

There was silence as she lifted the kettle on to the flames and waited for it to boil. Once the tea was scalded and poured she sat opposite Kate and sipped. 'That's nice,' she said. 'Nothing like a cup of tea.'

Kate murmured agreement and sipped too, feeling the tension between them as each of them wondered how to broach the subject that concerned them both: the future.

'You'll be leaving the factory soon,' the older woman said at last.

'I expect so.'

'You'll need to, when Jim comes home.'

Kate put down her cup. 'I'm going back to work in the salon, if they'll have me.'

Across from her, the other woman's face registered surprise. 'You're going back to hairdressing? How will you manage? Not that I won't lend a hand, and Dad. But it's you the lad'll want. I don't see how you'll manage, if you're working.'

'We'll need the money,' Kate said, trying to quell her panic. 'We'll want a place of our own eventually, and Jim'll likely need time before he goes back to work.' She had no intention of going back to the salon, but she had to kill the idea that she would be there twenty-four hours a day for Jimmy.

'Some of those men will never work,' her mother-in-law said gloomily. 'I can't listen to some of the tales – or watch the pictures.'

'We know Jimmy's okay,' Kate said encouragingly. 'They'd've said if there was anything really wrong.' She was not sure this was true. The bare missive from the War Office had simply stated that Pte Lucas, J, No.10554007, was alive and in Allied hands.

'Have you seen the paper?' The older woman's voice was suddenly anguished. 'It says the camps were hell-holes. The article is in again today.'

'Well, it's over now,' Kate said. 'It's over, and when we get Jim home we'll make it up to him.' She felt her own hypocrisy rise up in her throat, threatening to choke her.

'How long do you think it'll be before he's back?'

'I don't know,' Kate said. 'They say there's nearly forty thousand to get home, and some of them'll need hospital ships so it can't happen overnight. But they'll try, Mrs Lucas. You can bet they'll do the best they can.' Again she tried to fill her tone with a conviction that she did not feel. How else could you speak to an anxious mother?

On her way home she tried to work out what an anxious *wife* should feel, but it eluded her. On an impulse she turned into the dark doorway of the Catholic church, for Catholic churches were open day and night.

She had come into this church once before, when guilt threatened to overwhelm her. No one had taken any notice of her then, and it was the same today. She sat at the back of the church, watching the air quiver above the smoking candles until she was almost mesmerised by it, occasionally saying the Lord's Prayer or reciting 'Gentle Jesus, meek and mild', more often pleading with God to let it be all right. She didn't want to hurt anyone; on the other hand, she had a right to be happy the same as anyone else, hadn't she? The plaster faces of the saints were impassive; no hint of an answer there. In the end she bowed to the altar and slipped back into the sunlit street.

They had bubble and squeak for tea, potato and cabbage fried up together till it had a crisp brown crust on it. The meal was topped off with a piece of fatless sponge that tasted and smelled of liquid paraffin.

'I'm just going upstairs for a bit,' Kate said when everything was tidied away. Her mother's eyes were already closing as she sat down in her easy chair, but she managed to nod and Kate tip-toed up to her room.

She wanted Ben, needed to go to him now; but he was on the other side of the country at Burtonwood air base. She took out his last letter, written to her care of her charge-hand at the factory. 'I am coming to you soon, Kate. I need you so much I can hardly think sometimes, except that we have to be together one day and mustn't hurt Jim in the process. Everything will be clearer once he gets home and we can see the way ahead. I promise I'll come soon and take a room in a hotel. Pick one out ready. I want to hold you in my arms again and see that funny face of yours and call you "Babe", which always gets you mad. Oh, Katie, I wish I was back in Durham and we were together now.'

On the chest of drawers her wedding photo looked solemnly down at her. Who was the girl in that picture? It couldn't be her. She didn't feel married at all, much less the wife of one soldier and the mistress of another. She stretched out on the bed, the letter clutched to her chest, and cried then, for herself, for the two men and for the utter hopelessness of it all.

She must have slept when the crying was over for when she woke up the clock on the bedside table said seven o'clock. She got to her feet and went to the dressing-table. Her eyes were a bit puffy, but it was nothing that couldn't be explained away. Outside she could hear mothers calling children in from play, somewhere a wireless was playing; far off, a bell was calling worshippers to church. That was the real world, a place where decent people behave decently. She stood, looking out, her hands on the sill, until she heard her mother calling from below.

Kate came out on to the landing and leaned over the banister. 'What is it, Mam? I'm still busy up here.'

'Come down,' her mother said excitedly. 'Edie's brought a letter round, a government letter. It went to her's by mistake and she only got back tonight. It's postmarked Tuesday, so it's lain there for days.'

The OHMS envelope was brown and forbidding. The letter it contained was brief.

We regret to inform you that your husband, Pte J. Lucas, is unfit to travel and has been hospitalised in Australia for medical treatment. Further information will be forwarded as soon as it becomes available. Any communications on this matter should be addressed to the above.

So it was going to go on: the uncertainty. Kate handed the letter to her mother without speaking and walked out into the garden, where her father's vegetables stood row upon row. Above her, birds sped by on homebound wings. An evening hush was falling.

'Don't worry, pet. They'll get him better.' Her father had come up behind her, clearing his throat as he always did when uncertain of what to say.

Kate turned to him. 'I know, Dad. I'm sure they'll fix him up. They're clever.'

But even as she spoke aloud, she begged silent forgiveness for thinking, fleetingly, how much easier life would be if the clever doctors did not succeed.

27

IT WAS THE FIRST LONG train journey of Kate's life, and she felt scared as she settled into a window-seat to wave to her parents-in-law, standing anxiously on the platform. She had only been in the huge, echoing Sunderland station three or four times, and their offer to see her on to her train had been a godsend. Now Mrs Lucas moved forward to mouth through the glass, 'Tell Jimmy we love him.'

Kate nodded and mouthed back, 'I will.' It was Mr Lucas's turn then. He had already checked that she had her travel warrant and money for refreshments, but he still worried. 'Ask an MP to help you when you get to King's Cross.' Kate nodded, knowing she would never have the courage to approach a military policeman, who would be at least seven feet tall and forbidding in his red cap and huge boots. There were clouds of steam escaping from the train, and she prayed that it meant they would be under way soon so that this embarrassment would be over, but it was five minutes before the ordeal ended, time for many more exhortations and promises. Then the train was moving, and the anxious faces on the platform passed slowly from view.

Kate settled back in her seat, suddenly conscious that there had been no time for breakfast and the churning in her stomach was as much hunger as nerves. As they passed through Grangetown and Ryhope and she glimpsed the sea on her left, she unwrapped the first of the greaseproof-paper parcels provided by both mother and mother-in-law, and bit into a sandwich. It was cold black pudding and quite delicious. For the first time, she felt a small sense of adventure.

She was going to a London hospital to see Jimmy, who had been brought back from Australia but who was still in need of skilled care. Her trip had been arranged by the Army welfare authorities in every little detail, but Kate had added one small feature of her own: before she boarded her homebound train, she would be reunited with Ben. She licked in the last crumbs of the sandwich and decided to splash out on another, to get the day off to a good start.

The journey was long, nearly five hours, and eventually the excitement of each new station, thronged with service personnel from every Allied country, ceased to compensate for the boredom of the countryside in between. The guard, once he knew that she was the wife of a wounded serviceman, was kind and attentive, getting her tea from a WVS trolley at Doncaster and telling her to, 'Cheer up,' at Peterborough. 'It won't be long now, lass.'

Kate had felt confident of her ability to get to the tube station, armed with her official itinerary, but the sheer bustle of the platform as the train disgorged stopped her in her tracks. She stood, heart hammering at the ribs, fear drying in her mouth, until the guard reappeared and handed her into the care of two Redcaps. 'See to this one, will you? She's out of her depth here.'

Kate tried to look like a soldier's wife and square up to her challenge, until the older Redcap winked at her. 'It's a madhouse, this place, missus. I'm from Newcastle. Follow me.'

They put her on the tube with instructions to count off the stations until she alighted at her destination, Holloway Road. She felt heartened by his addressing her as 'missus', which seemed more respectful than 'lass', and managed to get herself out of the tube and along to the hospital, breathing a sigh of relief at being out of the bowels of the earth, where a hundred tons of earth and concrete could descend on you at any moment.

In the large redbrick hospital she followed the signs in the corridors, her nose twitching at the unaccustomed smell of antiseptic, her mouth becoming dry once more at the prospect of what was to come. However hard she tried, she couldn't remember her husband's face. Even when she stared at the photo in her handbag, it passed from her memory as soon as the bag snapped shut. And yet she had known Jimmy Lucas almost all her life, so why now did he seem like a stranger?

All her fears were reinforced when she was directed to his bedside by a slim, fresh-faced nurse in the uniform of St John. The gaunt man with the yellowed face was of a different generation to the fresh-faced boy who had so assaulted her on her wedding night. This man could hardly lift a hand to touch her hand when she offered it.

'Jimmy?' She bent to kiss the bony forehead. 'How are you?' The words were sterile and they brought forth only a slight shake of his head. She looked around for support but there was no one. She was on her own.

She turned to pull a chair up to the bedside and sat down, lifting her hat from her head and patting her hair back into place. 'Your mam sends her love. And your dad. And my mam and dad.' Her mind scurried hither and thither seeking something to say . . . anything! 'It's lovely to have you back, Jimmy. We'll soon get you home, once you're well enough, once you get built up.'

His lips were moving and a light had come into his eyes. She waited for his first words, part of her mind wondering if what he said would change things, make choices easier, or even sacrifice possible. And then it came: 'Any news about the team?' he said, referring to his pre-war passion, the Sunderland football club. That was all. A question about the club!

After that it was easier to talk about mundane things;

bomb damage in their hometown, her future at the factory, his parents and hers, the boys and girls with whom they had gone to school, scattered by the war and returning one by one to a Sunderland at peace.

Kate felt peaceful too. She had felt it descend upon her when he had uttered those fateful words, 'Any news about the team?' She was not the hub of his existence. She could slip away with Ben, leaving him to his mam and his mates and his Saturday at the match, and in time he would hardly remember she'd ever existed. She looked around the ward, noticing that some of the beds were surrounded by animated visitors, while others had only one or two silent relatives in attendance and the figure in the bed was hushed and still.

'I wish I could stay a bit longer,' she said when it was time to leave, 'but I've got to get back home for work. Besides . . . ' She didn't need to say it was impossible to stay on her own in this city. They both knew it.

'We'll be shipping him out next week,' the sister told her, appearing at Jim's bedside, her white cap flaring either side of her head, the proud insignia of the QAs pinned to her breast. 'He'll go to your nearest emergency hospital. Is there one near you?'

'A few miles away,' Kate said, smiling cheerily to show she could hardly wait. It was true; the sooner Jim was home and fit again, the sooner she would be free. She turned back to the bed. 'See, Jim, you'll be home in no time, and then we'll be with you every day.'

She kissed his mouth before she left, because he puckered up his lips and closed his eyes in anticipation.

'Don't expect too much at first,' the sister said as she walked Kate to the ward door. 'Now, turn and give him a wave. Don't spin it out. He's not up to it.'

On the tube train back into the city centre Kate cried, tears of relief, tears of remorse. Jim had been to Hell and back, and she had betrayed him. There were no two ways about it: she was a traitor. But it would all work out in the end. She would have to make that final decision, the choice; but Jim would benefit from it too. He deserved more than life with a woman who loved another man.

She was meeting Ben in a chapel in a place called South Audley Street, which he had said was in 'the American section', near Grosvenor Square. She couldn't work out how there could be an 'American section' in the capital city of England, but when she emerged from the tube exit at Hyde Park Corner and neared her destination, carefully following the directions Ben had sent her, she saw that the pavements were thronged with GIs, most of them with a dazzling blonde or an equally dazzling brunette on their arm.

The chapel in South Audley Street was surprisingly unpretentious for such a posh area. The houses surrounding it were huge and imposing but the chapel was small, not even as big as the Catholic church in Sunderland, and half the size of the C of E church. It was empty, too, and she slipped into a pew, kneeling down and bowing her head in prayer, before sitting back to gaze around her. The stone-flagged chapel was decorated in white and gold, shabby but distinctive, contrasting with dark oak pews. 'It's plain but it's beautiful,' she thought, looking at the arched window behind the altar through which she could see a tree in full leaf.

And then Ben was there, slipping into the pew beside her, bowing his head on his hand briefly before he reached for her hand and enclosed it in his own warm palm.

'I was afraid you wouldn't come.' They spoke in unison, and then they were both laughing and he was leading her out into the sunshine and raising a hand to bring a cab gliding to the kerb. He threw an address at the driver before he climbed in and then, as the cab pulled away, he took Kate in his arms and kissed her until her navy felt hat fell backwards off her head and she caught sight of the cabbie's amused eyes in the rear-view mirror.

They ate in a tiny café in a teeming street. The tables were close together, the place unbearably crowded, but the food was wonderful. 'Where do they get it from?' Kate asked in wonderment, but Ben only tapped his nose and closed an eye. 'Ask no questions,' he said. 'Just eat.'

When the meal was over and she had unbuttoned the top of her skirt to accommodate it, she told him about the visit to Jimmy. 'So you see, it'll be all right. I have to see him settled in, let him get his strength back, but after that . . . ' She was gazing into his eyes now. 'If you still want me . . . '

'Hush,' he said. 'Don't be foolish, Katherine. I can hardly get through the days without you as it is.'

They wandered the streets when they left the restaurant, dodging into doorways when they found a shop already closed for the evening to kiss and kiss again and pledge undying love.

'We've got to find somewhere, Katherine,' Ben said at last. 'I'm going crazy here. Let's take a room.'

'I've got to be on the train.' It was half past six and the minutes were ticking away.

'Say you missed it. Stay, Katherine . . . for God's sake, say you'll stay.'

'I can't,' she said, thinking of the accusing faces back at home. 'They know I've no money for hotels.' She thought for a moment. 'What time's the last train?'

He went into a phone booth and emerged, beaming. 'There are trains all night. You can leave when you like.'

The hotel was a large house with a huge wrought-iron staircase, and their room was on a corner with windows on both sides. They drew the heavy curtains and turned on the plopping gas fire, and then they made love, holding back each time they felt a climax approaching because this moment must be made to last. 'Hush,' he said, laughing, his eyes wild with pleasure. She had thrown back her head and moaned with relief, so that it seemed the whole hotel would hear. Then it was his turn to ride to fulfilment. Afterwards they lay talking quietly, limbs entwined, until it was time to dress and take a sorrowful road to the station and inevitable parting.

'It won't be for long.'

'Hardly any time at all.'

'I love you.'

'So do I.'

Now the train was pulling out of the vaulted station, and she was pressing her face to the window so that none of the other passengers should see her cry.

She slept after Doncaster, when the press of passengers eased and she could lie along the seat and close her burning eyes. There would be an inquisition when she got home, but she could plead ignorance of London. As the train rocked her to sleep she wondered if perhaps it was all a dream and she would wake up in bed at home, a schoolgirl again having nightmares about a war that would carry her from home to a city where she would commit adultery in a second-rate hotel with a foreigner who was not her husband. It would have been the scenario of a nightmare in those far-off, pre-war days. Now it felt less unreal by the minute. She bunched up her coat to make a pillow and closed her weary eyes.

28

KATE AWOKE TO THE SOUND of 'Hark the Herald Angels Sing'. In the street below, the Sally Army was blasting out carols. They came every Christmas morning, had done for as long as she could remember. In a moment they would rap on the front door and her mother would answer, coppers at the ready. There was something comforting about the ritual, repeated every year for as long as she could remember, and Kate snuggled down for a few precious minutes before the most confusing Christmas day of her life began.

She heard 'O Little Town of Bethlehem' and then 'O Come All Ye Faithful' dying away as the bandsmen moved on. It was time to get up and face her responsibilities.

The alarm clock showed eight fifteen. In three-quarters of an hour her father-in-law would roll up in a borrowed car, ready for the journey to the emergency hospital where Jimmy lay in a metal bed, his face still yellow from the Addison's disease that had affected him, his eyes wide as a bush-baby's in a wasted face. It would be her third visit to his bedside in one hospital or another, and still she could not look him in the eye.

She washed in cold water, peeling her vest down to her waist to wash under her arms and breasts, tucking it up to wash her bottom and thighs. She wiped her feet and between her toes with a soapy flannel, aware that she was performing some kind of purification ritual but uncertain of why. Last night she had dreamed of Ben, an erotic dream from which she had awoken guilty but satisfied.

Downstairs there was toast and dripping waiting, and a mug of yellow tea. 'It's only Puroh,' her mother said. 'There's no milkman today.' And then, belatedly, she remembered it was Christmas Day and moved to take her daughter in her arms. 'Keep your pecker up, pet. It'll all work out.' It was as near as she could come to sympathy and Kate felt her eyes prick. If only they could have been open with one another, discussed things woman to woman; but her mother could only see one choice, one acceptable course of action.

Kate shook her head to banish the threat of tears and sat down at the table. No use going on a car-ride on an empty stomach. She hadn't been in a car often but she knew what car-sickness was and it wasn't pleasant.

The car was a Ford Eight with leather seats and a dash-board of such highly polished wood that you could see your face reflected in it. 'Nice car, isn't it?' Mr Lucas said, holding the door open for her to slide into the passenger seat. She had a parcel of tit-bits her mother had begged, borrowed or stolen, and a jumper she herself had knitted on big needles, to save coupons on the wool and get it made in time. Her mother and father stood on the step to wave her off and she saw that several sets of curtains in neighbouring houses were animated, as they always were when a car came into the street.

They drove out of Sunderland, her father-in-law some-times grinding the unaccustomed gears and cursing softly under his breath as he did so. 'Mrs Lucas all right?' she asked, as they drove through Grangetown, and he nod-ded.

'Up to the eyes with the dinner, but she enjoys all that. She's taking a bit for Jim when she goes in tonight. God knows if he'll be able to eat it, though.' On either side of them the fields were black and stark, the hedges rimed with frost. Sea-birds showed white against the black earth, a sure sign of stormy weather to come.

The emergency hospital was a collection of hutted buildings hastily built in the grounds of a grim, old mental hospital. Men lounged in doorways, wearing the blue uniforms of wounded soldiers. Nurses flitted here and there, their navy capes scarlet-lined against the cold. There was holly on window sills and sometimes a few bits of pre-war tinsel, tarnished now but bravely proclaiming the spirit of Christmas.

In the sloping corridor they passed a young soldier on crutches, one leg of his trousers pinned up around the stump of his amputated limb. He had a piece of mistletoe held between his teeth as he chased a nurse, trim in a blue uniform, a red cross on the breast of her white pinafore. She eluded him for long enough to lend spice to the chase, and then allowed herself to be caught and kissed, holding the patient around the waist to make sure he didn't fall. They're happy, Kate thought, and was at once envious and amazed at what people could come to terms with if they must.

They were half-way down the passage that led to the ward when the sister spotted them. 'Mrs Lucas?' she enquired, although she knew Kate from previous visits.

'Yes.' Kate's mouth was suddenly dry with fear.

As if she caught the scent of it, the sister smiled. 'No panic. He's doing nicely, all things considered. Doctor wants a word, that's all.' She looked at Mr Lucas. 'You're father-in-law, are you?'

'Father,' he said proudly, and she smiled again. 'That's nice. Well, go on in and wish him Merry Christmas. I'll be in my office when visiting ends. Doctor will see you then.'

Jimmy was propped on pillows, his hands lying passively on the folded coverlet. He smiled at the sight of them but it was a mechanical smile, a gesture, no more.

'Merry Christmas,' Kate said, kissing his cheek. It was smooth and papery now, not rough and crêpe-like as it had been on her first visit. He smelled of disinfectant and her lips were conscious of how little flesh lay beneath the skin.

He'll need a lot of building up, she thought, resolving in one second to do it and in the next to make sure it was carried out when she had gone. I can't stay with him, she thought. He's a stranger. However, she must do her best for him; it was her duty.

Around them other visitors were bidding other patients a happy Christmas. At some beds the greetings were raucous, at others they were muted in deference to the patient's condition. Near the door one bed was screened off and nurses came and went from it at frequent intervals. Kate turned her eyes away and tried to concentrate on their own small space, racking her brains for things to say when her father-in-law fell silent and it was her turn to entertain.

'We've had a few people round asking after you,' she said cheerfully. 'You know, friends and such.' It was true that people did ask after him, but in the main they were other wives, other parents. Several of his friends had been killed in the war; others had married girls from other towns, even, in one case, another country. The old band of lads, larking about on the street corner and later in the pub, was gone beyond recall.

There'll be other men, she told herself firmly. Others in his position, for all I know, and there'll be girls too . . . women. You could pick out war-widows at fifty paces by their pallor and their anxious faces as they wondered what was to become of them.

They opened up the parcel before the bell went. There was a precious dried banana, brown and tiny, courtesy of a neighbour who got food parcels from Australia. There were a few hazelnuts in a red crêpe-paper poke and a piece of sponge cake with a thin line of watery marrow jam in the centre. Best of all, there were two mince pies, her mother's pastry crisp and golden and ornamented with pastry leaves.

'It's home-made mincemeat,' Kate said encouragingly, and for once her husband smiled.

'I get plenty to eat in here, Kathy. Too much. There's no need for your mum to give up her rations.'

'She wants to,' Kate said fiercely. 'We all do. I made you this.' Too late she saw the dropped stitch in the centre of the back of the jumper. 'I'll catch that up later,' she said, shame-faced. 'It's the first big thing I've knitted.'

'It's grand,' he said. 'I'll need it when I get out of here.'

'Any idea when?' His father's voice was eager but Kate contented herself with trying to look expectant as Jimmy shook his head.

'They don't tell you much. It'll likely be in a few more weeks.' He didn't seem to care much. In fact, Kate got the distinct impression that he was simply making conversation until the time came for them to leave.

He feels the same as me, she thought. He's no more keen to be married than I am. He never talked about the future, except in the most trivial of detail.

As if in answer to prayer, a nurse appeared at the entrance to the ward, swinging a brass bell vigorously with both hands. 'All right,' someone shouted. 'We can take the hint.'

As they left the ward the nurses were waiting, sprigs of holly in their caps now, standing by covered trolleys from which steam was escaping. 'What are they getting?' Mr Lucas asked.

The nurse to whom he had spoken rolled her eyes. 'They say it's chicken, it smells like chicken . . . but Sister thinks it's rabbit. Still, there's stuffing with it.'

'And it's better than they'd get at home,' he said, and went on his way to the door marked 'Sister'.

She rose from her desk in answer to their knock. Behind her the young doctor wore a khaki shirt and tie under his white coat. 'Mrs Lucas . . . and Mr Lucas, I understand? Well . . . ' He motioned to two upright chairs. 'Sit down and I'll lay out the facts for you.

'Your husband had a hard time, Mrs Lucas.' Kate nodded. The doctor was hardly more than a bairn himself and she could see he was struggling to find the right words. 'I'm glad to say we've stabilised his medical condition. His various wounds and sores have responded to treatment.

He'll need to continue his medication for some time – some quite considerable time – but we're reasonably content on that score. I'm not going to pretend he'll ever quite shake off the consequences of his treatment in Japanese hands. Few of our patients will. However, our main worry at the moment is his mental state.'

'What do you mean exactly, doctor?' Mr Lucas said, leaning forward in his chair, twisting his cap between his hands as they dangled between his knees.

'He isn't responding as most of the other men are.' The doctor raised his eyes to the ceiling, seeking inspiration. 'To put it in simple terms, he doesn't seem to care much about what happens. That's why we think he should go home as soon as is practicable . . . in the hope that familiar surroundings will do the trick.'

They were mostly silent on the drive back to Sunderland. 'He's going to need care,' Mr Lucas said once, and Kate agreed.

'Yes, he's going to need a lot of care.'

She made an excuse to be dropped off before her own house, saying she was going to visit a friend. 'I'll come round tomorrow and see what his mam thinks,' she said before she closed the car door, standing to wave as Mr Lucas drove away.

The car had rounded the corner before she began to walk, but she didn't turn for home. She struck away from Hendon towards the road that ran between the parks into the town centre. The pavements were still rimed with frost, in spite of the weak sun, and the park was deserted. She kept her head down and hurried, the cold striking through the thin soles of her shoes, her nose freezing and her lips drying even as she licked them. When she came in sight of the town hall clock she saw that it was twelve o'clock. She would have to be home by four or her mother would smell a rat.

She had not told a deliberate lie. She had simply hinted that, as a morning visit was an unheard-of concession and only permitted on Christmas Day, it might well run on into the afternoon. Her mother knew Jim's mother was going in in the evening, though, and that Mr Lucas would have to come back to collect her, so four o'clock was the latest Kate dare put in a reappearance. She quickened her speed, anxious not to waste one precious minute of the time Ben had managed to snatch away from his base.

The Commercial Hotel was in a street running parallel with Fawcett Street, the main street of the town. It was a large imposing building and she stood for a moment, plucking up her courage, before she pushed open the door and entered the lobby.

There was no one behind the mahogany desk, only a marmalade cat washing its paws on the counter-top. Kate put out a hand to ring the brass bell but her nerve failed her and she drew back. There was a register on the counter. Perhaps if she turned it round she could find Ben's room number and make her way upstairs, unobserved. Her fingers were almost touching the leather binding of the book when the man appeared.

'Can I help you?' He wore a stiff white collar and a blue bow tie and his eyes gleamed behind rimless spectacles.

Kate drew herself up and tried to look him in the eye as she spoke. 'I've come to see my husband, Mr Guyser. Mr Benson Guyser.' She put up a hand to wipe an imaginary smut from her chin, so that he could see her wedding ring. Was she over-sensitive, or was there a look of disdain on his face?

'Room seven,' he said. 'First floor.'

She couldn't see the stairs but she didn't dare to ask directions. She moved past the dusty oak chairs that lined the lobby, praying that stairs would open up in front of her. For once, her prayers were answered. They were there, leading off to the left, covered in a narrow strip of thin red carpet, held down by wooden stair-rods. Kate began to climb, conscious of the man's eyes on her, sure he knew that whatever she was, she wasn't the wife of a GI. She knocked on the door of room seven and when it was indeed Ben who opened it, her relief was so great that she burst into tears.

'There,' he said. And then again, 'There, there.' He pulled her over the threshold, smoothing the hair from her eyes, catching a tear with a fingertip, half laughing, half crying. 'Well, hey . . . this is some "Happy Christmas". Then he had drawn her to the warmth of the gas fire and loosened her coat, and there was cherry brandy in a toothglass and all was forgotten in the joy of being together.

They made love, fiercely at first, pulling at one another's clothes, half angry, half desperate when belts would not loosen or buttons give way. And then, when the first need of one another was met, they climbed inside the linen sheets and hairy blankets and lay, exchanging touch and conversation, until desire rose up in them again and they made love slowly. This time it was her turn to lie above and kiss his eyes and pull back when it appeared it might all be over too soon.

'I love you, Kate.'

'I know.'

'What are we going to do, Katie?'

She put out a hand then, to cover his mouth. 'Don't talk. Not now.' And when she felt his lips move as though to form words she closed them with her own. Impossible to tell him what the doctor had said or the burden of responsibility his words had laid upon her. 'Kiss me,' she said. 'It's Christmas . . . let's be happy.'

She had a present for him, wrapped up in her handbag. She could see his present to her, gift-wrapped on the dressing-table, but now, as they began once more the dance of love, they were giving one another the best present of all.

29

JIMMY WAS WAITING IN A wheelchair when they reached the ward, dressed in his blue serge suit, a kitbag, with his name and number stencilled on it, at his side,

'All ready?' Mr Lucas's face was flushed with emotion at having his son restored to him, but Kate felt a heaviness inside her, a compound of resentment and fear and determination. She tried to put on a dutiful, caring face. She *did* feel pity for the man in the wheelchair, but she couldn't love him; couldn't pretend it for a day, let alone a lifetime.

'Well,' she said brightly, 'let's get going. I hope you're wrapped up. It's freezing out there.'

'Now, now,' the male nurse said. 'He doesn't want mollycoddling, do you lad?' He put out hairy arms to grasp the chair. 'He'll be running in the National, the rate he's going.'

Through all of their banter, the boy in the chair had remained silent. Now he spoke. 'Have I got all my medicines?' There was fear in his voice and his hand twitched at the blanket that covered his legs.

'In your kitbag,' the nurse said. 'All ticketed, full instructions, your diet sheet, your appointment card, Uncle Tom Cobleigh and all.' Above his head the nurse's eyes flashed warning.

'Humour him,' the look said. Kate nodded acknowledgement. 'The least little upset and you're back here. Isn't that right?' the nurse went on.

'Absolutely,' Kate and her father-in-law spoke in unison, and then they were at the door and the ambulance men were lowering a ramp, assisting the patient to his feet and up into the vehicle. Kate followed him and sat on the narrow bench that ran down one side of the ambulance. 'Shove along,' her father-in-law said, and she moved obediently, to make room. They had come to the hospital by bus, discarding the car so they could both be with Jim on the homeward journey.

'We'll soon have you home,' the ambulance man said as he shut one door and bolted it. He looked at Kate and winked. 'We're used to this lot – ex-prisoners. Terrified of going home, some of them were. You can understand it. It just takes time.'

Shut up, Kate thought fiercely. She was tired of people telling her it would all be all right, easy, a piece of cake. She didn't know what to say to her husband during a half-hour visit. What would she do in a whole day, a week, a year? Ben had agreed to wait three months. 'Twelve weeks,' he'd said. 'That's no time at all. I'll write. We'll meet when we can. And all the time Jim'll be picking up. It's just a question of food with most of them. It's the same with our boys, I heard from home. You can hang in there, baby. It's not as if . . . ' He had hesitated then. 'It's not as if you'll be . . . he won't be . . . ' He was too embarrassed to mention sex, and his embarrassment was infectious.

'No,' Kate said, to set them both free. 'Of course we won't.' But there was only one bed in the room they were to share at the Lucases'. One high, oak-railed bed with a feather mattress and ticking pillows inside embroidered pillow-slips.

She cast the thought aside and put out a hand to her husband's arm. 'Comfy?' The ambulance started at that moment, moving slowly as it negotiated the hospital courtyard and then accelerating as it reached the road and turned towards Sunderland.

The ambulance men carried Jimmy into the house in a chair made of their crossed arms. They sat him down in the front room and departed, with a promise to collect him in a week for his outpatient's appointment.

'A nice cup of tea,' Mrs Lucas said, 'that's what you need.' Her bottom lip was trembling as she looked at her son, and Kate saw that she was making comparisons between the cheerful boy who had gone off to war and the withdrawn man who had just been returned to her. She followed her mother-in-law into the kitchen and began to assemble a tray for the tea. 'What d'you think?' her mother-in-law asked at last.

Kate put down a cup and reached for another. 'I think he's okay . . . at least, he will be. It's all a matter of time. The nurse said so.'

Mrs Lucas had turned to face Kate and now she put out her arms and drew her daughter-in-law to her.

'I'm sorry for you, Katie. You've had no real marriage, not even a week. And now this. But I'll help you. Dad and I will both help you. And you can stay here as long as you need to. Until our Jim's himself again. For ever, if you like.'

Kate let herself be clasped to Mrs Lucas's bosom. It was better than having to face her and risk her mother-in-law seeing what was going on in her head. But at last the duplicity of her silent acceptance forced her into drawing away. 'I'd better get this tea in,' she said. 'He'll probably want a nap soon. He usually sleeps around now.'

He did sleep, lying on the settee under a rug. At first his head rested uneasily on the arm of the settee and then the two women manoeuvred a cushion under his head, one of them gently lifting him, the other sliding the cushion along. Kate sat beside him, no sound in the room except the ticking of the clock or the occasional spitting of the fire. Her parents-in-law had withdrawn tactfully. 'Just call if you need anything,' Mrs Lucas said as she closed the door and Kate smiled as reassuringly as she could.

As he slept she watched him, seeing the changes captivity had wrought in him. He was only twenty-three but there

255

were flecks of grey in the thin hair that lay limply across his skull. His skin still had a greyish-yellowish tinge and his folded hands, twitching slightly now, were scarred, the nails bitten to the quick so that lumps of the nail-bed stood proud of the edge of the nail.

God help him, Kate thought. She moved quietly to the window and looked out on to the street. This was her home now, this tiny house with its neat bay window and pocket hanky-sized front garden; but not for long. For the few weeks it took, that was all. She turned back as Jimmy started to speak, muttering at first and then quite clearly enunciating a phrase: *'Goodbye, you land of stinking smells and sorrows . . .'*

Where had he heard that? She leaned closer but he was asleep, his eyelids twitching slightly but still shut. She straightened up as the doorbell went. When she crossed the room to peep from the windows she saw that it was her own mother and father who stood on the step.

She conducted her parents to the kitchen, explaining that Jimmy was sleeping.

'Don't disturb him,' her mother said. 'Poor lad, the more he sleeps the better.'

More tea was made, using the leaves of the previous pot, for tea was still on ration and therefore precious.

'I'm sorry,' Mrs Lucas said, apologetically, 'but I've got to make it go round. We did without before, when things ran out, but I couldn't see our Jim go short, not with what he's been through.'

'You won't go short,' Kate's father said. 'We'll see to that, won't we, Mother?'

'You'll have our Kate's ration book,' his wife said, 'and anything out of ours that'll help. It's the least we can do.'

'Now, isn't that nice?' Mrs Lucas said. They sipped their pale tea and smiled occasionally at one another, as minute gave way to minute and they all waited for the invalid to wake up.

At half past five the guests departed, contenting themselves with a peep at their still-sleeping son-in-law. 'Bye-bye,' her mother said when she kissed Kate on the doorstep; and then, leaning close to whisper, 'You're doing the right thing, pet. It'll reap its reward in the end.' Her father contented himself with squeezing her hand and clearing his throat, and then they were off down the road to the bus-stop and Kate had to go back into the unfamiliar house.

Jimmy woke at six o'clock, looking around him as though confused about where he was before hitching himself up on the settee and putting up a hand to wipe sleep from his eyes.

'That was a good sleep,' Kate said, wishing she didn't sound so much like an infants' teacher. This was a man. He had seen more in the last few years than his father or hers in a lifetime, except that they had both served in the Great War, so perhaps they had had their share.

She brought him tinned mulligatawny soup in a blue-and-white striped bowl and watched while he spooned it into his mouth. 'Nice,' he said at last, pushing it away half finished. She asked if he wanted to listen to the radio but he shook his head. 'Could I go to bed?' he asked apologetically.

Kate asked him to wait while she put in a bottle to air the bed in the yellow and green bedroom, but found that his mother had done it hours ago. She helped him to the stairs but in the end, much to her relief, it was his father who went with him into the bathroom and helped him to get ready for bed.

His wrists and ankles were huge and bony at the ends of his army-issue pyjamas, and the skin on his limbs was scarred purple here and there and looked thin enough to break if anything touched it. 'I'll be up in a while,' Kate said when he was tucked in. 'You try and get some sleep.'

She had intended to sit downstairs and read for a while – she was deep into a Daphne du Maurier novel and would have welcomed the diversion – but when she went downstairs the chairs either side of the fireplace were occupied by her parents-in-law, who both looked up in surprise when she entered the room.

'Is there something you need?' Mrs Lucas asked.

They expect me to be with him, Kate thought. Twenty-four hours a day. She shook her head. 'No, I just came down to say goodnight.' It was only twenty minutes to eight: twelve hours to daylight.

Perhaps I'll go mad, Kate thought as she re-mounted the stairs. She would be taken away then, and locked up in a room with bars, but at least she could cease pretending. It was not as frightening a prospect as it might seem.

She carried her nightclothes to the bathroom, with its embossed ducks on the wall, and undressed there before tiptoeing back to the bedroom, praying that Jim would be asleep already. He was asleep, muttering slightly under his breath, but asleep just the same. She stood looking down at him, listening to him moan and repeat certain phrases. Once he recited part of a rhyme again: '*An inch of rain today and none tomorrow.*' Once he even laughed, a bitter little chuckle that left his mouth half-open.

In the end, Kate put out the light and climbed carefully into the bed. It was nearly three years since they'd shared a bed, and she had forgotten what it was like to lie beside a sleeping man, not that he had slept much in that brief and greedy honeymoon. She turned on to her side, determined to think of something nice, like how it would be to sleep beside Ben, but Jimmy began to whimper. It was an animal-like sound that chilled her blood.

In the end she turned back and slid her arm around him. There was no response, but in a little while the whimpering stopped and his breathing deepened. It was then that Kate remembered she had not said her prayers. She wanted to get out and go down on her knees; she needed the penance that uncomfortable praying on lino could bring. But she couldn't disturb him and risk that eerie whimpering again. She contented herself with reciting 'Gentle Jesus' and on the last line, 'Find this little child a place', she closed her eyes for sleep.

When the church clock chimed half past ten and the stairs creaked as the Lucases came up to bed, Kate was still wide awake, her head a teeming mass of unbearable thoughts.

30

THEY SAT OPPOSITE ONE ANOTHER in an oak booth, a narrow cast-iron table between them, trying to make conversation . . . anything that avoided their own lives.

'Old Winnie made some speech!' Ben said.

Kate nodded. 'It scares me, all this talk of an iron curtain. What does he mean?'

'It's the Ruskies he's talking about. They're the threat now. They always were, really; it just suited us not to see it. Churchill's a wily old bird.' He mimicked the statesman's voice. '"The dark ages may return on the gleaming wings of science. Beware, I say. Time may be short."'

'No one listens to Churchill now,' Kate said, 'not since he lost the election. And some of us don't want to listen, not if he's preaching gloom and despondency.' Beside her, the red roses Ben had bought her gave off a heady perfume.

Ben put out a sympathetic hand. 'How's it been?' They couldn't go on pretending that everything was okay, not when time was so short.

'I can't go on,' Kate said desperately. 'I've tried. You know I've tried, but it's hopeless. We're no closer now than we were . . . less close, even. We're so polite to each other!

It's pathetic how grateful he is for the least little thing I do for him.'

Across the table, Ben's boyish face clouded. 'He's not a bad guy, Katherine. That's half the trouble. It would all be so easy if he was a hoodlum. How did you manage to get away today?'

'I told his mother I was going to see my bridesmaid, Heather. You've never met her. I'll not have to be long, though. They watch the clock if I'm away for a few minutes. I don't think they know how to manage when I'm not there.'

He took her hand in his. 'How long have we got?'

'A couple of hours. At the most.'

'Let's get a room somewhere.' There was an urgent tone in Ben's voice, but she shrank away.

'I couldn't do that again, Ben. These hotels know what you're up to. Let's go to the car.'

Ben had come in a borrowed car, driving all the way from Burtonwood so that they could be together for a few hours. 'Please, Katherine, let's get a room,' he said again. 'I'll go alone, and you can come up a bit later. Let's make the most of what time we have.'

But Kate was adamant and in the end he gave way.

They drained their glasses and picked their way between the tables in the smoky pub. Outside he drew her close, putting a protective arm around her. 'You'll freeze in the car.' It was parked under a tree in the corner of the car park, but by unspoken agreement they drove out on to the road and went in search of a more secluded spot: a field gate in the middle of a country lane.

Ben manoeuvred the car into the field and switched off the engine. 'Let's get in the back,' Kate said, and opened her door.

At first they came together to escape the cold, laughing and clinging, half weeping in the pleasure of contact, closeness, being alone. Ben picked at the buttons of Kate's jumper with numbed fingers, and she squealed when those same icy fingers touched her warm breasts.

'Sorry.' He sought a nipple with his mouth, and then she was tugging at sleeves and collars, finding warm, hairy, male flesh, saying, 'I love you, I love you,' over and over again. When he would have fumbled with a rubber, Kate was the one who forced the pace.

'It doesn't matter . . . now, now, now.'

When it was over, they were both spent. There was no possibility of rekindled desire after such a storm. They covered up as best they could, securing themselves against the chill, pressing against one another, pulling his greatcoat over them as if to shut out the world along with the cold.

Kate could feel her breath condensing as it left her mouth, feel his breath grow liquid on her cold cheek at the same time. 'What are we going to do, Katherine?' he said, and the despair in his voice brought out the tiger in her.

'We'll go away together. Jim's mother will look after him. She *really* loves him . . . ' She left unspoken the fact that she did not, because they both knew it.

'When?' Ben asked, and Kate did not waver as she had done in the past.

'I'll need a week. There are things to do, things to arrange. I want to behave as decently as I can. Come back for me next weekend. I'll be ready then.'

'I can't take these home with me,' she said, when it was time to go, gesturing towards the roses which lay on the dashboard.

'I don't want them,' Ben said. 'I bought them for you!'

'I love them,' she said fervently, burying her face in the fragrant, fleshy petals. 'I love them, but I can't take them with me.'

In the end they went into the Catholic church. Holding hands in the dim light, they laid the roses at the feet of the Virgin, seeing her eyes on them, unwavering. Help us, Kate thought. Ben lit a candle, dropping some melted wax and grinding the candle firmly down on to it to hold it steady. 'God help us,' Ben said, and then they turned and went back to the car.

He drove her to the corner of the street, stopping in

between street lamps to take advantage of the semi-darkness. She got out quickly: there was no goodbye kiss, because there was no need now. They would soon be together for ever. She felt cheerful as she walked up to the door, fishing for her key.

'I'm glad you're back,' Mrs Lucas said from the passage. 'Jim's been a bit upset.'

They had brought him his kitbag because he was anxious to sort out what could be put away and what could be disposed of. There had been a tin inside, full of odds and ends.

'Rubbish, really,' Mrs Lucas said. 'It was this that started him off.'

'This' was a grubby leaflet, stained with what might have been urine or tea: *To all Allied Prisoners of War*, it read. *The Japanese forces have surrendered unconditionally and the war is over. We will get supplies to you as soon as is humanly possible and will make arrangements to get you out but, owing to the distances involved, it may be some time before we can achieve this.* Advice followed. *If you have been starved or underfed for long periods do not eat large quantities of solid food, fruit or vegetables at first. For those who are seriously ill or very weak, fluids such as broth and soup, making use of the water in which rice and other foods have been boiled, are much the best.*

As Kate read it the paper began to disintegrate along the fold, until she held a piece of it in each hand.

'Where is he now?' Kate asked, when her eyes had skimmed to the bottom of the page.

'Dad got him to bed. He's up there with him now.'

Kate heard the weeping as soon as she reached the landing. Her father-in-law was wide-eyed as she entered the bedroom. 'Thank God you're back. It's beyond me, all this.' He was out of the bedroom even as she reached the bed, the words, 'You're his wife,' unspoken but hanging in the air. He had been a hero in the Great War, so they said, but he couldn't face his son's agony. Kate could hear a whispered altercation on the landing, but her attention was all for the man in the bed.

Jim lay on his side, his knees drawn up and his head turned down, arms tight around his knees as though to pull them into himself. It was the sounds he was making that horrified her; her scalp tingled, her breath caught her throat, as though she had inhaled ammonia. This was not the weeping of a man, it was the moaning of a creature – half-child, half-animal – a creature in agony.

She hesitated only for a moment, then she crossed to close the bedroom door and switch out the light. She shed her clothes as quickly as she could – smelling the odours of love on her as she did so, knowing that Jim would not notice, or care if he did – and felt for the folded nighty that should have been at the foot of the bed but wasn't. When she failed to find it, she dismissed the need for it, lifting the covers and slipping between the sheets.

'There now,' she said. 'There, there, I'm here now. Shush, Jimmy, shush.'

He turned into her arms, still curled up, but sobbing now, not howling. She went on holding him, rocking him gently, till the sobbing turned into the gulping of a child after a fit of tears, until the tense limbs relaxed, the body straightened, the head went limp and there was peace. She was not conscious of having made a choice. She knew only that she was doing what must be done.

BOOK 5

———————•———————

SOPHIE'S STORY

London
1993

31

SOPHIE HAD DREADED THE REUNION with Paul on her return from Nice. His bags were still dumped by the front door and he looked weary and unshaven, but his eyes lit up at the sight of her. 'You're back,' he said, and held out his arms.

Sophie had moved into their welcoming circle, glad to hide her bewilderment against his shoulder while she tried to work out what to say. She mustn't turn down a conciliation gesture; equally, she must not give the impression that anything had changed. Choosing, she thought . . . she was always having to choose.

In the end, and inevitably, they went to bed, avoiding meaningful conversation. The next morning they both dashed off to their respective jobs, tacitly agreeing not to make waves.

Now, it was the first Sunday since their reunion and the feeling of freedom was glorious.

'God, it's good to be sitting here like this,' Paul said, lifting his arms above his head and stretching.

On the other side of the table, Sophie nodded. 'No need to rush, no tube, no need even to get showered if we don't choose – '

'I always knew you were a shit at heart.' Paul strained

across to kiss her on the mouth. 'Did you miss me?' It was the first time he had referred to last week's separation.

'You know I did. The Riviera was wonderful, but I wish you'd been there. Incidentally, while you were out last night I had to listen to Chloe's San Francisco adventures. She enjoyed playing Mrs Bowker. It's the first time I've known her admit that marriage might have something going for it.'

Paul licked in a stray crumb of croissant from the corner of his mouth. 'If she imagines being married to a QC is all conference-time in San Francisco, she'd be in for a shock. It's being alone in a secluded London square most of the time . . . that, and charity work. They're a dull lot, the Bar wives, all Barbours and green wellies.' Behind him, the sun shone through the kitchen window, haloing his head.

'She'd be a "lady who lunches",' Sophie said, narrowing her eyes. 'I can see her now, straight from *John Freida* to the Dorchester or the Savoy. She'd adore it.'

'Well, enough about Chloe.' Paul pursed his lips. 'What about us? What shall we do today?' He reached out and covered Sophie's hand with his own. 'Apart from going back to bed, which I could easily accept.'

'I bet you could, but I'd like to do something different,' Sophie said. Her espadrille had fallen from her foot and she struggled to retrieve it. 'I'd like to have a long leisurely bath and then go off somewhere . . . but not anywhere posh. I want to slop around. We could go to Holland Park and picnic on the grass?'

'Too cold, and not special enough. Go and run your bath, and while you're doing that I'll think of somewhere really plebby.' Paul followed her into the bathroom and perched on the rim while she turned on taps and added bath-oil. 'Seriously, Soph . . . I wish you had come to Paris. I know you enjoyed Nice and seeing Kate, but it's daft that we should be apart unnecessarily – crazy.'

Sophie knew he meant more than a brief separation and she turned to check the towels on the rail so that she needn't meet his eyes. It was only a matter of time until the subject reared its head again. In the next few days the date of her departure for New York would come through, and judging by Paul's words that was when she'd have to make the ultimate choice between a relationship and a career.

Kate sat back as the bus wound its way along the Basse Corniche. Above, on the skyline, trees crowned the crest of the mountain like a weary Roman legion marching uphill. Below, the sea sparkled in the sunshine. The bus had come through a shabby area of shuttered houses and small, dark leafy gardens. Now the road clung to the cliff, and the turquoise sea below was edged with a spattering of bathers on the narrow fringe of pale gold sand. The Mediterranean was very beautiful, Kate thought, but she would be quite glad to get back to the North Sea, with its wheeling sea-birds and tides rimmed with coal-dust, the product of the pits that lay beneath the sea.

Besides, she wanted to find out how Sophie was. Ever since her granddaughter's departure a week ago she had chewed over what Sophie had told her about the prospect of America and leaving Paul behind. Kate closed her eyes as they reached the outskirts of Monaco, seeing Sophie's face as she walked to her plane, remembering her own feelings at that moment and the emotions they had stirred up from the past.

It had brought it all back: Ben, Jimmy's return, and the barren years that had followed. She opened her eyes to find a small child, a girl of two or three, her ears pierced, her hair screwed into Rasta braids, regarding her solemnly over the back of the seat in front. Kate smiled, but the child's unwavering gaze did not flicker, and she closed her eyes again, seeing instead that curled figure in the bed all those years ago. She knew now that it was called the foetal position; knew it from documentaries on the telly. Then, she had known only that she was looking at someone teetering on the brink of a black hole. She had not made a conscious decision to draw her husband back from it; she had acted instinctively, climbing into bed beside Jimmy and holding him like the child he had become because there was nothing else to be done.

He had slept in the end, still gulping from the effects of sobbing, but sleeping just the same. Once or twice he cried out, 'Tenko . . . tenko,' which later she found out meant a check parade. And once he called out, 'Sonkurai . . . naka Sonkurai,' which meant No 2 camp. Mostly, though, he called out, 'Sorry.' Just that one word: 'Sorry,' and each time she would feel his arms move up and down as though he were striking out at something.

It had been early morning when it all came out. She had got up when the birds started their chorus, just before dawn, and had gone downstairs to make tea. 'I'm coming straight back,' she said, seeing the whites of his eyes in the half-dark, sensing the need still in him.

When she came back he drank the tea, hunched over his knees, clasping the mug in both hands. It was then that he began to speak: of men dead of cholera, their corpses lying for hours amid the violent explosions of vomiting and diarrhoea that had caused their deaths; the big pit where their bodies were burned, layered with bamboo. He spoke of denghi fever and malaria, and how, when he was ill, he heard his heart beating inside his head until, suddenly, it stopped. 'I died then,' he said. 'I died and I knew it, and there was nothing I could do about it.' They had told him it was simply a symptom of cardiac beri-beri, but he knew better. 'I died then,' he said again, and sipped his tea.

Kate had hoped it would end there, but there was more. He spoke of small scratches or sores that ate into the flesh to become ulcers, which grew and grew and had to have the bad flesh scooped out with a sharpened spoon. 'I sharpened the spoons for them,' he said simply, 'on a little stone. And sometimes I helped to hold them down.' She had gasped then and he raised his eyes. 'It had to be done,' he said. Then, matter of factly, 'We held them down for amputations as well.'

In the end, when Kate feared she could bear no more, Jimmy handed her the empty mug and lay down again. Kate sat down on the bed beside him and stroked the coverlet as she would have done for a child, until the jubilant birds ceased their chatter and it was daylight.

All that had taken place forty-seven years ago; almost half a century. Kate looked out of the bus as it began to slow down for its entry into Monte Carlo, but there was no sign of the pink palace on the hill, only signs for McDonald's and Haagen Das ice-cream.

Elizabeth had no need of a hymn book. She knew most of the hymns by heart. *'Just as I am, without one plea, but that thy blood was shed for me . . . '* As she sang out she glanced sideways. Geoffrey's lips were moving but no great sound emerged, and she smiled to herself, thinking of him singing lustily in the bath, emerging shame-faced if he thought he'd been overheard.

She turned her eyes back to the altar, seeing Jesus with the fishermen in the stained-glass windows above, the bronze chrysanthemums below arranged by her on Friday, their fragrance wafting up as she measured and snipped and placed them in the brass urns with mathematical accuracy.

Her mind wandered as they moved into the second verse of the hymn. Kate's holiday would be over soon: let the aircraft land safely, God. And let Sophie forget the American nonsense. I want her married, Elizabeth thought. I want her safe. Marriage was security; bouquets on anniversaries, the Ladies Circle when you were young and Inner Wheel as you matured. Why can't she be sensible, God? Perhaps it was Kate coming out in her? Not that Kate wasn't respectable now, a credit even. But in earlier days . . . the smell of perm solution and ammonia was suddenly in Elizabeth's nostrils, the shuffling of curling papers on damp lino in her ears.

I was ashamed of my background, she thought. That was what had made her an easy target for a con-man and the illusion of power and affluence that surrounded him. And he had been good at his job. So good, she thought, remembering each tender gesture, his eyes limpid with love, his bewitching tongue and fingers that had possessed her, making everything that came afterwards meaningless. She felt her husband's arm, warm and solid at her side. I never gave him a chance, she thought.

Over the years she had followed other case-histories as well as John Stubbs', and that was the way of it with the successful ones, the con-men who almost made it. They were terribly good at their job, which was getting what they wanted. But why me? It was there in her head, the question that had echoed down the years and suddenly found an answer here, in a church filled with praise and the scent of flowers. Because I was pretty and untouched and ready to worship him. Because I was a snob. Her eyes burned and then filled and the tears were tears of shame.

'All right?' Geoffrey was bending to whisper his question, his eyes looking kindly towards her. They had always been kind eyes, right from the beginning.

'Yes, I'm fine. Just the sniffles . . . a cold starting, probably.' She turned back to the hymn book and blinked until her blurred vision cleared and she could continue singing. 'Just as I am, though tossed about with many a conflict, many a doubt.'

Paul and Sophie had settled for going down the river to Greenwich. Now they sat at the side of the boat as it churned murky, rolling water on its way past County Hall. 'What's the latest rumour?' Sophie asked as they looked at the massive building.

'The Japs are going to turn it into a hotel,' Paul said. 'I have heard that Madonna wants to buy it for a sex clinic, but that's unconfirmed.'

There was a babble of foreign tongues about them: German, Chinese, what sounded like Dutch, and Sophie felt a glow of pride that everyone – the whole world – wanted to see *her* country's capital. Love of tourists diminished slightly as an earnest oriental moved in front of her to take a photograph, but his smile and the bob of his head by way of thanks melted her annoyance.

'What do you want to drink?' Paul asked. 'There'll be a crush at the bar any moment.'

'Anything,' she said recklessly. 'Champagne, if possible. If not, surprise me.'

She turned her face into the wind as he moved away, closing her eyes and letting her worries slip away with the boat's wash.

'Here you are,' Paul interrupted. 'It's only gin and tonic in a paper cup but it's the best I could do.'

Sophie was sipping appreciatively when an American voice like a dentist's drill began a commentary to his companion. 'And that's the royal palace of Westminster . . . Westminster Bridge has seven arches . . . that's the Festival Hall.'

She couldn't get away from America, not even on the River Thames. If she left Paul behind in London, would he be faithful to her? Sophie thought of the girl in the leopard-skin dress, twisting to the music at the Condor party, and doubted it.

'Wonderful, isn't it?' Paul murmured. His face was turned into the wind so that he would catch the best view of St Paul's. 'I know I say these flippant things about "living for now, baby", but all this gets to you, doesn't it?'

The orientals were clustering to photograph Tower Bridge. Paul pointed to the bricked-up Traitors Gate. 'Britain's first one-way street,' he quipped, and then, suddenly serious: 'You couldn't leave all this, Soph, could you?'

Sophie wanted to say, 'If I have to, for a while, yes, I could,' but this was a day out. She held up her cup and said, 'Do we get seconds?'

After the scenic splendour of the Basse Corniche, Kate found Monte Carlo an anti-climax. She stood in the square in front of the casino, to her left the Café de Paris, to the right the Hôtel de Paris, behind her a hillside where modern flats tumbled down to formal gardens, with weird examples of modern art placed here and there.

She longed for Sophie's company once more as she sat

down outside the Café de Paris. They could have gossiped about the people passing by on the pavement and shared a giggle. The limping waiter was *very* French, *very* correct in his high collar and black tie, and *very* pleasant, but too busy to exchange more than a '*Merci, madame,*' when he served her coffee. She looked across the square at the signs that clustered around the casino. All the famous retailers were represented: Chanel, Wurz, Hermès, Lalique, Van Cleef and Arpels. How much wealth was represented there? Money, power, and decades of women kept in luxury. I've always had to fend for myself, Kate thought, but there was no pride in the knowledge.

A wave of perfume overtook her as a woman tottered past on three-inch heels. From behind she looked twenty but her face was the face of an old woman, and Kate's fingers strayed to her own face, seeking the reassurance of firmer flesh. I am ageing, she thought, and was afraid, pinching the back of her hand to see if skin could be separated from sub-cutaneous tissue, the ultimate symptom of decay. She was sixty-six, six years older than Joan Collins, and still looking good, but each month it was a harder struggle. Each time she looked in the mirror there was less for which to give thanks.

She raised her hand and summoned the waiter. '*Armagnac, s'il vous plait.*' She felt in need of a drink. There had been too much introspection lately, too much remembering, ever since Sophie had confided her troubles. 'What was it like for you?' That had been the question that raised the spectre of the past, a spectre that was ever-present, even on a sidewalk in Monte Carlo.

It seemed like a dream now, or rather, like a bad dream: those first few months of Jim's homecoming, trying to act the role of loving wife while she yearned for Ben. Being solicitous and caring . . . being amorous because it was so desperately important that she and Jim should have sex as soon as possible.

Later, as the baby grew inside her, she felt a sense of peace and, once her daughter was in her arms, a determination to succeed, to make a life for all of them.

As 1946 became 1947 they had shivered in the grip of one of the worst winters ever recorded. There had been a shortage of fuel, with coal-trains unable to overcome twenty-foot snowdrifts, and power-cuts at any time of day or night. Even Buckingham Palace had been candlelit, although it had been little consolation to know that royalty shared the common misery.

Jim had just returned to his pre-war job as a storeman in the Co-op when he went down with flu, and she had struggled both to nurse him and keep the baby warm. Elizabeth had been four months old then, a frail little thing with wispy fair hair. Now she was a formidable matron with lacquered waves that were never, ever out of place, and an almost permanent air of disapproval. How had the two of them grown so far apart?

It had been the little Elizabeth who had saved Kate from suicide. She had wanted to end it all a thousand times after Ben's letters stopped. At first he had turned up on street corners, his eyes imploring, his hands reaching out. Then he was gone, back to America, and the thought that there was an ocean and continents between them would have broken her heart if it hadn't been for his letters. For months she had watched for the postman, knowing that letters alone would not be enough. When eventually they stopped, she looked at the sad war widows, dressed in black, and tried to tell herself that she was lucky to have a husband, safely returned, and a healthy child. Yet still she had wanted to die. She was hardly more than twenty, and she had longed for death. Now she was sixty-six and terrified of it. She laid a one-hundred-franc note on top of the bill and went in search of diversion.

Paul and Sophie disembarked at Greenwich, which looked white and regal in the September sunshine. A seagull swooped on something in a gutter in front of them, found it to be trash, and returned it as they emerged into the street. The masts of a tall ship showed above the roofs and everywhere there seemed to be spires. They walked up narrow streets, past a shop full of dolls with piercing eyes and ranks of massed toy soldiers, into a market square bordered by craft shops and old pubs. Sophie drooled over gem-stones and twisted silver and the odd gleam of gold, but at last they came upon an antique shop. 'That's what I'd really like,' she said, her nose pressed to the glass. She was looking at a glass orb on a brass stand, inside which was a magnificent rotund Santa Claus, his head thrown back, his sack on his back, and snow around his feet that would swirl if the globe was shaken. The whole thing was no more than four inches high and the workmanship was exquisite.

'Would you like it?' Paul said, following her eye.

'Yes, but I bet it costs a bomb. It's Edwardian, Victorian, maybe. I'd be terrified I'd break it.'

'Shall I buy you a ring?' Paul asked. 'What about a tiger's-eye? That'd please your ma.'

'The ring would . . . I'm not sure about the tiger's-eye,' Sophie said, irked by the reminder of her mother's passion for matrimony.

'I would buy you a ring,' he said, suddenly serious. 'A plain gold one, if you wanted it.'

Sophie was uncomfortable. 'Is that a proposal?' she asked archly. Too archly. She wanted to say, 'Not now,' but that was a put-down. Paul was being serious, and all she wanted at the moment was not to think, for things not to get heavy.

'Well?' he said. He had turned to face her and she knew he expected an answer.

'Aren't you going to go down on your knees?'

'Stop mucking about, Soph. Shall we get married?'

It was too much. He was spoiling the day and she hated him for it. 'Why are you doing this?' She was half crying, beside herself with embarrassment. 'You know I can't commit myself now . . . with everything in turmoil . . . ' Her words tailed off at the sight of the fury on his face.

'You can't commit? *You* just can't commit? What have the last three fucking years been?'

Sophie was aware of eyes on her, all around, some shocked, some sympathetic, some frankly amused.

'How dare you!' she retorted. 'How dare you speak to me like that?' In her words and in her tone, she could hear her mother's voice.

They ate their tea outside, sitting at the white, wrought-iron table to eat finger sandwiches and Madeira cake. 'We won't be able to do this much longer,' Elizabeth said. 'Autumn is setting in now.' She hated autumn; loved it when October gave way to November and it was winter.

'There's a week or two left still,' Geoffrey reached for the teapot, lifting the embroidered cosy from it. 'More tea?' Elizabeth pushed her cup towards him and murmured a thank you as he added milk. Geoffrey always saw the bright side. She had often found that fact an irritation, but there were times when it could be a comfort.

I'm a pessimist, she thought. I have never travelled hopefully . . . But she must have done once, before Bruce Hartley-Davis – who was really John Stubbs – had entered her life. She had once cherished an ambition to be a nurse on a luxury liner and travel the world. I had forgotten that until today, she thought.

'I'm just going to tie up those chrysanths,' Geoffrey said.

Elizabeth watched him walk down the garden, his carriage upright, his step buoyant. He hadn't changed much with the years. The leather patches were gone from his jacket, and there was silver hair at his temples, but he was still recognisable as the boy he once had been. Elizabeth had revelled in that boyishness when he came back into her life; she had paraded his youthful respectability for all the world to see, because it was the antithesis of all that Bruce Hartley-Davis had stood for. Reading the papers each day, with the new details of his wife and children, his spells of imprisonment, the list of his victims, not only in Sunderland but also in other cities, in other towns, she had held up Geoffrey's ring like an amulet, to ward off the smell of corruption. 'I used him,' she thought, and was ashamed.

Neither Paul nor Sophie spoke on the journey back up-river.

Each of them raked an opposite bank with their eyes, as though trying to memorise every single detail of the shoreline. Paul held out a hand to help her alight, but she ignored it and the silence continued on their cab-ride home.

Sophie went straight to the bedroom, shutting the door behind her. She heard the television murmur in the sitting-room and then the sound of Paul's stereo. Vivaldi gave way to Bruckner and then – a complete change – Ella Fitzgerald singing, 'Every Time We Say Goodbye'.

Sophie lay on her back on the bed, her hands behind her head, the words of the song running through her mind. Was Paul making a point?

The record ended and for a few moments there was silence, until the bedroom door creaked open. It was not Paul who came through. It was a broom-shank with a white towel tied to its end. 'Pax?' Paul said from behind the door.

'Come in, you fool,' Sophie said, and burst into tears.

They sat on the bed, kissing and making up, each blaming themselves until they nearly fought again. 'I'll make some tea,' Sophie said at last, 'and then let's think of something nice to do to round off the day.'

She was filling the kettle when she heard noises from below. Voices raised in goodbye and then a door banging. She plugged in the kettle and stood, listening, hoping she was wrong in thinking she could hear Chloe ascending.

'It's only me.' Chloe was there, hair tumbled about her shoulders. 'I've had a glorious day,' she said. 'Is that tea you're making? I was hoping for something stronger.'

'It's tea-time,' Sophie said sternly. 'You know, that thing you make with tea-bags.'

'Tea is terminally uncool,' Chloe said. 'Still, if it's all there is . . .'

'Hi, Chloe,' Paul said as they entered the room. 'I thought you'd be off somewhere with Mr Justice Bowker.'

'That sounds wonderful,' Chloe said. 'He will be a judge one day, but tonight he's got some stuffy dinner party of Hilary's.'

'Shame,' Sophie said, hating herself even as she said the words. 'It's awful when a wife makes demands.'

'Ha ha!' Chloe was unperturbed. 'They don't have a real marriage. I wouldn't dream of interfering if they did.'

'Interfering?' Paul said quizzically. 'That's what they call it nowadays, is it?'

'You know what I mean, Paul. If you're both going to be beastly I'll go home.' Chloe sipped her tea and winced. 'If this is the standard of hospitality, I'm sorry I came up in the first place.'

'Shut up,' Paul said cheerfully. 'You know you're welcome. We're just trying to point out the error of your ways.'

'Seriously.' Sophie sought for the right words. 'Seriously, you could have any man – and don't shake your head because we all know you're not modest. Yet you continually go for married men.'

'I know why she does it,' Paul said cheerfully. 'We did a whole programme on it once. She's afraid of commitment.'

'I'm off,' Chloe said, replacing her cup. 'When you two go sociological on me, it's time to move.'

'It's true,' Paul said when Chloe was gone. 'Some people deliberately go for hopeless relationships because it saves them from having to commit themselves.'

He was using that word again: commitment. I fear it as much as he espouses it, Sophie thought. It was usually men who feared commitment and women who were supposed to crave it, so why were they two so different? But as she washed the teacups at the kitchen sink she could see why. Paul wanted a continuation of the warm entanglement in which he had grown up, while she was faintly uneasy about the atmosphere of her girlhood home. We are all part of a chain, she thought. One link forges the next, for better or worse.

32

S OPHIE TRIED TO KEEP HER mind on stock control but it wasn't easy. The print-outs in front of her kept fading as she thought how drastically things had changed since early summer. She had been really happy then. Ascher's had still been Ascher's, and Littlecamp Inc blissfully unknown. She had delighted in her job, enjoyed keeping house, and seldom if ever exchanged a cross word with Paul. Now, the early autumn weather seemed enervating; household chores were irritating; small spats escalated into huge rows. Chloe was a time-bomb and Ascher's was no longer the safest place in the world to be. Most of all, her relationship with Paul was under threat.

Sophie looked at her watch. Kate would be on her way home from France. Lucky Kate; nothing to do but come home and take up her life again. She was suddenly envious of her mother and her grandmother. They had always had easy lives. Kate had endured a war but she had not been alone in that; everyone had been in the same boat. Most of the men had come home, and life had gone smoothly on. As for her mother, the only thing she'd ever had to contend with was fabric-fade! Sophie snapped shut the files in front of her and went in search of something to take her mind off her troubles until her scheduled meeting with David was due.

Elizabeth had intended to go to a coffee morning in aid of Cancer Research. She wore her Windsmoor suit and pinned her Dior brooch on the lapel, the brooch that matched her earrings; but five minutes into the journey she turned the car away from the house where the coffee morning was to be held and headed back home.

The cuttings were locked inside a small shagreen box at the bottom of her lingerie drawer. She turned the key and lifted them out, seeing how fragile and yellow they had become. In a year or two they would disintegrate into dust. The most recent one was from 1983, the year Sophie took her O levels: *Judge calls man an excrescence on the face of the human race for robbing blind pensioner*. It was a scheme to cover funeral expenses into which John Stubbs had conned sixty or more elderly people. Elizabeth leafed through the cuttings. His cons had become smaller and more pathetic with time: never again a grandiose scheme like the marina. Bruce was never a great villain, she thought, only a pilferer. Even what he had taken from her had been as nothing compared with what she had taken from herself.

The phone in the bedroom rang, echoing the extension in the hall, but Elizabeth ignored it. She turned instead and crossed to the window. The garden was fading now that the season of mists was upon them. As she watched, a leaf spiralled down from the apple tree . . . and then another and another. As my defences are falling, she thought; one by one, until only my nakedness will be left.

The phone began to ring again but she ignored it. Instead she put the cuttings back into the box and carried it downstairs and outside, across the lawn, past the rockery with its alpine plants, to the edge of the compost heap where the incinerator stood. She opened the box so that the scraps of yellowing newsprint fell down onto the ashes below, then she went back to the house in search of matches.

* * *

As the taxi sped towards the airport, Kate turned in her seat for a last look at Nice. She would miss the palm trees, the exotic taste of an Africa just out of sight, but she was glad to be going home. Her flat would be warm and welcoming, with bread in the bin and milk in the fridge thanks to Oliver. It would be nice to be home . . . so why did she feel so unsettled? Why had she been so lonely after Sophie had left? She usually enjoyed her solitary holidays.

For years now Oliver had wanted to accompany her, but she had always said no. They had a good friendship; silly to spoil it. Besides on holiday, things could happen. She knew how Oliver felt about her, but it was ludicrous. Fifty-six was light years away from sixty-six . . . the sixties were another country. And yet I feel as though this is still the overture, she thought. I'm waiting for life to begin, and it's all passed me by.

She tipped the cab-driver handsomely for checking in her cases and then, relieved of luggage, went up to the bar for a final glass of wine. She treated herself to champagne at sixty francs a glass, but champagne drunk alone was only sparkling wine. She was glad when her plane was announced and she could pass through the boarding gate.

The seat next to her was occupied by a middle-aged Italian man with soulful eyes, which did not prevent him from immediately establishing territorial rights, spreading his legs and putting his elbow on the arm-rest between them. Across the aisle an enchanting little girl was smiling at her with narrowed, oriental eyes. She was Japanese, probably. Kate sighed. You couldn't go on hating for ever. She smiled back at the child and closed her eye in a wink.

The runway ran out towards the sea, and once they were aloft, she could see the paragliders and the yachts making for Villefranche. Suddenly she was filled with an unbearable longing to stay on the golden Côte d'Azur. If only she were going back to someone. Oliver's arms would open if she wanted them to, but it wouldn't work. I'm old, she thought. I don't know how it happened, but it's true. I was a girl, and now I'm an old woman, and I don't know what happened to the in-between.

'You'll love New York,' David said firmly. 'I wish I were going, I can tell you.'

'I've already seen it,' Sophie said mildly. 'It's not going to be a revelation.'

'Living there – living in any major city – is different to a visit. But you'd better not like it too much. I need you back here.'

'My replacement sounds good – on the telephone – and her track record's impressive. I've made arrangements for Sheila to show her the ropes and the department heads will help.'

'I'm sure she's good, but is she over here to spy out the land? What do they call them over there . . . ?'

'Stool pigeons.' Sophie grinned. 'You'll have to be on your best behaviour.' For a moment she was tempted to tell him about Paul's resistance to the idea of her going, but in the end she decided against it. It was all too easy to let your private life intrude into the workplace and it was never wise, especially for a woman.

She walked back to her office, smiling non-committally at people as she passed. Her secretary looked up when she entered the outer office.

'Paul rang. Can you ring him back?'

Sophie dialled the number.

'Well,' Paul said, when she got through. 'What happened?'

'Nothing *happened*!' Sophie tried not to sound angry. 'What did you expect? We talked. They want me in New York . . . you know that.'

'And . . . ?' He was giving no quarter, and it irked her. Didn't he understand how difficult it was?

'I'll have to go. There's no other choice. We've been through all this, Paul. You know I'm going.'

'What about us?' He was silky now: a prosecutor.

'I don't respond to threats, Paul. I never did.'

For a moment she contemplated conciliation, but the moment passed. There was a long silence, and then the unmistakable sound of the receiver being replaced at the other end.

'Damn you, Paul!' Sophie said fiercely. 'Damn you to hell.'

The restaurant was half empty and they had a table by the window which looked out on a fairy-lit garden. 'This is nice,' Elizabeth said. 'I'm glad you suggested eating out.'

'Where were you this morning?' Geoffrey said. 'I rang several times.'

'Coffee morning.' The lie came easily. She mustn't hurt him any more than she had to . . . than she already had done. 'For Cancer Research.'

If he knew she was lying, he didn't let on. His eyes fell to the menu. 'This looks good. I think I'll have fettucini, and the mushrooms to start. We'll have a very beautiful wine. Something special.'

'I'll have the prawns in garlic for starters,' Elizabeth said, 'and then the lasagne verde.' Once, on television, she had heard an agony aunt talking about marriage: 'You can't mend a broken marriage,' the woman had said, the drop-pearls in her ears quivering with earnestness. 'But if the ingredients are there, perhaps you can start again.' She had loved Geoffrey once . . . or at least liked him. If there had been no Bruce she might have married Geoffrey and borne his child with pride and enjoyed every minute of the last twenty-seven years. Instead she had seen him as a compliant fool, not realising how strong he really was. She thought suddenly of Sophie: poor Sophie, faced with decision, liable to choose wrongly, to spoil it and then to have to pay for it with the rest of her life.

'To us,' Geoffrey said, raising his glass.

Elizabeth chinked her glass against his and sipped, before raising it again. 'To Sophie,' she said. 'May everything turn out for the best.'

As they finished their first course, she heard herself saying, 'Tell me something. Have you ever had regrets?'

'Regrets?' She had Geoffrey's full attention now. 'Regrets about what?'

'About us? About marriage?'

'No,' he said firmly. 'Nary a one.'

Kate saw the flood-lit magnificence of Durham cathedral and castle and then the train was drawing into the station. The guard had already placed her luggage by the door and when she alighted, Oliver was there to meet her.

'Kate!' He kissed her cheek, gripping her arms quite roughly in the warmth of his welcome. 'Are these your bags?' He was lifting them eagerly on to the platform, and she felt the warmth of being cherished. What would her life be without him? And how much longer could she go on fending him off, before he looked elsewhere? He was handsome in his own way, his tweed hat tipped to the back of his head, his well-cut jacket just shabby enough to be distinguished. If she let the relationship ripen and become intimate, he would see her for what she was: an old woman with flat breasts, a sagging belly and age spots where cosmetics could not go. Easy to captivate in artificial light, with silk and chiffon and Estée Lauder to help you. But naked in the bath, the bed . . .

'Has everything been all right while I was away?' she said aloud.

'I missed you,' he said, folding her into the car. He was a stocky man, solid and sensible. His hands square and kind, especially when they touched polished wood or seasoned china. 'Did you miss me?'

'A bit. Now, don't be silly.'

Kate had expected him to smile, but even in the semi-light in the car she could see that he winced. She sought for something innocuous to say and found it in the Café de Paris lavatory. 'I saw the funniest thing in Monte Carlo,' she said. 'An automatic seat-lifter in the loo. You'll howl when I tell you . . . let's get home. By the way, did that Pembroke table sell?'

285

'Yes. Four hundred and eighty. I've made a meal at my place, so I hope you're hungry.'

She let him sweep her out of the car and into his house, and then his red setter was leaping to greet her and giving her a cover for her confusion.

Sophie had beaten eggs for an omelette and put a bottle of Chardonnay in the fridge. She had had a long talk with Chloe and was fairly sure that her neighbour would not reappear. While she waited for Paul to arrive home she chopped peppers and shallots and mushrooms and cut smoked ham into strips for the filling. He usually came straight into the kitchen, but tonight he went straight to the bedroom. She rinsed and dried her hands and went to find him.

As she pushed at the bedroom door she wondered if he was still angry after the phone call. Surely not? He usually cooled down quite quickly.

He looked up as she came into the doorway. 'Hello. We're eating in, I see . . . or rather smell. What is it?'

'An omelette.' So that was how he was going to play it – as though it had never happened.

He poured the wine and helped to carry the dishes to the table. 'I've had a jolly day,' he said. 'Pure, unalloyed pleasure from beginning to end . . . and if you believe that, you'll believe anything.'

'How did the abortion debate go?' Sophie said, willing to play the game his way.

'That wasn't too bad . . . it was the one bright spot. There was a man – some don or other – who made a good point: if a man has no rights over the unborn child, no chance of deciding whether or not it should exist, then asking him to pay maintenance is taxation without representation.'

'There's a flaw in that, somewhere,' Sophie furrowed her brow. 'He can't have a say, because if he does he takes away a woman's right to decide what to do with her body.'

'But why should she decide, any more than him?'

'Because it *is* her body.'

'It's his sperm.'

'Which he deposited . . . '

' . . . with her consent,' Paul finished triumphantly. 'No one's arguing about rape . . . that's a different ball-game.'

'Don't be smug,' she said, knowing that they were not fencing over abortion but over something much closer to home.

Paul continued to talk about work as they ate, recounting with relish how two episodes of the *What's It to You?* quiz were now in the can. 'Muna was as bitchy as ever. You know how she salivates when she's got her teeth into someone. It was poor old John Major. She also had a go at Glenys Kinnock, so you can't say she's biased! When she came off the studio floor she was panting . . . just like hounds after a kill. Sometimes I think I'm in a sick business.'

But you're not giving it up, Sophie thought. For better or for worse, it's your business and you're sticking to it. Aloud, she said, 'I had a good day, too. We've managed to land the Latoulle Spring Collection . . . exclusive in Britain.'

'Marvellous,' Paul said. 'That's what Britain needs at the moment – outfits at a thousand quid a throw. That'll lift morale among the unemployed.'

'God, you can be childish, Paul.' Sophie began to clash the plates together, before carrying them out to the sink. Too late, she saw the hurt in his eyes, the longing to stop squabbling and make up, but by then she was in full flight towards the kitchen. It was too late.

33

IT WAS STRANGE TO WAKE up again in the single bed. Sophie had slept in it, or its predecessors, for eighteen years, but all that seemed a lifetime ago. She turned on to her back and lay, her eyes closed, thinking of Paul, who was asleep no doubt in their double bed. They always slept late on Sunday mornings. At least, they stayed in bed . . . sometimes until eleven or twelve o'clock. Paul had used work as an excuse not to come north with her this weekend, but they had both known it was an excuse and not a reason. The row that had followed her meeting with David had rumbled on, degenerating into petty meanness on both sides until she was glad of the need to go home and relieved that he couldn't – or wouldn't – accompany her.

She opened her eyes as she heard a soft knock at the door. 'It's only me.' Her mother was carrying a tray of delicate china laid out on an embroidered tray-cloth. 'I thought you'd like breakfast in bed. You seem to have so little time off.'

There was an almost tearful note in her mother's voice and Sophie sat up and held out her arms. 'No, not the tray, silly. Put it down and give me a hug.' Last night, when she had confirmed that her American trip was going ahead her mother's eyes had filled with tears. 'I'm not going for ever, and I'll only be a few hours' flight away. You and Daddy must come to New York. You never go anywhere.'

'I know, I know.' Elizabeth sniffed and drew back, composing her face. 'Now get this breakfast down you while it's hot.' They fussed over placing the tray, each of them aware that there was more to say. At last, as Sophie scooped out her boiled egg, Elizabeth retreated to the window-seat and talked.

'I know I fuss. It's just that I love you so much . . . and I am worried about you and Paul. I thought, this time, that it would last, and that you two would marry.'

'What do you mean, "this time"?' Sophie asked indignantly. 'You make me sound like a bad lot.'

'Well, there have been one or two.' Elizabeth was trying to sound light-hearted, but her anxiety showed through. 'There was Gavin . . . and that awful Dave when you were at university. I didn't care for Paul much at first, but you've seemed so happy this last year . . . ' There was such regret in her mother's voice that Sophie's appetite died in an instant.

'That was lovely,' she said, putting down the spoon. 'I'd forgotten how nice boiled eggs could be.' She wiped her mouth with the folded napkin that lay on the tray and began to pour her tea. 'I'm only going on a secondment, Mum. I'm coming back. As for Paul, my feelings for him haven't changed, nor have his for me. You'll just have to be patient.'

'He won't like what's happening, Sophie.'

'No, he's not very happy about it. 'I'd've felt the same if he'd been going instead of me, but we both knew that our careers were important to us right from the beginning. He'll come round to it in the end.'

'You were going to buy a house,' Elizabeth said despairingly. 'I was so pleased about that.'

'And we probably still will buy a house. Paul won't stay in the flat for ever. He doesn't want to, even if he could. I expect he'll go on looking at houses when I'm away. It's not easy in London, you know. If he hasn't found something by the time I get back, we'll look together.'

Elizabeth smiled her gratitude for the reassurance and got to her feet. At the door she turned. 'I do admire your courage, Sophie. Whatever else I may say – or feel – I do admire you for that.'

Kate was in her garden when Oliver appeared at the gate. He was holding a small object in his hands, wrapped in a yellow duster, and by the reverent way he carried it up the path she guessed it was the precious piece of Derby he had acquired yesterday.

'What do you think of that?' he said triumphantly, when he had put it on the centre of her kitchen table and laid it bare of the duster.

'Lovely,' she said. 'Perfect?'

'A tiny chip on the base – there, just below the handle. A pity, but it's not much. I thought I'd hang on to it for a while.'

'Well, lawks a mercy, Mr Stone, fancy you doing a thing like that!'

Oliver was notorious for hanging on to favourite items. He shifted uneasily on his chair and then he grinned. 'Well, it is superb, Katie, you've got to admit it.'

The barrel-shaped mug was no more than six inches high, decorated with green bamboo and exotic birds in yellow and red. 'What's its date?' Kate enquired.

'About 1760, I think.'

'So it's pre-Chelsea Derby?'

'Yes. It'd be a few years after Heath and Duesbury bought out Planche. But it's very early . . . and very wonderful.' He was looking at Kate, his voice lingering lovingly on his words, and she felt herself blush.

'You're mad, Stone. Do you want some coffee?'

'I'm hoping for lunch, let alone coffee. We can go out to eat, if you like . . . and then afterwards we can go over the catalogue for next week's sale.'

'No,' Kate said firmly. 'I'm not starting to work on Saturdays. If I'd wanted to work at weekends I'd've opened a shop. That's why I only do occasional fairs, so that I can have most of my weekends. Anyway, Sophie's here, to make her goodbyes. She arrived last night and she goes back after tea, so I must keep some time free for her.'

'Fine,' Oliver said equably. 'I'll make myself scarce after we've had coffee.'

When he had gone, cradling his beloved Derby like a new-born baby, Oliver's image stayed on in Kate's mind. They had met at an antique fair when they had been given adjacent stalls. She had advised him on a piece of treen; he had told her a piece she was almost giving away was in fact a Gouda and worth at least fifty pounds, which in those days had been a lot of money. She had thought him a charming man then, who would never give an older woman a second glance, and she had been too wrapped up in her new profession to care.

It had been 1948 before she and Jimmy had got a place of their own: a council house on a run-down, pre-war estate. Kate had looked at utility furniture in the shops and found it hideous, turning then to second-hand shops where she found shabby, good-quality items at very low prices. She had brought them home, one by one, and polished them lovingly, but that did not satisfy her. So she had turned to the library, lugging home huge tomes on upholstery and French polishing and restoration. And so it had begun, the buying and selling of items as she improved her home, using something until she found a better replacement and then selling it off. Now, she was a local authority on English furniture of the twenties and thirties. She sighed and got to her feet. She didn't feel like an authority on anything this morning.

Sophie followed Susan into the garden, where the baby lay sleeping under a cat-net. 'I'll just see if he's awake,' Susan said, unfastening the net. The baby lay, eyes wide open, staring up at them. 'Who's a good boy, then?' Susan cooed, and the baby smiled and blew a bubble at its mother. 'Come on,' Susan said. 'Go to your Auntie Sophie.'

Sophie would have protested but it was too late. Susan

was already laying the warm, faintly damp bundle in her arms, and there was nothing to do but clasp it.

'I'm terrified,' she said, making a face.

'Don't worry.' Susan was reassuring. 'They're much tougher than they look. They can hang from clothes-lines as soon as they're born, or so they say – like little monkeys.'

'But he's so small!' The bundle in Sophie's arms felt more fragile than china and infinitely bendable.

'You'll feel different when you have your own.' Susan sounded distinctly superior. 'They say it comes in with your milk . . . a feeling of confidence. You don't think anyone can look after your baby as well as you can, not even midwives. You'll see, when it's your turn. When you get back from foreign parts . . . ' Susan's last few words were faintly disapproving, as though a trip to the United States was definitely a waste of time.

They carried the baby into the house and laid him on his plastic changing pad, unwrapping the complicated layers of his clothing to reveal tiny pink limbs that pedalled furiously as his nappy was changed. All the while Susan cooed and talked, keeping up a running commentary. 'Here's the lovely wipes, then . . . here's the lovely lotion . . . and a super, super clean nappy for a good little boy.' The baby cooed and pedalled faster and, just before the nappy was clipped shut, obliged with a lovely arc of water drenching everything within reach. Susan seemed to see this as a triumph and looked round to share the joke with her friend. Sophie grinned back, and tried to look suitably impressed, but she felt a real sense of relief when another disposable nappy was safely in place.

Could I ever get used to this? she thought, feeling at once both a fierce desire to hug the baby to her and an equally intense desire to see it put back in its pram so that she could go home.

'Do take care,' Susan said at the gate. 'Fancy you going to New York, you lucky girl!' The words were complimentary but the tone was faintly disapproving. 'Kiss Auntie Sophie.'

She held up the baby to be kissed and Sophie obliged. The baby's flesh was sweet and smelled of soap and powder. 'You'll have one of your own one day,' Susan said consolingly and Sophie, unsure of what to say in reply, was glad that she could fiddle with the car-key and then make a great play of fastening her seatbelt.

After lunch Sophie walked with her father, striding along the quiet roads, revelling in the clear air. 'We'll miss you when you're away, Sophie. Don't forget to ring. Reverse the charges; I can afford it.'

'So can I, Daddy.' She was glad of an excuse to joke. 'American salaries are astronomical in comparison to ours. I'll ring at least once a week, and when you finally give up work you and Mum can come and visit me and we'll see New York together. I've got a huge apartment, apparently. It belongs to my replacement at Ascher's. She says it sleeps four . . .'

She linked her arm in his for their return journey, and kissed him warmly as they turned into the drive. 'I love you both so much,' she said. 'Don't ever forget that.' If she and Paul didn't survive as a couple, her parents would be all she had.

She drove over to see Kate, borrowing Elizabeth's sedate Volvo, whipping along the A1 and then the A19 until Sunderland came into view. 'I wish I could've stayed longer, Kate . . . spent a night with you. Still, what chance of you and Oliver coming over?'

'I'll certainly come. I've already made plans. Judging by the things I've shipped to the States, that continent must be ready to sink beneath the waves. Perhaps I'll loot some of their early American stuff and redress the balance,' Kate replied.

They drank wine and half cried at the pain of parting until it was time to get in the car. 'Enjoy yourself,' Kate said firmly, holding her granddaughter by the shoulders. 'I know it's work, but it should be pleasure too.'

It wasn't as simple as that, Kate thought, as the car

vanished from sight. Sometimes it seemed that taking from life what gave you pleasure inevitably led to pain.

Elizabeth said goodbye at the house, controlling her emotions so that she gave brisk, practical advice and let her daughter go with a smile. Geoffrey drove to the station, the train was on time and Sophie was glad. Today had seemed like one long goodbye.

She waved to her father as the train pulled out and then sat back. She had two hours of peace before arriving at London. She hoped that Paul would be in a good mood when she got back. Perhaps we can really talk, she thought as the Yorkshire landscape flashed by. The thought cheered her. If they parted on good terms, he could fly over for odd weekends. She might come home at Christmas. Months would flash by, and then they would be reunited. It would be easy to be faithful to him: would he find it as easy to be faithful to her?

She didn't ring from the station, preferring to leap into a taxi at King's Cross and take him by surprise. She tiptoed past Chloe's door, exulting in her escape, and put her key quietly into her own lock. 'I'm home,' she called, when she was inside, but there was no response. She walked into the lamp-lit living-room, but there was no one there. All there was was a note, secured by an ashtray in the centre of the coffee-table.

Darling Sophie, it read. *I hope you had a good weekend. I've gone home. It seemed a good idea as I haven't seen Gary for a while. When I get back to London I'm moving in with Kieron. It seems the best way: no sad goodbyes, no arguments to spoil good memories. I hope you enjoy New York and do your thing there. As I said, I don't believe in love at a distance, so I want you to feel free . . . as I will feel. Maybe we'll make it in the end; who knows? For now, thanks for everything, and love. Paul.*

34

S OPHIE WALKED THROUGH THE CLOCK department, hearing the tick and hum of time and once the chime of bells.
Tomorrow was her last day at Ascher's and she was touring
departments today, to say a personal goodbye. The fact that
there was so much to do was the only thing that eased the
heartache that Paul's departure had caused.

She was moving towards the china department when she
saw her call sign flashing. Should she take it on the nearest
phone or go to the privacy of her office? The hope that it
might be Paul sent her racing for the lift . . . but it was not
Paul on the other end of the line. It was Alistair Dunbar,
the man she and Kate had met in Nice. 'I'm over here
for forty-eight hours,' he said. 'I wondered if we might
have dinner? Your grandmother told me you worked at
Ascher's.'

Sophie tried to sound regretful. 'I'm so sorry. I'm leaving
for the States in less than forty-eight hours, and you can
imagine the chaos. I haven't even finished packing yet, and
I'm going for an indefinite stay.'

'I see.' The disappointment in his voice was almost tangible.

'I really am sorry. If it had been any other time . . . '

'I don't suppose we could meet for a drink – just a quick one – on your way home?'

'Well . . . ' A moment later, and rather to her regret, it was fixed. Still, she didn't relish going home to the empty flat a moment earlier than she had to, and one drink with a nice guy couldn't hurt.

Kate put the decanter carefully down on the draining-board and dried the stopper before lifting the decanter up and shaking out the last drops of water. It was green crackle glass with a gilt rim to the neck and gilt bandings an inch below. She had paid fifty pounds for it, and would probably make another fifty in profit; not bad for a morning's work, especially as she had picked up some nice flatware too.

She felt the little thrill of excitement she always felt when she'd made an acquisition. Oliver would be pleased when he saw her purchase. They were not things either of them would want to hang on to, but they'd be easy to shift. As Kate dried her hands, she smiled to herself. Quite apart from the discrepancy of their ages, there was another good reason why she and Oliver couldn't ever get together: neither of them would part with a stick of their precious furniture, so no house would be able to hold them.

She began to assemble a salad, munching occasionally as she did so. It was silly, all this talk of marriage . . . but, like every fairytale, it contained a grain of truth. When first she had realised that Oliver was attracted to her, her only emotion had been incredulity. Then she had suddenly felt old. Another woman might have been flattered, even rejuvenated. Kate had felt threatened, unable to cope with the emotion of a love affair after so many years of channelling her emotions into her daughter, her granddaughter, and her beloved bits and pieces. If I'd been younger, she thought, squinting slightly in admiration of the green decanter. If I'd even been sixty, I might have risked it, but not now: far better to be safe than sorry.

They met in the American bar at the Savoy, managing to grab

a seat before it filled with homegoing workers anxious for that first sweet drink of freedom. He was taller than Sophie remembered, and more handsome. She held out her hand. 'It's good to see you again. I'm glad I didn't miss you.'

They drank wine and nibbled nuts and exchanged small-talk. He was thirty-two and had been with his present firm for four years. 'It can't be bad to be based in Nice,' Sophie teased. 'Where do you go for a break?'

He took her joking question seriously. 'I fell-walk. I'm horribly energetic when I'm off-duty.' Across the table his face was lean and tanned, his eyes creased to a smile. He's attractive, Sophie thought, but he's not Paul.

'How long will you be in New York?' he asked at last.

'I don't know. Littlecamp has a chain of stores. They've just bought up Ascher's . . . hence my trip to the States.'

'Your grandmother tells me you're a high-powered executive.' He was smiling, and Sophie grinned back.

'My grandmother says everything but her prayers. I'm an assistant manager, a very lowly position.'

'But you like it?'

'I love it. It's not what I intended to do. I fell into it as a holiday job . . . and I'm still there.'

I do love it, she thought, as he lifted his hand to summon a waiter, but I never bargained for this pain inside me. I never bargained for losing Paul.

When their fresh drinks came Alistair Dunbar cleared his throat. Here it comes, Sophie thought, knowing a move when she saw one.

'I was wondering,' he said, looking at her and smiling suddenly. 'What I mean to say is, I'd like to keep in touch while you're away. If you wouldn't mind, that is?'

He's nice, Sophie thought. I ought to leap at the chance . . . but he's not Paul. And besides, it wasn't a man she wanted, not now.

It was her turn to smile now, to soften her words. 'I have to be honest,' she said. 'I don't really want any kind of complication at the moment. This is a new job in a new country. I think I'll have my hands full.'

'Fair enough.' He was disappointed but he bore it well. 'I envy you going to the States. Tell me more about the job.'

When it was time to go they kept the goodbyes brief. 'Enjoy your trip,' he said. 'I hope we meet again.' The cab circled the horseshoe entrance and threaded into the traffic, and Sophie felt a sudden sense of terror at the loneliness of the empty flat waiting for her in Notting Hill until she remembered Chloe.

'Let her be in tonight,' she prayed. 'Tonight is the one night I want her knocking on my door.'

Geoffrey put on a Vivaldi CD and settled back in his chair. Opposite him, Elizabeth smiled and went back to her embroidery, a line of satin-stitch along the edge of a baby's pillow slip. 'That looks nice,' Geoffrey said, gesturing at her embroidery frame.

'It's for Susan's baby. You remember Susan Denham, Sophie's friend?'

'Ah yes, Susan of the dream bungalow.'

'I did go on about it a bit, I admit. I felt . . . well, I suppose I felt cheated. Moira Denham was having a white wedding for her daughter and a new house to plan, and I hardly ever saw my daughter.'

'That's a bit unfair. Sophie keeps in touch. I hardly ever wrote or telephoned when I left home. My conscience pricks me sometimes, now that I realise how much it means to a parent.'

'You were a model son,' Elizabeth chided.

'I wish, my love. I wish.' He pushed up from his chair with one easy lever movement of his arms. 'Shall I put a match to the fire? It's turning chilly.'

'Yes, it'll soon be time for the hour to come off the clock – or is it on? Anyway, I hate it.' She couldn't tell him how she hated October, or why; not now. If only she had been honest from the beginning. He could have helped me, Elizabeth thought. He's strong. I never realised how strong he is.

There was a large car parked at the end of the mews when

Sophie arrived home, and as she passed Chloe's door she could hear the murmur of voices. She was filling the kettle at the sink when she heard Chloe's front door slam, and then, a moment later, the sound of a car engine starting up. It hadn't been Desmond's car, nor had it been a man's voice she had heard through the door. She was putting the kettle on when she heard something else; an unusual sound. She froze by the cooker, listening intently. What she could hear was the sound of sobbing. It grew louder as she went down the stairs, a tea-towel still in her hand. The door to Chloe's flat was unlatched. Whoever had banged it had failed to secure it. She pushed it open and went in, moving towards the source of the sobbing: Chloe's bedroom.

She was there, sitting on the side of the bed. 'Who's done this to you?' Sophie said, looking aghast at Chloe's tear-stained face. Chloe raised her head.

'Come inside and shut the door.'

'What's happened?' Sophie asked again.

'Nemesis, darling,' Chloe said, wiping her nose on her sleeve. 'I think it just caught up with me.'

Once she was seated in the living-room her teeth began to chatter and her hands to shake. 'It's all right,' Sophie said, and cuddled Chloe until her shaking subsided and she could tell what had happened.

'Hilary's been here,' she said at last. 'Apparently I am becoming too close to Desmond and Hilary doesn't allow that, she says. It's okay for him to fuck me – her words, not mine – but he mustn't like me: that's the unforgivable sin. She says he needs someone for his excess energy, and she's a busy woman. Though he'd rather have caviar – again, her words – fish paste helps to quell his hunger pangs until she can oblige him. I'm not the first, she says, and I won't be the last.'

'Why doesn't she leave him?' Sophie said, horrified at Hilary Purser's cold-bloodedness.

'Why should she?' Chloe's eyes were wide now, her stare defiant. 'She has his house in Hampstead, and his name, and he's going places. She likes all that, and she needs someone for functions. He's useful to her.'

'Maybe he'll leave her?' Sophie said but Chloe shook her head.

'Oh no, he won't do that. He gets occasional sex, and has his own way. She makes sure his home is run to his liking, and she earns her own money. That's why a lot of men stay with their wives nowadays: because it's so bloody convenient.'

'Come on,' Sophie said. 'Come upstairs with me and let's have a drink.'

'You must have heaps to do,' Chloe said contritely. 'You go, and I'll come up in a moment. I don't know why I went to pieces like that. I must be mad.'

'Are you sure?' Sophie stood, unwilling to leave, certain that Chloe had no intention of following her upstairs.

'Yes, I'm sure. I'm fine.' But as Chloe pushed her friend out of the flat her chin was trembling.

As she mounted the stairs Sophie wondered why Chloe's normal chutzpah had been no match for Hilary Purser's ruthlessness. She could provide no answer, and it was a relief to get down to the mundane business of finishing off her packing.

35

THEY DRANK WINE IN DAVID'S office as a farewell. 'Safe journey,' he said, raising his glass to Sophie, 'and come back to us soon.' Around her, her colleagues wished her well and called her a lucky devil to get such a chance. Sophie smiled and nodded and tried to remember if she had tied up all the loose ends, packing her brain with details of Ascher business so that she need not acknowledge that Paul had not telephoned to suggest a farewell drink, or even to say goodbye. Should she ring him? She supplied a different answer to that question every five minutes, until at last she put it firmly away from her.

At twelve thirty a bouquet was delivered: red roses in Cellophane. Her heart leaped until she saw the signature on the card. 'Safe journey,' it read. 'Alistair Dunbar.' While her colleagues oohed and aahed over the romantic gesture, Sophie felt disappointment sour in her throat. Red roses from the wrong man did not work their magic.

David put her into a cab with her roses at twelve forty. 'We'll miss you,' he said. 'Show the Yanks how a store should be run.'

As she opened the door to her flat, the phone was ringing.

'It's me,' Kate said at the other end of the line. 'I was hoping you'd be at home. Things will be frantic tonight and worse in the morning, so I thought I'd ring you now to say that I love you, be careful, and for God's sake, keep in touch.'

Sophie felt tears springing up in her eyes. What have I done? she thought. I'm leaving everything, everybody I love. It has to be a mistake. They talked for a while, of aeroplanes and sightseeing and everything except the pain of parting with a loved one. 'Well,' Kate said at last. 'I'm glad you're going. So is your mother, although I doubt you'll get her to say it. We both married young, Sophie, and I'm glad you're giving yourself time to breathe. As for Paul, if he's meant to get you he will. You don't do a man a favour by giving him half a loaf, Sophie. That's one thing I'm sure of.'

When Kate at last rang off, Sophie gathered up the roses and went in search of Chloe. She wanted to make sure that Chloe was all right after her experience last night, but she was as much in need of comfort herself as Chloe might be. It was a while before she heard the door unlocking, but that hadn't prepared her for the sight that met her eyes. Chloe had cropped her wonderful, silky, foot-long hair, so that now it stood in uneven spikes all over her head.

'My God,' Sophie said. 'What have you done?' And then, in an almost involuntary gesture she thrust forward the roses. 'These are for you.' They stood for a moment, eyes locked, and then, unpredictably, they both started to laugh.

'Come in,' Chloe said, reaching out to draw her over the threshold. 'I know what we need now. It's time to open the Methuselah plonk.'

Kate took Ben's photo out from behind the picture of Elizabeth, aged eight, gap-toothed and earnest in school tunic and blouse. She had almost forgotten his face, and she smiled as she looked down at the young man in the forage cap and uniform jacket who she hadn't seen for forty-seven years. Perhaps Ben was dead now . . . but she hoped he was alive and happy.

She had tried to contact him after Jim died to tell him about Elizabeth, but her letters had been returned by the US army authorities, marked 'address unknown'. He had left the army, probably to marry and settle down in Maine where they grew blueberries and maize, and the earth was hard, to have children and forget what he had been forced to leave behind in England. She laid the photograph down and went to get ready. Tonight *she* was taking Oliver to dinner. 'My treat,' she'd said when she suggested it. 'You cook wonderful dishes and I give you rabbit food, so this is only fair.'

She put on her black velvet ski-pants and white highwayman shirt and topped it with a black, beaded matador jacket. I don't look too bad, she thought, when she had used eraser on her shadows and highlighted her eyes with blusher.

When Oliver arrived his whistle of appreciation proved that her efforts had paid off. 'Now, don't be silly,' she said. 'Let's get a move on. The table's booked for seven thirty.'

When they reached the hotel she had to stand close to Oliver in a lift filled with businessmen out on a spree. He put his arm around her to fend off the crush as they piled in and it was nice to be safe within his grasp. Her head came up to his shoulder and she felt his chin rest momentarily on the top of her head. The lift drew up at their floor and he fended a way for her into the hotel corridor.

Their table was by a window, its velvet curtains draped in the centre to show a glimpse of the darkness outside. 'What time does Sophie fly off?' he asked, when they were seated.

'Eleven a.m. tomorrow. Well, eleven thirty. I'll be glad when I hear she's safely there. Silly, seeing as the sky's the safest place to be nowadays.' He reached to pat her hand in reassurance and then they turned to their menus.

Kate was careful to keep the conversation light through the first two courses but over their Swiss ice-cream Oliver took command of the conversation. 'Kate, you know I'm fond of you?'

'Yes. I'm fond of you, too.' She smiled in what she hoped was a maternal fashion.

'Don't fence, Kate. What's that good old north-country expression? "Let's get down to pricky-bird." We're wasting time, you and I. Separate holdings, separate houses. It's daft . . . unless you don't care for me.'

Kate pushed her plate away and wiped her mouth with her napkin to gain time. She was trying to find a formula, something neat and final, but suddenly she opted for the simple truth. 'I'm too old, Oliver. Do you know how old I am?'

He shook his head. 'No. It's never seemed relevant.'

'I'm sixty-six.' She expected to see surprise in his eyes, perhaps even revulsion, but it wasn't there. 'I'm getting old, and if I'm truthful, I'm scared. Oh, it's all right now, you and I, but what about five years ahead – ten? You might tire of me.'

'I might. I might have tired of you if we'd married in our twenties.'

'I'm old enough to be your mother.'

'Hardly. Well perhaps, just – given a miracle. Socially, not.'

'I haven't slept with a man for ten years.'

'Then it's time you did.'

Kate thought of the mechanics of sex. Was it still possible? Did you wither internally as you did externally? She had been a widow for more than thirty years. There'd been men in that time but none of them had been much more than a one-night stand. Am I capable of it? she thought, after all this time. While she pondered Oliver reached for her hand, taking it in his this time and not letting go.

'I don't know if it would work, Kate, but I'm a grown man. I'm over the hill, too, come to that, and I know what I want. Dylan Thomas said you shouldn't go quietly, and I want to make a racket before I go. A hell of a racket.'

When the telephone rang Sophie's heart began to hammer, but it was her mother on the other end with a list of cautions a mile long. Sophie smiled tolerantly and promised to obey every stricture, but her mother's last remark took her by

304

surprise, in spite of Kate's words. 'I'm glad you're going, darling. It's made me think . . . I was against it at first, you know that, but now I think it's right to move forward.' There was such vehemence in her mother's words that Sophie was taken aback.

They exchanged goodbyes and there were tears in Sophie's eyes as at last she put down the receiver.

She was glad when Chloe appeared, her hair blow-waved into a halo that framed a face that was somehow more thoughtful, less defiant, than it had been.

'All packed?'

'I think so. You keep thinking you've forgotten something but, as far as I know, it's okay. Is it too early for another drink?'

'It's never too early.' They sat opposite one another, slightly tense, both aware of the minutes ticking away and the expensive booze running riot in their brains.

'I'll miss you,' Chloe said. 'Want me to see you off tomorrow?'

'Yes, please.' She had hoped Chloe would offer. There would be no one else.

'No more drink then,' Chloe said. 'The new sensible me says we've had enough. Well, perhaps there's room for one more.'

Elizabeth had established a code of early retiring from the beginning of her marriage. On most nights she was first in bed, lying back on the pillows until Geoffrey lifted the covers to climb in. She would hold out a cheek to be kissed, then say, 'Goodnight, get a good rest,' and turn on her side, her back to him. If by any chance he put out a tentative hand she would say again, 'Goodnight, dear.'

After a while he grasped that there would be an occasional night when she would stay on her back and there would be no goodnight, even when he put out his lamp. An approach made then would not be repulsed. Elizabeth would enter into foreplay for a while, long enough to make the act itself possible, and then she would urge him on to her and put her arms around him while he laboured away. When it was over she would wait for a second and then urge him gently back to his own place. After that it was, 'Goodnight, get a good rest,' and sleep.

As the years went by the welcoming nights were fewer, and Geoffrey seemed to mind less and less. Occasionally she would lie, and there would be no move on his part. She would wait for a moment out of duty and then go into the ritual, relieved.

Tonight she lay on her back, the memory of it all going through her head. She had begrudged him sex. Not only that; she had begrudged him her time. She had even, in the end, begrudged him the love of a dog. God forgive me, she thought in the darkness. She could hear him settling himself for sleep. He was fifty-one years old, and what did he have to show for it? Only his daughter . . . and now, for months he would not have her either.

'Goodnight, dear.' It was Geoffrey's voice. Elizabeth tried to say goodnight and turn away, but the urge to cry was overcoming her. She put out her hand and touched first his arm and then his rib-cage, sliding her fingers awkwardly under the flap of his pyjama jacket until they touched flesh.

'Liz?' He was turning towards her in the darkness. 'Are you all right?'

She started to laugh, then, silly gulping laughter at the thought that her touch did not provoke desire, only concern.

She heard a click and the lamp came on, but she shut her eyes against the light. 'Put it out, please put it out.'

'What is it, Liz?' There was another click, and she turned to him, hiding her face against him, moving her legs so that they lay parallel with his legs, pressing herself against him. She had to urge him at first. He was confused, and she was not surprised. She could not remember ever exhibiting desire for him; she had simply done her duty.

As he made love to her, she could sense the fear in him, the knowledge that all was not well. In the end she held his head in her hands, stroking the hair from his brow, laying her lips against his cheek when he was done. 'I love you, Liz,' he said, and she smiled in the darkness.

'I know,' she said. And then, after a pause: 'I love you too.'

Kate pushed open her front door and turned to Oliver to say goodnight.

'No coffee?' Oliver said.

'Not tonight. See your tomorrow. We need to talk about that Pembroke table.' She kept her voice deliberately business-like, and it worked. Oliver walked away down the path, and Kate felt instant relief. This made sense; and she would cool it even more in the weeks to come. There was no point in risking pain at her age, with so little time left to her. Except, if you couldn't go forward, perhaps you were dead already?

Oliver was putting his key in the door of the car when Kate called out his name.

As he walked back towards her, she fought back panic. If he came into the house now he would not go away, and she would be risking rejection, pain, and even loss. But then he was walking past her into the lighted hallway and she ceased to be afraid.

36

KATE WOKE AT DAWN, SLIPPING stealthily from the bed, leaving Oliver asleep. He lay on his back, one arm flung along the pillow, his face relaxed. She moved to the window and peeped through the curtains. The world was still asleep, except for birds already foraging in the garden below. She realised she was hugging herself, and tried to relax. Last night had been sweet, but far from perfect. It's only a beginning, she thought, but that was better than nothing.

She crept down the stairs and made herself tea, sipping it slowly until it was a decent hour and she could ring her daughter. 'I know how you feel today, Liz,' she said, when she got through, realising with surprise that it was the first time in years she had called Elizabeth by anything but her proper name. 'I know how I'd feel if it was you leaving for New York. I'll miss Sophie too . . . more than I can say. I want you to know how grateful I am that you gave me such a lovely granddaughter.'

At the other end of the line there was silence for a moment and then Elizabeth spoke. 'I love you, Mum . . . and I won't call you Kate, whatever you may say. You're my mother and don't you forget it.'

*　　*　　*

The early morning London streets were almost deserted, but wood-pigeons were cooing as Sophie walked through the gates of Holland Park. The bed of red busy Lizzies had been replaced since her last visit, but the stone cherubs were still there, a dolphin peeping between them. She would miss Holland Park, haunt of lovers and squirrels and Tony Benn types with books under their arm. At first the dense Victorian greenery had been off-putting. Now she loved it all: every laurel bush, every clipped hedge, the carpet of leaves beneath her feet, the mother suckling her baby on a wooden seat, her foot resting on the undercarriage of the pram.

She was suddenly reminded of Susan's baby, blowing bubbles, focusing its eyes, saying mama soon, for all she knew. She didn't know much about babies. She herself would probably take the pill for ever, or till the menopause, whichever came first. Except that she couldn't imagine ever making love again now that Paul was gone, so the pill had become redundant.

A grey squirrel with a foot-long tail was foraging in the leaves near the duck pond. It looked up hopefully as she passed, but she had nothing to give. There was a curious sense of timelessness about the place. Perhaps she could sit here for ever and not bother about the packed bags, the airline ticket, the office waiting on the other side of the Atlantic?

She turned before she reached the café with its dirty white plastic tables and orange chairs; they would break the spell. Besides, it was time to go home. Perhaps Paul would ring, just to wish her well, for old time's sake?

She thought of Kate and her mother as she retraced her steps. They had been lucky not to be so bewildered with options as she was. I can do anything I like, she reminded herself. I have total freedom. At least, she had sexual freedom . . . but whether or not that was the same thing as total freedom Sophie was not sure. Perhaps there was no such thing, except as a concept. Perhaps women had never been free, and never would be.

She saw another squirrel scurry across the path in front

of her, looking neither right nor left. It reminded her of the petrified baby rabbit she had seen on the walk with her father. It was easy to get petrified by too much space. The trick was to fix your eye on a single object and move forward. One day at a time, Sophie thought, and put out a hand to touch the gate in farewell. She would never really know why she and Paul had parted. It wasn't just America. It was the pressure of work on two people. It was not seeing enough of one another. It was the difficulty of sustaining a sexual relationship when your legs ached and your brain teemed with left-over detritus from your working day. And perhaps, too, it was her need to grow.

There was no winking light on the answering machine, but she had not really expected one, so it was all right.

Elizabeth put down the phone and went upstairs. She always made the bed as soon as Geoffrey left the house, then it was down to the kitchen. Today though, she left the duvet unsmoothed, the pillows awry, and went instead to her dressing-table. It was here in the right-hand drawer, the tiny diamond star with the sapphire centre that had cost thirty-seven pounds and ten shillings all those years ago. She had once intended to give it in part-exchange for something grander but now, winking in the morning sun, it seemed to have an added charm. They had chosen it together. Or rather, Geoffrey had chosen it because Liz had not cared, as long as she got a ring to show the world. It had to be forced over her knuckle, but it went on to her finger eventually.

She looked at it for the moment, seeing how small it was. But a ring was a symbol of strength. It could withstand almost limitless pressure.

Through the window she could see Geoffrey working by the bonfire. 'Dangerous to leave it smouldering all night,' he'd said, and gone out to rake the embers.

The fire gave one last defiant burst of flame, sending sparks shooting into the air. It would be November the fifth soon, and then Christmas. Geoffrey would retire and spring would come . . . another year. Elizabeth went out into the garden, walking towards him over the grass, feeling the smoke sting her eyes.

He turned at her approach and smiled. 'Nearly done.' She moved closer, wanting to speak but not finding the words. 'Missing Sophie?' he said. 'Me too. She won't be on this island any more, so we can't rush to her . . . it's the first time in her life I haven't felt that I can protect her. Funny feeling.' He looked down at Liz. 'But we've got each other.' He put an arm around her and drew her closer. She wanted to tell him the truth: that she didn't deserve his love, had never returned it, but somehow the words wouldn't come. It seemed right to be there, in the curve of his arm, her eyes smarting from the smoke, the last dying embers of the fire burning out at her feet.

'I've been thinking,' she said. 'We ought to get another dog. I've missed Pepsi too. We can kennel it – him or her – when we travel. We'll get a sensible dog this time, though. You choose.'

Geoffrey was looking out over the autumn garden. 'Look at those leaves,' he said. 'I'll try and get back early and get the incinerator going. They're treacherous under foot if they're left.'

'You'll have more time for the garden soon.' Elizabeth had not meant anything by the words, but her husband smiled wryly.

'Don't worry, my love. I'll keep out from under your feet. Anyway, it's not for three months yet.' He looked up at the sky. 'It's a nice day. Good flying weather.'

'Yes,' Elizabeth said, thinking of her daughter setting out to the unknown, a strange city, in a strange country, with no one she knew for support. And I'm afraid of my shadow, she thought.

'Geoff . . . ' She moved away so that she could face him. 'There's something I have to tell you, something I should have told you long ago, before we married.'

He leaned his rake against a post and turned back to her. 'I know . . . at least, I think I know what you're going to tell me. It's about John Stubbs, isn't it . . . Bruce Hartley-Davis?'

Shock robbed Elizabeth of speech, and in a little while Geoffrey carried on. 'I've always known, Liz. I worked in the town clerk's office, remember? He took the council for almost five thousand, and that was a fortune then. The reports we got mentioned you – that you had known him and been interviewed – but there was never any question of your being prosecuted.'

'Did you come back because you were sorry for me?' she asked.

He reached out to grip her by the shoulders. 'Sometimes, my dear wife, you are an idiot. I never went away. I merely bided my time. I knew I had more staying power than him. I'd never have let you go. You ought to have known that all along.'

She put up her hands to his face, cupping it tenderly. She wanted to say something but the words wouldn't come, until she saw the gleam of moisture in his eyes. 'I love you, Geoff,' she said, and knew that for the first time in a long, long while, she was speaking the truth.

Heathrow was quieter than usual when Sophie and Chloe arrived. They went up into the bar when Sophie had checked in and sat at a table overlooking the concourse. 'Are you watching for anyone special?' Chloe asked, as Sophie's eye kept straying to the glass partition.

'No. Of course not. Like who?'

'Like who? It's me, Chloe! We both know who.'

'He won't come now,' Sophie said. She thought of the letter Paul had left her and its finality. 'I never expected him to come, but it's okay between us. We're friends.' They sipped their Bloody Marys for a while in silence, Sophie trying hard not to look out at the mass of faces moving below.

'Don't look so scared,' Chloe said at last. 'I envy you.'

Sophie grimaced. 'I'm going out there to work, Chloe. Like a dog, probably. The Americans don't go home at night, so they say. Think of me toiling while you're lolling back, sipping champagne with some . . . ' Again she hesitated but Chloe shook her head.

'Some other Desmond? I don't think so. I've done some thinking in the last two days. I think I know why there was Desmond, and all the others before him. I wasn't sure I could make it on my own, you see, so I swanned around in their limelight, hoping it would rub off on me. Terminally uncool, wasn't it? Now, I want to make it on my own – like you. I wrote five hundred words last night on the subject of dead-end affairs. So it's eat your heart out, Tina Brown. I'm hot on your trail.'

'I'm so proud of you,' Sophie said. 'And I love your hair. It makes you look . . . intellectual.'

'Steady on, Sophie, no hyperbole, please! I'm still suffering from last night. That wine was wicked. The one good thing Desmond ever did for me.'

They were calling Sophie's plane now, and the two of them moved towards the departure lounge. 'Take care,' Chloe said, and hugged her. She pulled away then, to dive into her leather bag. 'This is to open on the plane. Treat it gently, it's fragile.'

Sophie took the parcel and went through the barrier, turning to wave as often as she could until the corridor swallowed her up and she could no longer see her friend.

At eleven thirty Kate walked out into the browning garden and looked at the sky. Up there Sophie was flying to a new future in the country of the grandfather she had never even known existed. 'Godspeed,' Kate whispered, 'Godspeed.'

EPILOGUE

The seatbelt light went out and Sophie settled down. She felt desolate now, the journey ahead an ordeal, the prospect of making a new life in a strange country suddenly terrifying.

'All right?' The hostess's face was kind, and Sophie nodded.

'I'm fine.'

She would sleep in a while and when she awoke she'd feel better.

The parcel Chloe had given her was in her lap, and she removed the paper to reveal a cardboard box. As she pulled off the lid she saw the glass dome and knew what it was, even before the Santa Claus figure came into view, the Santa Claus she had seen with Paul at Greenwich, surrounded, as she turned it, by swirling snow. The card bore two words, in Paul's familiar writing. *See you*.

When Sophie closed her eyes for sleep, she was smiling.